prepared to do nothing else but read once you start this book!"
—Fresh Fiction

"Six stars—Stina Lindenblatt has a skill to write heroes with some depth like few can."—Collectors of Book Boyfriends & Girlfriends

"I Need You Tonight is one of those books that you go into thinking one thing and end up getting your mind blown because you were not expecting the emotion that this made you feel. Honestly, this had to have been the best book of the series because of that."—Life of a Crazy Mom

"There are so many, many things that I loved about this story. . . . I hadn't realized I'd been missing and I was craving the Pushing Limits boys until this one came along. And it came with a bang!"—Collectors of Book Boyfriends & Girlfriends

"I. LOVED. THIS. BOOK!!!!"—Seeking Book Boyfriend

"I love Stina's writing style. It's very emotive, and flows beautifully. I felt connected to the characters from very early on and cried several times at the pain these characters go through"—Reading Realm Blog

"This was an amazing read, I could not out this down. The author really wrote this one so beautifully. Let me say that the author's writing bought out so many emotions from me, I just loved it"—Lustful Literature

"...a truly unique and utterly swoon-worthy romance." —Mary Dubé at Frolic/USA Today's HEA

ALSO BY STINA LINDENBLATT

Contemporary Romances

Carson Brothers Series

One More Chance

One More Secret

One More Betrayal

Pushing Limits Series

This One Moment

My Song For You

I Need You Tonight

Spicy Romantic Comedy Novels

By The Bay Series

Decidedly Off Limits

Decidedly with Baby

Decidedly with Love

Decidedly with Mistletoe

Decidedly by Chance

Decidedly with Luck

Decidedly with Wishes

Visit stinalindenblattauthor.com for more books

ONE MORE BETRAYAL

HIDDEN SECRETS TRILOGY BOOK 2

STINA LINDENBLATT

*To every woman striving to rise
from the ashes...*

ONE MORE BETRAYAL

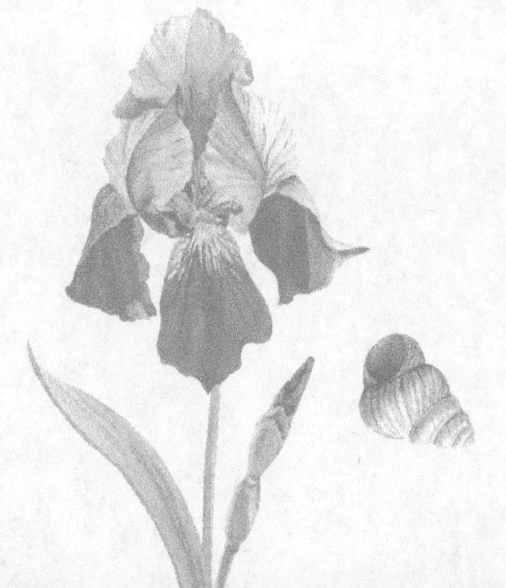

1

TROY

June, Present Day
Maple Ridge

The forest leaves rustle in the wind and whisper secrets. But not the secrets I want answered. Not the secrets telling me what happened to Jess in the past. Not the secrets telling me where the two missing hikers went.

The last time anyone heard from the father and son was three days ago. Shortly after eight this morning, I received the alert from the Maple Ridge Search and Rescue organization—following a night of taking my relationship with Jess to a new level. When I made love to her. When, for a short time, her past wasn't a dark shadow looming nearby.

That was roughly nine hours ago. Nine hours and still no sign of the two hikers.

I stop walking. "Joseph! Christopher!" My voice carries in the wind, but who knows if it's being carried in the right direction. I listen for a reply. Nothing.

A twig cracks to my left, but it's only Ethan Philips, the newest member of the search and rescue team. So far, none of my crew has found any indication we're even in the correct area.

All we know is their car was found in the parking lot. No signs of foul play. We can only assume they started along the trail as planned. Thankfully, the father had enough foresight to tell his wife which campsite they were staying at. The only reason it had taken so long for them to be reported missing is because they'd planned to camp out here for two nights.

But who knows when they actually disappeared?

I focus on the terrain, the sky growing dimmer with the thickening storm clouds. But even with my Marine and SAR training taking priority, a memory slips into my thoughts. Of Jess, of her silky-soft skin as I eased into her. As I made her come. Memories of how she felt in my arms. Of her scent. Of her moans.

Next time, I want to make love to her in the light of dawn as its golden rays stroke her face so I can see her fall apart as we come together.

If not for the missing father and nine-year-old, I'd still be in bed with Jess, enjoying this new landmark in our relationship. Enjoying the small piece of trust she has given me. The trust I'm slowly building with her—and nearly blew to pieces when I opened her nightstand drawer and looked at the photos of her niece.

A magpie squawks somewhere in the trees above my head. A gust of wind rustles the leaves again, warning of the approaching storm. If we don't find the missing hikers soon, they'll be in for a bad night.

And we'll be forced to return to base camp until the storm passes and it is daybreak.

An hour later, my crew enters a clearing and the end of the grid we've been searching.

"We'll take a ten-minute break," Sheldon, the team leader, announces.

We scout out a patch of ground to sit on and lower our asses onto the dirt. A blanket of dead leaves and pine needles litters the area, the leafy undergrowth pushing through it and growing thicker beyond the trees.

Voices come through Sheldon's walkie-talkie from the other crews, all announcing their grids are clear.

"Where the hell did those hikers go?" Garrett asks, sitting a few feet from me. Kellan and Lucas were assigned to two other crews.

"Wish I knew." I unscrew the lid of my flask and sip the coffee. It's not the best coffee in the world, but it's not the worst either.

My thoughts slip back to Jess this morning in bed, and my index finger subconsciously taps a Morse code message on the metal flask.

I repeat it, and slowly the words behind the dots and dashes infiltrate my brain.

I'm in love with you.

My heart hiccups a beat, and my finger pauses mid-tap. Bit by bit, everything about Jess has been slipping under my guard, wrapping around my heart. I'm not a cynic, my heart cold to the possibility of love. It just wasn't something I was looking for. Not at this point in my life.

Before Jess showed up in Maple Ridge, I'd been too busy with work and the cabins for the Wilderness Warriors program to worry about a relationship.

But here I am, on a mountain, searching for two missing hikers, and the truth behind my feelings is as bright as lightning against a storm-gray sky. But the Morse code message is one I sense Jess still isn't ready to hear. Whatever happened to her in the past has put her heart into a vault, and who knows if she'll ever hand me the key?

Patient. That's what I need to be. And in time, hopefully I can convince her to fully trust me. Only then can we have a future together.

"How's the festival planning going?" Noah takes a drink from a flask that reads "World's Best Uncle." The Maple Ridge police aren't normally involved in search and rescues in the mountains, but Noah helps out whenever his schedule allows.

"It's getting there," I reply. "George Ottaway and Susan Hodges have been booking acts." I list some of the individuals and groups.

Ethan gives an impressed whistle. "Isn't Pushing Limits a major rock band?"

"It is. The lead singer had PTSD at one point, which is why the band volunteered to be part of the festival lineup." I explain the purpose for the festival since Ethan recently moved to Maple Ridge and might not be aware of it. Or he might not be aware of the goal for it: to raise money to help victims of PTSD and their families.

"My best friend died last year because his PTSD became too much, and he ended his life." And I didn't do enough to prevent that from happening. "I want to make sure other sufferers get a better chance in life than he did."

I want to make sure other families aren't left to mourn the loss of a loved one with PTSD.

"I'm currently looking for more donors and sponsors to help pay for the equipment rentals needed for the festival," I tell the men. "So if you know anyone who might be interested..."

"I should be able to swing something," Sheldon says. "We can talk about it some more after we locate the father and son." A wry grin spreads across his face. "I heard there's gonna be an auction where women can win dates with sexy bachelors." He chuckles.

I can't believe that rumor's still circulating. "I don't know where you heard that from…" Rose, Delores, or Samantha, no doubt.

"So it's not true?" Sheldon still looks amused, the corner of his mouth twitching.

"Definitely not."

"Why not?" This question is from Ethan, who I guess could fit under the title of sexy bachelor. I'm not exactly an expert on the topic. As far as I know, he's single. "Seems to me something like that would raise a fair amount of money."

"Philips is right about that." Sheldon eyes each of us in turn like some all-knowing wizard. "There's a reason romance novels are a billion-dollar industry."

"And you know this because…?" Noah takes a swig of whatever's in his flask.

"My wife. I made a dumbass remark about the half-naked man on the cover of the book she was reading and received a ten-minute lecture about the romance-novel industry. Word to the wise." Sheldon wags his finger at us. "Never underestimate a woman's love for those books. Never mock them, unless you appreciate getting blue balls for the week. Plus, there're definite perks to women reading those books, if you get what I mean." His eyebrows do a jig up his forehead, his expression smug.

He's right about women loving that genre. Zara, Emily, and Simone all read those books. I've heard them go on about the ones they're reading.

Jess is the only one out of the five of them who doesn't seem to read romance. But I could be wrong. I've only seen the titles of some of the paperbacks and library books she's read, and all of them are historical fiction, as well as Garrett's latest release. It's not like I've snooped through her phone, checking the e-book apps.

"I bet you'd make a shitload of money if the guys from Pushing Limits participated in the auction." Sheldon laughs, knowing damn well the five rock stars would never go for that. I doubt their women would let them.

A smirk slides onto my face. "I'll be sure to mention that to the entertainment committee and see what they think."

Garrett snorts. "You're only saying that because you won't have to do it. You've got a girlfriend."

"That won't matter." Sheldon points his flask in my direction. "Unless Troy's married by then, he'll still have to participate. Same deal with Noah. But it's for a good cause, so I'm sure your girlfriends won't care. It's not like you have to sleep with or kiss the winning date."

Ethan pushes to his feet. "No girlfriend in her right mind would let her boyfriend go out with another woman because she won a date with him in an auction."

Sheldon shrugs, lifting the flask to his mouth. "The girlfriend would if she trusted him."

I inwardly flinch. Trust is something that's still missing from my relationship with Jess. She doesn't trust me enough to tell me what led to her PTSD.

Sheldon's walkie-talkie crackles to life, and he listens to what Command has to say. "We're on our way. Ten-four." He stands and gathers his daypack. "Break's over. The hikers have been spotted. Now, we just need to rescue them from the ravine they've found themselves in."

"Any injuries?" I ask.

"The father possibly has a broken leg, but the boy sounds like he's fine. Just scared. The team needs experienced climbers to get them out."

Which means me and Garrett.

The wind cranks up again, sending dried leaves cartwheeling across the ground.

2

JESSICA

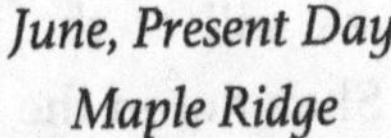

June, Present Day
Maple Ridge

My head pounds. My thigh screams. My ribs ache. I pry my eyes open, hoping that will end the pain. Hoping I'm just experiencing a dream that feels too real.

But I'm not.

I'm in the driver's seat of a truck. Troy's truck? And it's lying on its side. Beyond the cracked windshield, the world is nothing more than trees and rocks. At an angle to me...as if the truck is on a steep incline.

The inside of the cab is dim. Rain hammers the windshield and the metal exterior of the vehicle.

And I'm alone. So very alone.

A pained groan reaches my ears. My groan, barely heard over the wind roaring through the valley.

Despite the throbbing in my head, I try to slot the other puzzle pieces together, but a third of them are missing.

A vague memory fades in, fuzzy around the edges. Of a deer leaping onto the road. Of me swerving to avoid it. Of losing control of the truck.

A wave of panic wells up, threatening to pull me under. *Breathe. You'll never get out of here alive if you don't keep yourself together.*

"Bailey! Are you okay?" My voice comes out weak, raspy, pained.

I don't hear her panting breaths or whines or any other sound she might make.

Images flicker in my head. Finding her lifeless body in the living room. The vet told me that Bailey had ingested poison but would be okay. She's still at the vet clinic so they can monitor her condition. She's not in the truck. Relief floods me at that realization. But it's only temporary.

A long gash slices across my bare thigh, blood spilling from it. I need to staunch the flow of blood first and then figure out what to do next. I look around the cab, but the only thing I can use is the T-shirt I'm wearing and the sweatshirt in my daypack.

My trembling fingers locate the seat belt buckle. I yank on the strap while pushing the button. *C'mon. Release the goddamn seat belt. PleasePleasePlease.* Nothing. I jerk on it hard. Still nothing. I try again and again, my movements becoming more frantic and utterly useless.

C'monC'monC'mon. Unclick, dammit, before I bleed out...or something worse.

Something sticky drips down my face. Tears and raindrops join it. A strong coppery smell mingles with the normally soothing scent of pine.

Don't panic.

Channeling everything I've learned in yoga, I breathe out

an exhalation that isn't as slow as it should be. But it's enough to help me coordinate my efforts, and the seat belt clicks open.

I shift toward the daypack. It's still where I left it on the floor, wedged against the passenger side of the console. I hook my fingers on the strap and yank it. The bag smacks the gash on my thigh, sending a fresh wave of pain coursing through my leg.

A whimper escapes me, but I don't let the sharp pain deter me from my task. I unzip the daypack and pull out my sweatshirt. The better option would be to use my T-shirt as a bandage and put my sweatshirt on to stay warm. But the T-shirt is sweaty and dirty from hiking and too small for that idea to work.

I wrap the sweatshirt around my thigh, tying the sleeves to secure the top in place. It's not great, but it will have to do until I get help.

Help. My phone isn't in the cupholder where I'd left it. My gaze searches the cab for where it could have gone, but I can't see it anywhere.

A surge of panic pumps through my body, sending my heartbeat thundering. My breathing comes in fast and tightness spreads through my chest. *No, no. NoNoNoNoNo.* The phone barely had any battery power left, and I'm not even sure I can get cell reception out here, but the phone definitely won't be of any use if I can't find it.

It could be anywhere in the truck. Or maybe it fell out of the smashed window and it's on the ground somewhere.

Rain falls through the broken side window above my head. I shiver. Perhaps I can climb back up the slope and wave down a passing vehicle and ask the driver to call 9-1-1. It's that or wait until someone spots the truck. If they spot it.

I examine my options for escape. I can try kicking out the cracked windshield, but I'm not sure my thigh would be too thrilled with that. Plus, the steering wheel is in my way. But if that's what it comes down to, I will attempt it.

The dropping temperature runs its icy fingers along the exposed skin on my legs. Goose bumps pile on top of goose bumps. God, why did I dress in shorts and not jeans for hiking? Why didn't I bring more layers with me—like Troy would've done?

I wiggle out from under the steering wheel and clamber awkwardly to my feet, keeping my weight off my injured leg as much as possible. My stomach lurches, and it's all I can do to keep the contents down.

I reach for the passenger door, but it's too far away. Pain rips through my rib cage, almost knocking the breath from me. My ribs don't feel broken, but they do hurt like hell. Everything is beginning to hurt like hell.

The ache in my ribs is familiar. I've experienced it on more than one occasion. X-rays weren't on the menu then either.

I scan the cab once more but still can't find my phone. No one knows I'm out here. No one knows I've been in an accident.

I want to scream. I want to cry. I want to kick the dashboard. But none of those things will help me.

I place my foot on the steering wheel and use it to try to reach the passenger door. I strain upward, biting my lip to distract from the pain wracking my body. "C'mon. C'mon. C'mon." A wave of dizziness sweeps through me, forcing me to close my eyes for a second. *I can do this.* I've got to do this. It might be my only chance of survival. If my phone is outside the truck, I just need to locate it and call for help...as long as I have cell reception.

The front end of the truck points toward the edge of a forest of towering pines several yards away. I shift around and look out the rear window. As far as I can tell, it's a fair distance between where the truck ended up and the road. The incline is steep, but I don't have any other choice but to climb it if I can't find my phone.

The passenger window is shattered, but sharp edges grip the frame like teeth of a great white shark. I would need to pull away the pieces of glass to go through it. But the door...the door thankfully isn't locked. As far as I can tell, that's my best chance for escape.

With the help of the steering wheel and the console between the two bucket seats, I get into position. I harness my waning strength and push the door open. Pain slams into my ribs, and a brittle cry falls from my lips.

The door stays precariously upright, aided by the direction of the wind, which is stronger now than it was when I left the hiking trail.

I push and pull myself out of the truck, my ribs and thigh protesting. A whimper slips between my gritted teeth.

I tumble to the ground with a thud and a groan, the air knocked from me. I scramble to my feet. My head spins; my stomach lurches again. I barely have time to double over before the contents splash on the incline of mud and rocks and pine needles.

I turn to the truck, and dread becomes a dead weight in my stomach. Troy's truck is totaled. And it's my fault. If I hadn't gone hiking, if I hadn't swerved to avoid the deer, his truck would be in one piece.

Oh, God. Oh, God, Oh, God. My body stiffens, bracing for the blow.

"Savannah." My husband's voice comes from the hallway. My body tenses. It's the tone that always sends icy fear shooting through my veins, but I don't know what I did to deserve it this time. Correction. I usually don't know what I've done to deserve it. His fits can be so unpredictable, so explosive.

"I-I'm in the kitchen." The words sound as though they're traveling through cement. My fingers grip the edge of the counter.

His tall, broad-shouldered frame appears in the doorway. "What the hell did you do to the car?"

"W-what do you mean?"

"There's a scratch on the bumper." His tone turns darker.

I shake my head, but I don't know what exactly I'm shaking it for. To deny his allegation? To tell him I have no idea what he's talking about? To plead for him not to touch me?

I register the sound of the slap before I notice the stinging in my cheek.

Tears prick my eyes, blur my vision. I clutch the roof of the truck, steadying myself, and shove away the memory.

Troy's gonna be furious.

A tremor assaults my body. Somewhere in the fog of my thoughts, another voice tells me Troy isn't my husband. He's kind. He won't hurt me like my husband did time after time.

The voice keeps telling me that, but my fear of what his reaction will be swells like a deadly tsunami. The truck. He needs it for his job. He needs it for everything he does.

I wasn't responsible for the scratch on my car's bumper my husband accused me of, but I am responsible for wrecking Troy's truck.

My body still trembling, I limp around the area, searching the wet dirt for my phone and listening for sounds of an approaching vehicle. Another wave of dizziness rushes over me, and I sway on my feet. The wind doesn't help my cause. It pushes me to the side, makes me unstable.

The dizziness passes after a moment, and I continue combing the ground. At this rate, by the time I find my phone, the battery *will* be dead.

I glance up the steep incline. My stomach sinks. The slope is steeper than I first realized. I study it, determine the best route to take, and stumble forward. The pain in my head and the dizziness intensify.

Rivulets of muddy rainwater stream downhill. Heavy

chunks of mud cling to the soles of my sneakers as I walk, and I can barely find the strength to keep going. With each step, my feet keep sliding down the slope.

A harsh breath blows past my lips. The sky grows steadily darker, and there's no sign the storm will be ending soon.

Shelter. That's what I need. I head for the tree line and continue walking toward the towers of pine and spruce. I stumble over protruding rocks and roots and tangled undergrowth. The wind howls through the trees and rattles the branches.

Just keep swimming. Just keep swimming.

Dory's words spring to mind. Amelia loved *Finding Nemo* as a toddler. And I loved watching it with her.

A shudder grips me, strong enough to cause the ache in my side to intensify. My legs stiffen from the cold and my fear, making it more challenging to even limp.

Just keep swimming. Just keep swimming.

A loud crack splits the sky—a bright and sudden flash its encore. Seconds later, a resounding boom sends my teeth chattering.

Or maybe they were already doing that and I'm only now noticing.

Shadows loom around me, hiding the most dangerous creatures in these parts. Bears. Cougars. Wolves. As I slowly back away, my eyes try to make out the blurred shapes and shadows. Nothing moves. Nothing lunges toward me.

But that doesn't chase away the feeling that something is watching me.

It only emphasizes how alone I am out here.

3

ANGELIQUE

June 1943
France

When I was twelve years old, my sister, our parents, and I visited Munich. We were living in Austria at the time because my British diplomat father was stationed in Vienna. I don't remember much of Munich beyond the metallic taste of fear and the pounding in my chest. I remember wondering if angels were real and if I was about to see one.

I remember the glint of metal, the pistol aimed at my father.

The only difference between then and now is, the last time I stared down the barrel of a gun, we were being robbed by a stranger. And it wasn't the middle of the night.

This man...this man who is about to shoot me is no stranger. He's Captain Johann Schmidt, the German soldier who has done nothing but surprise me time and again since he

14

moved into the farmhouse. The German soldier who is hiding his Jewish family in Jacques's barn.

"I'm not going to harm them." My voice is a soft whisper, a tremor looping the French words.

Johann doesn't lower the pistol.

I raise my hands slowly, not giving him a reason to shoot me. "I only want to help. I can get them some food."

The pistol remains in place.

"I promise your family is safe. But we have to get them out of here. If the Gestapo or SS or Milice find them here, they'll kill us all." A chill wraps around my body, reminding me I'm standing outside Jacques's barn in the middle of the night, wearing a nightgown and a robe.

I had stepped out of the house to get air after waking from a nightmare. I hadn't expected to stumble across Johann or his family in the barn.

"They aren't my family." Johann lowers the gun, but even then, I cannot breathe.

"But...but the little girl called you *Oncle* Johann."

He doesn't reply, and my mind is spinning, trying to devise a plan to help the family. I have connections, but none who can help get a family out of the country. And that's exactly what needs to happen. Whoever they are...they can't stay in France. It's too dangerous.

"Where are they from?" I ask. Johann spoke to them in German, so they aren't originally from France.

"Oskar"—he points at the barn—"Dieter, and I grew up together in Austria." Johann's tone is somewhat stiff, a newly erected wall now between us. And I feel, once again, the sorrow at the loss of his friend Dieter, who was executed for desertion.

"How did they end up in France?"

"Several months before Hitler invaded Poland, Margrit's father became worried. He knew Hitler hated Jews and was a dangerous man. He didn't predict the annexation of Austria to

Germany, but he did know it wouldn't be safe for them to stay there. Margrit's parents begged Oskar and Margrit to join them. They escaped the only home Sonja had ever known."

"Why France?"

"Because they thought it would be safer here." There's a challenge in his voice, as if he's expecting me to tell the Gestapo he's hiding a Jewish family. Expecting me to do whatever I can to protect my father and myself, regardless of what it costs anyone else.

"We all thought the same thing until Pétain sold us out to Hitler." The bitterness behind my words is neutralised in my soft tone. "How long have they been in the barn?" How long has Johann known about the hiding space?

"I brought them here this evening. I discovered the trapdoor under the bales of straw a few weeks ago." He levels a warning gaze at me. He knows exactly what the storage cellar was used for prior to his arrival at the house. He would have to be an imbecile not to piece everything together once he discovered the camp bed and the few other amenities in there.

"My father has nothing to do with it. Please believe me." I maintain eye contact with him, praying it is enough for him to see the truth. At the same time, I know I have revealed I've been involved in something that will get me tortured and killed if the Nazis find out.

But why should he believe me? He doesn't trust me. How could he?

Silence settles over us like soot, the uncertainty of Johann's next move smothering my breath. I count the seconds in my head as I wait for him to respond. *One. Two. Three.*

"I believe you."

He might say that, but the wall between us is still there, fully fortified. Neither of us can afford to trust the other, but we don't have any choice. Too many innocent lives are at stake.

His words don't bring me a sense of relief. If anything, the tension in my muscles increases.

I nod, a truce between us, an acknowledgment we both need to trust each other. For now, anyway. "They must be hungry. I can get them some food."

"I'm sure they would appreciate that. Thank you."

I leave and return a few minutes later with all the food I can scrounge up. Most of it is what Johann provided. If not for that, I wouldn't have much to give the family.

I enter the barn to find his three friends sitting on a bale of straw. Johann introduces them to me.

Sonja, who cannot be more than six years old, is barely awake, her eyes half-closed. She's leaning against her mother, who has her arm around her. Sonja clutches to her small chest the teddy bear Johann gave her, as if the toy gives her an inner strength none of us can imagine.

Margrit brushes her hand over her daughter's hair. The soothing touch is the same one Mum used whenever I was scared as a young child. But there is a monstrous difference between a thunderstorm and the nightmare Hitler has inflicted on the Jews.

My heart aches for everything Oskar's family has been through and for everything they still have to face. "I'll get you some blankets to keep you warm."

"We don't want to be a bother." Exhaustion slopes Margrit's frail shoulders, saps the glow from her face I imagine was there before the war.

I crouch in front of her and take her hand. Her skin is cold and dry and rough. "It's no bother. Whatever I can do to help, I will try."

When I return to the barn a short time later, I am dressed and carrying blankets and hand-stitched quilts. The sun will be peeking above the horizon soon. There's no point in me trying to go back to sleep.

Sonja has fallen asleep in her mother's arms. Even in her sleep, the little girl looks worried. She should be spending her waking hours playing and laughing and learning. Instead, she's spending them in hiding and fear.

"You need to rest," I tell Oskar and Margrit. "You can stay in the hiding spot"—I avoid Johann's gaze—"while we figure out how to get you to safety."

"Thank you," Oskar says. "We're indebted to you."

My lips slide into a sad smile, and I attempt to shift it into something more optimistic. But all I can think about is what the Jews in Europe are going through, all because of the hatred of the Nazi party and the misguided beliefs of its supporters. Allaire is concerned with how Christian wants to add communists to the *Cashmere* network, communists who share the German anti-Semitic views. Is there really any place where Oskar and his family will be safe?

The anti-Semitic views aren't isolated to Germany. England has plenty of people who share the same horrendous beliefs. I've witnessed men and women look down their derisive noses at their Jewish neighbours. Heard stories of secret meetings among society members who support shunning Jews.

Johann and I watch Oskar's family descend into what will be their new home for hopefully only a few days. Johann closes the trapdoor, shutting them away from the cruel outside world.

We leave the barn and walk to the house.

"Do you have any idea how you're going to get them out of France?" My words are whispered so only Johann can hear them.

"No." He looks determined but also resigned to the difficulties he faces with regards to saving his friends. "I've heard rumours of families in Germany and Austria who tried to hide their Jewish friends. It didn't end well for all concerned."

I study the face of the man who is a paradox. Johann's sister is deaf, a target for Hitler. The same sister and his mother are trying to escape the Gestapo. His best friend is dead at the hands of the Nazis for desertion. And his other close friend and his family are fleeing for their lives, fleeing from prosecution because they are Jewish.

Yet he is a captain with the German Army, the country that is responsible for all his anguish.

"Why do you fight for Germany? You're not even German." I'm stepping into dangerous waters with my question, but I need to know. I need to know what kind of man he is and how much I can trust him.

"According to the *Anschluss*, Austria is now part of Germany. And therefore, the Austrian Army is part of the German Army." Johann glances up at the house where Jacques's room is located, and he threads his calloused fingers with mine. "Come with me."

My hand recoils at his touch, almost jerking out of his grasp. But if going with him means getting answers to my questions, I need to give him a chance to explain. I need to trust him, even if he has only earned a tiny taste of it.

But I'm also not naïve. I've heard Wehrmacht soldiers are raping French women. If I go with him, am I putting myself at risk of that happening to me?

"I swear I won't hurt you," Johann says as if sensing the reason behind my reluctance to go with him. "I just need to talk to you. To explain things without the risk of being overheard."

My hand relaxes in his, and I nod while praying I'm not about to make a costly mistake.

He takes me to the pond, his safe haven. It's far enough away from the farmhouse and road to not be seen or overheard. The early rays of dawn poke above the horizon, the sky a striped pattern of muted indigo, mauve, and orange.

He releases my hand and sits on the grass near the bank of the pond. I sink down next to him.

Johann doesn't say anything, and I don't push for him to

start talking. The quiet, awakening sounds of nature fill the silence, helping me to temporarily forget the war. Allowing me to breathe.

After what feels like ten or so minutes, he releases a long, slow breath. "When my mother first heard the early rumours about Hitler rounding up certain groups of Germans he felt were a burden on society, she ignored them." Johann's voice is almost distant, as though he's reading a schoolbook relaying the facts, but the subtext of emotion is buried deep within the words. Easily missed. "Austria wasn't part of Germany, and she had no idea if the rumours were true or not. She didn't know who was being targeted and what was happening to them. She turned a blind eye to it. Then she heard how the Germans were performing surgeries so those individuals couldn't have babies. Again, she ignored the rumours. She finally grew worried when she learned the SS was targeting deaf people—including children."

I close my eyes against the pain I imagine would be on Johann's face if I were to look at him. I would be horrified, shocked, furious if Hitler's hatred targeted Hazel for something like this. Any of this.

"Anja, my sister, was attending a school for the deaf in Vienna. Our mother begged her to come home. She told Anja she needed her help with the shop. That saved my sister's life, because eventually it wasn't safe to be deaf and living in Austria. The teachers at the school told the SS where they could find the deaf adults and children. The people who were supposed to protect them practically handed them over to the murderers." Johann's tone tightens, anger and pain and worry streaking his words like blood from a wound.

"My mother knew they couldn't stay in Austria anymore. But she also knew it wasn't safe to tell anyone where they were going, including me. I found a note hidden in a place my mother knew I would look. She told me they couldn't contact me because it was too dangerous."

My throat and heart ache for what he is going through, losing his family that way. Not knowing where they are and how they are doing. At least I know Hazel is safe in Bristol. It's my whereabouts she knows nothing of.

Johann's mother was right to believe it was too dangerous to contact Johann. If the SS had tried to torture the information from him, he might have broken and given them what they wanted. Even if he hadn't wanted to give it to them. That's why each member of the SOE and the resistance networks and circuits knows as little as possible. If one of us is captured and tortured, we don't know enough to bring down the main networks.

"I joined the Wehrmacht because I thought by joining the Army, it would ensure Anja and my mother are safe. The Germans would see I am cooperating with them. I joined the Army and not the SS because I didn't want to be any part of the Nazi regime."

"But isn't the Wehrmacht also part of the regime?" I know some details about the German Army based on my SOE training. The original Army officers didn't support Hitler and were executed or forced into retirement. Members of the Nazi party replaced them.

"Most of them, yes. But if you are viewed as not supporting the party, you're at risk of being accused of being communist or socialist or some other threat to the regime. And that would result in imprisonment and possibly death."

Germany isn't Johann's birth country, but Austria is now part of Germany. From what I've heard, the majority of Austrians welcomed the *Anschluss*. They willingly joined the German Army. They willingly threw in their support for Hitler.

"Why are you telling me this?" I ask, uncertain of his motive for revealing his family history and his reason for joining the Wehrmacht.

"Because I want you to understand. I'm not here because I want to be. If I had my way, there would be no war, my mother and sister would be safe, and I would be doing the job I loved."

"But you could still turn around and tell your commanding officer about the hiding space in the barn. As soon as you've relocated your friends, there's nothing stopping you from turning against my father and me." And I have no doubts that Major Müller would either kill us himself if he knew about the hiding place in the barn, or he would turn us over to the SS or Gestapo.

My heart pounds hard and heavy in my chest at that possibility and my skin prickles with fear. Even the brilliant colours of the sky do nothing to ease my body's reaction.

"You're right. There is nothing stopping me. But I won't do that. No one else needs to know about the hiding spot. But I do ask you not to take any more risks. Risks like what you were using the cellar for. My presence here doesn't keep you safe, Angelique. Just the opposite. Major Müller is curious about you."

An uneasy feeling slithers into my belly. "Why is that?"

"Because you're a beautiful woman. And you live under the same roof as me. In his mind, there is something going on between us. He's jealous. He wants what I have. I wouldn't be surprised if he wants you to be his lover." The harshness in Johann's tone sends my gaze shifting from the breath-stealing sunrise to him.

I'm not sure how to respond to any of that. It is one thing to be friendly with Johann to gain information. It's another to be that way with Müller.

"The man is ambitious and dangerous," Johann says. "Never forget that."

Yet another reason to forgo the plan of hiding the wireless

set in Jacques's barn. As it is, I will need to discuss the latest turn of events with the circuit leader. I don't want her showing up in the middle of the night and scaring Oskar, Margrit, and Sonja.

I look at Johann for a heartbeat, his concern and compassion weaving through me like silk thread. But at the same time, a wave of dizziness washes over me with the weight of his words.

"Thank you for the warning." I push to my feet. "I should return to the house. My papa is probably up now, and he will be wanting to eat before he begins his work."

As I approach the farmhouse, a military Jeep stops in front of it. I can't see who is in the back seat, but that doesn't keep my heart from stumbling over itself at one possibility.

The driver opens the rear door, and the loathed man Johann warned me about steps from the vehicle.

Major Müller.

4

TROY

June, Present Day
Maple Ridge

From the top of the cliff, I study the bruised sky above us. The wind picked up a short time ago, and the team doesn't have long before the storm hits hard. If Garrett and I fail to get the father and his nine-year-old son up soon, they'll be forced to stay on the ledge until the storm has passed. And by then, it will be too dark for us to get to them, and they'll have to wait another night to be rescued. No one wants that, least of all the father and son.

I step into my climbing harness and make sure it's secure. "Ready?" I ask my brother.

Garrett nods. "Ready."

We double-check that our lines won't fail us when we rappel down the cliff, and we get into position. "Okay," I yell to the father and son. "We're coming down." The father is reclining with his legs stretched in front of him, his bent elbows propping him up. His son is huddled beside him.

The father says something to the boy. "Okay," the boy yells up, waving his arm at us.

Garrett starts his descent first, with me close behind. Our rappelling partners keep an eye on our lines.

The wind is strong, but not strong enough to push me off-balance. It's situations like this, with an approaching storm, when my years of climbing experience pay off—both recreationally and with the Marines.

It takes us a minute or two before we're standing next to the two hikers. The father is flat on his back now, his son clutching his hand. My chest tightens at how scared the boy is, his face pale, body shaking. He's the reason I volunteer with SAR. I grew up on these mountains. My grandfather taught me how to respect them and how to survive on them. Most of the kids the team rescues aren't equipped to survive in these conditions like I am.

I kneel next to the boy and give him a reassuring smile. "Hey, Christopher. Everything's going to be all right. I'm Troy. And this is my brother, Garrett." I point to Garrett, who nods at him. "We're gonna get you and your dad out of here. Do you think you can be brave a little longer? You've been doing a great job so far."

The boy eagerly nods, his eyes wide with fear.

Garrett checks the father's injured leg. The man is even paler than his son. Perspiration dots his forehead, betraying his pain.

"It looks like it could be broken," Garrett says. "We'll get you two out of here as soon as we can."

I remove the walkie-talkie from my jacket. "It does look like the father's lower leg is broken," I tell Sheldon.

The rescue stretcher and another harness are lowered. Each second we wait for them puts us that much closer to the path of the oncoming storm. Each second racks up the tension in my muscles for the same reason.

"Garrett will take your father up first," I tell Christopher. "Then you and I will climb up together."

The boy's face crumples, and my chest tightens some more.

I put my hand on his shoulder. "You'll be fine, Christopher. I won't let anything happen to you. You've got this. I promise." The victims claimed by the mountains, my Marine brothers who I've lost to war, and Colton have all left dings in my soul. I have no desire to add Christopher to the mix. "And just think of the cool story you'll have to tell your friends."

That gets a slight smile from him.

Garrett and I get Christopher's father into the stretcher. Once he's securely fastened in, the crew waiting at the top of the cliff pulls him up. Garrett goes with him.

His eyes big and round, Christopher watches his father while I help him into his harness. I fasten it, ensuring it's secure.

"Don't worry, Christopher," I tell him with a confident smile. For his benefit. "We'll be out of here in no time. You just need to do exactly what I tell you. Can you do that for me?"

He slowly nods his head, looking no less worried than before.

"You see those men up there?" I point to the guys peering over the cliff edge.

"Yes." Christopher's voice is small and hitched, his fear a fist around my heart.

"They're gonna pull you up. That's why you're wearing this harness. It will keep you safe. Do you like Spiderman?"

More nodding.

"Well, that's who you're gonna be. You're gonna climb this cliff like Spiderman."

His eyes grow wider. "Like a superhero?"

I smile again, keeping my concern about the growing wind from my face. "Exactly like a superhero."

I instruct Christopher on what I want him to do and tell the two men assisting us from the top of the cliff that we're ready. Garrett and Christopher's father are almost at the top.

"You'll need to move quickly," Sheldon says on the walkie-talkie. "The wind's picking up."

"Ten-four." I release the button. "Okay, Christopher. We need to start climbing." I keep my voice calm and even. I've been in countless dangerous situations and have come close to losing my life more than once. I've been able to work with a level head, powering past emotions that only serve to defeat.

It's different when kids are involved.

A little boy's life, his future, is in my hands.

I get him into position, praying the wind will hold back long enough for me to get him to safety.

He cautiously moves up the cliff face, following my instructions. He's a natural. A real Spiderman. I use my body to protect him from the elements.

"You're doing great, Christopher," I call out over the increasing wind. The roar of the wind and the flapping of the nylon fabric of my zipped-up windbreaker make it more challenging to hear what I say. Shit, why couldn't the wind have held off a little longer?

Raindrops splatter on Christopher and me. *Shit.* If we hadn't already started to climb, we would've been forced to wait until after the storm.

Not. Much. Farther.

The wind continues to howl and whistle through the valley, rivaled only slightly by the loud beat of my heart encouraging me on.

Only two more yards to go. "Attaboy, Christopher. We're almost there." The wind drowns out my words.

Any other time, I'd keep my body close to the rock face, but that's not possible now. Not when I'm using it to shield Christopher. He's my first priority.

A strong gust of wind knocks into me, causing me to lose my grip on the wet rock face. The slippery surface doesn't help with getting a foothold. I'm flung sideways.

I put my arm out to brace for impact a fraction of a second before I'm slammed into a huge rock jutting from the cliff. Pain shoots down my arm. *Fuck.* I'm pretty sure I've just dislocated my shoulder.

Christopher screams and clings tightly to the rock.

"Hold on, Christopher!" Garrett yells, peering over the edge. "I'm coming for you."

He still has his harness on and rappels the short distance to where Christopher is located.

"How're you doing?" Garrett asks me over the howl of the wind.

"Dislocated shoulder," I manage to get out through gritted teeth.

"We need help here," he calls up.

"I can manage," I tell him. "It's not much farther. Just worry about Christopher."

The brief gust of wind dies down long enough for Garrett to help Christopher up the rest of the way. And I drag myself to a route that's climbable.

My rappelling partner pulls me up via the rope while I do what I can to climb one-handed, my injured arm held against my body. Adrenaline assists in temporarily muting the intense pain in my shoulder.

Garrett and Noah help me onto the ledge and I collapse, looking up at the sky, the rain falling on my face as I fight to regain my breath. At the same time, I try to breathe through the throbbing in my shoulder and distract myself with my thoughts on the last time I saw Jess, a sheet wrapped around her chest.

Christopher is kneeling at his father's side, crying but also keeping his chin held high.

Garrett squats next to me. "You think you'll be able to walk out of here?"

I push to a sit and wince at the pain. "Yeah. But my shoulder'll need to be stabilized first." I inwardly curse myself for getting injured. Helping Jess with her renovations will be more difficult while the shoulder heals.

The father's stretcher is carried off to where the ambulance will be waiting. Noah walks with Christopher, his hand on the boy's shoulder, keeping him close and safe.

Garrett applies the sling to my injured arm and secures the arm to my chest with a wide bandage. "I'm sure there're way better ways of getting laid tonight." Lines crinkle at the corners of his eyes. "You didn't have to go for the sympathy fuck."

I smack him on the shoulder and chuckle. "Dumbass. You're just jealous I thought of it first."

He laughs. "Don't you know it?" He helps me to my feet. "Let's get you out of here."

GARRETT AND I HEAD TO TOWN IN HIS SUV. AS SOON AS I GET cell reception, I text Jess.

> Me: Found missing father and son.
> Heading back. Have to swing by hospital
> first. Will come over once I'm finished
> there

It takes an additional forty-five minutes to get to the hospital, and I still haven't received a single text from Jess by the time we arrive.

She's probably busy with her friends. Our friends.

In the ER, I head to the triage desk. "Hey, Troy." A brief

smile flickers on the nurse's face. "What happened to your arm?"

"I dislocated my shoulder during a search and rescue." Now that the adrenaline surge has receded, the pain has intensified. I inwardly curse.

Her eyes widen. "You were the one who rescued the boy and his father?"

"Yeah. Me and Garrett. Are they okay?" I ask even though I know she can't tell me anything. It's against hospital policy.

"They're in an exam room. If you want to visit with them, I can check if they're up for that."

"Yes, please." I want to make sure Christopher is all right.

She has me sit in the triage room and asks questions about my shoulder while briefly examining it. Then she leaves and returns a minute later. "The boy is in Room Four. You can wait there until an orderly takes you to radiology. The physician will need X-rays of your shoulder before he can pop it back in." She points in the direction I need to go for Room Four.

Garrett and I walk down the hallway. Even with the renovations several years ago, the hallway feels familiar. Growing up, I had more than a few hockey and skate-boarding accidents that landed me in the ER. It was almost a second home, much to Mom's dismay.

Christopher's sitting on the bed, studying the phone in his hand, when we enter the room. An IV tube is attached to his other arm. Noah's sitting on the chair next to the bed.

The boy is smiling at the phone, his face no longer devoid of color. I can't imagine how frantic his mom must have been, not knowing where her son was and if he was okay. Not knowing if she would ever see him again. Not knowing if she would get to wrap her arms around his warm body, his smile directed at her.

"Hey, how's it going, Christopher?" I ask him, happy to see the kid's physically okay.

He glances at Garrett and me. Dried tears stain his dirty face. "Daddy's getting X-rays."

"His mom's on the way," Noah informs me. "How's the arm?"

"Just waiting to see the physician. But I wanted to check on Christopher and his father first. And how are you doing?" My question is directed to the boy.

"I'm getting an IV because of..." Face scrunched in a confused frown, he glances at Noah.

"You were dehydrated," Noah says. "Your body was incredibly thirsty."

Christopher goes back to looking at the phone and tapping at the screen, his expression one of concentration.

It's the same expression I've seen on Nova's face when she's playing one of her games on her mom's iPad.

"You playing a game?" I ask him.

He turns the screen to show me. "Minecraft." He nods at Noah. "It's his phone."

Noah shrugs. "My five-year-old nephew likes playing the game. So I downloaded it on my phone for him."

Garrett and I stay with them until Christopher's father returns from radiology, appearing grateful. Grateful to be alive. Grateful his son's okay. Grateful he'd told his wife where he was taking their son camping. Things could have gone so differently if he hadn't done that.

The nurse walks into the room with an orderly. "We're sending you up to get that shoulder of yours X-rayed now, Troy," she tells me and gives Christopher a warm smile.

I give the wheelchair the orderly is pushing a disgruntled glance, which must have looked funnier than I realized. Christopher bursts out laughing.

I flash him a grin and climb into the wheelchair.

"I'll call Lucas and Kellan while you're up there," Garrett tells me as the orderly pushes me toward the door.

"Can you text Jess that I'm here?" She still hasn't responded to the one I sent earlier.

"Will do."

Once I'm finished in radiology, another orderly wheels me to the ER and into a different exam room than the one Christopher and his father were in. "Any luck getting through to Jess?" I ask Garrett.

"Nope. I can try calling her if you want."

"No, that's fine. I'll call her once I'm sprung from here."

Samuel enters the room with an intern. "Hey, Troy. Garrett." We fist-bump Zara's older brother. Then he switches to ER-doc mode, his gaze directed on my fucked-up shoulder, eyebrows raised. "What happened to your shoulder?"

"A cliff and I had a minor disagreement, and the cliff came out the winner. My shoulder slammed into it while I was climbing."

"I heard you were in the mountains on a rescue mission. Let's have a look." He checks the X-ray on the viewer attached to the wall. "Have you seen the latest pictures of Jerome and Kim's daughter?"

"You mean the ones Kim sent two days ago?"

"Nope. She sent out a new batch today. I swear my niece is the most photographed baby around."

I chuckle. "That's because Sidney wins the prize for being the cutest baby. And her mother is a highly successful photographer."

"True." Samuel examines my shoulder. "You have an anterior dislocation, but no broken bones or fractures. I can easily pop it into the socket. You need to ice it for twenty to thirty minutes every three hours for the next few days and wear the sling. I'll give you a prescription for an anti-inflammatory drug to help with the pain."

"How long will it take to heal?"

"About twelve to sixteen weeks."

"Great," I grumble. I'd suspected as much. "Looks like I'll finally have time to catch up on my paperwork, huh?"

Samuel and Garrett grin, knowing how much I hate that part of my job. I'm very much a hands-on guy when it comes to my company and being at the worksites.

Garrett's phone pings, and he checks the screen. "Mom just texted. You're supposed to call her once you're finished here."

"How does she know where I am?" Given the gossip grapevine in this town, she could have found out from any one of numerous sources."

"I texted her while you were in radiology. Figured you'd rather she hear from me instead of from a hospital employee."

"Good thinking." I'd never hear the end of it if she'd found out via the grapevine.

With the help of an intern, Samuel pops my arm into place. And mother of all fucking hell, that hurts. Even with the pain meds and while thinking again about Jess in the sheet.

By the time I leave the hospital, my arm in the sling, the rain is coming down hard. I check my phone. Still no word from Jess. That's strange. I'd have thought by now she would've responded.

Something twinges in my gut, but I ignore it. The search and rescue must have made me slightly edgy, even though everything turned out all right in the end—other than my dislocated shoulder.

Since she has my truck, Garrett drives me to her house. The truck isn't parked in her driveway or on the street. I try ringing her doorbell, but no one answers.

Damn, where the heck is she? Maybe she's visiting a friend. Like Violet Wilson. Or another friend I don't know about. Jess doesn't seem to know many people in Maple Ridge, but she could have friends she hasn't mentioned to me.

Or does this have to do with yet another secret she's keeping from me?

Back in Garrett's SUV, I call Jess but end up in voicemail. "Hi, Jess. I'm at home. Call me when you get this message." I end the call. "You might as well take me to my place," I tell Garrett.

He drops me off at my house. I jog over to my neighbor's front door. The wind battles against my body, trying to veer me off course, and the rain switches to hail. Pea-sized ice stones pound me and bounce off the ground, creating a thin layer of white on the grass.

The lights are on in Katherine's living room, peeking through the slats in the closed wooden blinds. I ring the doorbell.

An answering bark comes from the other side of the door, but it's not Butterscotch.

The door opens. Katherine's smile vanishes from her wrinkled face the moment she spots my sling. "What happened?"

"I dislocated my shoulder while rescuing two hikers from a ledge."

Worry creases her forehead, lifting her gray eyebrows. "Are you going to be okay?"

"I'll be fine." Following rest and physical therapy. But Christopher is doing well and is in one piece, so that's the main thing. "I don't suppose Butterscotch is here, is he?"

The lines on her forehead deepen. "No. Is he supposed to be?"

"I left my truck and Butterscotch with my girlfriend when I got called in for the search and rescue." Jess hasn't agreed yet to us using the girlfriend-boyfriend label, but Katherine doesn't know that. "They're not at her house or mine. I thought I'd check to see if she dropped Butterscotch off with you."

"I haven't seen her since the last time she was at your house."

Which was last week.

Unease stirs in my gut, stronger than the twinge I felt there earlier. Stronger and sharper than the hail hammering the ground, the house, the cars on the street.

And this time...this time I can't ignore it.

If Jess isn't at her house and she's not at mine and she's not answering her phone, where the hell is she?

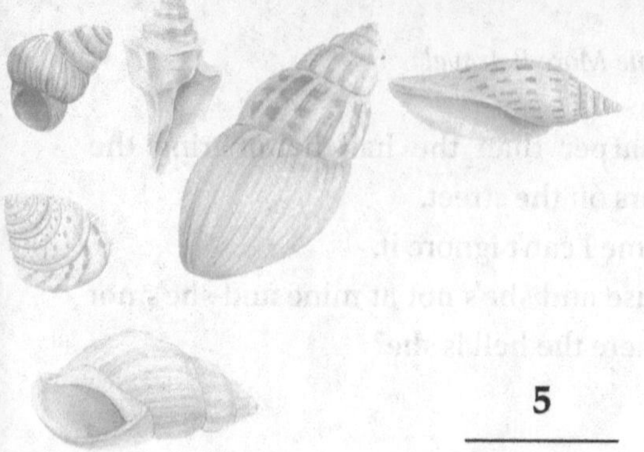

5

JESSICA

June, Present Day
Maple Ridge

The rain continues to pound me. Water streams down my face and the nape of my neck. Everything about me is soggy, including my hope.

The incline is too steep, the ground too slippery, for me to get to the road. But what if the slope isn't so steep farther along? Then I can scramble up it to the road and wave someone down.

Except I don't think anyone has driven past since I tried to avoid the deer and crashed through the guardrail. The road is too far away to hear approaching vehicles through the rain, so I have no idea if anyone has noticed the broken guardrail or Troy's overturned truck. I only know no one has leaned over the metal rail to see if the driver is all right.

I'm alone. Alone with an unrelenting throbbing in my head.

I shudder, partly from the realization at how alone I am and partly from the cold. The pain in my body intensifies, annoyed at the unnecessary movement.

I don't mind the pain. God knows I've suffered enough of it over the years. The pain reminds me I'm alive. If I can survive my husband's abuse and the assaults in prison, surely, I can survive this.

I have no idea what time it is. It's impossible to tell with the thick clouds, but it's dark enough to know nightfall is coming soon.

And I have no way of getting to safety.

There's no sign of a hiking path leading into the forest that could possibly get me to the road where the incline isn't so steep. No easy way out of here.

I sway on my feet, still lightheaded. The sweat shirt I tied around my thigh is wet and heavy from the rain and my blood.

Even if there is a path nearby, I'm not sure I could make it far with my injured leg.

I lean against a boulder. Maybe I can rest for a few minutes, then return to the truck to see if I can find my phone or something I can use to wave down a vehicle. I just need a second.

I sit on the ground and rest the back of my head on the wide rock. It provides a small amount of shelter from the wind and the diagonally falling rain. The forest swims around me, and I'm forced to close my eyes. *Just for a moment.*

I'm so tired. Tired and cold. I just want to sleep. Sleep and only wake up once I'm home again. With Bailey.

My body shivers harder, draining what little energy I have left.

It doesn't help that I went hiking before this. At the time, I figured I would go home and have something to eat and drink. I wasn't worried about surviving the night out here.

I didn't even have the foresight to leave Troy a note to tell him Butterscotch is with Rose and not Katherine and to tell him where I went. It's not as if I were Angelique, unable to leave a message in plain sight at the risk of the Gestapo, Milice, or SS stumbling across it.

My only hope is Troy will return home and discover his truck and I are gone and...and then what?

A flash of lightning brightens the sky as if to answer the question.

I didn't even think to tell Rose where I was going. I only told her I'd be back in a few hours.

Just one more minute...and then I'll figure a way to get help.

"Get up, Jess. Find a way to get back to me."

Troy. I let the deep, smooth sound of his voice weave into my consciousness, and I imagine him smiling at me with the sexy grin of his.

"Just one more minute...one more minute...one more minute..." I whisper, my voice growing weaker by the second.

If I don't find help soon, I won't get to hear Troy's voice again. His real voice, not the one playing in my head.

The wind abruptly shifts direction, and without warning, a deluge of small pebble-sized hail releases from the clouds. Its stinging touch pummels me. I release a gasped shriek, unable to find the will to stand up.

Unable to find the strength to seek better shelter than the boulders.

6

TROY

June, Present Day
Maple Ridge

My phone rings from my coffee table. I stop pacing, snatch it up, and check the screen.

Shit. It's Simone, not Jess.

I go back to pacing and accept the call. "Hey, Simone." Disappointment clings to my words. "What's up?"

"Do you know where Jess is?"

"No, I've been trying to figure that out myself. She has my truck, but she's not at her place. Bailey and Butterscotch aren't there either."

"Butterscotch is at Grams's. She phoned me because Jess left Butterscotch with her five hours ago but hasn't returned. And now Grams is worried."

The concern coursing through me a moment ago spikes to full out worry and fear. "Did Jess tell her where she was going?"

"No. She told Grams that Bailey somehow ended up eating

39

poison and has to stay at the vet clinic overnight. That's all Grams knows."

"Do you have any idea where Jess might be?"

"No. I texted Em and Zara to see if they've seen or heard from her. They also have no idea where she could be, and she isn't answering any of our texts."

"What about Violet Wilson? She and Jess were in yoga together. And I know they've met up for coffee a few times." I don't know Violet personally, but I do know she's married to that asshole I went to school with. That asshole who liked to bully me as a kid.

"You don't by any chance know Violet's phone number, do you?" Simone asks. Jasper's bark comes from her end of the line.

"Nope. But Rose is in yoga with them. Maybe she can ask their instructor for Violet's number."

"I'll try that," Simone says. "Thanks."

"Let me know what you find out."

Five minutes later, Simone texts to tell me Rose got Violet's number from their yoga instructor, but Violet isn't answering her phone. We're no closer to figuring out where Jess went than we were ten minutes ago.

And she has my truck, so I can't exactly drive around town searching for her.

I call Noah's cell. "Hey, can you help me?" I explain the situation to him. "Can you check if my truck's been involved in an accident?"

"Sure. Give me a moment. What's your license plate number?"

I tell him, and he phones back after a few minutes to let me know nothing's been reported.

"Let me know if you need any help locating her," he prompts.

"If you can keep an eye out for her, that would be great. I

don't know if I'm overreacting"—because I'm in love with her—"or if my gut instinct is right and something's wrong." The twisting in my gut is the same feeling I'd get in the Marines right before things went to hell. The way the air molecules seem to shift and shrink and splinter.

"Will do. You might want to fill in a missing persons report. Have you checked the hospital in case she's there?" There's a solemn quality to his tone, like he's hoping he's wrong—she hasn't been injured and is unable to talk—but he still has to ask.

"I'll try that next." I thank Noah and call the hospital.

"I'm sorry," the woman on the other end of the phone replies, "but we can't tell you anything. Patient confidentiality."

"So you're saying she *is* there but you can't tell me anything?" I ask.

"No, I'm saying unless you're family, I can't release any information. Period."

Crap. Now what? I call Samuel and leave a message for him, asking if Jess has been admitted to the hospital, and then I call Lucas.

He answers immediately. "What do you need?" It sounds like he's grabbing his keys and heading to the garage.

"I need a ride to Rose's to pick up Butterscotch. And if you happen to have a crystal ball that can tell me where Jess vanished to, that would be great." I figure Simone has filled him in on the situation. I don't need to explain it to him.

"I can do the first request. Sorry, fresh out of crystal balls. But if you want, after we get Butterscotch, we can drive around Maple Ridge and see if we can locate your truck and Jess."

"Thanks."

While I wait for him, I text and phone Jess again. "Where the hell are you, Jess?" I mutter.

I go back to pacing, not caring I'm supposed to be resting. I'll rest as soon as I find her.

A flash of lightning streaks across the sky. A resounding boom follows it.

For the first year after Lucas was honorably discharged from the Marines, thunderstorms would trigger his flashbacks. He's not the only vet I know who suffered from thunderstorm-induced flashbacks.

Jess has never mentioned having issues with storms. But there are a lot of things about her past she hasn't admitted to.

Lucas picks me up and we drive to Rose's house.

"You gonna let me be your PT once your physician gives you the green light?" he asks.

I smirk. "That depends. Just how over the part where I accidentally drove over your bike in high school are you?"

He laughs, the sound not quite a low chuckle. "Don't worry. I've moved on. I won't be taking out the loss of my favorite bike on your shoulder."

My smirk widens into a full grin. "Phew. That's a relief." The smile falls away. "Yes, you get to be my PT. I don't trust anyone else with my shoulder."

"You do realize everyone who works in the clinic is a skilled PT, right? They're some of the best around."

"I know, but you're my brother, and you know my revenge will be swift if you fuck up my shoulder." I toss him another grin, even though my shoulder is aching.

His laugh this time is loud and abrupt. "Fair enough."

Lucas parks his SUV in front of Rose's house, and we both go to the front door. I ring the doorbell, and a second later, Butterscotch's bark is heard from the other side.

Rose opens the door and lets Lucas and I in. The smell of fresh-baked gingersnap cookies greets us. We both kiss her cheek, and Lucas hugs her. I manage to give her an awkward one-armed hug. She might not be our biological grandmother, but she's always been like a grandmother to us.

"What happened to your arm, Troy?" She stares at the arm in question. I give her the abridged version.

Butterscotch peers up at me, his round dark eyes hopeful. I kneel by his side and fuss over him. "I heard your little buddy was sick." He gives me an answering bark. Christ, if anything happens to Bailey, it could set back Jess's recovery. If I can find her, that is. "I don't suppose you know where Jess is?" Another bark, which does nothing to solve the mystery of her disappearance. I straighten. "You have no idea where Jess could've gone?" I ask Rose.

"Sorry. No. She told me what happened to Bailey and asked me to look after Butterscotch for a few hours because there was something she needed to do. But then she never came back. I tried calling her, but she hasn't answered the phone or returned my call."

It's not like Jess to not respond to texts and calls. The only time she couldn't quickly respond to them was when she was working at Picnic & Treats or at yoga. She's never gone this long without responding.

Something's definitely wrong.

But unless I know the sequence of events leading up to her disappearance, it will be next to impossible to figure out where she is.

Lucas, Butterscotch, and I return to Lucas's SUV. "Do we report her missing to the police?" he asks, but judging from his expression, he thinks that's a waste of time. He doesn't have much faith in the Maple Ridge Police Department after they arrested him last year for the possession of narcotics with the intent to sell. Narcotics he had nothing to do with. And the police did little to find out who was responsible for the fake tip or how the drugs ended up in his house.

"Noah suggested that. But we have no proof she's missing. For all we know, she isn't answering her texts because she's driving back from Eugene after going shopping there." She didn't say she was going shopping in the city, but since she doesn't own a vehicle, why not make the most of my truck? "There's no indication her disappearance is an emergency."

The police won't care about my gut feeling.

My phone rings, and I answer it. "Is she there?" I ask Samuel, the question tumbling out before I have a chance to catch my breath.

"No one has been admitted under her name, and no one in the ER has seen a woman fitting Jess's description. Sorry I couldn't be of more help."

"No. That was good. Thank you, Samuel. I owe you."

"No problem. Good luck finding her." He ends the call.

"She's not at the hospital," I tell Lucas.

He starts the engine and turns on the windshield wipers. The rain hasn't let up since we returned to Maple Ridge. "We could ask her neighbors if they saw anything. Maybe one of them talked to her before she disappeared, or they saw something suspicious."

"Good idea."

He parks in Jess's driveway. There's still no sign of my truck or Jess. The lights are off in her house, other than the one in the living room that's on a timer. I ring her doorbell, but still no one comes to the door.

We split up. Lucas goes door-to-door on Jess's side of the street. I cover the other side, but it quickly becomes clear no one noticed anything out of the ordinary about Jess or her house.

"She was carrying Bailey when I last saw her," Delores says, sounding heartbroken, her short gray hair glowing in the porch light. "She was putting her into the back seat of your truck, Troy. Rose told me the poor puppy accidentally ate poison. Is that true?"

"I only know what Rose told me. You never saw Jess after that?"

Delores shakes her head.

"I did." Samantha's voice comes from the other side of the front door. Delores opens the door wider, revealing her friend shuffling toward us. "It was several hours ago. I was pulling up to Delores's house, and Jess was walking to your truck."

"Any idea where she went?"

"None at all," Samantha says. "Sorry."

I thank the two women and move on to the next house. My wet clothes stick to my skin, and a chill creeps into my bones. The chill won't go anywhere until I've located Jess.

By the time Lucas and I return to her house, neither of us has learned anything beyond what Samantha told me.

"Could she have gone somewhere to shoot photos?" Lucas asks.

"She loves taking photos of the sunset, but with the storm, that wouldn't be possible."

"Maybe she was taking photos of the storm and the lightning. I bet it was impressive over the lake."

I lift my good shoulder in a half shrug because I have no idea if that's something she would do. Or could do with an iPhone camera. "Sounds pretty risky to me." She's not a Marine. She's not the epitome of a risk taker.

"If there's one thing I've learned from Kim, it's that photographers will do almost anything to get a great shot."

I walk to Jess's garage and check the door. It's locked, like I knew it would be. Lucas joins me. I peer through the garage side door, but it's too dark to see if her bike's inside.

I pull my phone from my jeans pocket, turn on the flashlight, and shine it into the garage. The beam of light lands on her bike. "She doesn't have her bike with her."

"We'll check the parking lots at the lake to see if your truck's there. Other than that, I don't know where else to look."

We try all three lake parking lots near Maple Ridge. All are empty. The rest are much farther away, and I can't see her going to any of them just for a photo. At this point, there's not much more I can do.

The only thing left is to go home and wait for Jess to show up or for her to call me or for the worst-case scenario to happen. For the police to call me to tell me my truck has been found and she's...she's badly injured or dead.

My chest constricts at that last possibility, frenzied thoughts robbing me of my breath.

Lucas drives Butterscotch and me to my house. "Call me if you need anything, or if you hear from Jess."

"Will do."

I'm entering my house when my phone rings. Kellan. "What's up?" I ask him.

"Em just told me that Jess is missing."

I get him up to speed on the situation. "Do you have any idea where she might be?" An unsettled feeling in my gut tells me she's told him a lot more about her past than she's told me.

A tortured silence vibrates for a beat from the other end of the phone. "I hate to say it, but it's possible she's on the run."

What the hell's he talking about? "On the run from what?"

More silence. The type of silence that comes from deliberating one's options.

"What aren't you telling me, Kellan?" My voice comes out rough, beyond frustrated.

A quiet sigh reaches my ear. "Someone might be looking for Jess because of who she is. Or it's possible someone found out who she is and threatened to expose her." His words are even and without a hint of emotion. He's just relaying the facts.

I clench the phone tighter. "What the hell are you talking about?"

"All I know is, it's possible she's not coming back."

"You're wrong!" Christ, I hope he's wrong. "She'd never leave Bailey behind. She loves Bailey. And she bought a house."

"None of that matters if she feels like she doesn't have a choice."

Lava boils inside of me, churning in my gut. Why isn't he telling me anything that will help me figure out where she's gone? "Why can't you give me a straight answer, Kellan?"

"Because I don't have an answer I can give you. I'm sorry, Troy. If I knew where she might be, I would tell you."

I believe him. He would tell me if he knew where she was—it's just everything else she's told him he isn't willing to share that has me...

I kick the side table in the hallway hard enough to jostle it. The ceramic vase topples onto its side and rolls over the edge before I can make a move to stop it.

The vase crashes onto the wood flooring and shatters into several bits. *Dammit.*

"What was that?" Kellan asks, his voice tight.

"Nothing. I accidentally knocked over a vase." And now I have to one-handedly clean up the damn pieces. "Has she told you where she would go if she felt she had to leave town?" My teeth are one step away from being ground to dust.

"No."

"Do you really think she's in trouble?" The volume of my voice drops to just above a whisper, the words pushing past a dry throat. "Is it possible someone has hurt or threatened her?" I've never felt this fucking helpless, felt this lost, until now.

"I really don't know," Kellan says on a sigh. "Anything is possible."

That wasn't the answer I'd been hoping for.

Jess, where the hell are you?

7

ANGELIQUE

June 1943
France

A smile absent of any pleasantry curves onto Major Müller's loathsome face. And Johann's words echo in my head: *"The man is ambitious and dangerous. Never forget that."*

"Bonjour, Madame D'Aboville." Müller's eyes roam over my body, and I gauge the distance from where I'm standing to the front door of the farmhouse. The sky above us has turned light blue now that the sun has risen above the horizon.

Fear and nausea churn in my belly. My heart gallops in my chest. I can't get to the door without crossing him. Müller is an arm's length from the path leading to the house.

I stay planted where I am, praying Oskar and his family don't make a sound. "Are you looking for Captain Schmidt?" My face gives Müller no reason to believe his presence unsettles me.

"Major Müller. I was not expecting to see you here this morning." The deep, soothing voice Johann used at the pond has been replaced with the hard edge of respect for a superior. The words are spoken in German.

I turn to see Johann walking towards us along the same path I took.

Müller lifts his arm in salute. "Heil, Hitler."

Johann salutes without hesitation, but I can't help but wonder at what cost to him. Is that why he disappears to the pond in the evenings? To pray for God's forgiveness because of his involvement in the war? To give solace to his soul?

"I have arranged for the rest of the officers to meet us here so we can discuss our upcoming mission," Müller says.

My throat tightens. Jacques is still inside the farmhouse, and I know how much the Germans' presence in his house angers and pains him. There's nothing I can do about it, though. Jacques and I aren't supposed to be here. Our presence in the house, I now realise, is the only act of defiance Johann can afford.

The act of defiance Müller knows about.

The one he doesn't know about is hidden in the barn.

"Madame D'Aboville, would you care to make us breakfast?" Müller's rhetorical question is spoken in French. I'm not a houseguest. I'm the unpaid staff, the cook.

I nod my acquiescence to his command.

He instructs his driver to take the food into the house.

The soldier carries out Müller's orders, and I follow him. While this is not how I had hoped to spend my day, there is a chance I'll overhear something to share with Désirée later. If I'm going to ask for help with Oskar and his family, it will aid my case if I also have information that will benefit the local resistance group.

Once all the food supplies have been brought in, the soldier disappears, and I am left alone to cook breakfast.

German recipes, translated into French, are included with the supplies.

I hear Jacques leave through the front door without a word from the occupants in the drawing room and without eating his breakfast first.

I survey the food I've prepared. There is enough to feed at least a dozen men. Would anyone notice if I hid some to give to Oskar, Margrit, and Sonja? They need it far more than the officers, and I doubt I'll have a chance to steal some of it afterwards, even if there are leftovers.

I grab several bread rolls and whatever else I can fit on a large plate and hide it in the cupboard. No one will go looking in there; of that I am certain.

I take the food into the dining room and set up the table. I avoid making eye contact with anyone, and that includes Johann.

They sit down and I am dismissed. I return to the kitchen, but instead of tending to the dishes or cleaning the stovetop and counters, I stand by the door and listen. The men don't bother whispering since they believe I cannot understand a word they say.

I mentally make note of everything said about an upcoming attack on one village and the plans to quickly erect a bridge to make the transportation of tanks into one region faster than it is currently. I silently curse I cannot journey to Paris to relay the information to Allaire. There is too much to tell him using our typical means of communication through coded messages.

I cannot even ask the new operator to transmit the message to Baker Street. It won't be possible until he has a safe place to transmit from. And now that Oskar and his family are hidden in the barn, it is unlikely the operator will have a safe place to transmit from soon. But that would be true even if Oskar and his family were not here. It doesn't matter if Johann is against the Nazi regime—he won't sit idly by while a wireless operator is sending messages to London. Not if he believes that in by telling his commanding officer about the operator, it will ensure his mother's and sister's safety.

The officers' conversation switches to a grand ball in Paris next month. A high-ranking officer will be in attendance with his wife. It will be quite the affair. Johann and several officers in the room will also be attending.

"Perhaps I should ask Frau D'Aboville to attend with me as my guest," one of the officers says. I recognise his voice. The officer reminds me of a toad, only not half as pleasant. His tone is light with mocking condescension, and it makes my skin itch with disgust.

The other officers laugh.

"That is not a bad idea." Müller's words feel like a noose around my neck, cutting off the air to my lungs. "She's certainly pretty enough to impress General von der Osten and his wife. She doesn't understand German, so she'll be what a woman should be: silent and nothing more than an adornment."

More laughter from the officers.

"I disagree." The gavel-hard tone of Johann's response echoes through the room, and I am able to breathe once more. I'm not interested in escorting the toad to the event. He can go on his own.

"You disagree she's pretty, or that a woman should be silent and nothing more than an adornment?"

I can see, in my mind, Müller peering down his arrogant nose at Johann.

"I disagree she should go with Second Lieutenant von Bock. I shall be the one escorting her. She's too beautiful to be with the likes of him. People will notice her, and he will be invisible." Johann's tone shimmers with humour but also hints at the seriousness that lies beneath the surface.

Laughter filters into the kitchen from the dining room once more. "He has a point," one of the men says, still laughing.

"I agree," Müller intones, laughter absent from his voice. "She is a better match for Captain Schmidt. Just makes sure she understands her place. It won't reflect well on you if she does act as anything but a docile companion."

My heart rate kicks up. Not from fear but the realisation this might result in the break Baker Street is looking for in the war. It's my chance to do my job, to do what Allaire hoped would happen once Johann moved into Jacques's home. What better way to learn about the Nazis' plans in the war than to be among a group of high-powered officers who are likely to brag about upcoming operations?

The faint sound of a distant explosion reminds me of just how in the middle of the war I am, and my muscles tense. It's far enough away that the ground doesn't tremble.

At the rapid scraping of a dozen or so wooden chair legs across the dining room floor, I hurry to the sink and begin washing the dishes. My body braces for another explosion. There isn't one. Was it an Ally attack? It wasn't the work of a resistance circuit. They wouldn't do that during broad daylight.

Or at least I don't think they would.

The officers and Johann rush from the house. Soon after, I hear the rumble of engines drive away.

I wait a few minutes while I tidy the kitchen, then check through the window to make sure all the German soldiers are gone.

Satisfied no one has lingered behind, including Johann, I remove the food-laden plate from the cupboard. I put it on the counter and fill another plate with what little food remains from the officers' breakfast. I carry both plates to the barn.

Inside the barn, I remove the bale of straw from the trapdoor. "It's Angelique. I have some food for you." I pull open the trapdoor and climb down the steps, carrying one of the plates. I pass it to Oskar.

"Was that an explosion?" he asks, worry pinching his brow.

I nod. "But you should be safe here. Whatever it was is over." Or I assume it is.

Sonja is asleep on the bed. Her parents look as though they might have successfully squeezed in an hour or two of sleep since Johann and I left them.

I go back up to retrieve the other plate and hand it to Margrit. "Sorry for the delay." My voice is quiet so as not to wake Sonja. She looks so at peace. I can't imagine the last time she felt that way. The last time we have all felt that way. "Johann's commanding officer was here, along with some other Wehrmacht officers."

Margrit's face pales and she gasps. Oskar wraps his arm around her shoulders, but his expression and tense body conflict with the comforting action.

"It's all right," I assure them. "They're gone. No one suspects you're here. For now, you're safe. I have to go into town. Is there anything I can get you before I leave?"

Oskar smiles softly, the strain of their situation a stain on his face. "No, we should be fine. Thank you for your kindness."

I return his smile, struggling to make it brighter, more reassuring than I feel. My smile is nothing like it was prior to the war. I wonder if it will ever be that way again. "You're welcome."

After I leave the family hidden in the barn, I go into the house and pack food for Jacques, putting it in a basket. Then I head towards the part of the vineyard where he told me he would be midday. I pause at the top of the slope and appreciate the view of neat rows upon rows of grapevines attached to the long trellises.

The view is also a reminder of how much work the vineyard is for one man to manage, beyond what I do to help when I can. But I am a poor substitute for his son and the other man who used to work here until they found themselves in the German prison camp.

I walk down a row of grapevines and relish the peace. It's just me and the leafy plants and the silence.

The sun is high in the sky when I come upon Jacques. He's inspecting an inline stake in one of the trellises.

He accepts the food basket. "Are they gone?"

"Yes." I assume he is referring to the soldiers.

Jacques peers into the basket. "Who is the family he's hiding in the barn?" He speaks so calmly; I would think he was referring to a warm spring day. A heavy weight drops in my stomach.

So he does know about them.

I try to gauge his reaction to the unexpected guests. He's used to hiding downed Allied pilots in the barn, but this is no doubt the first time a German has hidden someone in there.

"How...?" I stumble over the word. "How did you find out?"

He bites into a stale piece of baguette, his expression giving little away. "I saw him take them into the barn last night. Who are they?" Jacques still doesn't look at me, his eyes moving to the horizon.

"A Jewish family he knows from Austria."

That draws Jacques's attention to me. "Thought the Germans and Austrians all hate the Jews."

"I guess not all do."

I trust Jacques with the work we do for the local resistance circuit, but I don't know what to expect when it comes to his hatred of and distrust for Johann. I can only hope he doesn't turn his back on the family just to spite the captain.

"How do we know he won't tell his Nazi friends we're hiding them?" Heat flares in Jacques's voice with enough intensity to burn down the vineyard and everything in a ten-mile radius. "Have you considered it might be a setup?"

I reverse a half step from the force of his words. In the short time I've been living in his house, I've rarely seen a show of temper from him. "You're right. It could be a setup, but I don't think it is. He has known about the cellar in the barn for a few weeks but hasn't told anyone about it."

Jacques grunts but doesn't say anything. He takes another bite of the baguette with the ferocity of a tiger tearing the meat from a bone. I only hope he's imagining the bone comes from a Nazi and not from me.

———

DÉSIRÉE IS STANDING ON THE GRASS, WATCHING AFTER A GROUP of small children in the village park when I arrive. The children are running around, trying to forget their hunger. Trying to forget their fathers are missing because of the war.

I can feel the scorching gazes from a few women by the fountain, can hear their silent condemnations because Johann is billeted with me. To them, I'm a collaborator.

I walk towards Désirée as if I have not a care in the world and smile at the children as they run past me. It's not a bright or happy smile. It's just the slight upturn of my lips. That's about all I can muster with the weight of what I am about to confess sitting on my shoulders. The smile is meant to bring a little comfort to the children. That, and to mask my nervousness at what I am about to ask Désirée.

I stop next to her and keep my eyes on the children. "I need your help," I tell her, knowing we don't have much time if we want to avoid drawing any attention. Attention from those who believe I am a collaborator, and attention from the German soldiers. "There's a Jewish family hiding out in Jacques's barn. We need to get them out of the country."

A short and abrupt laugh rises from Désirée. "There are lots of Jewish families wanting to get out of Europe. The escape line is only for downed pilots and agents. It's not for Jewish families wanting to escape to Britain."

"Not even if the Jewish family is hiding in Jacques's barn

because a certain German soldier snuck them in there?" I turn my head to her, widening my smile while attempting to keep it looking natural.

Désirée's eyes go round. "Ronan, please don't pull on your sister's plaits." Her voice carries over the sound of the children playing. "Are you telling me there might be a tiny soul in Captain Schmidt, even though he's one of *them*?" The volume of her voice drops, hidden under the nursery rhyme a pair of girls are chanting with little enthusiasm.

"It would seem that way."

"It won't make a difference for the escape line. Downed pilots and agents only."

"Not even if the family's presence puts us all at risk? If the SS finds them there, they'll believe Jacques and I are responsible. It will put my mission in jeopardy."

Désirée releases a weary sigh. "I'll see what I can do. But I can't make any promises."

"I also need your help with something else. Major Müller had an impromptu meeting at Jacques's farmhouse this morning."

She curses under her breath, and I can see in her eyes she understands my desperate situation with Oskar's family.

"I overheard details about one of their upcoming missions Baker Street needs to know about," I say, keeping my eyes alert to our surroundings and whether we're drawing any unwanted attention. "But it's too tricky for me to go to Paris right now and relay the message to Allaire."

"Our wireless operator can send it."

"That will not work. We can't hide his set in Jacques's barn. Not with the family there. And now that Captain Schmidt knows about the hiding space, that option is no longer feasible."

"Agreed. But for now, the operator has a temporary location. He should be able to send your message to London." She tells me where to meet the cut-out tomorrow. The newly recruited member of the local resistance circuit will pass my message to the wireless operator.

"Give me three days," Désirée says, her tone brisk yet soft, "and hopefully I'll have some news about what we can do with your other situation."

I give her a small nod of understanding.

A tiny flicker of hope sparks inside me. If we can get Oskar and his family to safety, it might go a long way in helping me gain Johann's trust. That would benefit Baker Street when it comes to ending the war if it means gaining information to use against the enemy.

And the end of the war will bring me that much closer to seeing my sister again. To repairing things between us.

My reason to survive.

8

———

TROY

June, Present Day
Maple Ridge

D aybreak hasn't even arrived when I push myself upright in bed with my good arm.

My injured shoulder curses me. The painkiller I took four hours ago has long since stopped working.

I have no idea why I even bothered going to bed. It's not as if I slept much. Between my aching shoulder, getting comfortable in a position I don't normally sleep in, and Jess going missing, I barely got in more than two hours of sleep.

I grab my phone from my nightstand and check it. There are no texts or missed calls from Jess. No texts from Zara or Simone or Emily to tell me they know where she is. No messages from my brothers.

No missed calls from the police department—which may be a good thing, considering Jess has my truck. It means they haven't found it crashed somewhere.

58

But as much of a relief as that might be, it means I need to file a missing persons report. It isn't like Jess to disappear.

Except...I've only known her three months. What do I really know about her? Maybe her disappearing is exactly what she's like.

Kellan's words from last night replay in my mind: *"Someone might be looking for Jess because of who she is. Or it's possible someone found out who she is and threatened to expose her."*

What the hell was he talking about?

He knows something she hasn't shared with me. He's being loyal to her, which says a lot. He's more concerned about protecting her than he is about what the secret could mean for me or our friends or our family.

I have to trust him. And I do.

But that still doesn't solve anything. What am I supposed to tell the cops? She's missing, and so is my truck.

I go downstairs and feed Butterscotch, make some extra-strong coffee, and pace in my living room. I think back to all the conversations Jess and I have had over the past few months. Hints of where she could be.

I think about the people she knows outside of Maple Ridge, but other than her grandmother who died more than five years ago and a niece, Jess has never mentioned anyone else, including a sibling. Whenever I try talking to her about her life before Maple Ridge, she quickly changes the topic.

I check the time on my phone. Someone at the vet clinic might have an idea where she went. But it's Sunday, which means it's closed—except for emergencies and to pick up animals who can go home after staying overnight.

It's also too early to drag any of my brothers out of bed and ask them to drive me to the clinic. Or in Garrett's case, to drag him away from his latest manuscript. I turn on the local news, then call the Maple Ridge Police Department's non-urgent phone number and tell the man who answers about the situation.

"Do you want to file a stolen vehicle report for your truck, sir?"

"Unless someone has abducted my girlfriend and is using my truck as the getaway vehicle, my truck isn't stolen. I loaned it to her." I don't need a cop pulling Jess over after locating her and scaring her to death because they think she stole my truck.

He asks me all the necessary questions, like: When did I last see Jess? What was she wearing? What is the make of my truck and the license plate number?

Once the report is filled out, I'm asked to email a recent photo of Jess. I don't exactly have many because she's more comfortable being behind the lens than in front of it. I send the only photo I have of her on my phone, but she's not even looking at the camera in it.

Then all I can do is wait. Wait for the police to call me if they find anything out. Wait until I can call Garrett to help me search for her.

I spend the next two hours pacing while listening to the news. Nothing is mentioned that sounds like it has something to do with Jess. I call Garrett. "Hey, I need a lift to the vet clinic."

"Is this for Butterscotch, or did you want to check on Bailey?"

"The second option," I reply, "and to see if anyone there knows anything about Jess's disappearance."

"You do realize it's Sunday? No one's going to be working there other than one veterinarian nurse."

"And maybe she talked to Jess yesterday and has all the answers I need."

"Alright. I'll be at your house in ten." Garrett ends the call.

We swing by Jess's house first, but like yesterday, there's still no sign that she's home.

The vet clinic is in an old house off Main Street. The small parking lot is empty except for a single car. The early morning sun promises a warm day, the blue sky reflecting in the puddles scattered on the ground.

I ring the after-hours doorbell. A few minutes later, Ambrosia opens the door, her textured curls a cloud around her smiling bronze face. "Troy? Garrett? What are you doing here?"

"I came to see Bailey, Jessica Smithson's dog. And I wanted to ask you a few questions."

She looks behind me. "Where's Jessica?"

"I'm hoping you can tell me."

Ambrosia's forehead pinches into a confused frown. "Why are you hoping I know where she is?"

"She's my girlfriend and she's gone missing," I explain. "And I'm hoping you can tell me something from when she was here yesterday that might give me a clue where she vanished to."

"I'm not really sure I'll be much help, but c'mon in. I bet Bailey would love to have a visitor." Ambrosia opens the door and leads me to the room where the sick animals are housed. Each animal is in a cage with blankets. The sharp tang of pine disinfectant lingers in the air.

Bailey is in a large cage, big enough for her to lie down in but not do much else.

Like a number of the animals in the room, she lifts her head and gazes in our direction.

Ambrosia unlocks the metal door and steps aside so I can stroke Jess's puppy.

"Hey, girl. How're you doing? I don't suppose you have any idea where Jess went?"

Bailey whimpers.

"How's she doing?" I ask Ambrosia.

"Definitely better than when she came in yesterday. Her poor owner was scared Bailey wasn't going to make it."

"She loves Bailey." For so many reasons. "You talked to her yesterday? Jess, I mean."

"Not really. It was Dr. Cummingham who mostly spoke to her. She was too stressed to talk to anyone else when she first arrived."

"Is he coming in today?" I continue stroking Bailey, doing my best to make up for Jess not being here.

"No, not unless there's an emergency. He's on call."

"Do you have his number? I need to find out what he and Jess talked about."

"I'm not supposed to give out any of the vets' home numbers." Hesitancy lingers in Ambrosia's words.

"It's an emergency. Maybe he knows where she is."

Ambrosia glances at Bailey, who chooses that moment to flash her sorrowful pleading puppy eyes. "Okay, let me check with him."

Ambrosia leaves the room and returns a few minutes later. She picks up the phone receiver on the wall, punches in a few digits, and hands it to me. "He'll talk to you."

I take it from her. "Hello, Dr. Cummingham?" I say into the phone.

"Yes. Ambrosia said you want to talk to me because you think I might know something that will help you find your missing girlfriend?"

"That's right." I've known Dr. Cummingham for forever. He used to come to my elementary school when my brothers and I were kids and talk about his job as a veterinarian. He knows me. Trusts me. *I hope.*

"I'm not sure how much I can help you, but I can try."

"What did you two talk about yesterday when she was in with Bailey?"

"We talked about what happened to her dog, and that I wanted to keep Bailey overnight to monitor her condition."

"Did Jessica mention she was going anywhere specific after she left the clinic?"

There's a pause for a beat, as if he's mentally replaying his conversation with her. "Sorry, Troy, but we only talked about Bailey. She never mentioned any plans for the rest of the day. I wish I could be more help."

I thank him for his time and apologize for disturbing him on the weekend.

"That's fine. I hope you find her."

Garrett and I return to his SUV.

"Now what?" he asks. "Any ideas where she could possibly have gone?"

"No. None." I glance around the parking lot as if the answer to Jess's disappearance is here.

Ambrosia's green Honda Civic sits at the far end of the small lot. A blue SUV drives past on the street. A magpie hops down from the low fence and pecks at a discarded paper cup on the ground. There's nothing here to tell me where Jess could have gone.

We drive over to Picnic & Treats. Zara isn't working today, but maybe someone there saw Jess before she went missing.

Amy is leaving the café as we walk up to it. "Hi, Garrett. Troy." Her gaze lingers on my brother for a beat longer than necessary. It's no secret Amy once had a thing for him.

"Hey, Amy," I say. "You haven't seen Jess Smithson in the last twenty-four hours, have you?" Jess mentioned they're in the same yoga class, so Amy knows who I'm talking about.

"I think I saw her yesterday afternoon. Maybe. I saw someone who looked like her from a distance. Except, she was alone."

Hope stirs to life, but I wrangle it under control. "Where was this?"

"I was hiking with my brother and some of his friends

yesterday. We were in the parking lot, getting ready to return home, when I thought I saw her walking toward the trailhead."

I suck in a breath. "Which trail?"

She gives a quick shrug. "Who knows? They all seem the same to me. It's the one that's about thirty to forty minutes from here."

I know the trail she means. It's one of Jess's favorite hikes.

"But you're not a hundred-percent positive it was her?" Garrett asks.

"I was too far away to know for certain. But from where I was standing, it looked like her. Same height, body, blond hair in a ponytail. Bailey wasn't with her. And since those two are inseparable, I'm not absolutely positive it was her. Is something wrong? Why are you looking for her?" Amy's gaze slides between us, eyebrows raised in alarm.

"Because my girlfriend has gone missing." I immediately regret the terseness in my tone. It's not Amy's fault that her news has put me further on edge when it should have the opposite effect. At least we're closer to figuring out where Jess went than we were ten minutes ago. "Sorry. I'm worried about her."

"I hope you find her soon. I was surprised to see anyone heading out on the trail so late, but I figured the woman knew what she was doing."

Garrett and I thank her for her help.

"What do you think?" he asks me. "Do you think it was Jess?"

"It's possible. She was stressed about what happened to Bailey. Her therapist has been encouraging Jess to do more things that relax her. It would make sense for Jess to go hiking and take photos." The unease in my gut from last night has turned into a five-alarm heartburn. If she went hiking yesterday afternoon, why the hell hasn't she returned?

Garrett and I exchange concerned glances. Either something happened to my truck and it didn't start—but that's unlikely because I keep it well maintained—or Jess is injured and possibly lost in the mountains.

We race to his SUV, which is parked on a side street. As soon as my door slams shut, I'm on the phone, calling Kellan and Lucas on a conference call. Garrett pulls onto the street and heads toward the route we need to take to get to the trail.

Kellan picks up with a grumpy, "Any luck finding her yet?"

"Amy Clayborne saw her yesterday afternoon." I get him and Lucas up to speed. "More than likely, Jess is lost and injured." And scared. For all I know, something triggered a flashback while she was hiking and she fell.

All kinds of terrifying possibilities charge through my head, and my grip tightens on my phone.

9

TROY

June, Present Day
Maple Ridge

arrett and I head to the closest trail. Lucas and Kellan are driving to two other locations where I've taken Jess hiking, in case she went to either one of them. The first step is locating my truck. The second will be calling in search and rescue once I find evidence of where she is.

The tension in the SUV stifles all conversation. Even if Garrett were talking, I wouldn't hear a word he was saying. My attention is focused on our surroundings. Pine trees pass us in a blur.

Ahead of us, the metal guardrail that separates the road from the steep incline catches my eye. The railing should be upright and continuous. It shouldn't be ripped from the road and split in two.

Long black marks streak the road. Skid marks leading to the broken guardrail.

"What the hell happened here?" I ask, not expecting an answer.

Garrett pulls over to the shoulder. A black truck lies on its side farther down the incline, the roof dented. The bumper is facing uphill, and I can make out the familiar yellow sticker. The Marine Veteran bumper sticker.

My bumper sticker.

A frigid chill settles in my bones, steals my breath. "Shit!"

"What's wrong?"

"I think that's my truck." I scramble out the passenger door. There's barely enough space between Garrett's SUV and the guardrail for someone my size, but I squeeze past and stare down the steep incline. Stare at the wreck and search for signs of life.

Stillness stares back, giving no indication Jess survived the crash or is even in the truck.

"Jessica!" I yell, praying she can hear me.

If she replies, it isn't loud enough for me to make out her voice.

I tear my gaze from the mangled wreck and survey the area for a way to get to it. I take a step toward the gap in the guardrail, ready to run down the slope if I don't have any other choice.

Garrett grabs my good arm before I can do exactly that. "You won't get to it that way. The ground's too wet. And you're gonna fuck up your shoulder again if you attempt it."

I yank my arm from his grip. "I have to check on her. I have to make sure she's okay."

Garrett's usually good at keeping his emotions off his face. It's something that was grilled into us when we were in the Marines. But this is one time even he fails to keep the flicker of what he's thinking from his expression.

And what he's thinking pisses me off.

"She's alive," I grind out. She has to be. She's already survived a lot. I'm not going to lose her now.

He heads to the driver side of his SUV and out of sight. I vaguely hear him talking to the 9-1-1 dispatcher. My attention is focused on finding another way to my truck.

But there is none.

Ignoring the truth of Garrett's words, I start walking down the slope. It's not a sheer drop like the one I rescued Christopher and his father from. I have that in my favor.

The ground is muddy from last night's storm, but if I perform a switchback instead of going straight down, I might be able to get to the truck without sliding onto my ass.

I can't just stand on the sidelines, waiting for someone to rescue my girlfriend.

"Idiot!" Garrett shouts. He might be right—I would call him the same if our places were reversed—but I currently don't give a damn what he thinks.

I carefully hike, zigzagging my route. If it weren't for my shoulder and if Garrett still had my climbing gear in his SUV, I could have easily descended.

As I draw closer, I call out Jess's name.

Again, no reply.

I don't bother to check where Garrett is. I assume he's by his SUV, waiting for the emergency vehicles to arrive.

I keep going, my hiking boots slipping every few feet. The muscles in my lower body strain with each step, taut with tension at the thought of finding my girl's mangled body in the wreck. Taut to keep me from falling or losing control of my descent.

The pain in my shoulder intensifies with each step. But hell if I care about that.

"Jessica!" I yell her name every ten or so strides.

Each time I call out her name, I'm met with silence.

My heart hammers in my chest, the force of it vibrating through my body. *Please be okay. Hang in there, Jess.*

After what feels like too many hours, I arrive at the truck. Sirens wail in the distance.

Holding on to the wreck with one hand, I move along the length of it, searching for signs of Jess through the rear window. The glass is cracked, but it's still in place. She didn't try to get out that way.

What could be footprints in the mud lead away from the truck, but it's hard to tell if that's what they are. The rain has partially washed them out. They look like they belong to the same person. It doesn't appear as if any first responders have already been down here. There'd be more footprints trampling the area if they had been.

"Jess?" I move to the front of the truck and peer into the windshield. It's cracked, but like the rear window, the glass is in place.

And still no sign of Jess.

A rush of air forces its way out of my lungs, and I scan the area for signs of where she might have gone.

It doesn't take me long to find what could be the remains of Jess's prints. I'm not experienced at tracking and interpreting what the different tracks mean, but she might have been limping.

"Jessica!" I follow the footsteps until they disappear under a carpet of dead leaves, fallen needles, and undergrowth beyond the tree line. I have no clue which way she went. "Jessica! It's Troy!"

Again, no reply.

I curse. Why didn't she stay with the vehicle? The slope would've been too slippery last night for her to climb it. But her only chance of getting out of here was to get to the road and not to go into the forest and get lost.

But if she had a head injury, she likely wouldn't be thinking clearly.

My training tells me I should stay at my truck and wait for the first responders so we can do a systematic search for Jess. But I also know they'll have to call in Maple Ridge Search and Rescue to find her.

I remove my phone from my pocket, but the cell reception is weaker here than from the road. I try anyway.

"She wasn't in the truck," I say as soon as Garrett answers my call. "It looks like she went into the forest." I keep walking, alert for clues as to where she could've gone, my brain in search-and-rescue mode.

"Okay, I—" Static crackles in my ear, garbling the rest of Garrett's words...and then the line is dead.

Great.

I retreat a few steps until the bars indicating cell reception reappear. I call Garrett again. "Contact the hospital to see if she's been found." There's no evidence first responders or anyone else has been here since the accident, but she might have made it to the road and flagged down help. Something has just kept her from calling or texting me. "If she isn't there, you need to call in the SAR team to help me locate her. Unless the police or hospital can confirm she's been found, we have to assume she's still out here somewhere.

"If the hospital gives you bullshit about not being able to tell you anything, call Samuel." I resume walking. This time when the line goes dead, I don't bother calling my brother. I continue searching for Jess and yelling her name.

The ground squelches under my boots, but the promised heat of the day will leave it solid in a few hours.

I scan the tree line. Shit, she could be anywhere. I cup my hand around my mouth. "Jessica!"

The only answering replies are the wails of the sirens as

they draw closer to where Garrett is waiting by his SUV. I'm guessing he's still there. I can't see him from here.

I glance back at my truck and turn in the direction Jess was last headed according to her footprints. For now, I have to assume she continued going in that direction and do the same. Maybe her trail picks up once I get beyond the tree line. If it was raining while she was out here, she might have gone into the trees to look for shelter.

Or, she might have looked for shelter in the group of large boulders several yards away.

I head for them in case they created some sort of shelter on the other side. A better shelter than what the trees provided.

The sirens stop and I can only guess that Garrett is updating the first responders on the situation.

I round the boulders and stumble across Jess, fully exposed to the elements. She's curled up on the ground, eyes closed, face pale, other than where her right temple is starting to bruise. My body turns cold with fear. *She's gonna be okay. She's gotta be okay.*

Her shorts and T-shirt are wet and muddy. A blood-soaked sweat shirt is tied around her thigh, but I can't tell how much blood she's actually lost. Last night's rain and the wet fabric might make things look worse than they are.

"She's over here!" I yell to anyone who can hear me.

I drop to the ground and gently shake her shoulder, taking care not to spook or move her. "Jess."

She doesn't stir. *Please be okay. Please be okay. Fuck.* I was away on a routine rescue for two missing hikers while Jess needed me. I wasn't here for her when she needed me the most. And now...

Please be okay.

I press my fingers against her carotid pulse. Her pulse is weak and thready, her breathing shallow, her skin cold. I inwardly curse for not bringing a jacket with me. It's a pain to put on with my shoulder, so I left it in Garrett's truck.

I can't even scoop her in my arms and warm her up. I'll end up possibly worsening her injuries and doing more damage to my shoulder. But if I can't come up with a Plan A, I'll do what I can to heat her.

"Jess, I'm here. You're safe now." I gently open her left eyelid. Her pupil is dilated. I check the other one. It too is dilated. But that might be because the boulders and trees are shading her from the sunlight. Without the use of my other hand, I can't check if her pupils respond to the flashlight on my phone to see if she has a possible brain injury. *Fuck.* "Hold on, sweetheart."

Please be okay.

I stand and yell, "She's over here!" I crouch again. "Jess, I'll be right back. I have to make sure they know where you are." I can't see the first responders, but I can hear their distant voices.

I move closer to the tree line and grab my phone from my pocket. Once I have cell reception, I call Garrett. He answers on the first ring.

"I've found her. She's unconscious."

"The first responders are on their way down."

"They need to go down to the tree line and to the left to where there's a large group of boulders," I tell him. "She's behind them."

"Got it. I'll relay the message."

I return to Jess's side, scared of leaving her alone for too long. I need to check on her. Make sure she's still breathing, her heart's still pumping.

It feels like the world has stopped spinning, dragging time to a standstill. A muffled quiet reaches my ears. Only the caw of a crow and the rustle of leaves penetrate it.

"What's taking them so long?" I mutter, too low for even Jess to hear.

Time stretches endlessly before I finally make out the sounds of the first responders drawing near.

I stand and wave my good arm. "She's over here! In the tree line." A partial surge of relief washes through me. The rest of it will come once I know she'll be all right.

Two men approach carrying a backboard and a first aid kit.

"She's unconscious and unresponsive," I tell them.

I step away, giving them room to work. They check her vitals, put a neck brace on her, check her for injuries other than the one on her right thigh, and insert an IV needle into her arm.

"Are her pupils reactive?" I ask. *Christ, please let her be all right.*

The paramedic nods, but that doesn't mean she's out of the woods. He doesn't have to tell me that. I can see it on his face. She's still at risk of increased intracranial pressure from her head injury.

The men lift her onto the backboard and secure her to it.

I go with them to the base of the steep slope, stroking her hair, touching her shoulder, reluctant to let her go. By the time we get there, several members of my SAR crew are climbing down the incline, guide ropes attached to their harnesses. Kellan and Lucas are with them.

They're waiting for us when we arrive at my truck.

"We'll take her up first, and then come back for you." Sheldon shakes his head like a disappointed parent. "You just had to try to rescue her, even though you're off duty for the next few months because of your injured shoulder." His expression also says he didn't expect anything less from me.

"I couldn't stay up there"—I jerk my chin toward the road—"knowing she was probably injured."

I want to hold Jess's hand, so she knows she's not alone, but her hand and body are bundled securely in the yellow blanket. I lean down and kiss her on the forehead. "I'll see you soon."

I watch as the men carry her up the steep incline with the help of the guide ropes and harnesses.

"You think you can get up the slope with the harness and without reinjuring your shoulder?" Ethan asks. "Or should we get them to lower a stretcher?"

"I should be able to walk up it with the harness. I can do it one-handed."

"You sure about that?" His tone disagrees, challenges, insinuates that I'm being an idiot.

"I've dealt with tougher while injured."

"I don't doubt it." His tone remains the same, and I roll my eyes. He's not a Marine. What does he know?

Ethan helps me get into the harness since that part is challenging when you only have one operational hand.

Once I'm in the harness, I walk up the slope. Lucas walks alongside me, either as encouragement or to ride my ass for hiking down the slope when I'm injured, I'm not sure. Or maybe he's here to ride my ass to distract me from what happened to Jess.

She may have been located, but she's barely breathing. She might develop a brain injury, or she might have some life-threatening injury the paramedics don't know about yet. *Christ, let her be okay.*

10

TROY

June, Present Day
Maple Ridge

Time trudges slowly when waiting for news about a loved one.

Lucas, Kellan, Garrett, and I have been camped out in the ER waiting room since we arrived forty-five minutes ago. And still we haven't heard a word about Jess.

Movement near the ER doors pulls me away from my pacing. Simone, Zara, and Emily rush toward us. Avery and Noah are right behind them.

"What happened?" Emily asks me, worry widening her eyes. "Is Jess gonna be okay?"

"Code Blue!" a female voice announces through the hospital speakers. "Room Five. Code Blue!"

My heart feels like it's the one going into cardiac arrest. *It's not Jess. It can't be Jess.*

Memories of the night Colton ended his life rush in. Of

sitting with Olivia in the waiting room while the ER staff worked on him. That feeling of helplessness, of frustration at not knowing what's going on.

It takes everything I have not to go rushing through the doors leading to the ER exam rooms and demand to see Jess.

"We don't know," Garrett responds, not at all fazed by the code blue. I'm not in the mood to talk, so I let my brothers do it for me. "As far as we've pieced together, she went hiking. But for some reason, she lost control of Troy's truck on the way back and went through a guardrail."

Lucas puts his arms around his wife's waist. "We don't know the state of her injuries, but it looks like she could have a concussion."

He's coating it with a big bag of sugar. Jess might have a concussion and she might have a more serious brain injury. No one has told us anything.

I want to punch a wall. She wouldn't have been left to fend for herself overnight against the elements if I'd realized yesterday where she'd gone. I had been rescuing Christopher and his father while Jess was injured and alone, not knowing if anyone would find her before it was too late.

Zara's gaze jumps to something over my shoulder, and she walks past me. I turn to see Samuel, his expression the opposite of what it was yesterday when I ended up here as a patient.

He hugs his sister, who grips him as if he's her lifeline.

"How is she?" The words power from me, rough and raw.

Samuel looks at each of us in turn, his expression no less somber. But there isn't the same strain around his eyes he'd had when he told Olivia that Colton hadn't made it. I allow myself to take a small breath of relief at that. A very small breath.

"She's back from radiology and is conscious," he tells us. "She has a concussion, and we want to admit her overnight for observation. She also has bruised ribs, a laceration on her thigh that we've stitched up, and she'll be sore for a while. But she's lucky things weren't more serious."

Dizzying relief rides on a long exhalation, and I barely restrain myself from hugging Samuel. *She's gonna be okay.*

He steps toward me and pulls me to the side, away from our friends, and that relief is short-lived. Something about his expression has my insides tightening. Our friends glance our way but get the hint Samuel wants to talk to me alone. They stay where they are.

"Do you have any idea how she got the scars on her body?" His voice is low, preventing anyone else from overhearing the question. Quiet murmurs fill the waiting room that have nothing to do with us, everyone else locked in their own private conversations.

"Scars? You mean other than the two on her face?" The volume of my voice matches his.

"That's right."

I frown. "What kinds of scars?"

"I can't tell you that. I just assumed you'd seen them..." He leaves his words hanging, letting me fill in the blanks. He assumes I've seen Jess naked.

He's halfway correct. She was naked when I had sex with her yesterday morning and the night before. But she'd insisted the lights stay off. Was that because she didn't want me to see her other scars?

"How bad are they?" How bad are they for Samuel to comment on them?

"It's not my place to tell you. It's something *she* needs to talk to *you* about." The concern on Samuel's face doesn't diminish.

"Are they recent scars?"

Samuel shakes his head, the movement small. He sighs, a barely audible rush of air from between his lips. "Some are. Some are several years old. And some showed up on the X-rays.

I suspect I'd find more if I had ordered X-rays for the rest of her body."

"What are you saying?"

"I'm saying the number of scars is alarming for a woman her age. For a woman of any age. When I asked her about them, she shut down and wouldn't say anything. I shouldn't be telling you this, Troy, because you aren't her family, but I am concerned about what happened to her. I thought you might have some idea what caused the previous injuries. And if whatever caused them is still a threat to her."

The tightening inside me increases. *Shit.* I knew something had happened to her to cause the PTSD, but I wasn't expecting any of what he's telling me. "I had no idea. She has PTSD, but she hasn't told me what caused it. Thanks, Samuel. I appreciate the heads-up."

"Is she seeing anyone? A therapist?"

"She is."

"That's good. You can visit her in a few minutes. But only two of you at a time." He leaves, but my legs refuse to move. I can't walk. I can't pace. I can't talk.

What the hell happened to her?

Years. That's how old some of the scars are. But he also said some of them are more recent.

Thank God I pushed for her to see Robyn.

"What's going on?" Kellan's low and steady voice comes from behind me. I can't even turn to acknowledge his question.

"You knew." Heat rises in me and accusation drips from my words.

"Knew what?"

This time I do pivot...and glare at him. "You knew someone hurt her before she moved to Maple Ridge."

Kellan closes his eyes and curses under his breath. His eyes reopen. "What exactly did Samuel tell you?"

"He's not allowed to tell me much of anything. But you know. You know what happened to her in the past, don't you?"

"It's not my place to tell you. It's up to Jess if she wants you to know." He remains infuriatingly calm, not giving anything away.

I glare at him, but he's right. There are things I've done and seen while in the Marines I don't want to share with anyone. Things I'm not allowed to share with another living soul.

I get it, but it doesn't mean I have to like it when it comes to Jess.

And I don't like that he knows more about the woman I'm in love with than I do.

"Don't push Jess about it," Kellan says. "If she wants to tell you, she will. It's not easy for her to talk about. She's scared more than anything."

His words from yesterday replay in my head: *"Someone might be looking for Jess because of who she is. Or it's possible someone found out who she is and threatened to expose her."*

"Does this have to do with what you said when you thought she was on the run?" Somehow, I manage not to growl out the question. *Is whoever might be looking for her responsible for the scars?*

Kellan flinches, the movement barely visible, but otherwise keeps what he's thinking from his expression. "I shouldn't have told you that."

"Yes, you should have. There're a lot of things you should be telling me, but you aren't."

"There's not much I can do about that." Kellan shrugs in the infuriating way that tells me he's going to continue playing Fort Knox with Jess's secret.

In a way, I'm thrilled he's being a loyal friend to her. Kellan has a hard time letting people in after everything he's been through. He doesn't easily trust. When he does trust someone the way he has with Jess, that's big.

But it doesn't mean I'm not pissed at him for keeping from me what he knows about her.

I cross my arms, the tension vibrating in my muscles, my body rigid. As if I'm facing down the enemy, even though my brother isn't one.

Kellan's stance and expression matches mine. We're eyeing each other like elk ready to fight over the right to be protector.

A nurse enters the waiting room and approaches our group. "I can take two of you back to see Jessica. Who will it be?"

I step closer to her. "Me. I'm her boyfriend."

"I'm coming with you." Kellan says it in his don't-bother-to-argue-with-me tone.

I shoot him an I-don't-need-a-chaperone glare.

He levels his gaze at me as if to say, *I don't give a fuck what you want.*

Lucas clears his throat.

"Fine," I grumble at Kellan. "You can come with me."

"She needs rest," the nurse informs us as the three of us walk to Jess's room. "So you can only stay a few minutes. And try not to upset her."

I assume this means not asking the questions prowling in my thoughts.

The nurse pauses outside a door. "She's been given pain meds, so she's going to be a little groggy. The state police will be here soon to ask her questions about the accident."

We enter Jess's room, and my heart almost crumples at how broken she looks, how pale her skin is compared to the white pillow behind her head. Pale and bruised. She looks so fragile, except she's anything but that. She survived an accident that came so close to killing her. She survived being lost in the wilderness overnight without anything to protect her from the elements.

She survived that...and who knows what else?

I stride over to the bed and tenderly kiss her forehead. I try to ignore the beeping of the heart rate monitor and the IV in the back of her hand. Try to ignore how battered she looks. Try to ignore Kellan is here with me.

I thread the fingers of my good arm with her hand that's free of the IV needle. "Hey, how are you feeling?" It's a stupid question because I imagine she feels like shit.

Her gaze slowly drinks me in as if she hadn't expected to ever see me again. Her eyes land on my sling, and her forehead wrinkles into a frown. "What happened to you?" Her words are slightly slurred.

"The idiot injured his shoulder while rescuing a boy and his father," Kellan says from the doorway.

Jess's eyes move to him, and a smile flickers on her lips. "Hi."

A shot of jealousy torpedoes through me at how she's smiling at him but I didn't get the same reaction. I knock it aside. I'm not about to ruin what Jess and I have, what we could have, because I'm jealous of my brother and their friendship.

I should be happy they *are* friends. Happy he's accepted her in a way he's never accepted my past girlfriends.

Kellan moves closer to her bed. "You had him going crazy looking for you." His tone is gentle, teasing. I don't remember him ever talking to a woman that way, not even Em. I get the feeling he understands Jess in a way I never will, and I can't figure out why.

Not knowing the why kicks my internal tripwire. Jealousy spills through my veins once more, with curiosity mixed in.

Jess looks at me, and this time I'm the recipient of her smile. It's nothing like the smiles I'm used to from her. It's softer. The fist around my heart, which I hadn't noticed until now, loosens a tiny amount.

Her smile vanishes and her muscles tense. Her eyes go glossy and her hand in mine shakes. "I-I'm so sorry about your truck, Troy. I-I'll pay you back. I never...I never should have taken it hiking. I'm sorry." She sounds terrified—like a serial killer is chasing her through the forest.

"Hey, it's okay," I tell her, trying to figure out what triggered her reaction. "It's only a vehicle. It's you I'm more worried about. You could have died out there." I could have lost her.

I release her hand and reach toward her bruised cheek to stroke it.

The heart rate monitor beeps faster and Jess flinches like I'm going to hit her or something. I drop my hand to the bed and frown at her reaction. Like I said, it was only a vehicle. As it is, my heart is still reeling at how close I came to losing her.

She shifts on the bed like she's trying to get comfortable. "I need to go home now."

I thread my fingers with hers again. "Sorry, but Samuel—Dr. Thompson—wants you to stay overnight for observation. And the state police will be here in a few minutes to ask you questions about the accident."

If I thought Jess was pale before, that's nothing compared to how pale she goes at the mention of the police. She pulls her hand from mine and jerks the cover off her, revealing her hospital gown. "I have to go."

"You can't. You're not well enough to leave the hospital. You have a concussion." I keep my voice even and the words come out slow, as if that's all it will take for her to see reason.

"I'm fine. I just want to get Bailey from the vet and go home." She makes a move to rip the IV out.

I grab her free hand, stopping her. "What are you doing?"

"I don't need any more painkillers. And I can drink fluids when I get home."

"Jess, it's only one night. I can pick up Bailey on my way home." Except I can't drive anywhere. It was my truck that crashed through the guardrail, which means after I leave the hospital, I'll need to deal with my insurance company and make arrangements for a new vehicle.

"I don't want to talk to the police." The fear and stubbornness in her voice are palpable, and I can't help but wonder if her reaction has to do with her past. It's like she's scared of the police.

"Why not?" I ask calmly. "All they're gonna do is ask you what happened."

Kellan steps closer to the bed. "What did happen out there, Jess? How did Troy's truck end up down the slope?"

"I was driving home after I went hiking and a deer jumped onto the road. I swerved to miss it." She frowns as if the memory causes her pain.

Her explanation fits with the skid marks I saw on the road at the crash site.

The door opens, and the nurse from earlier enters. "The officers are here to ask Jessica a few questions, and then we'll be moving her to another room. You two should go so she can get some rest."

"I'm not staying." Jess pulls her hand from mine and reaches for the IV in her other hand. "I can't stay here."

I cup my hand over the IV site. "Let's talk to Samuel first before you remove this. Okay?"

Two state troopers enter the room. One of them is a woman, her brown hair pulled back in a no-nonsense bun. "Jessica Smithson? We need to ask you a few questions about the accident."

My hand is still covering the IV needle, which is why I notice the trembling in Jess's hand intensify. She's not looking at the woman. She's staring at the male officer.

He's tall with short, dark-blond hair and hard blue eyes. There's nothing noteworthy about him, other than a small scar on his chin.

Jess pulls her knees to her chest, ducks her head, and gently rocks. My heart clenches. She's having a flashback.

I can't tell if the cops triggered it or something else did.

"Ma'am, we need to talk to you about the accident," the male officer says.

My eyes are still locked on Jess, but I hear the rustle of his uniform as he steps closer to the bed.

Jess's trembling intensifies. I feel so goddamn helpless, not knowing how to end her inner torment.

Still not looking at the officer, I raise my hand to tell him to stop. "She's having a PTSD flashback," I tell him. To Jess I say, "Jess, you're safe. You're in the hospital. You're not wherever you think you are. Can you describe the room to me?"

She doesn't answer. She doesn't even acknowledge I'm here. It's not the first time I've felt this helpless over PTSD destroying someone I love, and I can't imagine it will ever get easier.

"Can you question her later?" Kellan asks them. "She told us a deer darted in front of the truck, and she swerved to miss it."

"Is she okay?" The woman officer doesn't seem to have heard my brother's explanation. She's staring at Jess. Both officers are staring at her.

"No." I don't feel like explaining, especially since I don't know what's going on.

But I bet Kellan does.

I glance over my shoulder and see the distrust on his face. That's nothing new when it comes to cops. But there's another emotion there, a protectiveness that's also nothing new—when it comes to his family and close friends.

"We'd prefer to hear it from her ourselves," the male cop responds, his tone stiff.

"Well, you can't. Not right now." I keep my voice soft, but that's mostly for Jess's benefit, and not for his.

"We'll wait." The female cop's tone is not quite as unbending as her partner, but it is still all business. Her eyes remain locked on Jess, her eyebrows pulled together in what seems to be concern.

"It might be better if you two wait in the hallway," Kellan says. "We don't know if something about one of you caused this."

I nod. "He's right. And maybe if only one of you comes back to ask her questions, that might help too."

The cop responds with a nod, concern unwavering on her face. "We'll wait in the hallway, and you can come get me once she's ready to talk."

Both officers step out of the room. I have so many questions I want to ask Kellan, but I know he won't tell me anything, even if he does have an idea what caused the flashback. Jess has obviously asked him to keep whatever they've discussed between the two of them. To keep me out of the loop.

I just wish she would open up to me the way she does with my brother.

Just wish I didn't feel like the outsider in my relationship with her.

11

JESSICA

June, Present Day
Maple Ridge

"**Y**ou're having a flashback, Jess." Troy's voice breaks through the fuzz in my head. The deep, grounding sound of it brings my world into focus, but the *throb-throb-throb* of my brain turns my stomach queasy.

I unhook my arms from around my bent knees and blindly reach for Bailey. My hand searches for her, my fingertips brushing the rough hospital sheets. Then I remember she's not in the hospital with me like I wish she were. My source of comfort, my lifeline is recovering at the vet clinic.

She's going to be okay. I got her to the clinic in time.

I switch my focus before I fall down the tunnel of despair, and I knead my arm like Robyn taught me to do.

Breathe in. Breathe out.

The slight squeeze-release-squeeze sensation on my biceps

helps to further ground me. Helps to bring me back to the here and now. Back to the ER exam room.

Think of a happy memory or about something that makes you smile.

Robyn's instructions slip in past the throbbing. I dig deep, pulling up a memory of Amelia toddling ahead of me on the beach, wearing only her swim diaper. High above us, seagulls squawk and glide on the gentle, sea-salted wind.

She spots a shell half-buried in the sand and squats to inspect it.

I crouch next to her. "What did you find, sweetie?"

She points to it, a beautiful grin on her face. "Shell!"

"Should we dig it up?"

She nods, the movement bunny fast.

I dig the yellow plastic shovel into the sand and unbury the small treasure.

I show her the shell. "How 'bout we put it in the sea for the mermaids and pretty fishes?"

She nods again, and I take her hand. Her skin is soft and warm, her hand small and chubby. Everything about her is beautiful and precious. Like an angel.

We walk to the water's edge. The cool water washes over our feet and tickles our toes. Amelia giggles.

Breathe in. Breathe out.

Fuckers, I miss her. Miss her so very much. Her absence hasn't just left my chest with a gaping hole—the black hole of despair. It's left me with an ache that will never go away. An ache that makes it hard to breathe some days.

"Jess," Troy says, pulling me away from the beach and back to the ER. "Can you describe the room?"

"It's a hospital room. With no windows." My gaze shifts to the IV stand next to my bed, the bag half-full of clear fluid. "And there's an IV machine. Do I have to keep describing the place?" It's kind of depressing and the pounding in my head makes me want to focus on something more uplifting. Something filled with beauty, not pain.

"No, that's fine."

I straighten my legs on the bed. The two cops who came into the room a moment ago are no longer here. "I had a flashback, didn't I?"

The one perk to the flashbacks is I never remember what happens in them. But maybe it would help if I could remember—then it might be easier to eventually banish them.

"Looks like it. Do you remember what happened before it started?"

I look between Kellan and Troy, attempting to get a read on the situation. The full story. A hint.

Neither man's expression gives anything away.

Darn Marine training.

I lift my shoulders in a hell-if-I-know shrug. "Can you tell me, or are we turning this into charades? Because right now my brain isn't on board with that. So how about we skip to you telling me what happened?"

Troy leans down and kisses my forehead. I'm not sure if that's supposed to chase away my headache—which it doesn't —but the action is sweet. My mouth slides into a smile, not enough to irritate my headache, but enough to let Troy know he can kiss me anytime he wants. Preferably, on the lips.

I'm still absorbing how he didn't get mad at me for wrecking his truck. I'm not talking about a small scratch on the bumper. I'm not sure the bumper was even still attached to the truck when I last saw it.

"Two state police officers came in to ask you a few questions about the accident," Troy tells me.

My smile vanishes. A tidal wave of fear obscuring it, wiping it away. Kellan's normally difficult-to-read expression is gone, and the one he is wearing sends a jolt of panic through me.

I'm not surprised I had a flashback when I saw the male

cop. In a way, he reminded me of Lincoln, my late husband's younger brother. Something about the way Lincoln looked at me and the way my husband seemed meaner whenever they got into an argument always left me feeling unsettled around that brother.

Not that he had ever done anything to warrant a flashback.

"Did something happen in your past that has to do with the police?" Troy asks.

"Troy!" The slap of his name from Kellan startles me. The reprimanding tone I recognize, but it isn't the same harsh one I'd heard countless times from my husband. It's the tone Granny used when I was a kid and did something I knew she wouldn't approve of.

My gaze drops to the IV in the back of my hand.

"Jess, one of the officers is female," Kellan says. "Would you be more comfortable if you just spoke with her?"

Would I?

None of the officers who came to the house were females. My husband hadn't approved of women on the police force. But...but plenty of the prison guards were female. With...with a few exceptions, they were no better than the men.

The idea of talking to anyone in a police uniform worsens the throbbing in my head, but I don't have a choice. And the more I refuse to talk to them, the more questions they'll have about why that's the case. Besides, it shouldn't take long. There's not much to tell.

If they have to ask me questions, it must mean the deer survived. I didn't hit it. Its poor body wasn't found at the scene of the accident. A small amount of relief bounds through me.

"Okay," I say, knowing I don't have a choice, and praying the officer doesn't recognize me from my past life. "I'll talk to the female officer. But I meant what I said earlier. I don't want to stay here. I want to go home. I want to see Bailey." I want to make sure she's still okay.

"I'm so sorry about your truck," I tell Troy and the image of the bent and twisted metal flashes in my head.

My body stiffens, automatically bracing for the blow.

The punch to my stomach.

The foot to my back.

The gun to my head.

My body shakes again and my vision swims in and out. I'm an 8.9 magnitude earthquake. Every part of me is unstable. Every part of me is at risk of crumpling under its force.

A warm hand rests on my cheek. "Hey, Jess. It'll be okay. It wasn't your fault." Troy's soothing deep voice makes its way through my shattered thoughts, reminding me I'm here with him. I'm not reliving my past. "It's just a truck. It's you I'm more worried about."

"I'm going to get the female trooper," Kellan says, "so you can get this over with."

"And then I want to go home," I tell Troy.

"I'll talk to Samuel and see what we can do about that. But I'll do that after you've spoken with the state trooper. I'm not leaving your side while you talk to her unless you want me to go." He weaves his fingers with mine.

His firm touch roots me to the spot, making me feel safe and secure against the storm battling inside me and the one I'm about to face.

Please tell me the officers didn't recognize me. Please tell me my secret's still safe.

I tighten my hold on his hand. "No, please stay."

The room door opens, and the female officer enters. She wasn't the one who triggered the flashback. That dubious honor goes to her partner.

The woman is nothing like the prison guards who lorded over me. She's shorter than I'd expected. And younger. Maybe only twenty-five or twenty-six years old. She has seen things, but they haven't hardened her yet. She gives me a brief but compassionate smile.

But I still can't relax. All I need is for her to recognize me, and my secret will no longer be hidden.

"Hello, Ms. Smithson," she says without a hint of recognition, and I allow myself to relax a tiny bit. "I'm Officer Campbell. I have a few questions about the accident."

"There's not much to tell. I went hiking in the mountains. While I was driving home, a deer leaped onto the road and I swerved to avoid it. It was raining at the time, and I must have lost control of the truck." That part is kinda blurry.

"You had a flashback a few minutes ago. Do you have them often?"

Define often.

My hand grips Troy's, possibly cutting off his circulation. This isn't something I really want to discuss with her or anyone else associated with a police department. So I just shrug, letting the vague response be my nonanswer. I still have flashbacks once or twice a week, which is an improvement.

"Is it possible you had a flashback while you were behind the wheel, and that's what made you lose control of the truck?" There's no hint of accusation in her tone, but I can't help feeling that's exactly what she's doing. Accusing me of wrecking Troy's truck because I had a flashback and not because of a deer.

"I didn't have a flashback." My voice sounds weary to my ears. Hopefully she doesn't have many questions. I slowly blink, my eyelids weighing a ton. "I was fully aware of what was going on at the time of the accident. Like I said, I swerved to miss the deer."

"It's usually best that you don't try to avoid hitting an animal on the road," she tells me, her tone matter of fact. "Often the damage is greater when you try to swerve to avoid the animal than if you keep driving straight."

I'm sure the animals who leap in front of vehicles would disagree.

I nod my response, my mind growing sluggish.

"Why didn't you stay with the truck once you got out of it?" she asks. There's no judgment on her face. Just curiosity as she tries to piece together what caused me to go deeper into the forest.

"I thought if I could find another way back to the road, I could flag down a car and get help. I was looking for a path when the storm worsened. So I took shelter there and passed out."

I can't remember the last time I felt this tired. I blink again, attempting to chase away the exhaustion. My eyelids are also sluggish, and it takes all my energy to pry my eyes open.

Even then, they aren't fully wide.

"If you have any questions about the report," the officer says, "please contact me." She hands me her business card. It's heavy. Surprisingly heavy. My hand falls to the bed and she leaves.

My thoughts grow fuzzier, and I'm floating, floating, floating.

"HOW'S SHE DOING?" THE QUIET FEMALE VOICE BREAKS THROUGH the fog in my head.

"She's still sleeping." *Troy.* His words are hushed.

Other sounds slide into my thoughts. People talking. Their voices quickly fade away.

I slowly blink my eyes open, and it takes a moment for the fog in my head to dissipate and for my vision to clear.

Troy's sitting by the bed. "Sorry, didn't mean to wake you."

"How long have I been asleep?" Drowsiness gravels my voice.

"Just over two hours.

The nurse inspects the IV bag. "We're moving you to your room now. It's ready for you upstairs."

The hospital smells that I was too sluggish to notice earlier are now strong. Too strong. Each one is linked to the last time I was in a hospital. The disinfectant odor mocks me. Reminds me of what it felt like to be treated like a rabid dog. They thought I was a killer. Someone unworthy of compassion or respect.

"No, I'm not staying here. I'm fine." I tear the bedding off me and swing my legs to the side. But Troy puts his hand on my shoulder, pinning me in place.

"Weren't you going to ask the physician to let me go home?" I say when it's clear he's not letting me leave. The aching sting of betrayal turns my tone quiet and rough.

"I was. But you fell asleep, and I didn't want to leave you alone."

"I just want to go home to my own bed. I don't like hospitals." I rub my wrist, the memory of the cold press of metal handcuffs on my skin still fresh.

"You don't have to worry about the cost," Troy says, apparently not getting the problem. "My company's insurance plan will cover it."

"Th-that's not what I'm worried about. P-please, Troy." My heart thuds rapidly in my chest, my anxieties and fear taking over all reason. "You promised you would talk to the physician. I'm not staying here. It's not prison. They can't make me."

I have the right to walk out of here. They can't hold me against my will.

Kellan is standing in the corner. I can see on his face the moment it all clicks for him. My past. My comment about the hospital not being a prison. He gets it.

Dr. Thompson walks into the room, presumably to check on me. Troy explains I don't want to stay.

"I would rather you stay overnight, Jessica." Dr. Thompson gives me a smile that under other circumstances might have been reassuring. He does look like his sister. The same copper-brown skin, same chocolate-brown eyes, same all-consuming smile.

Kellan pushes away from the wall. "What if someone stays with her at her house? That way she's not alone."

"She can stay at my place," Troy says.

"Right, you're both injured. So that won't work," Kellan points out. "Jess's leg was sliced open, which means she won't be able to walk on it for a few days." He looks at Dr. Thompson for confirmation.

Zara's brother nods, though I get the feeling he's not giving the red light to small things like going to the bathroom.

"How are you planning to help her, Troy?" Kellan asks.

"I'll be fine," I jump in since I have no intention of staying in the hospital, regardless of what everyone thinks.

"Or she can stay at my place," Kellan goes on as if I haven't said anything.

Troy's eyebrows lower into a scowl. "Hell if that's going to happen."

Dr. Thompson and I stare at the two men for a beat. I'm half expecting them to charge at each other, horns ready to gouge. Zara's brother appears highly amused.

"I can sleep on Troy's couch if it comes to that," I rush to say. "But I'm sure I can manage to walk upstairs to go to bed and shower." I shoot Dr. Thompson a pleading look. "I promise I'll take it easy. I just can't stay here. I don't like hospitals."

I swing my legs over the side of the bed, making it clear that one way or another I won't be spending the night here.

"I can't stop you from leaving, Jessica," Dr. Thompson says. "I can only strongly recommend you don't. But I will feel better if you stay with someone who can keep an eye on you. I can swing by Troy's place on the way to the hospital tomorrow morning."

I glance at Troy to make sure it's okay with him, willing him to say yes.

"I'm more than happy to have you stay with me, Jess," Troy replies with a soft smile, and a relieved breath *whooshes* softly over my lips.

Before I can thank Troy, I catch the look in Kellan's eyes. A warning look. *Troy knows.*

Knows what? The unease stirring inside me tells me I'll find out soon enough.

"Your clothes are wet and muddy," Kellan reminds me since I'm currently wearing a hospital gown. "I'll go track down some dry clothes for you and ask Em to pick up some more from your house to drop off at Troy's." He holds out his hand to Troy. "She'll need the spare key."

The key that Troy has because he's been helping me with the renovations.

12

ANGELIQUE

July 1943
France

A week after I discovered Oskar and his family hiding in Jacques's barn, Johann paces on the dirt-covered ground inside the building. Restlessness seems to fuel his steps. The pre-dawn light isn't enough to cut through the dim space. He's a tall, dark shape moving through the shadows.

"I'll be gone for four days," he tells them in German, referring to the mission he and his unit will be away for. He hasn't told me what the mission is, though, and I have a feeling he has even spared Oskar those details.

He rakes his hand through his hair. I can't see his face clearly, but I can hear the pain and uncertainty simmer and burn in his tone.

"We know." Oskar keeps his voice low so not to disturb his daughter who is sleeping on the bed in the hiding place. He

96

replies in German, then switches to French. "We will be fine while you are away. Angelique is a charming host."

I don't have to see his expression to know Oskar just grinned at me. In the short time he, Margrit, and Sonja have been here, I've gotten to know them. Oskar and Margrit have shared amusing stories about Johann from when they grew up together. I've witnessed the love the four of them have for each other.

None of them view Johann as the enemy. The same cannot be said about Oskar and Margrit's view of the Wehrmacht and Nazis. Their fear for the enemy echoes what I feel every time I see one. My nightmares are plagued with the monsters in their grey-green military uniforms and sneering faces.

"Thank you," I tell Oskar. "You are a charming guest."

A charming guest who will be in England soon if everything goes according to plan.

"God, I wish I didn't have to leave." Johann pivots and paces in the direction he came from. "I can't protect you if I'm not here."

"You don't have a choice. If you don't go, they'll kill you. They'll kill you like they killed Dieter." Determination and pain flare in Oskar's tone, breaking through cracks in his otherwise steady voice. "And if they come here looking for you, they'll find us and kill us. Sonja, Margrit, me, Angelique—we're all at risk if you don't go."

"I'll keep them safe," I say, relieved Johann cannot see the truth on my face in the dim light. The truth he doesn't know about. The truth I will share with Oskar and Margrit once Johann leaves for his mission. "You have my word."

Johann stops pacing, and I can just make out the hunched lines of his shoulders. "You're right. I have to go." He releases a hard breath that hints he still isn't convinced but doesn't have a choice in the matter.

Oskar and Margrit return to their daughter, and Johann closes the trapdoor.

He and I return to the house without a word. He stops at the front door. "There is something I need to ask you," he says.

"What is that?"

"There is to be a grand ball on the twenty-fourth of this month. I would like it if you could come with me. As my dinner date. It will take place in Paris."

Ah, the ball Müller had mentioned and Johann had said he would bring me as his guest. This is the first time he has brought it up with me. I thought he had perhaps changed his mind.

"Are you certain you want me as your date?" I ask, even though it would be the perfect opportunity to gain intelligence for Baker Street.

"I am." The smile he flashes me is sweet and charming. It's one any woman would have a hard time turning down.

I return the smile, mine more on the demure side. "I...I would like that. To get to see Paris. Thank you."

His smile widens, and we enter the house. He goes upstairs. I go into the kitchen and turn on the tap. Dirty breakfast dishes sit in the sink.

I am scrubbing the cast-iron frying pan when Johann enters the kitchen. I pause a moment to take in his drawn yet handsome features. He's nothing like I expected when he first arrived at the farmhouse with the documentation that stated he was moving in. The kind and compassionate man before me is a juxtaposition to what his uniform stands for.

"Thank you." Johann's voice is a whisper, the words meant only for me. I am not completely sure of what he is referring to. Does he mean how I have not betrayed his friends' presence to the Germans? How I am treating them like guests? Surely he does not know about my plans to get them out of the country and to safety. Does he suspect something?

"They'll be safe," I say, praying what I'm telling him is true. Their journey will be no easy feat, especially with little Sonja. But their daughter is the reason they risked everything to escape Austria, the country that embraced Hitler.

Johann steps towards me, and something about the way he looks at me makes me think he's going to wrap his arms around me, to make me feel protected and safe—something I haven't felt since parachuting into this country. I doubt I'll ever feel safe again. This bloody war has robbed me of that.

"I got word that your brother, Yvon, is in a prisoner of war camp, but he is alive and well. Could you perhaps relay that message to your father?"

His words touch my heart. I cannot believe he did that. For Jacques. Neither of us had asked him to find out about Yvon. I only wish I could give Johann the same reassurance about his mother and sister.

I smile at him, pretending it is my own sister he is talking about instead of the man who I have never met but who is supposed to be my blood relation. My smile is heavy with relief and gratitude. "I can. He will be relieved to hear that. Thank you."

The crunch of tyres on gravel outside the kitchen window interrupts the moment between us. Johann retreats and turns to leave. "*Au revoir*, Angelique." His tone is tender. It's the same one he uses with Sonja and Margrit.

He's out the door before I can echo the goodbye. He's unwilling to give the driver a reason to get out of the Jeep. The fewer Germans on this property, the lower the risk of Oskar and his family being discovered.

I wait ten minutes to be certain Johann is gone, then hurry upstairs to my bedroom. I remove the short strand of white thread strategically placed on the edge of the rug and lift the rug and the broken floorboard beneath it, revealing the hiding space. It's too small for a wireless set but perfect for hiding documents, large amounts of money, and the gold compact Major Maurice Buckmaster gave me the day I departed from England.

I take out the three recently forged identity papers and some money. I replace the floorboard and the rug and return the white thread to its usual location. Half of it lies on the wooden floor, letting me know if someone else disturbs the hiding spot. I rush downstairs.

I stash the identity papers in the secret compartment of my handbag, load a satchel with some food, and return to the barn. I move the bales of straw from the trapdoor.

"It's me. Angelique," I say somewhat hurriedly, my pitch low, and pull open the door.

Oskar and Margrit peer up at me from the floor where they're seated. Oskar's arm is around her shoulder in comfort. It's not comfort offered in fear; it's based on love.

"What is wrong?" Oskar's eyes are wide in alarm, his voice a concerned whisper.

I descend the ladder and crouch in front of them. "I'm here to help you escape out of France."

His features pinch into a frown. "What do you mean?"

Sonja begins to stir, and her eyes slowly blink open.

The less she knows, the better. War and what she has been through has robbed her of her childhood, but she still possesses the innocence that could be dangerous if she repeats something she overheard us say. "We should talk in private," I tell him.

Oskar follows me up the ladder. Margrit stays with their daughter.

I lead him over to the far side of the barn, past the old tractor that sits forgotten due to the lack of petrol to run it. We stop at the hay bales piled near the far wall, the amount barely enough to get the horses through the next few months.

Rays of the early morning sun stream through gaps in the wooden walls. Dust motes dance in the pale warmth.

"I realise you don't know me well enough to trust me, and there is a lot I can't tell you," I say, keeping the volume of my voice to little more than a whisper. "It's not safe for me to reveal everything to you. It's dangerous for you to know, and it's dangerous for me to tell you. Too much is at stake."

The frown returns to his face. "I don't understand."

"I have connections that can get you and your family to safety and far from Hitler and his regime. It won't be easy. Every step of the way will be dangerous, for you, for Margrit, for Sonja. But it's the only way to get you as far away from the Nazis as possible."

"Does Johann know?"

"I have not told him the plan. He's a German soldier with an allegiance to Hitler..."

Oskar vigorously shakes his head. "He's not—"

"I know he doesn't like the man. But Johann is still a German soldier. It will be equally dangerous for him if he learns the truth about me. His commanding officer would like nothing more than to make an example of him if he ever discovered the truth about you and your family and about Johann's sister. Like he made an example out of Dieter's desertion." My words come out swift, my desperation for him to see reason fuelling them.

"I am to take you and your family to Dijon," I explain. "My connection there will help you and your family get to Lisbon. From there, you will board a ship that will take you to safety, but I can't tell you more than that."

Oskar studies me, uncertainty showing in the wary lines around his eyes. I cannot say I blame him. If our places were reversed, I would feel the same way.

"We should wait for Johann's return." Determination and

bloody stubbornness hang on his tone and make me want to stomp my foot. Stomp my foot and shake some sense into him.

"It's too dangerous for him to know about this," I point out. "He's a German soldier. An enemy to France. An enemy to the Jewish people. I've seen the roundups of Jews in Paris. There's a reason Johann is desperate to hide you and your family."

"But Johann is a good man. He is not like the rest of them. No, I think we should wait for him to return. I'm positive he will go with us. He has always talked about one day living in America. Perhaps then he will follow his dream of going there."

I can see why Oskar was a lawyer before Hitler took that away from him.

But I can be equally persuasive. I've learned that skill from being the daughter of a diplomat and from working at a law firm. "He won't go anywhere as long as he believes staying in the Army is the only way to protect his mother and sister."

Oskar's sigh is heavy with frustration and sadness and the weight of the world with Hitler in it. "He still clings to hope they're alive. It's the only thing that keeps him going. Otherwise, I know he would have deserted the Army with Dieter." His voice splinters with grief on his friend's name.

"Is it true his sister is deaf?"

"It is. Prior to my family and I escaping to France, I heard rumours Austria wasn't safe if you were disabled. Disabled children were required to report to special medical centres. Operations were being performed to sterilise them. Other disabled children went missing or were reported dead. At the time, all of this was nothing more than rumours, ghost stories. But if those rumours were true, what did that mean for Jews? Hitler had no use for us either."

"Do you think his mother and sister are still alive?"

"I pray they are. But no matter where they went and no matter what happened to them, Johann will never give up hope they are both alive. He would do anything to keep his mother and sister safe."

"And that's why we cannot wait for him to return. He's fighting for Germany, not because he wants to, but because he hopes that will protect his mother and sister. But if you and Margrit and Sonja stay, the SS or Milice will eventually find you. None of us will survive if that happens, and that includes Johann."

Oskar looks over where the trapdoor lays open and releases another sigh, the world on his shoulders growing heavier. He turns back to me. "Okay, we'll go with you. For Sonja's sake."

Thank God. A momentary jolt of relief pulses through my veins, only to be quickly replaced with fear for what will come soon.

We return to the cellar, and he explains the plan to Margrit and the still sleepy Sonja.

I hand them the forged *carte d'identités.* "Your name is Ava," I tell Sonja. "It is very important you remember that."

Her lips push into a sad pout. "But I like my name."

I crouch to her level and smile, making sure she sees nothing on my face that betrays the turmoil inside me. "It's a beautiful name. But for now, you are called Ava. It's a pretty name too. *Non?*"

She seems to contemplate my question for a heartbeat and nods.

"And it's very important you don't mention your uncle, Johann," I tell her. "Or anything to do with this place. You should try not to talk when you're around other people, just to be safe."

She peers up at her mother, worry furrowing her small brow. Margrit repeats in German what I said. Sonja nods, but it's not enough to smooth out her frown.

"It's best you don't speak German," I remind her. "That will raise too many questions." Especially because her German is more fluent than her French. "Stay here and I will come back for you shortly," I tell them and leave the barn, praying they will make it out of France alive. Praying they will make it safely to their final destination, together.

UNLIKE THE PREVIOUS TIMES I TRAVELLED FROM THE LOCAL train station, German soldiers now demand to see our *carte d'identités* before we can approach the platforms. I don't recognise these two soldiers. I haven't seen them around the village.

Oskar goes first and hands the soldier his papers. He isn't wearing the armband identifying him as Jewish. None of the family are.

Margrit and Sonja watch the soldier check Oskar's papers and the satchel with food. They don't acknowledge they know me. I'm just another passenger who happens to be standing behind them in the queue.

The soldier inspects the *carte d'identité* and Oskar's face, then hands the papers to him. The entire time, Oskar is calm as though none of this is a big deal. It's nothing more than a minor inconvenience like everything to do with the war.

Margrit's hand shakes as she passes hers and Sonja's *carte d'identités* to the soldier.

He gazes down at Sonja and smiles. "You look like my daughter."

His French is broken, but it's enough for Sonja to understand. She gives him a shy grin and hugs the teddy bear Johann gave her tighter to her chest.

Good girl. I could not have asked for a better response from her. She is doing as I instructed. *You beautiful, brave little girl.*

The soldier gives hers and Margrit's papers a cursory scan, quickly searches through Margrit's handbag, and waves them on. They walk with Oskar to the platform without looking back at me.

I glance over my shoulder as if expecting to find Johann there, wondering why I'm flaunting his friends in plain view of the Germans. But the only people behind me are those waiting to board the train.

I hand my papers to a soldier. He inspects them and searches through my handbag, unaware of the secret compartment with the wad of money to fund the journey. He returns the bag to me without so much as a raised eyebrow.

It's not until I'm near Oskar and his family on the platform that I can finally breathe. For now, anyway.

The train trip goes smoothly.

The sun is high in the sky and the heat is stifling when we arrive at the entrance to the park in Dijon.

Oskar removes a coin from his coat pocket and hands it to me. It's an Austrian coin that is old and damaged and has a hole in the centre. "Give this to Johann. Tell him it really is a lucky coin. He will know what that means."

Oskar scoops Sonja up in his arms. Margrit hugs me. "Thank you so much," she whispers in my ear. "I hope one day, once this war is over, we will see each other again."

I hug her back. "I hope so too. Take care and stay safe."

I give Sonja a quick kiss on her brow.

They enter the park. I wait a minute and then follow after them, keeping a fair distance from them as if I do not know them.

A soldier stands at the fork in the path leading away from the pond. He isn't the only soldier keeping watch on the area, but he is the one closest to the meeting spot.

A woman matching the description I gave Oskar—blond hair, pink and green scarf, green dress—is waiting by the pond, watching several ducks swim near her feet.

Oskar puts Sonja down. She runs over to inspect the birds

in the water. Her parents follow her at a more leisurely pace. While they might look unconcerned, I imagine they are trembling in the soldiers' presence.

Oskar and Margrit approach the woman and make a show of pretending they have bumped into an old friend, like we rehearsed. And, like we rehearsed, they give each other the secret code phrases so there are no mistaken identities.

The fear thrumming through my body and the tension-ladened summer air send my heart racing. I walk towards a nearby empty bench and try not to think about the risk we are all taking, praying that will be enough to keep me from looking suspicious.

I sit on the bench and pretend to check for something in my handbag. I pretend the folded newspaper inside it is in my way and put it on the bench. I pretend to find the watch I was searching for in my bag, the watch strap broken, and pretend to check the time. I pretend to be distracted by a woman wheeling a pushchair past me, a young toddler sitting in it.

I stand up and walk away, leaving the newspaper with the money behind.

I don't have to look behind me to know the partner of the woman by the pond will be intercepting it, and I walk in the opposite direction from which I came. Walk while praying to a god I don't believe in for Oskar and his family to be all right. Praying one day I will see them again, happy and safe.

Praying Johann won't believe I betrayed them.

Because my life will be forfeit if he believes exactly that.

13

JESSICA

June, Present Day
Maple Ridge

Zara's brother arranges for my hospital discharge papers. While we wait for them, Troy contacts the vet clinic and asks how Bailey is doing. He gets the green light to pick her up.

Kellan returns to my room with a nurse and an oversized men's T-shirt in light blue that says Maple Ridge Hospital on the front and a pair of drawstring shorts that aren't quite as oversized. "Sorry, this is all I could find."

"That's fine," I tell him, grateful I don't have to wear my wet clothes for the trip to the vet clinic and to Troy's. Besides, they're still a lot better than my old prison garb. "Thanks, Kellan."

The two men leave to give me some privacy, and the nurse helps me get changed. And then Kellan drives us to the clinic.

I've never been happier to see Bailey than I am when

107

Ambrosia walks her into the waiting room. Tears prick my eyes. Happy tears. And a smile stretches across my face.

I carefully lower myself to the floor, every muscle in my body grumbling. I ignore them and hug my dog. "I'm so glad you're okay."

She licks my face, which only makes me smile more. I laugh. My ribs ache at the movement, but it's worth it just to be with Bailey again.

Kellan drives us to Troy's house. Butterscotch is waiting by the front door when Troy unlocks it, and the two dogs take a moment to get reacquainted.

Kellan heads to Troy's living room. Troy and I follow him.

We walk past the hall table. "Where's the vase?" The ceramic vase that usually sits there is missing.

"I wasn't paying attention to where I was going," Troy explains, "and bumped into the table. The vase fell over before I could stop it."

"Oh, that's too bad." It was a nice vase.

I sit on the couch, relieved to get off my feet. My body happily sinks into the dark-gray cushion.

Troy puts a small navy cushion in front of me on the coffee table. "Put your foot on this." His deep, gravelly voice turns my insides quivery, and I steal a second to savor the sinful sound. Last night, I thought I'd never hear it again.

I rest the foot of my injured leg on the cushion, and Troy adjusts it so I'm comfy. He leans down and gives me a quick kiss, his lips lingering on mine for less than a heartbeat, and heads for the kitchen. I wish it could've lasted longer.

Bailey jumps up next to me on the couch. My fingers sink into her silky hair. With each stroke of my hand along her warm body, the tension lurking inside me from the past twenty-four hours begins to subside.

Troy hands me a glass of water and sits next to me. Kellan is in an armchair. I sense Troy would prefer it if his brother left us alone. I also sense Kellan has no intention of doing that yet.

Troy knows.

Kellan's silent warning in the ER room rings in my head, echoing against my tender brain. But just how much does Troy know? As much as I told Kellan? Or do they both know more than I'd originally shared with him?

"Samuel told me..." Troy's gaze shoots to Kellan, who meets it with a look sharper than a dagger.

"Told you what?" My words sound as dry and scratchy as my throat feels. *Keep stroking Bailey. Keep stroking Bailey...*

"He mentioned your body is covered in scars. And scars showed up on the X-rays."

I swallow, pushing down the years of pain that resulted in those scars. Each one tells a story—a story I don't want to share. I should have known that was what Kellan's silent warning was about. Zara's brother had questioned the scars when he'd first seen them.

"They aren't important. They're from my past, and that's where they're going to stay." That's exactly what I told Zara's brother.

Troy's expression is that of someone who's been sucker-punched in the gut with a spiked glove. "You don't trust me. Do you? Not enough to tell me the truth. I'm your boyfriend, yet you can't trust me enough to tell me. But I bet you told Kellan what happened."

"Troy!" Kellan snaps, a warning for Troy to stop right there.

My body tenses. Bailey whimpers.

I continue stroking her. "Technically, we agreed to no labels for what's going on between us," I point out, careful to keep my tone from sounding accusatory, smoothing out the rough edges.

The lack of labels excuse is lame, but he's right. Trust is not something that comes easily to me. Not anymore.

But maybe it's time I told Troy the truth. To try on for size the ability to trust. Because Troy will always be wondering what happened to me. Will always be poking at the peeling wallpaper haphazardly covering my secrets.

The question is, can he handle what's beneath the surface?

"You're right," he says. "We did agree to no labels. But I still think of you as my girlfriend, Jess." His tone is steady, unbending. It's my stomach that's struggling to find stable ground. "And since when have I given you reason to believe you can't trust me? I'm not the asshole you were involved with before you came to Maple Ridge."

"Maybe not the same asshole, but you're still acting like one." The undertow of Kellan's words is dangerously rough. "If you want, Jess, you can stay at my place."

My gaze jumps between the two brothers. Both are angry at each other. Because of me.

I can't let my own stupidity—my past actions—damage their relationship. They are family.

I'm not.

I'm expendable—as my parents proved.

"You don't owe Troy an explanation." Kellan's tone is gentle, the Band-Aid to a wound that has trouble healing.

But he's wrong. I do owe Troy something. If it weren't for him, I wouldn't be where I am now. I wouldn't have Bailey. I wouldn't be going to therapy. I wouldn't have a job where I don't have to worry about flashbacks.

Kellan only knows I was wrongfully convicted and was in prison for five years. He doesn't know the rest of it. And while I do plan to tell him the full story, it's Troy who should hear it first.

I move my hand from Bailey. "I need to tell him, Kellan. And I need to tell him things about my past I haven't told you yet. I will. But I need to tell Troy first."

Kellan nods, no sign of judgment or hurt on his face. He

already knew I hadn't told him everything. I'd kept to myself what I had been falsely accused of.

He stands. "Let me know if you need anything, Jess."

I smile, the way I imagine I would if Kellan had been my real brother. "Thank you. Thank you for everything you've done for me."

I drop my gaze to my lap and wait until I hear the click of the front door. I fiddle with the hem of my shorts. I find little comfort in the action, but it does save me from seeing Troy's reaction to what I must tell him. I breathe in through my nose, letting Troy's scent of mountains and sunshine and hope settle inside me.

Em's voice comes from the front door. Kellan's low voice tells her something, probably to let her know Troy and I need time alone. She's here to drop off some of my clothes and toiletries.

The front door clicks shut, and a moment later, the sound of two engines can be heard driving away.

Troy doesn't say anything, but I can feel the gentle weight of his gaze on me.

I continue staring at my lap. "I'm married."

A sharp inhalation, heavy with questions, cuts through the air, but I still don't look up.

"Well, more specifically," I clarify, "I'm a widow."

I shift my attention to Bailey, as if telling her my next words will help the truth go down easier. "My husband was a cop. He was also abusive." I draw air through my nose like Robyn taught me to do and release it. *I can do this.* "He wasn't at first. He made me feel loved at a time when I thought I was unlovable. My parents didn't want me. My grandparents were the ones who showed me what love was. And I thought my husband loved me too."

"I'm sorry your parents made you feel that way," Troy says,

his quiet voice slightly rough. "And I'm sorry about your husband."

I nod but still can't look at him. "I have lots of wonderful and fond memories of being with him, especially in the beginning. Which only made it harder for me to leave. I kept remembering those times and doubting myself. I believed his lies, his empty apologies. He had a way of causing me to convince myself that I deserved his mean words. I really did think everything he did was my fault. And if I did better next time, everything would be fine."

I shake my head, remembering how foolish I'd been—how I'd naïvely believed his words.

Or perhaps it was hope that kept me there—hope that one day things would be different.

"In time, he made it more and more difficult for me to visit my grandmother, and he isolated me from my friends." The friends I had before I married him. "I didn't realize it until I tried to escape him after my grandmother died. I had no money —well, no money I could easily access at the time. I had nowhere to turn. And because he was a cop, he made it impossible for me to leave." I never truly became friends with the wives and girlfriends of his friends and colleagues. Maybe he also had a hand in that too. I don't know.

I can't explain to Troy how my late husband made it impossible for me to leave. To do so means revealing the one thing I'm not ready to discuss yet—Amelia.

My husband had used her as a pawn. Leave him, and I would lose my parental rights. No judge would grant me custody. I didn't know if what he'd told me was true or if he'd been bullshitting his way to have complete control over me. I couldn't take the risk in case he was telling me the truth.

So I'd stayed.

Stayed and prayed one day his job would kill him. Maybe it did in the end.

"You said you're a widow," Troy says, his voice still rough, still soft. "What happened to your husband?"

"Someone broke into the house and murdered him. I was there at the time. But I'd been drugged, and the cops and DA decided it was a failed murder-suicide. With me as the murderer." I finally drag my gaze from Bailey to Troy. Bailey jumps down from the couch. "They figured I botched my own suicide."

"Shit." The word is a soft breath. "Did the cops ever figure out who did kill him?"

"No. Whoever murdered my husband did a great job of framing me. I was found guilty and spent five years in prison before the police realized their mistake." I shift my gaze back to Bailey. She's playing with one of Butterscotch's chew toys. "Five years branded a cop killer. Five years of being attacked by inmates and ignored by guards."

I can feel the door to my soul shutting with a resounding boom. I'm in an empty cell. No furniture. No pictures. No toilet. Nothing but the familiar cold that filled me for all those years.

My body, my arms, my hands shake—adrenaline fueled from ten years of memories. "I-I..." I can't get the words out. I'm shivering too much.

Troy grabs a plaid throw from behind him on the couch. His mother gave it to him for Christmas. I haven't even met his parents—and I probably won't now.

Five years. Five years spent in prison, and I'd changed into a different person. A person who'd given up hope. Who'd expected each day to be her last—and had abandoned the will to live after giving away her parental rights for her daughter.

Kellan's family didn't turn their backs on him after he spent time in prison.

But I'm not part of their family.

I might not be a murderer, but I have done time in a maximum-security correctional facility. I'm not the kind of woman you introduce to your mom.

Troy spreads the throw over my shoulders. I pull it around me, shielding myself from more pain. I flash him a sad smile.

A loud *squeeeeeeaaaaaak* fills the living room. Bailey is shaking a fire-hydrant chew toy and looking adorably silly.

An unexpected laugh spills over my panic-dried lips. The sound comes out less of a full-fledged laugh and closer to a tear-choked giggle.

"I have no idea if the police are close to figuring out who killed him." I pull the throw tighter around my shoulders. "But ever since my husband's death and my trial, the media has been unable to let go of the story. I just wanted to collect the pieces of my broken life and start over. I couldn't do that with them hounding me with questions, demanding answers I don't have." Panic leaks into my words like a faucet set on dribble.

"That's why I didn't tell you before. I can't risk my true identity being discovered. I'm scared of what people will think of me if they find out I was locked up in maximum security for five years." I'm scared they'll drag out the metaphorical pitchforks and attempt to chase me out of town.

Troy's brow wrinkles into a slight frown, but other than that, he seems to be taking things in stride. Or he's doing a stellar job at hiding his real emotions. Something he's good at. "True identity? Your name isn't really Jessica?"

"It's Savannah Townsend."

Recognition ghosts his face at the name, as if he's not one-hundred-percent certain it's a name he's heard before. "Which name do you want me to call you—Jess or Savannah?"

"Jess. I don't want people to know who I really am. And I haven't felt like Savannah in a long time. She's not who I am anymore."

"Alright. Jess. So what made you decide to come to Maple Ridge?"

"A mutual friend of Anne Carstairs contacted her about me staying at Iris's house." That's close to the truth. I hadn't known Florence prior to her picking me up at the prison following my release. But if it hadn't been for Florence, Anne, and my brother-in-law, Craig, I don't know what I would have done. "Anne knew I was dealing with a traumatic event and needed a place to recover for a few months while I pieced my life together. She doesn't know the full story of what happened."

"And Kellan knows all of this?"

I shake my head. "He figured out I was an ex-con."

"You're not an ex-con, Jess," Troy says, his tone gentle, the words forceful. "You're an exoneree. Big difference."

I lift my shoulders in a *whatever* shrug. I'm not sure if other people would view it the same way. "A few weeks ago, I was walking from the library after working at Picnic and Treats. It was the day I had the flashback when the power went out. I saw a cop car coming toward me and my body shut down. Kellan witnessed it and confronted me about it. He'd already suspected I was an ex-con."

Troy raises an eyebrow. I ignore the reminder because it's the truth. Kellan hadn't known then that I'd been exonerated.

"I told him I had been wrongly accused of a crime, and the cops recently realized they'd made a mistake and I was released. I didn't tell him I'd been accused of murder. And I didn't tell him about my husband, or that I had been married. Only you know the full truth." Minus the part about Amelia.

Troy's lips kick into a faint smile. "Thank you for telling me. I know it wasn't easy for you."

I mirror his smile because he's right. At least he realizes it. "Some people still believe I'm a cop killer, that I got off on a technicality. There are tons of conspiracy theories circulating about that. There are some who believe that while I might not have directly killed my husband, I was the mastermind behind his death. And others claim my story about being an abused wife is a lie. If my husband had abused me, I could have just left him." As if it's as easy as that.

"Fuck," Troy mutters. "You tend to avoid Noah whenever possible. Is that because of what happened to you?"

Of course Troy noticed that about Noah. Kellan had too. Who else has wondered the same?

"Yes. He's a nice guy." As far as I can tell. "But he's still a cop. And I have trouble trusting cops. They haven't given me a reason to."

"Has anyone in town recognized you?"

"No. No one yet. I dyed my hair blond, and the media keeps showing old photos of me from when I was married. My face wasn't scarred back then." My finger goes to the scar stretching from the corner of my mouth to my jaw. "I used to look a lot prettier and...and different."

I used to wear more makeup. A pretty wife meant fewer beatings.

"You're still gorgeous." Troy traces his thumb along my cheekbone, and the way his eyes drink me in tells me he believes it.

My face is bruised and cut from last night, but even so, he thinks I'm pretty. Heat blossoms in my chest, spreads throughout my body. *Gorgeous.* The word patches up old wounds. Eases a decade worth of pain.

It's the rest of it I'm worried about. What happens when the rest of the town finds out about my past? Will he still want me then? It's a lot to expect him to be able to look past that. A lot to not expect doubt and uncertainty to plague his thoughts.

In the end, will he decide that's too much to deal with?

14

TROY

June, Present Day
Maple Ridge

My blood boils. Jess's ex treated her like a punching bag.

I'm glad the asshole is dead. I'm sorry he didn't die sooner.

And I'm pissed as hell someone framed Jess for his murder.

But knowing the only reason she told me about her past is because of the accident...if Samuel hadn't seen the scars and asked me about them, who knows if Jess would have told me the truth?

She didn't trust me enough to tell me the truth until she was backed into a corner. Until she felt like she didn't have a choice. Even Kellan knew she'd once been wrongfully imprisoned.

But he didn't know about her husband.

Knowing that's true gives me very little satisfaction.

I lean back on the couch, my thoughts still reeling from everything Jess told me. Her reaction in the ER at what happened to my truck now makes sense. Christ knows what her husband would've done to her if it had been his vehicle. "You're moving in with me."

She flinches even though I didn't say it harshly. Resentment lights her eyes. "You can't tell me what to do. I've spent the last eight years living like that—never given a choice."

I mentally curse myself for not considering her past before giving commander-stripes to those words. "I'm sorry, Jess. You're right." She's never going to trust me if I keep pulling bullshit stuff like that. "I care about you and...and it pisses me off what you've been through. All of it." The abuse. Prison. PTSD. The accident. "I just want to keep you safe."

I failed my best friend. I can't...I *won't* let that happen with Jess.

"I get that. But what exactly are you trying to keep me safe from? The media hasn't tracked me down. No one knows my secret. I haven't received death threats because I live here."

"You set up traps on your doors and windows because you don't feel safe," I point out. "Those aren't infallible. You thought someone broke into your house because the tape came unstuck. What if someone had? We don't know for sure what happened to the tape."

Jess releases a long and frustrated breath, the movement deflating her shoulders. "I know, but I have to do what's right for me, Troy. And I have to be the one who gets to determine what that is."

"I get that." I really do. "But I spent four years as a Marine. Protecting people is what I do."

The corners of her mouth twitch. "Are you going to whip out your cape next, or throw around your giant hammer?"

"Nothing that extreme. Though the giant hammer might be useful." A wry grin spreads across my face. My gaze shifts to Bailey, who's now dozing in the sunny spot next to her partner in crime, and the grin drops away. "Does the vet have any idea when or how Bailey was poisoned?"

Jess's own amusement flatlines from her face. "Not a clue. She didn't eat anything she shouldn't have when I took her for a walk yesterday. She was with me the entire day."

"Is it possible someone poisoned her food?"

"I don't know." Jess seems to shrink in on herself at that suggestion, and I silently curse some more, only this time it's directed at the person who stole her sense of security.

"Are you gonna move in with me so I can keep you and Bailey safe?" I nod at the two snoozing dogs on the floor. "I know someone who'd love to have Bailey around."

Jess laughs, the sound slightly brittle. But at the same time, it's just an inch short of my favorite laugh. "You mean as a pillow." Butterscotch is using Bailey's body for that purpose.

The grin flickers back on my face. "Partly for that." The smile fades and my resolve to keep Jess safe hardens. "So, are you moving in with me?"

"No. For once I'm living where I want to live. Where I can come and go as I please..."

Shit, I hate this. Hate feeling helpless at not being able to protect her. "You wouldn't be a prisoner in my house, Jess. You don't need my permission to leave whenever you want. I'm not your late husband and I'm not a prison guard."

Husband.

Widow.

I still can't link those two words with Jess.

Not Jessica. Savannah.

"I know I don't," she says. "But it's more than that. I'm finally getting to make my own choices. I'm not ready to give that up.

I'm enjoying being free again. And that includes living in my house."

"Can I at least install a security alarm in it? Think of it as not only for you but also for Bailey."

She doesn't answer.

"That's why you're constantly looking over your shoulder, isn't it? Because of what your late husband did and because of your time in prison?"

"It's been trained into my nervous system. My husband stalked me during our marriage because he didn't trust me. Every move I made, he knew about. It got worse later on, before he was murdered. But it's similar to how it is for you and your brothers. You're all vigilant—constantly on alert for danger."

She's right. My brothers and I haven't gotten that out of our systems. I'm not sure we ever will. Our synapses have been rewired that way. "We're not talking about me and my brothers. We're talking about you, Jess. You didn't ask for any of that to happen. The abusive husband. The prison sentence. The PTSD. The constant need to be alert."

"And you and your brothers did?" She raises an eyebrow as if to challenge me. "I'm working on it, Troy. Robyn is helping me to learn to trust and not be hypervigilant. I don't know if I'll ever feel safe again. But I'm also learning that I can't stop living while I try to make it happen."

"So is that a vote for the security system?"

"Would it make you happier if I said yes?" Her voice sounds...not resigned...but...soft. Placating.

Well, shit, I'll take whatever I can get if it keeps you safe. "It would let me breathe again knowing you're safe while at home. I've lost people I loved. They either died because of a flesh-and-blood enemy or because of an invisible one. Because of PTSD." I swallow down the pain at the memory of those I have lost. "Our pasts have changed us both. Before the Marines, I wouldn't have been so overprotective. If it makes you feel any better, it drives my mother nuts too."

Jess leans into me on the couch, and I put my good arm around her waist. "Is it also that way for your brothers?" she asks.

"We've all had to deal with our own demons, and we've dealt with them in our own ways. We're better, but our time in the Marines has left scars—both physical and psychological."

Her gaze travels over my face as if she's attempting to get a better read on me. "Okay, I'll get the security alarm. But can you not say anything about what I told you to anyone else? I'm going to tell Kellan about my husband. But I'd rather no one else knows. I...I'm...he..."

My heart breaks at the pain and shame paling her face, and I nod. I can't know what she went through, but I can guess what she might be thinking. And she's wrong. No one will blame her for what happened. It wasn't her fault. Everything that happened to her was her late husband's fault. And the person who framed her for his death.

"I won't tell anyone, and that includes Garrett and Lucas. If you want to tell them, that's up to you." I brush my thumb under her shadow-crested eyes. "Maybe the security alarm will help you sleep better."

"Maybe." She doesn't sound too convinced.

My thumb moves to her mouth. "Are you gonna stay in my bed tonight so I can keep an eye on you?" A teasing smile slips onto my lips, masking the real reason I want her to be with me.

"Do you think that's a good idea?"

"I do. Neither of us can do anything. Between my injured shoulder and your bruised ribs, we'll have to be a little more creative for a while with sex." I brush my mouth against hers. "We should probably wait at least a week before we attempt it." Another brush of my mouth. "But that doesn't mean we can't kiss."

"We can definitely kiss. And…and maybe now you know the truth about my past…" Something flickers in her eyes. "Maybe we can change our relationship's no-label policy. I mean, if that's what you want."

Hell, yes. That's exactly what I want. "You mean I get to officially call you my girlfriend?" I grin once more, pouring what I think of her suggestion into the smile. Pouring everything I feel about *her* into it.

"Yes. That's what I mean."

"Let me just clarify—you're going to refer to me as your boyfriend? Because that's also what I want." So there's no doubt in anyone's mind we're together—in case they didn't get that from our hand-holding over the past month.

I briefly press my mouth to hers again.

"Yes to all of that." She parts her lips and lets me deepen the kiss. And, Christ, I've missed kissing her. I always miss kissing her, especially when we're working together given her strict no-kissing-at-work policy.

"And I'm thinking I should go on the pill," she says. "Since I'm going to be your girlfriend."

"If you're okay with that…going on the pill, I mean."

She smiles against my mouth. "I am."

The doorbell rings.

I ignore it and keep kissing Jess.

Or try to.

She pulls away. "You should probably answer that."

"Nope. I should keep kissing you." My mouth tilts to one side. "In fact, I'm positive that's what the doctor ordered."

She laughs harder this time and winces, her ribs no doubt reminding her of their injured status. "Nice try, Troy."

The doorbell rings again.

Sighing, I push to my feet and walk to the foyer. Jess's suitcase is where Emily must have left it.

I peer through the peephole. Mom's standing on the porch,

a casserole dish in her hand and a cloth bag dangling from her other arm.

I hide the suitcase in the hall closet and let her in. "Hey, Mom. What're you doing here?"

"I came to check on you and bring you some dinner. How's your shoulder doing?" She gives me the same concerned expression I was a recipient of whenever I skinned my knee as a kid.

"It's fine. Nothing PT with Lucas won't solve."

Mom removes her sandals and heads for the kitchen. I don't bother to stop her. I'm more than ready to introduce her to my girlfriend.

She smiles at Jess on the couch, but then the smile wavers. And I can only guess it's because of the bruises and scrapes on Jess's face and her bandaged thigh. Even from the kitchen, Mom can see them. "Hi, I didn't realize Troy had a visitor."

"Mom, this is Jessica."

Mom's face brightens. "So you're the Jessica I've heard so much about. I've been wondering when I'd finally get to meet you. I'm Joanne." She walks toward the couch.

"It's nice to meet you, Joanne," Jess replies, smiling in the way that always causes my heart to stutter several beats. She lowers her leg and makes an effort to stand.

"You're supposed to be resting your leg," I remind her with a playful glare that has Jess grinning.

"Don't get up on my account." Mom waves for Jess to sit again.

Butterscotch comes into the kitchen with Bailey trailing behind him. He gives Mom a small welcoming bark. Bailey joins in on the game, adding a slightly deeper bark.

Mom puts the dish and bag on the counter. "Hey there, Butterscotch. Who's your new friend?" She crouches to fuss over the two dogs.

"That's Bailey," I tell her. "Jess's dog. Jess is training her to be a service dog." That's all Mom needs to know for now.

"Aren't you adorable," she says to Bailey and straightens. "Soooo, is it true you're dating my son?" The question is directed at Jess, and Mom gives her the same *Are-you-going-to-give-me-grandbabies?* grin she gave Lucas and Simone when they got engaged.

"Yes, I am." Jess throws me a panicked expression that's so fleeting, I'm positive Mom didn't notice it.

"Jess was in an accident and needs her rest. So now's not a good time to ask all those questions I know you want to ask her." My tone is gentle, teasing, but my message is clear.

Mom turns to me. "Kellan did mention that." A snorted laugh threatens to push free from me. That's probably the only thing Mom got out of Kellan.

Her gaze returns to Jess on the couch. "How are you doing, dear?" she asks my girlfriend, ignoring the message. "I hope you fared better than my son here when he rescued the father and son who got lost hiking."

"Neither of my shoulders was injured," Jess points out, "so I'm thinking that's a yes."

Mom turns to me. "And how's your truck?"

"It was totaled."

"Oh, no! You loved that truck."

Jess flinches as if bracing for a physical blow. Like she did in the hospital. I can only imagine where her thoughts are. Mine are murderous toward the man who made her that way.

"It was just a truck, Mom." The loss of that I can survive. I don't know if I'd survive if something bad happened to Jess.

"Very true. Anyway...there's another reason I'm here, other than to drop off the casserole." Mom nods at the dish on the counter. "Your father's been itching to use his new barbecue. So we're having a big family get-together next weekend. I hope you can make it, Jess."

That's news to me. "How come I didn't know about it?"

Mom flashes me a grin. "Well, I'm telling you now. I hope you can make it, too, Troy." She looks back to Jess. "What do you think, Jess? Will you be able to join us next weekend?"

15

JESSICA

June, Present Day
Maple Ridge

Two days after the accident, I sit on Troy's couch with my laptop, go online, and check the amount in my bank account to make sure it's still as it should be.

Almost a quarter of a million dollars magically appeared in it earlier today. My heart bounces into my throat, and I suck in a hard breath. "Holy fuckers!"

Why would the State of California deposit money into my account?

I'm still staring at the screen, positive I'm imagining things, when the sound of Troy entering the house through the garage door reaches my ears. I blink. Nothing changes. The amount in my account is the same as when I logged in a few minutes ago.

"Are you okay?" Troy asks, and I finally tear my gaze from my laptop. Worry lines crinkle his brow. "You look like you've seen a...well, you look stunned."

That's a good way to describe it.

"For some reason, the State of California deposited almost a quarter of a million dollars into my bank account." My voice comes out sounding like one of Bailey's squeaky toys when she's playing with it. I clear my throat.

Troy studies my face. "Is this the first time the state has done that?"

I nod slowly, still dazed over the amount.

"And you really don't know what this is?" Based on his tone, I'm the only one who's clueless about why I received the mysterious deposit.

"No clue."

He drops next to me on the couch and rests his hand on the lower curve of my spine. "My guess is, it's a restitution payment for the five years you were wrongfully imprisoned. Didn't anyone mention you were getting it?"

"Maybe. I don't know. I wasn't in any sort of condition to comprehend much when I was released. I did meet with someone from the prison or a lawyer or some government official before that, but I don't remember who. They told me a bunch of stuff, but I was dealing with the emotional and physical stress from being stabbed. Everything was pretty much a blur—until I arrived here." I had no idea I was due to get money because of the years I spent in Beckley, innocent of the crime I'd been accused of. "I just figured the government didn't care what happened to me. I wasn't their problem."

The money is greatly appreciated, but it doesn't make up for the abuse I suffered while in prison. Nor does it make up for the loss of my daughter in my life. If not for the justice system failing me, I would still be her mother. I would be the one who got to hug her, to kiss her boo-boos better, to read her bedtime stories. I would be the one who got to love her, who got to hear her say, "Mommy."

I would give up all the money if it meant getting to be her

mother again.

Troy's mouth curves into a soft smile. "You know this means you don't have to work for me if you don't want to? You're set for a while."

"No, I want to." It's not my dream job, but it does give me a sense of accomplishment. That was something I didn't have when I was married. "I need to think about the long term. The money I got won't last forever."

"Okay, if you're sure."

I nod, the movement less dazed than before. "I am."

"Glad to hear that. You're a great office assistant." He captures my mouth in a brief kiss, then pulls away, the frown back on his brow. "I can't believe it's taken this long for them to deposit the money."

I laugh, the sound slightly hollow. "Guess they weren't all that excited to give it away. Or I temporarily fell through the crevices. But at least someone finally fixed that mistake." Now if only they could fix the mistakes that led to me losing my daughter.

I STARE AT THE PHOTO ON MY CRACKED PHONE SCREEN. THE LATE morning sun pokes through gaps in the thick clouds outside the living room window, the dim light painting mottled patterns on Troy's couch and me.

The driver from the towing company found my phone in Troy's destroyed truck when he retrieved it from the ravine. The crack misses my beautiful twenty-month-old daughter as she held out her floppy puppy when I took the picture. The photo of the original print means Amelia is always with me.

I trace over her sweet face. "I miss you so very much." The words are a croaked whisper. Saying them any louder will only hurt more.

The accident happened three days ago, and I'm alone in Troy's house while he's at work. He wanted me to recover for a few more days before I return to my job. Restlessness gnaws at my insides. I need to get back to work since it's about the only thing I can do while the laceration on my thigh heals.

I keep staring at Amelia's photo. All I want is to hear her voice. To talk to her. To see her.

Bailey, in her *Service Dog in Training* vest, whimpers next to my feet, seeming to sense my warring emotions. She's good at that.

"What do you think?" I ask her. "Should I call Craig and Grace? I've been working hard to turn my life around. I've got a job and a house. I've even got you." I smile at the ten-month-old puppy. "Surely that's enough to prove I'm regaining my footing." After spending five years at Beckley.

I pull up my list of contacts, and my finger hovers over Grace's name. Maybe they've been waiting to hear from me, to make sure I'm okay. They must have heard by now that I bought Iris's house since Anne Carstairs is a friend of a mutual acquaintance of theirs.

Before I have a chance to talk myself out of calling Grace, I tap on her number.

I can do this.

The phone rings a few times. My palms grow damp and my pulse races in my ears.

"Hello?" Grace says from the other end of the line. I can only assume it's her voice. This is the first time I've called her.

"Hi!" The greeting comes out as a strangled sound. I cough past my dry throat, attempting to clear a path for my next words.

"Mommy! Where are my favorite sandals?" A little girl's voice dances through the phone and clutches at my heart.

"Give me a moment, Lia." Amusement colors Grace's tone, a

reflection of the smile I imagine on her face. "I'll help you once I'm off the phone."

The band around my heart tightens at Amelia's shortened name, and useless tears prick my eyes. Amelia was my grandmother's middle name. I'd never planned to shorten it to Lia. The nickname is just one more reminder Amelia is no longer mine.

"Oookay," Amelia calls out. She sounds so beautifully happy, and I manage a teary smile.

A bark comes from her end of the line, followed by the giggle.

I squeeze my eyes against the ache in my chest. The pain from my bruised ribs is nonexistent in comparison.

"Hello?" Grace repeats into the phone. "Can I help you?"

Amelia starts singing in the background, and all the air in my lungs rushes out on a hard breath. I used to sing all the time to her. I can't remember the last time I felt like singing.

"This is...S-Savannah." The name still tastes foreign on my tongue. I swallow, my mind suddenly blank as to what to say next. "H-how are you doing?"

"Good." The word is drawn out, hesitant, unsure. "What can I do for you?" Grace's voice isn't unfriendly, but it's also not welcoming. It's as if I'm a telemarketer who she's about to hang up on.

I can do this.

The voice in my head sounds less certain this time.

"I was hoping I could see Amelia. In person. That...that I could be part of her life again. But not as her mother." I rush out the last part so Grace doesn't get the wrong idea. So she doesn't feel threatened. I know what it's like to lose a child. I'm not going to put Grace through that. She doesn't deserve that kind of pain. She's the one who saved my daughter from going into the system. Who loved Amelia when I couldn't be there for her.

"I just...I just would like to see her again." The final words fall, sandpaper to my tender throat, rendering my voice gritty. My heart is beating so hard, I'm positive Grace can hear the rapid *boom-boom-boom* through the phone.

A thickening silence fills Troy's living room as I wait for Grace's answer.

I stroke Bailey. Her silky hair runs through my fingers and keeps me from going numb.

Grace clears her throat. I close my eyes, preparing myself for whatever she's about to tell me.

"I'm sorry, Savannah." Her voice is so quiet, I can barely hear it over the phone line. "But I don't think it's a good idea. It's too soon. You just got out of..." She leaves the rest of the sentence hanging, but I know which winding road of disappointment it was headed down. She does sound sorry, but other emotions sit in her tone. Emotions that feel like the door is being slammed in my face.

My vision swims in and out. I bite back the building sob. "I have a job and a home. I...I'm seeing a therapist. I'm getting my life back together." Somehow, the words come out smooth and even, the curtains closing over how much *her* words shred me on the inside.

"That's great. I'm happy for you." She actually sounds genuine. "But it's more complex than that. We just need more time. You need more time to—"

"Moooooommmmyyyyyy," Amelia calls out, interrupting what Grace was saying, and giggles.

"How much more time?" I ask and wipe at the rebellious tear.

"I've got to go. Bye, Savannah." Grace ends the call.

And I'm left staring at the phone again, my past mistakes repeatedly stabbing me in the heart.

I swat at another tear. I feel cold.

I feel empty.

I feel lost.

I just want to curl up on the couch and sob until I have nothing left to cry. Enshroud myself in a blanket of grief and never let it go. I just want to pull the familiar numbness to me and try to make it through each day as the shell of the woman I once was.

"When you feel anxious, I want you to do the five, four, three, two, one exercise." Robyn's words flutter in my thoughts. *"What do you see?"*

"I see a dark-wood coffee table, Bailey, the TV remote control, the thriller Troy is reading. I see the framed photo on the shelf of Troy, Olivia, Colton, and eight-month-old Nova all smiling and looking like a happy family."

"What do you hear?"

"I hear the hum of the fridge in the kitchen, the purr of a lawnmower outside, the neighborhood kids playing in the street, soft music from someone's yard. I hear the emptiness buzzing in my ears."

"What do you feel?"

I lean down and stroke Bailey.

"I feel Bailey's hair running through my fingers, the soft texture of the couch, the short pile of the rug under my feet, the movement of Bailey's chest as she breathes." I touch my leg. "I feel the bandage on my stitched-up thigh."

I continue with the exercise. It might have helped if not for the sound of the young girls giggling outside of the living room window. It's the tether to my grief. The thing that reminds me of everything I've lost.

I pull my feet onto the couch, wrap my arms around my bent legs, and lower my forehead to my knees. My body shakes with the intensity of my sobs.

I'm vaguely aware of the front door clicking open and shut. Of Butterscotch scampering into the living room, his nails clicking against the floor. Bailey moves from beside me, and a moment later, Troy takes over her place on the couch. His scent of mountains and hope envelops me.

He strokes his hand down my back. "What happened?"

I shake my head, still not looking up. I can't tell him. It was hard enough to tell him the truth about my husband and prison. I can't reveal this secret too.

Troy pulls me to him, and I rest my head on his chest. My tears soak through his T-shirt. I want to ask him what he's doing home so early, but I can't find it in me to form the words. I can only let my tears fall.

Troy continues holding me and doesn't push for me to tell him what's wrong. He's the stalwart against all my storms, supporting me when my base crumbles.

I'm not sure what I would do without him.

"TELL ME HOW YOU FELT WHEN GRACE ENDED THE CALL WITHOUT answering your question," Robyn says from her chair. She's wearing her Army-green shirt and skirt, her ankles crossed to the side. I'm sitting on the couch in her office.

My gaze flicks to the plants on the corner shelves. "Frustrated. Jealous. Powerless."

"Tell me why those emotions."

I had a therapy appointment scheduled for this afternoon, and I finally admitted the one truth I had omitted before. I told her about Amelia, about her adoptive parents, and about their connection to me.

Amelia's voice replays in my head, and the air is yanked from my lungs, making it difficult to breathe. I never thought I'd get to hear her voice again. Every day while I was in prison, I would imagine what she looked like and how she sounded.

And now I know. I know how she sounds when she's happy and when she's singing.

"I'm jealous Grace knows what my daughter looks like in the morning when Amelia gets up for school." I say the words as if they're barbed, and if I'm not careful, I'll shred myself to pieces from the inside. "That Grace gets to read her stories. Gets to sing with her. Gets to know all those details only a mother would know about her child. I'm jealous Grace is the one who tucks Amelia into bed at night and is the one who hugs away her hurts."

I drop my gaze to the cream-colored textured rug beneath my feet. "I feel frustrated because I know why Grace doesn't want me to see Amelia. I don't blame her. Why should she trust me? I'm an ex-con. I'd be scared of me too, if our places were reversed." My chest squeezes tightly just thinking about it.

"But you're not an ex-con, Jessica. You're an exoneree. And you're a woman who found herself in an impossible situation. But you've also shown that you always put Amelia's needs above your own. You gave away your rights to her because you love her that much. It doesn't sound like you've done anything to give Grace a reason not to trust you when it comes to Amelia."

My eyes find Robyn's. I wish her words were true. I haven't given Grace a reason to not trust me. But that doesn't matter. Our fundamental beliefs mold our perceptions. If she believes environment shapes the person we become, she might also believe prison negatively impacted how it reshaped me, no matter how good a person I was beforehand.

Which in many ways is true.

"Legally, your brother-in-law and his wife don't have to let you see Amelia," Robyn says. "It's up to them what they want to do about you visiting her."

I nod. I do know that.

"I'm not sure you are ready yet to be in Amelia's life, Jessica." Her tone isn't cruel, just straightforward and with a note of compassion. "Yes, you have a job and a home, but you need to be in a healthier place for the sake of your mental well-being." Robyn leans forward in her chair. "Why don't we set a goal for you to strive for?"

"What kind of goal?"

"You want the chance to be in Amelia's life, but first you need to work on the guilt you're holding on to because of what happened. You did nothing wrong. That was all on your late husband and whoever killed him." I'm sure Lincoln, my husband's younger brother, would disagree. "We also need to address the shame you're experiencing. So how do you feel about setting the goal of dealing with those two emotions, so you're in a better place mental-health wise?"

"What about the PTSD?" The reason I'm seeing Robyn to begin with.

"The PTSD, the feelings of shame and guilt—all of it is part of the bigger picture. We can't just focus on one element, ignore the rest, and expect everything to be fine in the end. Mental health and healing doesn't work that way."

"Okay. If it increases the chance of seeing Amelia again."

Robyn seems to consider her next words. "I can't promise you that once we've dealt with those two issues, Grace and her husband will let you see Amelia. That might take time. And it might never happen because of their own concerns and worries when it comes to their daughter. That's their job as her parents. To worry about her and protect her."

I inwardly flinch at Robyn's reference to Amelia being their daughter, even though that's what she is. "I understand. I'm just not ready to give up yet on that possibility. I miss her so much it burns in my chest. I see other kids and can't stop wondering what Amelia looks like. Can't stop wondering what she's doing at that moment. Can't stop wondering what she loves to do and what she's not a fan of." I wring my hands in my lap.

"She was my reason to keep breathing on the days when I felt like giving up. Both during my marriage and while in prison." Until the day I finally gave up my will to live after I was literally stabbed in the back.

"Do you still feel that way?"

I think on the question for a beat. "Sometimes. She's not my reason for getting up each morning like she once was when I was married." But she is my motivation for the renovations in the second bedroom in my house. My motivation for turning my life around. I'm not ready to admit that to Robyn, though.

"How do you see her when it comes to your life in general?"

"What do you mean?"

"Does she have an impact on any of your decisions?"

Darn it. It's like Robyn can read my mind. "Not really."

"Not really?"

I shrug, unwilling to articulate the truth.

Robyn doesn't say anything. She watches me as if waiting for me to elaborate.

Which I don't. My decisions about my life aren't necessarily focused on what's best for me, but they are what will bring me closer to seeing my daughter again. And seeing her again is what's best for me. It means I can see for myself she's happy and thriving.

"No, she doesn't impact most of my decisions," I say, deciding to give Robyn that much of the truth.

"That's good." She leans back in her chair. "You mentioned you felt powerless when Grace ended the call without telling you how much time she and her husband need before they'll consider letting you into their daughter's life. Tell me about that."

"I feel like no matter what I do, they will never be ready to let me see Amelia. Grace didn't give me any specific milestones I need to reach first. She just said she and Craig need more time."

"Why do you think she said that—that they need more time?"

I twiddle with the fabric of my skirt. "I don't know." I don't know them well enough to know for sure.

"It could be they really do need time to adjust to you being in their lives and Amelia's again. They were kind enough to help you secure a place to stay while you got your feet on stable ground. They didn't have to do that." Robyn gives me a small smile.

"I suggest giving them that time while you focus on yourself." Her smile inches wider, and she sits up even straighter. "Take that opportunity to find something that makes you feel more grounded. You've mentioned before that you feel like you've lost all sense of purpose. Which is quite understandable with everything you've gone through, Jessica. This is a good time to examine what would give you back that sense of purpose in life. Something that shows you're establishing roots here. Something not connected to Amelia."

I guess she's right. In college, I had a burning desire to change the world. That's why I went into journalism. Working for Troy doesn't give me a purpose like I once had. It gives me a paycheck—for which I'm extremely grateful.

"Right now, your mental well-being is a concern," Robyn says, "and your feelings of powerlessness make sense given what you've been through over the past ten years. You were stripped of all power in your life. We'll work on regaining it. And you can start thinking about the things that interest you that might give you the sense of purpose you're looking for. Or at least something you're passionate about. How does that sound?"

I nod, the makings of a smile twitching on my lips, because I would like to regain control of my life once more. To banish the powerlessness that still thrums through my body.

To find my purpose.

To find myself.

And in doing that, strengthen my relationship with Troy.

16

JESSICA

June, Present Day
Maple Ridge

Thursday, after a busy first day back to work as Troy's office assistant, I head to the grocery store. Bailey walks alongside me wearing her *Service Dog in Training* vest, and we practice some of the commands we've been working on.

My ribs are still sore, so I'm taking things easy, but my leg is getting better. As it is, I had to practically beg Troy to let me return to work.

And let me go back to living at home.

I go into the store, focusing on Bailey's training each step of the way, and head for the produce section. Violet is there, checking out the display of peaches. Sophie is in the shopping-cart seat, cuddling her toy lamb.

"Hey, Sophie." I wave to the little girl. She waves back, grinning, and waves at Bailey.

I instruct Bailey to lie down and give her a treat to reward the behavior. "Hi, Violet. I called you Tuesday afternoon." I reach for a peach, taking care not to stretch too far and irritate my ribs. "Did you get my message?"

She shakes her head stiffly and continues inspecting the peaches.

The unsettled feeling that something's not right with Violet, the same feeling I'd experienced the day of the accident when she wasn't home, returns. I had brushed it off as me being paranoid. Now, I'm not so sure. "Is something wrong?" I give Bailey another reward for remaining down and to encourage her to stay there.

Violet shakes her head again, her attention on the peaches.

But it doesn't matter if she's not looking at me, I can see the faint bruise on her cheek. Her makeup hasn't completely covered it. "He's hitting you, isn't he?" My words are barely louder than a whisper.

"No one's hitting me, Jess." Her voice is small, soft, as if it too has gone into hiding. She picks up a peach and inspects it.

"I know what it's like." I keep my volume hushed. A few other customers are also in the produce section, but they aren't close enough to overhear us. "I've been there, where you are, and I barely survived. If you need someone to talk to, I'm here for you, Violet." I don't know if her husband is hurting their daughter, but I do know his abuse will impact her both now and in the long run.

"You've got it all wrong," she says, her voice still soft, and returns the peach to the display.

She walks away, pushing the shopping cart. Sophie waves goodbye, her chubby hand gripping hold of my heart.

I wave back and attempt to stretch my lips into a smile.

I give Bailey another reward and do my shopping while continuing our training session.

I don't run into Violet again in the store. I can't text or email or phone her. If her husband is anything like mine was, he'll be monitoring all that.

Like what usually happens when I walk with Bailey, I feel the gazes of the people who spot her vest as we walk around the store. Their curiosity about it prevents me from being invisible like I was before she came into my life.

I keep my head down, hiding my face.

I pay for the groceries, and Bailey and I walk back to the building where my bike and trailer are parked.

Taking care not to aggravate my ribs, I pedal home, thankful Iris's bike is a comfort bike instead of a regular one. The higher handlebars put less strain on my ribs than a regular bike would. But even then, I have to pedal slowly and walk up any slopes that are too much for the healing cut on my thigh to manage.

I park the bike and trailer in the garage and unlock the back door to the house. Bailey walks past me as I punch in the alarm code. I shut the door, lock it, and reengage the alarm.

It's only then I let what happened in the store with Violet replay in my head. The bruises. The denial. The shell-shocked voice. And my mind slips to another time and place, when my husband had accused me of cheating on him. I had taken a beating for that lie. I tried to escape with Amelia the next night, promising her we would go somewhere he wouldn't find us. But that didn't happen. A cop pulled my car over while I was driving to a motel.

And all the comments from the few months prior had returned in droves. Comments from my husband's colleagues about postpartum depression. Recommendations that I get help. All part of his plan to manipulate me. To make sure I couldn't get custody of Amelia.

I shake the memory away. My husband is dead. He can't hurt me anymore.

Unfortunately, my life didn't start over once he died—not in the way I had dreamed of so many times.

But now, I'm finally getting my new start. In Maple Ridge. With a man who makes me feel happy, appreciated, safe. I'm getting the chance at the life I'd once dreamed of.

A life minus my daughter.

That part hurts.

Robyn feels I'm not ready yet to be in Amelia's life again— I'm still too much of a mess. Grace doesn't trust me enough because of where I spent the past five years. Which I get. I really do.

Maybe one day soon Violet will get to live the life she dreams of and share it with her daughter.

And I hopefully, by then, won't still be trying to prove myself worthy of seeing Amelia.

17

ANGELIQUE

July 1943
France

The late afternoon breeze brushes strands of hair into my face as I pedal towards Jacques's vineyard. But the breeze isn't enough to cool my heated body.

Baker Street recently approved a new drop zone, so while Johann was away, I've been busy recruiting safe houses. My body is ready to call it quits after I spent the past two days cycling almost non-stop.

Johann is due back this evening, and then I'll have to explain to him about Oskar and his family's disappearance. It's a conversation I'm not prepared for. No matter how many times I've thought it through, I haven't been able to think of a way to break the news.

I steer down the driveway and approach the barn. The door is wide open. I know I closed it when I left this morning.

142

Jacques must have forgotten to shut it after retrieving some equipment. Or perhaps he is still in there.

Or...or the Nazis decided to search the property. A collaborator reported us. Someone from the local resistance group was captured and pointed a finger at me.

Anything is possible.

But if that were the case, the Gestapo or SS would still be here. *Unless they didn't find the hidden cellar in the barn or any of my SOE-related items hidden in my room.*

I dismount my bike.

Johann steps out of the barn, his expression winter-storm dark. The pistol grasped in his hand is pointed at me.

"Where the hell are they?" Johann's tone isn't just angry. The anger is laced with accusation. His eyes burn with loathing, with despair, with grief, and my chest tightens, forcing air from my lungs.

A shudder grips my body. I have been in the presence of Nazis, and I have been closer to SS soldiers than I ever want to be again. But the fear I felt then is nothing compared to now.

This—Johann's reaction—is so much worse.

"I-I can explain." The words are sand in my throat, rough, crumbling apart. "W-we should go into the house."

Unless Jacques has called it a day earlier than normal— which I have never witnessed him do—he will be working in the vineyard. He won't be inside.

Johann nods but keeps the gun trained on me.

I wheel the bicycle to the barn, lean it against the wall, and walk to the farmhouse with Johann following behind. I can only hope that is a positive sign. He is willing to listen to what I have to say. Whether he will believe me is another matter.

Inside the house, I look at him to see where he wants to conduct this interrogation. In retrospect, I should have taken him to the barn. That way if he did shoot me, he wouldn't get blood all over Jacques's possessions. The consequence of my actions wouldn't be a stain on the furniture.

Johann appears to consider his options for a second and points to the drawing room with the pistol.

I sit on a chair, a bergère I hope doesn't have too many memories for Jacques attached to it. Johann doesn't sit. He stands several feet in front of me and nods for me to talk.

"They're safe." *For now.* "I can't tell you anything." I gesture to his uniform with the wave of my hand. "It's not safe for them or for you if you know where they went. I will tell you that I'm trying to get them as far away from Hitler and his deportation camps as possible." I release a long shaky breath. "Oskar asked me to give this to you." I remove the old Austrian coin from my pocket and hand it to Johann. "He said to tell you it is a lucky coin. He said you would know what that means."

Johann inspects the coin, and a small smile twitches on his mouth. But the smile isn't directed at me. It's for whatever memory is linked to the keepsake.

He lowers the gun to his side. "Are they really safe?" His voice is scratchy, and my heart squeezes into a grenade-sized lump at what he must be thinking.

No one is safe as long as Hitler is in power.

"Are they safe? Or is that wishful thinking?" The emotion in his voice is gone. His tone is like marble, hard and cold and dangerous when wielded as a weapon.

"To be honest, I don't know. Nothing is predictable. We can only hope it will be all right." My breathing is shallow as I wait for him to strike. My SOE training didn't prepare me for something like this. It prepared me to be tortured, to die for my country. It didn't prepare me to die because I was trying to save a family from possibly being murdered. "I promise you everything is being done to protect them. I can't tell you where they will end up because I don't know those details either. That is to keep everyone involved safe, including you."

"Will you be able to tell if they are all right? Or will we never know what happens to them?" Some of the hardness has faded from his voice.

"If I had a radio, I might find out when they arrive at the destination." I am hardly going to admit I have one hidden in the house. Jacques and I listened to the BBC France news while Johann is away. Radios are forbidden in the country. To be found with one could result in death.

Johann sits in the wingback chair across from me, places the pistol on the small table next to him, and drops his head into his hands, elbows on his knees. "God, this is all my fault," he says in German.

He has lost so much due to this war. I still have my sister and friends back home. Although that might change if Hitler cannot be stopped.

God, I miss Hazel. All I want right now is to hear my sister's voice. To hear about her day and about her dreams once the war is over. Are Hazel and Charles expecting their first child yet?

Is Charles still alive?

During those infrequent times when I've been able to listen to BBC France, I've heard about RAF pilots who have been safely returned to England after their planes landed in enemy territory. But there is no way for me to know if Charles is one of them, or if his code name was mentioned during the many times I couldn't listen to the reports.

The anger I felt towards him, the sting of betrayal he caused —none of it exists anymore. It has faded. Disappeared. It took too much energy to be angry at him and Hazel. Energy I need to survive this war.

And maybe Hazel was right. I hadn't loved him as much as I thought I did.

The sound of an engine pulling up to the house alerts me to approaching danger. My head jerks up.

Johann jumps to his feet. "Upstairs. Now."

I don't argue. I run up the stairs to my room and shut the door. I press my body against the wall and listen to what's happening downstairs. The front door opens and closes, but I don't hear anything beyond that.

Then the engine starts up again, and the sound of gravel crunching under tyres tells me whoever it was is driving away.

Or the vehicle's driver is leaving and the passenger remained behind.

I wait for Johann to come to tell me the coast is clear. Silence settles over the house and stretches with each passing second. And still, there's no indication if the threat has gone.

I check the clock on the dresser. I don't know where Johann is, but there is still enough time for me to bike to the village and see if the cut-out has left me any new messages.

I walk downstairs and pedal to the village. A wooden structure that wasn't there the other day sits in the middle of the town square, its ominous purpose unmistakable. Loops of rope dangle from the structure.

I duck my head, not daring to look at it for any longer than I already have, and go into the café.

The place is empty other than one other customer. The man is reading a newspaper, a coffee cup in front of him on the table. I don't recognise him. He's wearing a suit that is threadbare at the elbows and does not fit as well as I imagine it once did. His brown hair is prematurely greying and slightly messy.

My gaze flicks to Danielle. The short, thin woman, with grey hair slipping from her bun, doesn't appear too ruffled by him being here. She's busy wiping the top of the glass display.

I walk to the counter. "*Bonjour.*" I keep my voice appropriately cheery and place my order. I pay for it. Danielle accepts it and hands me the change, the exact amount indicating there was no message today.

A commotion outside snares our attention. Shouting and

screams come from the village square. Danielle and I exchange worried glances and rush to the window.

Two SS officers are dragging a man to the wooden structure. Even without seeing his face, I recognise the man who is my friend and fellow resistance fighter. The man who kissed me when two German soldiers stumbled upon us during a parachute reception. *Please, no.*

The SS officers stop beneath the structure and turn the man to face the crowd.

At the sight of Pierre's bleeding and beaten face, my hands slap against my mouth.

It's all I can do not to scream.

18

JESSICA

June, Present Day
Maple Ridge

Three days after I run into Violet at the grocery store, Troy picks Bailey and me up in his new truck and drives us to his parents' house. Their neighborhood is pretty much like mine, only several decades newer. The houses here have vinyl siding instead of wood or stucco, and they're larger than on my street, with porches and longer front yards. Tall, thin trees skirt both sides of the wide street—between the road and the sidewalks—providing a leafy shade from the sun.

Troy pulls up in front of a two-story, charcoal-gray house with a wraparound porch, and my heart scampers into my throat.

Bailey and I step down from the truck, and I open the back door for Butterscotch. The dish with the homemade dessert bars is balanced on my free hand. Butterscotch goes running up the porch steps. Bailey has on her *Service Dog in Training* vest, but I can tell if given a chance, she would be chasing after her friend.

The path leading to the porch is made of cobblestones. It branches off into a narrow pathway that meanders through several flowerbeds, each trimmed with low hedges. The entire front yard is peaceful and quaint. It's similar to what I would love to adopt for my house one day.

The house and garden are perfect. It's the kind of place one can't help but fall in love with.

A direct contrast to me.

I'm imperfect, damaged, unlovable. I'm the house with cracked and chipped stucco and warped floorboards.

I stare at the house, and the feeling of peace from a moment ago vanishes. All I can do is stare at Troy's childhood home, unsure what I'm doing here. I'm not used to dealing with parents. Not even my own.

Especially not my own.

Troy comes over to my side of the truck. "Hey, breathe, Jess. You've met my mom. And my dad's also gonna love you." He lowers his mouth to mine. His lips are soft and soothing and sensual, and I let myself get lost in the kiss.

But kissing him has the opposite effect than the one he was after. My heart rate picks up and my palms grow annoyingly damp.

I pull away, but not far enough to lose his warm breath on my face. "My late husband's parents are both dead. I never got to meet them. He loved his mother and couldn't stop talking about her. And later, he couldn't stop comparing me to her. I always came up short." I glance back at the house. I already know Troy's mom is perfect. "I can't even make a casserole."

His brow scrunches into a clueless frown. "What do you mean? You've made a casserole before."

"Not like the one your mom brought you last Sunday." His

mom's casserole was like a touch of heaven. Like the casseroles Granny used to make.

Troy hooks my chin with his finger and turns my head to him. "Your casseroles are delicious too, Jess. And that's not gonna happen with my parents. My mom likes you. You put up with my dumb ass, so my father will automatically like you. And I'll never compare you to my mother. You're an amazingly strong and beautiful woman, Jess. You'll never come up short." His lips brush mine once more.

A rush of relief surges through my veins. Admitting the truth to him—some of it, anyway—is like having a whale-sized weight knocked off me. I'm no longer being dragged beneath the surface. No longer gasping for air.

But there's one thing I'm not ready to tell him about—the one thing I wonder if he already knows.

Amelia.

She's a minor, and none of the news stories I've read have mentioned her. That's to protect her—in more ways than the media can appreciate. But maybe there's a story out there that does report I have a daughter. Or at the very least, a child. A news story from shortly after my husband was murdered.

All Troy has to do is google my name, and he could stumble over my remaining secret.

"Have you googled me yet?" I didn't mean for the words to slip out, a touch of accusation poisoning them.

"Have I googled Jessica Smithson to make sure no one has figured out who you really are? Yes. Have I googled Savannah Townsend? No. It wasn't easy for you to tell me what you did about your husband...or even to admit you had one. I want you to be able to trust me. And that won't happen if I snoop into your past."

I consider his words for a second, roll them around in my mind.

I haven't imploded from telling him about my husband and

about the conviction. He hasn't pulled away because I spent five years in Beckley.

Even knowing that, I still can't admit to my one biggest failing. I can't admit to losing something that means more to me than my life.

Troy pulls me to him with his good arm. "I really hope you trust me, Jess." He kisses my forehead, and the tenderness of it sends a shiver sashaying up my spine.

I smile up at him. "I do." For the most part, that is true.

"Butterscotch," he calls out. "This way." He leads me down the side of his parents' house, to the wooden gate. His dog comes bounding after us.

Troy opens the gate, and we enter a garden that looks like something out of one of Iris's magazines. We walk past colorful flowerbeds and rock gardens to the expansive pond in the middle of the lawn. The greenery and rocks surrounding the odd-shaped pond give it a natural feel. Like the water was here first, and the house came later.

I peer at the light-pink water lilies, delicate and beautiful. "I love the pond."

"Garrett built it," Troy says.

"He did?"

"Yup. Mom kept saying how great the yard would look with a pond. She'd been saying it for several years. Two years ago, she and Dad were on a cruise to Alaska. Garrett was struggling with a book he was working on. And, well..."

I laugh, knowing where Troy's headed with this. In the few months I've gotten to know his brother, I've learned the man could start a landscaping business if he ever quit writing. He's responsible for several of the gorgeous gardens in Maple Ridge. All because whenever he struggles with plot points or some other aspect of his political thrillers, he gardens. A lot.

Whatever it is about gardening for him, it certainly works. I've read a couple of his books. They're addictive and filled with so many twists and turns, it's impossible to predict what's going to happen next.

"Maybe I should become an author if this is what my garden will look like while I'm writing." A soft chuckle tickles the back of my throat as I imagine turning my garden into an oasis with a pond and a deck where I can write from. Where I can write those articles for the With Hope festival. The articles I still need to interview some PTSD survivors and their families for.

Troy's responding chuckle is a sexy rumble in his chest. "Let me know if you need help lifting the heavy stuff."

I pointedly check out his injured shoulder. He no longer needs the sling, but the joint is still a long way from being healed. "We might need to wait a while longer on that."

"Hey, don't underestimate my abilities." The corner of his mouth lifts into a smirk. "You weren't complaining about my arm last night."

I grin. "You might be right about that." Although him going down on me might not have been what the doctor ordered when it came to my ribs. But the orgasm? Definitely worth it.

Simone, Zara, Garrett, and Lucas walk over to join us. "Wow, you two look happy." Zara carefully hugs me and then Troy. "I don't remember you ever smiling this much, Jess."

Her gaze flicks between us as if waiting for us to make a big announcement. A diamond-on-the-finger announcement.

I hug Simone. "I was just admiring Garrett's work." I point at the pond. "It looks great," I tell him.

"Thanks. Let me know if you want me to add a pond to your backyard."

"Stuck on a plot point?"

"Nope. Things are going great. Well, maybe not for my protagonist." He flashes me a wry smile. "But that's good news for me."

"It's a miracle he's even here," Zara says. "He disappeared

into his story and forgot he was supposed to be at his parents'." She smacks him on the arm. "If I hadn't gone over to his house, he would still be typing away on the computer."

Garrett shrugs, clearly having no defense for almost missing his parents' dinner.

A man in his early sixties approaches our group. The brothers' father, if their similar good looks are anything to go by. He smiles at me, and there's no missing the same warm-brown eyes he shares with Troy, Garrett, and Lucas. "You must be Jessica. I'm Ian." He holds out his hand for me to shake. His grip is firm but welcoming. "I've heard so much about you. It's about time I got to meet you."

I return his smile. "Thank you. I'm happy to finally meet you too."

"You boys ready for your first Wilderness Warriors clients?" Ian asks them. "I can't believe they come in less than two weeks."

"We were ready until Troy here got himself injured." There's no malice in Garrett's tone. Just the usual teasing between brothers.

"It's not like you guys can't run it without me," Troy tells them. "Am I pissed I can't participate yet? Yup. I was looking forward to the upcoming canoe and climbing trips. But what can I do?"

Ian chuckles in what seems to be sympathy. "And how's the festival planning going?"

"Good. Right now, I'm busy trying to find sponsors to pay for the equipment rentals." A lot of sponsors from what Troy has told me. Running a fundraising festival isn't cheap. I anonymously donated five thousand dollars, which only Troy knows about, but he didn't want me to donate more than that.

"Your restitution payment is for your new life," he'd told me when I'd offered to donate a large chunk of what he still needs. "I'll find another way to get the money."

"How's that going?"

"Slow. But I'm hoping to reach our goal very soon. Because if we don't, we'll have to cancel it. I'd rather not do that if I can avoid it. People's lives are at stake. Individuals like Colton and their families."

Troy's dedication to making a difference to those who struggle with PTSD fills me with warmth. I just want to hug him and show him how incredible I think he is.

"Have you asked Anthony Bell?" Ian asks.

"The owner of Bell Automotives?" Troy shakes his head.

"It's worth a try. The worst that can happen is he says no."

Kellan joins the group. "Dad, Mom needs you. She's ready for you to put the food on the grill."

Ian nods at him, a warm smile on his face. "Thanks, son."

As he walks, he draws my attention to the picnic table where his wife is standing. His movement is proud and distinguished and belies his former Marine training. It's much like the way his sons walk.

Emily enters the garden through the kitchen door. She's glowing. And it's not only her blond hair that's glowing due to the angle of the sun. She's glowing with excitement like she *is* the sun.

"Hi, Jess." She gives me a careful hug and steps away. "I've got a new wedding client, and she's looking for a photographer who specializes in the photojournalistic style you excel at." The flood of words rushes out, making it difficult to know what to grasp hold of first.

"Hi, Em," I say on a light laugh, buying myself a little time before responding. "I'm not a wedding photographer. I don't know the first thing about it." Just like I didn't know anything about photojournalism until I took courses in college and practiced. A lot. "And I don't think wedding photographers use their iPhones to shoot wedding photos."

I love being able to use my phone to take photos, but I miss the feel of a DSLR camera in my hands. Miss using different lenses depending on what I'm trying to do. I don't have that option with my phone.

But as much as I miss having a DSLR camera, I'm not ready to buy one or the rest of the equipment just yet. The camera I want—the model like I used to own—is expensive. And I'm not sure it's a good idea to use my restitution payment for it.

"I bet you could find an online course on the topic," Simone says. "There's a course for everything these days."

Emily brightens, and I sense she's only inches from bouncing on her toes at the idea. "She's right. I've been posting wedding photos on my Instagram account, and I get ads for all kinds of wedding-related services."

"I don't have an Instagram account." Or any other social media site. I don't need to make it any easier for the trolls and conspiracy theorists to find me.

"But you do have a computer." Em pulls out her phone from her skirt pocket and taps on the screen. A moment later, she shows me the results of her search. Several interesting-sounding courses pop up. I take the phone from her and click play on a video that tells you what the instructor's course will cover.

It's his attention to detail that grabs my interest. His work looks like something from a wedding magazine. Not just the photos of the bride and groom, but also the parts they spent a year planning. The dresses. The flowers. The decorations. The reception tables.

It tells a story. And telling stories is why I fell in love with photography.

"Okay."

Emily's eyes practically sparkle. "You'll shoot her wedding?"

"I'll check out the course." Maybe wedding photography will be my calling. The thing that will make me feel more fulfilled—to help with my mental well-being—and put me on the right track to seeing Amelia again.

Em throws her arms around me and gives me a gentle hug. "Thank you, thank you, thank you."

I chuckle and pull away from her. "I haven't agreed to anything yet."

She grins in that confident way she has. "But you will. You should meet Theresa. You'll like her. She's super nice. Her wedding is August first."

Damn. That's in just over a month.

"So soon? I thought people spent a year planning the perfect day."

"You can. But some people are looking for something more intimate. They aren't looking to have the ceremony and reception in a location that needs to be booked far in advance."

"Em pulled Lucas's and my wedding together in about a month." Simone beams proudly at Emily.

"Wow, you really couldn't wait to get married?" I mean, I kind of get it. Simone and Lucas have known each other since they were kids.

Zara snorts a half laugh. "That's 'cause they didn't get married for love like most couples. They got married for business reasons."

"Only we didn't know that at the time," Emily adds, sounding slightly grumpy despite the amusement gleaming in her eyes. "We thought they were marrying for love."

"But they did fall in love in the end, so it was all worth it," Zara points out.

"You do realize Lucas and I are standing right here?" Simone rolls her eyes.

Zara and Em level her with a satisfied smirk.

"I can set up a meeting with Theresa next week if you want, Jess. And you two can discuss the photos." The hope in Emily's expression shines at me like a beacon in a lighthouse.

"That sounds great."

"You're coming to the Fourth of July event and fireworks, right, Jess?" Emily asks.

I nod with a hesitant smile. "I'm looking forward to it. Especially the fireworks." The only thing I'm not looking forward to is I can't bring Bailey with me. The crowds will be too much for her. But I'll have Troy there by my side. That will make things easier on me.

"The girls and I signed up to volunteer. I'm helping with the hayride, but the person who was going to work with me had to cancel." Em casts me a wide-eyed pleading expression. "How 'bout you sign up and join me? We'll have so much fun."

"Um..." *Do it.* The old me, the pre-married me, would have jumped at the chance to do something like this. "I don't know anything about hayrides and horses."

"Don't worry. There's not much you need to know. We're just helping to load people onto the wagons." She presses her palms together in front of her chin.

I grin, and a small laugh tumbles free. "Okay. I'll help you."

Emily releases a tiny squeal. "Thank you, Jess."

"You're welcome." I turn to Troy. He's talking to Kellan, Lucas, and Garrett. "I'll be right back," I tell the girls. "I just have to say hi to Joanne and give her these dessert bars."

I walk toward the long table covered with a blue gingham tablecloth. Ian is standing at the open barbecue, a spatula in his hand. Troy's mother is talking to a woman who's maybe a little older than her.

Joanne's gray-streaked brown hair brushes across her shoulders as she talks, her head bobbing animatedly. She picks up a plate laden with food and moves it to the other side of the table.

The other woman tucks her chin-length gray hair behind her ear and looks over her shoulder at something. She turns back to Joanne.

"I can't understand how a mother could ever leave their daughter behind," Joanne says as I approach them. "I mean, what kind of mother would do that to a child?"

Everything inside me turns into a pointy shard of ice, even though I have no idea the context of what she's talking about.

I take an awkward step back. God, if she ever finds out my true identity, she'll hate me. If she finds out my mother left me with my grandparents and never looked back, Joanne won't want me in her son's life. She'll think I inherited my mother's selfish gene for abandoning those we're supposed to love.

If she finds out I have a daughter...

Joanne glances in my direction, and a grin spreads across her face. "Jessica!"

I fix on a smile that feels like a bra that's too tight and approach the table. "Hi, Joanne. I brought some dessert bars." I pass her the plate.

"Thank you. These look delicious." She puts the plate down in an empty spot. "Have you met Tuuli?" She nods at the other woman.

I offer Tuuli a friendly smile that's genuine. "Hi. It's nice to meet you."

"Jessica is Troy's girlfriend." Joanne is now beaming.

"Ah, so you're the infamous girlfriend I keep hearing about," Tuuli says, her eyes sparkling with amusement. "You definitely couldn't have done better than Troy. He's as good as they come. As you no doubt know."

I'm not sure how to respond, so I just nod.

She's right. He is the best thing in my life right now. But Troy could still do a lot better than having me as his girlfriend—as his mother will attest to if she ever finds out the truth about my identity.

19

TROY

July, Present Day
Maple Ridge

Thursday afternoon, I enter the building for Bell Automotives and walk past several shiny antique cars on display.

A light-haired woman in her late fifties is sitting at the desk outside of Anthony Bell's office. "I can fit you in on August sixth to see him," she says into her headpiece. She looks at the computer screen in front of her. "That's right....No, it would have to be either ten a.m. or four p.m....That's right....Okay, four p.m. it is." She smiles, her gaze still on the screen. "You have a nice day too. Goodbye."

She ends the call and looks up at me, her smile not fading. "Hello. How can I help you?"

"I have an appointment with Mr. Bell. I'm Troy Carson."

"Thank you." She types on her keyboard. "Troy Carson is here to see you....Alright..." She nods. "I'll send him in." She returns her attention to me. "Just go on in, Troy. He's leaving in about ten minutes, so he won't be able to talk for long."

She had mentioned that when I booked the appointment on Monday. The work he does on classic cars is in such high demand in Oregon and the surrounding states, I was lucky to even get this appointment. Otherwise, I would've had to wait another month to talk to him.

I enter his office.

Anthony is sitting behind his desk, studying something on his computer and wearing a dress shirt and green-striped tie. The man is in his late sixties, his hair completely white, but he's in good shape for someone his age.

He shifts his gaze from the computer to me, and a smile appears on his face. "What can I do for you, Troy?" He stands and leans over his desk, offering his hand for me to shake. He's not the only one dressed up. I don't usually wear suits, but I figured it couldn't hurt to wear one for this meeting.

I shake his hand and take a seat. "I'm not sure if you've heard, but I'm currently organizing a fundraising festival. The money will go to help military vets and first responders who are struggling with PTSD, as well as to help their families."

"Katelyn did briefly mention that to me." Katelyn being his daughter. He leans back in his chair. "Tell me more."

I spend the next few minutes explaining the specific goals for the money I hope to raise. He doesn't say anything. Just listens intently.

"As you can imagine," I explain, "it's not cheap to run a festival. Everyone involved in it is volunteering their time. And that includes the entertainment. But we still need to pay for the various permits, the marketing, and the equipment rentals. So I'm looking for sponsors."

"How much more are you looking at?"

"We still need twenty thousand dollars." The majority of our sponsors and donors were able to give amounts in the several thousand-dollar range, but nothing like what we still need.

He steeples his hands in front of his chest and nods, the bob of his head slow and thoughtful. "Not to sound cutthroat or anything, but how will I benefit if I help sponsor the event? I mean, business is business after all. As you can respect being a business owner yourself."

"Everyone who sponsors the festival will get recognition and their name on the promotional materials and signage at the event." The usual sponsorship perks—which of course adds to the additional costs of the event.

"It all sounds good. Especially what you plan to use the money for." Anthony leans forward and folds his arms on the desk. "But what's the real reason you decided to organize the festival?"

"Excuse me?" An uncomfortable feeling twists in my gut.

"Something tells me you aren't organizing the festival to help promote your construction company, Troy. Or because you woke up one morning and decided to help those individuals struggling with PTSD. What's the real reason you're doing it? The blood-and-guts reason. The thing that inspired you to throw yourself into planning this."

"My best friend was a first responder. He was diagnosed with PTSD after working at the site of the horrific bus accident last year that took the lives of all those junior hockey players. He wasn't the same after that." I explain to Anthony what happened to Colton and how it has impacted Olivia and Nova.

I can tell from Anthony's expression he remembers the accident. The details of it are tough for most of us to shake because it happened so close to Maple Ridge. And for a while, there was a lot of media coverage.

"Okay," Anthony says after a moment. He looks at his computer screen and stands. "I'll donate twenty thousand dollars. I need to leave now, and I'll be away next week at an antique car show. But book an appointment with Angela for next Friday, and you and I can hammer out the details then."

I stand and shake his hand once more. "Thank you so much, Anthony. Your support means everything." It means I can breathe a little easier when it comes to the event.

I leave his office and drive to the Wilderness Warriors property. The first group of military vets arrive a week from tomorrow, and I want to finish painting the trim on the final cabin before the festival-planning meeting this afternoon.

I unlock the cabin door and step inside the space that's about the size of a large hotel room. Like all the cabins my brothers and I built, it's wheelchair accessible. I go into the large bathroom. Several pink sticky notes cling to the mirror. All with the recognizable Morse code dots and dashes.

It doesn't take me long to decipher Jess's Morse-coded message.

Have fun at Game Night. If you win, I will give you your prize tomorrow night. Nudge, nudge. Wink, wink. Are we still on for a movie at your house?

I pull my phone from my shorts and type a reply.

> Me: Yes, we're still on. Looks like I better win. I want my prize. Nudge, nudge. Wink, wink

I hit send on another message.

> Me: Are you sure you don't want to join us tonight?

We ended up switching Game Night for today. It's Thursday, but Lucas and Simone have plans for tomorrow.

Jess responds a minute later.

> Jess: Yes. I'm sure. See you tomorrow!

I type back.

> Me: I could go over to your place instead
> of going to Em's for Game Night

> Jess: No. Don't miss out on that because
> of me. I've got lots to do tonight. But
> tomorrow night you're all mine ;)

20

JESSICA

July, Present Day
Maple Ridge

Troy's front door opens. The man who already has my heart beating fast flashes me a smile, and my heart flutters into overdrive. Bailey pushes past him to find her friend. She's getting a break from her service-dog training.

"Hi," I say, barely getting the word out, my voice soft and husky.

Troy grabs my hand and pulls me to him. I loop my arms behind his neck and loosely grasp my wrist. His arms go around my waist, and his mouth finds mine.

His tongue plunges into my mouth, hot and ready, and my legs go wobbly. God, I feel...feel so. My body...I'm...damn, I've missed him. I've missed this.

Sure, I saw him for a short while at work, when he dropped by between meetings and before he left for his PT appointment. But my no-kissing-at-work rule, which I seriously need

164

to rethink, kept me from getting to enjoy more moments like this.

Troy maneuvers to the side and shuts the front door. My back is pressed up against it, and nothing else exists outside the bubble we've carved for ourselves. His lips pull away from my mouth, and I release a needy whimper.

His mouth finds my neck and his teeth gently scrape my skin. The sound that slips from me this time is a down-and-dirty moan. If his shoulder wasn't healing and if I wasn't recovering from bruised ribs, I'd climb him like a maple tree.

Butterscotch barks from the direction of the living room. We keep kissing.

The intensity of it slows, easing away to tender kisses. The brushing of lips. The gentle touch of our mouths. My breath comes out on a stuttering sigh.

"I've made the popcorn." Troy's breath coasts my lips.

We head for the living room. Bailey and Butterscotch are playing with some of Butterscotch's squeaky toys. Troy opens the door leading to the backyard so they can play out there, and he and I get comfy on the couch. I lean into him. He puts his good arm around my waist. The bowl of popcorn sits on the coffee table in front of us.

"What did you do today?" Troy asks as he skims through the movie options.

"Trevor Dumas asked me yesterday if he could move the interview to today for the PTSD articles I'm writing. He and his family decided to go to Seattle next week. So I talked with them." I look up at him. "Thanks for setting that up with them. It went great. And I also started the online wedding photography course. So nothing too exciting. What about you?"

On top of all that, I spent more time reading and transcribing Iris's journals. For Anne. And, well, because I'm curious to find out what happens next. How the hell did Iris escape back to England? She never told her great-niece about her time as an SOE agent. Did the Nazis capture her, and that's why she was silent about the war? Did she end up in a concentration camp like so many SOE agents who were captured? From what I've read, few survived.

I don't mention that part of my day to Troy. I still haven't admitted to anyone, including Anne, about the journals, the heart pendant, and the medal. Once I've finished transcribing the journals so Anne can easily read her great-aunt's words, I'll give everything to her. And she'll learn about that part of her great-aunt's life she never knew about.

"I had the meeting with Anthony Bell yesterday." Troy grins like a little kid on Christmas morning after Santa left him the bike he asked for.

"And?" I knew about the meeting, but when Troy didn't say anything about it, I thought maybe Anthony wasn't interested in helping sponsor the festival.

"He's donating the rest of the money we still needed."

I didn't think it was possible, but the grin on Troy's face grows wider.

My own smile matches it, even with the scar between my mouth and jaw trying to keep it from forming, and I squeal. I throw my arms around his neck. "I'm so happy for you. This is incredible news."

AFTER THE MOVIE, TROY AND I GO OUTSIDE AND SIT ON THE wicker love seat in his backyard. A fire burns in the firepit, but even then, the air is on the cool side. I snuggle deeper into Troy's soft sweatshirt that smells like him.

Bailey and Butterscotch have opted to stay inside. Both were snoring from Butterscotch's bed in the living room when we stepped out.

"I still can't get over how amazing the stars are here," I say, glancing up at the dark sky. Stars and sunsets and flowers are a few of the things I missed while locked away. But I don't remember the stars ever being this breathtaking.

"That's one of the best parts about living in a small town. Nowhere does The Great Cock Constellation look as spectacular as it does from Maple Ridge."

"The wh-what?" I know I'm not a wiz at astronomy, but even I know there's no such thing as The Great Cock Constellation. Or at least I don't think there is.

Troy points to a cluster of stars. "There it is. The Great Cock Constellation." The corners of his mouth quirk and his eyes have a wicked gleam. But otherwise, his tone is that of an astronomy teacher telling his students the name of a constellation.

I bite back a laugh and say in an equally serious tone, "And let me guess, that's the Boob-a-licious Constellation?" I point to a random group of stars to the left of his cluster.

He chuckles, the low rumble shooting straight to the spot most desperate for him between my legs, and it reminds me of the promise I made him yesterday. The one I left in Morse code. "Absolutely correct. I take it you also took astronomy in college?"

"Of course. And I seem to remember getting an A." I move to stand between Troy's knees and drop to mine. The paving stones aren't the most comfortable things to be kneeling on, but I don't care. "I also remember promising you a prize if you won last night." Zara told me Troy won when she, Emily, Simone, Avery, and I met up for lunch.

The wicked gleam in his eyes returns. "And what prize is that?"

I run the tip of my tongue along my lower lip in anticipation, and his Adam's apple jerks up and falls down in a move that gets me more excited. For this man. For what I'm about to do. "I guess you'll find out soon enough." I unzip his jeans.

His length is long and thick and grows thicker under my perusal.

He helps me lower his jeans and boxer briefs over his hips, giving me better access to my own prize. I give his length one long, satisfying lick and take the tip into my mouth.

"Christ," Troy says on a hissed-out moan, and his fingers knot in my hair.

My fingers wrap along the base of his cock. The other hand gently grabs his balls.

I'm rewarded with another "Christ," and I smile around his hard length.

I bob my head, his panted breaths my musical accompaniment, his groans my motivation. My blood simmers in my veins, heating me more than the fire behind me ever could. I keep going, relishing every sound and movement he makes. I've never felt more powerful than I do in this moment. Never felt more wanted.

His fingers tighten in my hair, driving me on. I release his tip from my mouth and lick it, the wetness from my mouth almost sizzling from the heat of his velvety skin. I take him back in again.

"I'm going to come." Troy's words carry on a long groan.

Good. He can come all he wants. I'll be there to catch it, to catch him.

His balls tighten, and a salty heat jets into my mouth. I swallow it, which elicits another moan from him.

I gently release his cock from the depths of my mouth and give him a minute to collect himself.

I push to my feet and sit next to him as if I hadn't just caused him to come undone. I grin. "Congratulations for winning last night."

Troy puts himself together and guides me to straddle him. His hands move to my waist, and his thumbs brush under the hem of the sweatshirt.

He looks at me, longing in his eyes. "Stay the night." The smooth rumble of his voice coats his words, melts me to the core. "I want to wake up tomorrow with you in my arms, Jess."

His fingers knot in my hair once more, and he guides my head down to his. His kiss consumes me, sets me on fire again. I'd be more than happy to stay this way for now and forevermore.

"Okay," I murmur against his lips, mine curved in a dreamy smile. "I'll stay the night."

21

TROY

July, Present Day
Maple Ridge

A movement next to me in bed jerks me awake. Early morning sunlight stretches through the closed curtains in my bedroom.

A foot lashes out and hits me in the shin. Jess's foot.

Her thrashing stops and she turns to me. Her eyes appear slightly dazed, and she slowly blinks several times, seemingly to bring the room into focus. "Troy?" The disbelief and longing in her voice—as if she's longing for me not to be a figment of her imagination—almost guts me.

I shift closer to her and kiss her cheek. "Yes, sweetheart. It's me."

"Thank God. I was having a nightmare."

"You want to talk about it?"

"Not really. I'd rather you help me forget it." A coy smile unfurls on her lips.

170

I kiss her jaw. The shell of her ear. "I can do that." The word rumbles in my chest. She moans a sound that makes me hard in record time. "Are you sure that's what you want to do?"

"Positive."

"We don't have to be at the Fourth of July celebrations until noon. I can think of lots of things we can do in the meantime." I flick my tongue along the shell of her ear. "And all those things require me seeing you naked." I kiss the corner of her mouth where her scar is. "Without it being dark in here." My tone is a reverent whisper.

I haven't seen her naked. Not in the light where I can appreciate the sight of her better. She's only let me make her come when the light is off. But that's because she didn't want me to see her scars. The scars I still haven't seen.

But it's been two weeks since she told me about them and about her previous life. I want to see all of her.

I want to kiss each scar and chase away her pain.

She swallows, her eyes uncertain. "Okay."

"Let me know if it gets to be too much." I cup her face and stroke my thumb along her cheek. "I've got you, Jess."

She nods and her eyes turn dark and beautiful.

I slowly peel the sheet down, giving her a chance to change her mind.

She's wearing one of my T-shirts, the hem bunched around her hips. The cut on her leg from the accident is now free of stitches. It's the small round scars peppering her upper inner thighs that have me inwardly cursing.

I don't have to ask her what caused them. There's only one thing they could be. Cigarette burns. Anger flares in me at what that prick did to her, but I carefully school my expression to keep the anger from my face. Instead, I kiss each scar, silently promising her body, the woman who has captured my heart, that I'll never treat her like he did.

I'll only worship her.

I push the hem up, exposing her stomach. It's there I witness the rest of the roadmap of abuse. I have no idea which scars were the result of her husband's hand, and which were from her time in prison. All of them make me want to curse everyone responsible for her pain—including the police and prison guards who failed to protect her.

I take the time to kiss each scar. I don't ask her what caused them, and she doesn't volunteer the answers. Her fingers reach for the scar on my arm, jagged and white.

"Shrapnel wound," I say.

She pushes herself up to sit, the hem of my T-shirt pooling around her hips. Her fingers shift to the small scar on my chest. "Is that what caused this one?"

"Yes, but from a different incident."

She's not the only one with scars on their body with different stories to tell.

Her fingers brush across a thicker scar that cuts through my healthy shoulder. None of these old wounds are new to her. She's seen them when I've been shirtless while working on her renovations.

"That one wasn't from the Marines. I was in a car accident during college. Colton was in the car too, and he saved my life. That's what made him decide to be a paramedic." Instead of the accountant his old man had been pushing for.

Her fingers continue to the tattoo on my arm. The tattoo of a mountain scene inside a maple leaf. Two hockey sticks form a diagonal cross under it.

"This is beautiful," she says on a hushed whisper. "The details are so realistic. Did you get this because you love hiking?"

"Yes, partly because of that. Colton and I lived for the mountains. Even as kids. The hockey sticks are because we played hockey together as kids and in college. I got the tattoo last year after he died."

"To keep him with you." This time her whispered words seem to be more directed to herself than to me. She traces over the picture, and her touch sends a surge of desire through my veins.

"Exactly."

"It's a great idea. And so beautiful." Jess peels my T-shirt over her head, tosses it to the floor, and lies back on the mattress.

I join her and kiss her long and deep, consuming her like she's consuming me. My hand skims along the curve of her hip, down her thigh, and brings her leg to wrap around *my* hip. I slip my hand between us, and my fingers push the edge of her panties aside. I stroke her heat, spreading the wetness waiting for me like it's a gift from the gods.

A small moan slips from between Jess's lips, and I grin. "Enjoying that, are you?"

"Very much," is her purred response.

I slowly drag the cotton down her legs, my fingertips caressing her smooth skin. *So. Fucking. Beautiful.* How could anyone treat her like she's anything other than a goddess?

Inwardly shaking my head, I slip the panties over her ankles and drop them next to my T-shirt on the floor. I lie back down next to her, and my finger finds her heat once more.

I slide my finger inside her, and I'm rewarded with another of her moans.

I add a second finger, stretching her, teasing her, driving her to the brink. Each whimper, each groan goes straight to my cock, making me harder. I want to plunge inside her and worship her soft heat. But knowing what she's been through, knowing her husband repeatedly raped her, I take my time. I'm not going anywhere.

This is about more than just sex. It's about me giving her pleasure. It's about her healing.

I let her body and her soft sounds guide me. She's the one

in control. In control of what we do. In control of my heart. I want to kiss her and tell her I love her, and I know some women would be all for it, but it's too early for that with Jess. So I show her with my hands and with my mouth.

Jess's hands are also busy. They explore my body, caress my scalp, stroke my length. "I want you inside me, Troy." Her voice is low and husky, and it sends the remaining blood in my body rushing to my cock.

"Are you sure you're ready for that?"

Her ribs are still healing. My shoulder is too, but I'm more worried about Jess.

She pulls away from me and rearranges the pillows on the bed. A soft smile curves across her face, the heat in her eyes unmistakable. "Sit up. I'll ride you."

I do as she requests, and I grab a condom from the nightstand drawer. I open the package and roll the protection onto my length.

She moves to straddle my legs. I put my hands on her hips to keep her in place. "Not yet. There's one thing I'm craving first."

"What's that?"

I lean forward and pop a nipple in my mouth. I alternate between sucking and flicking it with my tongue. While my mouth is busy, my hand is no less idle. I pinch and tug on the other nipple, enjoying the moans I draw from her. Jess's back arches, and I put my arm around her, holding her in place. Her hand cups my balls, and I think I'm gonna come right there. I groan and release her nipple from my mouth.

Jess grins at me. "Like that, huh?"

I return the grin. "Very much."

"Now can I have you inside me?" Her warm, calloused fingers circle my cock, and I make a strangled noise.

This isn't the first time I've made love to Jess. We had sex a couple of times the night before I was called away for the search and rescue. But it is the first time since then. The first time since I learned the truth about her husband and her wrongful conviction.

She positions herself on my tip and eases herself down until I'm fully sheathed. She's so warm and tight and heavenly, I'm surprise I don't lose my load.

She rocks her hips. I move my fingers between her legs and caress her mound, letting her sweet sounds guide the pressure.

The sun is shining brighter in the room compared to a few minutes ago, giving me a spectacular view of Jess's face as she comes apart in my arms. The dazed look in her eyes. Dazed from disintegrating into a billion pieces. Of trusting each piece will slot perfectly together.

Her head falls back, exposing the length of her neck, and she cries out my name. Her inner muscles clamp around my cock. I keep going, savoring the silky heat squeezing me, and I pump into her. Thrusting. Holding out as long as I can.

And then I can't hold back any longer. I plunge into her one more time. A flash of white heat consumes me, and I'm catapulted up, up, up. Tonight's fireworks will be a letdown after the ones I'm now experiencing.

I groan out my release, eyes closed. Jess's heat convulses around me in smaller waves, and our breaths come in hard and ragged.

We lie together on the bed, regaining our senses. The warmth of the sun sinks into our skin. And I feel more content than I have in a while.

Jess carefully lifts herself off me, and I go deal with the condom.

She's under the covers again by the time I return to my room. I join her and gather her in my arms, my chest against her back.

I kiss her shoulder. "Are you okay?"

"I am now." I can't see her face, but there's a smile in her tone. She snuggles closer to me, and I love keeping her like this—keeping her safe and content.

She looks up at me, and I capture her mouth in a long kiss, showing her once more how much I love her. Showing her I would do anything to protect her. And that includes protecting her from the nightmares that intrude on her dreams.

"Would you tell me about your nightmare?" I ask, hoping she'll open up to me once more like she did when she told me about her dead husband and about her grandparents.

"Nope. I just want to lie like this and not think about the dream."

"Okay." I'm not giving up on this yet, but I'm also not going to push her out of her comfort zone until she's ready. "I'll admit I'm all for spending all day in bed with you and skipping hanging out with our friends and my family," I murmur on the crown of her head.

She laughs, the low, smoky sound sleepy with satisfaction. "I'm sure your family will have something to say about that."

"You might be right, other than Lucas. I'm sure he'd rather spend the entire day in bed with Simone."

Jess chuckles. "I bet she feels the same. But as tempting as it is to spend all day in bed with you, I promised to help Em with the hayride this afternoon."

A bark comes from the other side of the door. I groan and cover my eyes with my forearm. "I guess Butterscotch has figured out we're up."

"You were a Marine. Aren't you trained to wake at the crack of dawn?" Her voice is featherlight, amusement wrapping around each syllable.

I peer at her from under my arm. "I untrained myself."

Jess laughs again. "I'll go feed the dogs and take them for a W.A.L.K."

"I have a better idea. How about we both take them for a you-know-what, and then we can shower together afterward?"

She twists in my arms, and her face transforms into a wince. A smile swiftly replaces the pained expression. "I like that suggestion."

"How're your ribs doing?"

She presses her lips to mine. "They're good. Definitely getting better."

"You sure about that?"

"Positive. I can handle a little pain. Especially after that orgasm." She gives me another quick kiss.

While she gets dressed in the shorts and the pale-yellow T-shirt she was wearing last night, I go downstairs and feed Butterscotch and Bailey. Jess appears in the kitchen as they're chomping down their food.

"You know, you can always leave some of your clothes here." I hand her a mug of coffee.

She takes a small sip from it. "Is that your way of getting to leave *your* clothes at my place?"

The corner of my mouth tugs up. "You're right. That's part of my genius evil plan for world domination."

"Well, in that case..." She kisses me lightly on the lips. "Okay, I'll leave a few items at your place, and you can leave some stuff at mine."

My smirk transforms into a full-out grin at how she's trusting me with more of herself, and my insides heat with relief.

By the time we've finished our coffee, the dogs are ready to go for a walk.

Jess pulls on one of my clean sweatshirts and we go outside. It might be July Fourth, but the morning mountain air is cooler than she was used to in San Diego.

I thread my fingers with Jess's. The move feels so natural now, I can't imagine not holding her hand while we walk.

We turn the corner and head toward the park. A front door bangs shut a few houses down, and Katelyn hurries along the path leading to the sidewalk. It's only once she's walking our way that she notices me.

Her gaze drops to our joined hands and lingers there for a beat. "Hi, Troy. Jessica. I didn't realize you two are dating."

"We've been dating for a few weeks now. Didn't you see the latest *Who's Dating Who* update on Maple Ridge's Facebook page?" I'm joking, of course. Or I assume I'm joking. Maybe there is an update on the page.

But she must have known we're together. We were holding hands and kissing at the festival we saw her at last month. Although at that point we weren't officially a couple.

"Must admit I missed that." Her tone is the same one she uses when working at the Veterans Center. The politely friendly tone. The respectful tone. The tone she doesn't usually use with me, so I can't figure out why she's using it now.

"Are you going to the fireworks celebration at the lake tonight?" Jess smiles at Katelyn, her expression not giving away if she notices Katelyn's acting different.

"Of course. Everyone goes. It's a town tradition. Maybe I'll see you guys there." Katelyn turns and walks away. "I'm meeting with my sister," she calls over her shoulder.

Jess watches Katelyn climb into a car parked on the street. "I didn't realize she had a sister."

"She has an older sister who lives in Eugene." My phone rings in my pocket. I check the screen. Maple Ridge SAR. *Shit.* I accept the call. "What's up?"

"Troy, I know you're on medical leave for the next few months," Sheldon says. "But we're short-staffed due to the holidays and a couple of climbers have gone missing. We need you to be the leader for the command post. That way Jeff can join us for the search."

I release a long, relieved breath that it's not a missing kid this time. Those are always the most emotionally draining—especially when things don't end well. "Okay, I can do that."

He tells me where the meeting spot is, and I end the call. "Sorry, looks like I won't be able to spend the day with you after all." I explain everything to Jess.

"Hey, that's okay. You go be a superhero." She kisses me on the cheek. "I'll be fine. I'll call Zara and she can pick me up." She rolls her bottom lip between her teeth and fidgets with the hem of her sweatshirt.

"Are you sure?"

"Positive. And I'll tell your parents what happened if I see them." She lets go of her hem. "I'll take Butterscotch and Bailey to the park first and then call Zara."

"Christ, why does this have to feel like *déjà vu*?"

"Things will be different this time. For one, I have no intention of going hiking on my own. Lesson learned."

I hate this, but I can't let the team down. And I can't let whoever needs rescuing down.

I kiss her, taking a little longer than I probably should. Kissing her deeper. Telling her without words that I love her. "Hopefully I'll be back before the fireworks tonight." She's been looking forward to them after five or more years of going without seeing any.

I sprint to my house to retrieve my truck and gear, but my heart remains with the woman on the sidewalk.

22

ANGELIQUE

July 1943
France

I don't realise I'm moving towards the café door until I feel Danielle yank on my arm, halting me. "You can't," she hisses. "It's too late."

I jerk my arm away, hating that she's right. If I run outside to the village square, it won't change anything. The only thing it will accomplish is to give the SS officers a reason to end my life along with Pierre's.

Or maybe that is also coming soon.

I cannot even go out there so my face is the last one he sees. It's too much of a risk. The soldiers could put together that I'm also responsible for the crimes he's clearly been accused of.

Angry shouts come from somewhere near the front of the crowd. I cannot make out what the man is saying, but it's drawing a frown from the SS officers. They don't push through the crowd to grab him. They just resume their task of breaking my heart.

It is not a gunshot that ends his life. A noose robs him of it.

Tears wet my face as I remember the man who was my friend, the man who made me laugh while the world is at war. The man I trusted with my life. We might not have always agreed, such as when he accused Johann of being a Nazi, right before I found Oskar and his family hidden in Jacques's barn. But Pierre and I knew we could always rely on each other.

My legs begin to crumple under me. A strong arm steadies me and guides me to a nearby chair. I sit but cannot draw my eyes away from the window. I'm vaguely aware of the man taking a seat opposite me.

I want to scream, to throw a knife at the SS monsters, to claw their eyes out. To steal their life like they're doing to us.

What's the worst that could happen if I did any of that? They murder me too?

Except I know death isn't the worst thing that could happen. Death is when the torture would end. When the pain would stop.

Death would be what I'd pray for, beg for.

Did Pierre pray for the same?

Once it's clear Pierre is no longer with us, the crowd disperses. Tension is visible in their shoulders, in the lines on their faces. No one says anything, their attention directed at the ground in front of them.

The soldiers don't take him down. They leave him as a reminder of what they do to traitors.

My tears come harder, but I don't make a sound.

"It won't do you any good to keep looking at him," the man who was in the café when I arrived says sombrely. "It won't bring him back to life. Was he your boyfriend?"

I tear my gaze from the square. "No. He was a friend." That is all I will admit to him.

Danielle places the coffee I didn't order on the table in front of me. "He was well liked by everyone in town. He will be greatly missed." Her eyes rake over the man, taking in the features I have already catalogued. "I haven't seen you before."

"I'm passing through from Paris. I was hoping to get away from that." He nods towards the village square. "I guess that was too much to wish for."

Neither Danielle nor I respond.

I just take a long sip of what is supposed to pass as coffee—crushed walnut shells instead of coffee beans.

The café door opens and one of the men who is part of the parachute reception enters. Danielle leaves to serve him at the counter. A murmur of voices comes from them, but I cannot make out what they are saying.

The door opens again, only this time I'm met with a glare from a woman much older than myself. "It's your fault, you German-loving whore!" She limps to my table as I stand, bracing for her vitriol. "Pierre is dead because of you." She strikes me across my face.

Stunned silence fills the room. The woman is not known for her anger. She's observant. And she could easily get me killed by turning me in to the Gestapo because she knows I'm lying about Jacques being my father.

"Did you tell your lover before or after you fucked him that he should kill that poor boy out there?" She points towards the village square with a flick of her arm.

"That's enough, Lilian," Danielle says. "You don't know what you're talking about."

"I know plenty enough." The woman growls the words at Danielle and turns to me. "It should be you up there." This time she points at the village square with more force behind the movement. "You're nothing more than a disgusting collaborator."

She raises her hand once more, but the man who helps

with the parachute drops grabs her wrist. My skin still smarts from when she struck me.

I don't attempt to defend myself. If the stranger is working for the Germans, I don't want to reveal I am a threat to Hitler and his regime. I also don't want the older woman to get herself into trouble with the Germans for the same reason.

A quick glance at the stranger is met with a neutral expression. He's not going to give away what he's thinking if he can help it. I make a move for the door.

Danielle rushes to my side. "Will you be all right?"

Her words could have so many meanings. Can I expect to be next in the noose? Or will I be all right after the loss of Pierre's life?

I respond with a small nod, even though I have no idea the answer to either question. If the reason Pierre is no longer with us is because of me, I cannot live with myself knowing something I did cost him his life.

And I have no idea if I am next on the Nazis' list.

Danielle walks outside with me. "No matter what she thinks, it wasn't your fault."

I scan the area for SS or Wehrmacht or Milice. None are around, which makes me more nervous than it should.

"He knew the risks. We all did." Her words are too quiet to be heard by anyone but me.

"I know. But I can't help feeling responsible for what happened. Did he tell you why they"—my voice splinters, and I nod to the café where the other resistance circuit member is— "why they killed him?"

"They suspected him of collaborating with the local resistance group. They arrested him. It's unknown what, if anything, Pierre may have told them." She smiles and laughs, but the sound is strained at best. It's not enough to fool anyone. "There's a chance he didn't tell them anything. They didn't break him. They haven't arrested anyone else in the area yet, so maybe it means they don't know who was working with him."

"I hope you're right about that." Because while the *Cashmere* network has maintained a level of anonymity vital for keeping those who are part of it safe, the resistance group in the area has grown since I arrived in France. It's not about a member only knowing one or two people in the group. Too many members know too many other individuals in it.

And that might lead to the downfall of us all.

THERE IS NO SIGN OF JOHANN WHEN I ARRIVE AT THE VINEYARD. While I wait for his return, I focus on cooking the evening meal and pretend I'm home in Bristol, preparing supper for my imaginary husband and children.

I imagine my husband entering the kitchen and wrapping me in his arms from behind. Him swaying us in time to the music on the radio. Him kissing me on the cheek while our children are playing and giggling in the drawing room.

I imagine my sister, my brother-in-law, and my adorable nieces and nephews arriving for dinner. The squeal as the girls run off to play with their dolls.

The front door bangs shut, and I'm unwillingly dragged back to my present reality. Heavy footsteps approach. I don't have to turn to know who they belong to. It means Johann will be the one I see when I do turn around, not an SS uniform.

Relief eases through me. But it also means I will have to face a man who is angry because he thinks I betrayed his friends.

But instead of thinking of the last time I saw Oskar and his family, it's Pierre's image in the village square, his life no longer part of him, that flashes in my head. I close my eyes, forcing away the tears that have resurfaced.

"Did you know him?" Johann's voice is low and gentle and free of accusation. Is he talking about Pierre? Does Johann know I was in the village? Did he see me?

Still unable to look at him, I nod. There is no point pretending I don't know what he's talking about. "Everyone in the village knew him." My voice cracks, and I will myself to be stronger.

The SOE recruited me not only because I am fluent in three languages. They were impressed with my inner strength that isn't so easily dented, other than during the whole kerfuffle with my sister and fiancé. But even then, I didn't curl up in a ball and become a useless lump. I continued to prove my worth to the WAAF, the Women's Auxiliary Air Force.

"I'm sorry about your friend." The sincerity in Johann's tone is almost my undoing. It would be easier if he were a callous monster like those men who killed Pierre. Then I could hate him like I'm supposed to.

I nod again because I know he is sorry, but that doesn't change anything. The SS killed Pierre because they had evidence linking him to the local resistance group.

I turn to tell Johann the meal is ready, but his expression stalls the words. Hope lights his eyes—or I assume it is hope.

"Is it true, what you said?" he asks. "Are my friends going somewhere that will keep them safe?"

"That is the plan. The plan is for them to escape to freedom so Sonja can grow up in a world that doesn't know hatred towards Jews." Or a world that knows less hatred than what the Nazis stand for.

"Perhaps they will go to America one day?"

"If that's where they wish to go, maybe that's where they will end up. After the war." As long as they're not captured on their journey to Portugal—their first destination after going over the Pyrénées Mountains. A ship from there will take them to wherever they are headed after that. It is the same escape route the downed pilots travel.

"Thank you." Johann's mouth curves into a relieved smile, and the tension in his body appears to lessen.

Our gazes lock, and my breath comes a little faster than normal. There's a fluttering in my chest that doesn't belong there, and the longer we stare into each other's eyes, the more it intensifies.

I cannot explain it. Cannot explain this intense connection between us, especially after the devastation of the day. Or perhaps that is why I feel it. A connection has been steadily growing between us since the day I learned his sister's life was at risk in Austria because she is deaf. With everything we are dealing with—the loss and the fear—it makes sense that things between us have dramatically shifted.

"The meal is ready," I finally tell him.

"I'll eat with you," the gruff voice that doesn't belong to Johann says.

Jacques is standing in the doorway to the kitchen, eyeing Johann as though he isn't sure what to make of him. Distrust still scars Jacques's features, but ever since he found out Johann was hiding a Jewish family in the barn, his distrust for the man has softened slightly. Hearing the news the other day his son Yvon is still alive also helped ease the tension. Until Johann relayed the news to me, Jacques had no way of knowing if his son was among the living.

Johann offers him a quick smile, accepting the olive branch, and heads upstairs.

He returns a few minutes later in clean clothes that do not belong to him. I've never seen Johann out of his uniform. The shirt is made for someone a bit smaller. The cotton skims his muscles like a second skin. The trousers reach his ankles, but that doesn't appear to bother Johann.

"Yvon's clothes," Jacques mumbles by way of explanation, digging into the stew.

"They were on the bed. I hope it's all right with you if I wear them for the meal."

Jacques nods without looking up. "Good stew."

"Charles," my sister calls from her seat at the dressing table. I'm sitting behind her, on the bed, her toddler daughter on my thighs. I bounce my legs, giving the little girl a horsey ride. She giggles in glee.

"Did you remember to grab the theatre tickets?" Hazel calls to her husband, who is downstairs. She puts on her pearl earrings, the finishing touch to her beautiful burgundy gown. The low back reveals her pale skin and shoulder blades, and the hem of the skirt pools around her feet. My gaze shifts to the mirror in front of her, to the dress's deep V-neckline. The gown is stunning. My sister looks truly stunning.

"Are we going to have fun while your mummy and daddy are out tonight?" I ask the little girl, grinning at her. She bounces on my legs, indicating she wants the horsey ride to go faster.

A loud bang comes from downstairs as if the front door has been blown open by the storm brewing outside. The sound is followed by the stomping of boots on the stairs. So many boots.

The little girl presses her hands over her ears, trying to block out the terrifying noise. The bedroom door flings open and SS soldiers flood in. My blood turns to ice. Oh, God. This can't be happening.

One grabs my crying niece and hauls her off my lap.

"Noooo!" I scream. "Leave her alone! Please give her back!"

Several others grab me and Hazel and drag us struggling and screaming to the bedroom door.

And then I'm standing in the village square, staring at the dangling body of a woman dressed in a beautiful burgundy gown that flutters in the wind. Her head is covered with a sack, but there's no doubt who it is.

I release a scream, and I keep on screaming. "Oh, God, nooooo! Please, no. Please."

I jerk awake, gasping for air, and push up to sit in the bed. The room is dark due to the blackout curtains, but I know without a doubt where I am. *It was only a nightmare. Hazel is still alive.*

Tears wet my face. I pull my feet to me and wrap my arms around my legs. My body is trembling at how real the dream felt. I close my eyes, trying to push away the memory of the nightmare, but I cannot stop the loud sob that escapes me.

The floorboard creaks with the weight of someone walking across it. A moment later, a hand rubs my back, the gesture soothing. "It's okay." The words are in French and spoken softly against my temple. "You're safe, Angelique. I'm not going to let anyone hurt you." A slight German accent is buried within the words.

My eyes snap open. The bedroom now glows softly in the light of a candle, and Johann is sitting next to me, shirtless. The flickering candlelight dances over his muscular stomach and chest.

My gaze darts to the doorway. Jacques is standing there, his night clothes and hair rumpled, his expression more drawn than usual. Fear flares in his eyes, and it takes me a few seconds to understand why. Did I cry out in my sleep? Or worse yet, did I cry out in English or in French?

I close my eyes briefly. When I reopen them, Jacques is gone.

Johann wipes his thumb under my eyes, drying the tears away, and tenderly kisses my forehead. The heat of the candle flame is nothing compared to the one in my belly at his touch.

Johann's expression holds a mix of understanding and fear, but most of all, desire shines back at me in his eyes.

I should feel embarrassed a man who is not my husband is seeing me dressed in my nightgown. I should, but I don't. It's not as if I am still a virgin. I foolishly gave that to the man I thought was going to be my husband one day.

"I'm scared," I whisper in French, being more honest with Johann than I have been with anyone lately.

He kisses my temple. "I am too. I'm scared for my mother and my sister. I'm scared for Oskar and his family. And even though I haven't killed anyone, I'm scared for my soul."

With those last words, the final barrier between us is pulled down. I search his eyes for the truth hidden there, the way I suspect he's doing the same to mine. Then we shorten the distance between us, and our mouths brush. We pause, our lips a hair's breadth apart, our rapid breaths misting over them.

Our mouths touch once more and move together in a soft kiss.

My heart flutters in my chest in a way I can't remember it doing before. We pull away a fraction of an inch, our breaths still intermingling.

I don't say anything, but he must see the plea in my eyes for him not to stop. He lowers his mouth to mine once more.

Our kisses become a slow exploration, a source of comfort, the weaving of souls.

I lie back in bed, and the kisses continue. Some are nothing more than a tease, a taste of what is to come. A promise. Others are more heated, taking my breath away. And with each kiss, tiny pieces of me the war has stolen are restored.

Johann's hands roam over my body, but he takes care not to overstep any boundaries. Mine do the same to him. His touch is addictive, making me buoyant, but all too soon it's not enough. I crave more. I crave him.

"I want you," I whisper. "I want to have you inside me." I press my lips to his. "I want you to help me forget my nightmare." Another kiss. "I want you to help me momentarily forget everything else." I search his eyes, their depths reflecting my feelings for him.

"Yes," he murmurs, not removing his gaze from mine. "I can do that." He smiles, and it's like we're in another place, another time, thousands of colourful butterflies fluttering about. A place where only love and happiness are possible. A place where war is not welcome.

He pushes himself off the bed. "I should probably shut the door first. I don't think your father wants to see me in your bed in the morning, holding you, like I plan to do when I wake up."

My lips curve into a soft smile. "You might be right about that."

He closes the door and unbuttons his trousers. I strip out of my nightgown.

Awkwardness wraps around me. I've only been naked in front of Charles. But I could die tomorrow or next week or next month, and how I feel right now will be irrelevant.

I shuck the awkwardness off like a winter coat on a hot day and watch as Johann removes his trousers and underwear.

I draw in a quick breath at the sight of him. Nothing about him reminds me of Charles. Whereas my ex-fiancé is lean and more on the lanky side, every part of Johann reveals his strength. Charles enjoys watching cricket. Johann's body is that of an athlete. And he was blessed when it comes to the hard length between his legs.

He rejoins me on the bed. "You are sure you want to do this?"

"Yes. I'm sure." I reach for his hand and pull him down next to me.

We start kissing again, taking our time. We have the whole night ahead of us.

Our hands explore, worship, take each other to the stars. We get a taste of what heaven is like, and I don't ever want the moment to end.

Johann eventually slides inside me, and it's nothing like I have ever felt before. His movements are slow, deliberate. As if he's memorising every part of me, memorising every second we're together.

Outside the window, the world is ugly, full of hatred and pain. Inside...inside the room, it's beautiful. Like a garden after a storm, lush with colourful blooms that sparkle in the sun from the raindrops still clinging to the petals.

And when our bodies become one, the intensity exploding between us, we're the rainbow in the sky.

The hope.

The future.

We lie in each other's arms while we recover, neither of us saying anything. We just hold one another, keeping our fears at bay. Johann caresses my arm. I stroke his clean-shaven jaw with my thumb and revel in the beauty of this man, both inside and out.

A single thought blares in my head like an air-raid siren: What does it say about me when I'm falling in love with the enemy?

23

JESSICA

July, Present Day
Maple Ridge

Butterscotch, Bailey, and I continue down the sidewalk of Troy's street, my thoughts on the kiss Troy gave me before he left following the call from the search and rescue team.

The dull ache in my ribs reminds me they're not fully healed. But I wouldn't have changed this morning in bed with Troy for anything, healing ribs be damned. "I'm not going to be much use when it comes to throwing your balls," I tell the dogs. "Butterscotch, your daddy was going to do that. But maybe I can bowl them instead?"

The grassy area of the park is busy with families getting ready for the Fourth of July celebrations. We continue to the off-leash section, and I unclip Bailey's and Butterscotch's leashes. Bailey doesn't have on her *Service Dog in Training* vest. She gets to be a puppy for now.

I throw their balls underhand. The balls don't go far, but the dogs don't seem to care. They race after them and drop the balls by my feet for me to toss again and again and again.

"Okay, you two," I say after we've been doing this for at least thirty minutes. "Time for us to go. I'm volunteering with Emily at the hayride this afternoon, and I still have to shower and get ready."

We head back to Troy's house, passing a family playing soccer on the grass. The mother and father are playing alongside their two young kids and cheering them on. The kids are giggling and chasing the ball. And for a beat, I allow myself to slip into my old childhood fantasy of being part of a loving family like this one. With Troy.

I quickly disregard the thought.

As the dogs and I draw closer to the bench seats, I notice a lone figure on one of them with a toddler on her lap. *It's Violet.* Her shoulders are hunched as though the air has been knocked from her lungs. She looks...defeated.

"Hi, Violet."

She startles, and her eyes go wide. I recognize the fear and the hollowness in them. The fear and hollowness that stared back at me in the mirror when I was still married.

Sophie spots the two dogs and reaches out to them, a toothy grin on her face.

My heart squeezes, remembering Amelia also responding the same way whenever she saw dogs. She would point her chubby little hand at them, giggle, and say, "Doggie!" in the sweetest voice.

Craig seems to be the opposite of his brother in so many ways, including his love for dogs. Amelia's family has a dog. His brother—my late husband—despised them.

The memory of my dead husband sends a shiver creeping up my spine, its cold touch spreading through me. I scan the area, searching for signs that Violet, Sophie, and I aren't alone. Searching for signs Chief Wilson is lurking in the shadows.

Once I'm certain he's not here, I sit next to Violet and Sophie.

I don't speak. I focus on my breathing and focus on my happy place. In the canoe. With Troy and the dogs. I imagine the soft splash of the paddles breaking free of the lake surface. I try not to let Violet's reality pull me back under. Try to fight it so my own dark memories don't drag me down too.

"You were right," Violet says, her gaze directed away from where I'm sitting. "What you said in the store the other day. You were right. But you can't tell anyone. He'll hurt me if he finds out I told you."

"Do you have anywhere you can go?"

She shakes her head, shame and fear twisting the corners of her mouth. "And even if I do try to leave him, he won't let me. He has too many connections. He'll track me down and kill me if I attempt to escape him."

Those were the same words I'd told myself so many times during the worst points of my marriage. Shards of fear stab me. Fear for what Violet is going through. Fear I'll never truly escape the damage my husband inflicted and I'll never see Amelia again.

"My husband was a cop too," I tell Violet. The little girl playing soccer with her family kicks the ball and it rolls across the grass toward the goal. Her father pretends to make an attempt to stop the ball. It rolls between the two pylons.

Pretending.

Pretending.

Pretending.

Sometimes there's nothing wrong with pretending and make-believe. But sometimes...sometimes it's a dangerous trap. "At first, I thought he was wonderful," I tell her. "He seemed sweet and funny. It wasn't until we'd been married for a year that things changed. Or maybe they'd been changing all that time, but by the time I noticed, it was too late."

Violet nods as if she knows exactly what I mean, her gaze on the dogs by my feet.

"He used to beat me, rape me, demean me," I continue, my mouth dry, the words scratchy. "It was a sport for him. When he forgot he shouldn't bruise my face...those were the days I dreaded most. It meant I couldn't leave the house. I wasn't allowed to go out until after the bruises were healed. I know what it's like to be trapped, Violet, thinking you'll never escape the monster."

She turns to me, and her expression...it's as if she's seeing her own reflection in my face. The same reflection I saw every morning in the mirror after my husband left for work.

But at the same time, there's also a seedling of hope in her eyes. "But you did. You escaped him."

I laugh, the aching sound hollow and humorless. "I'm not sure you ever truly escape the abuser. Yes, my husband is no longer physically in my life...or on this planet. But he still haunts my dreams. My thoughts. My actions. I'm seeing a therapist now. She's helping me realize what happened wasn't my fault. It was my husband's fault. Every lash of his tongue, every punch, kick, hit—it was all on him. You don't have to live like this, Violet. But I also know you can't do it alone. You need help to escape him."

She scoffs. "Easier said than done. I have a child. He'll never let me take her, and there's no way I can leave her behind."

"I get it. I really do. He's using her as a pawn. My husband did the same with my daughter." My voice cracks, the splinters rough against my throat, and my gaze drops to my lap.

"You have a daughter? Where?"

"Seattle. But she's no longer mine. Not legally anyway." I shelve the pain and think about the bedroom I hope Amelia might see one day. Once it's renovated. "My husband was murdered. I have no idea who killed him, but the evidence pointed at me. I was sentenced to twenty-five years. I thought I'd never see her again, and I didn't want her to be ashamed her mother was thought to be a cop killer. I wanted her to finally have the new life I had promised her so many times when I'd dreamed of escaping my husband. So I gave her up for adoption to one of my husband's brothers." I describe the family dynamics between the two men, and how Craig had been estranged from the family, which is why I trusted him with my daughter.

"She's in a loving home with all the opportunities I could never give her," I explain. "I miss her so very much. But she likely doesn't know I exist. And if one day I do get to see her, she'll never know I'm her biological mother and I love her more than I can bear. No one in Maple Ridge knows about her, and it needs to stay that way." A plead threads through my words, begs for Violet to understand my wish to keep my daughter a secret.

She nods.

I cover her hand with mine, wishing that was all it would take to protect Violet from her monster. "I don't want you to go through what I did. I don't want you to lose your daughter like I lost mine."

Tears fill her eyes, but I don't know who they're for. For me and everything I lost? For Sophie? For herself? Or maybe the tears are for how helpless she feels, like how I felt. How I still feel sometimes.

"You escaped because your husband died. I'm not going to be so lucky. He's like a prison warden. There is no escaping—"

"Are you all right, Mrs. Wilson?" a deep voice says to the side of us.

My body tenses from the warning buried beneath the surface of the words, and I can feel Violet's body do the same next to me.

A uniformed cop approaches us. My body shifts into overdrive, and a feeling of *déjà vu* squeezes air from my lungs. I wrap my fingers around my biceps and squeeze-release-squeeze-release the muscle as I focus on my breaths like Robyn taught me to do. I breathe in through the nose. *My stomach is a balloon, gently filling with air.* I breathe out a little longer than the inhalation, my lips pursed.

Breathe in. Breathe out.

Don't let him see you have a panic attack.

The cop's eyes search us. For what, I don't know. "Are you all right, Mrs. Wilson?" he repeats, the unspoken warning still there.

"I-I'm fine. I-I was just taking Sophie to the playground, and I ran into a friend from yoga."

Except the playground is on the other side of the park. We aren't even in her neighborhood. Violet lives closer to my house than she does Troy's home.

"I'll escort you there," the cop says, his command-chilled tone setting off another round of *déjà vu*. "You can never be too safe on a day like this. Too many strangers in town for the celebrations."

God, it's all too familiar. The explanations. The excuses. The lies.

During the final year of my husband's life, whenever he couldn't be there to stalk me in person, he sent his friend, a fellow cop, to do the deed. To keep me in line. To remind me how powerless I was. Is this...is this what's happening to Violet?

Violet gets to her feet, her arms protectively around Sophie as if she's afraid the cop will take away her daughter. She gives me a brief smile that seems more wilted than genuine. "Bye, Jess."

"I'll talk to you later." *Be careful.*

Without another word, she walks away. She doesn't even glance in my direction.

The cop walks two steps behind her. He doesn't see the air

expel from my lungs in a long, dizzying breath, my breathing technique already forgotten.

I slide off the bench and drop to my knees next to Bailey and Butterscotch. My shaky fingers sink into their fur, and I stroke them until the tremor in my body fades.

I watch Violet walk away with Sophie in her arms. She admitted it—whether Violet knows it or not, that's the first step in escaping her husband. Violet wants to be saved.

The question is: how the hell am I going to help her?

24

——

JESSICA

July, Present Day
Maple Ridge

Emily is talking to an older couple who she knows as we wait for the horses and wagon to arrive for the next group. The early afternoon sun warms my bare arms, and I let my gaze wander over the area where the Maple Ridge Fourth of July celebrations are taking place: an open stretch of land on the edge of town, near the lake.

Zara and Simone are also volunteering, but they're at the petting zoo.

The event isn't huge. The bustling crowds I've witnessed at celebrations in San Diego don't exist here. But the place has seen a steady stream of people, laughing and talking and walking around. Kids eating ice creams that would be dripping down their arms if this were San Diego.

It's all so...wonderful. It's been forever plus a day since I last enjoyed the holiday.

199

In the background, country music plays through the nearby speakers.

I spend the next few minutes people-watching, trying to guess their stories. Like I did when I was studying journalism. The smiling teenage couple, their hands stuffed in their partner's back pocket. The elderly couple strolling arm in arm. The mother with her rounded stomach, her young daughter perched on the shoulders of a broad-chested man.

A raw emotion pinches my stomach. They remind me of the happy family I'd once imagined being part of.

I hold my phone at waist height and practice shooting photos like I learned to do during one of my photojournalism courses. I have no idea how the pictures will turn out because I'm not supposed to look at the screen while I shoot them. That's part of the fun.

My gaze lands on another young family, standing in front of a police officer with short, dark-blond hair. The officer folds himself to the level of the two boys and shakes their hands. The boys' faces glow as if he's a magical creature they revere.

The parents are beaming at the trio, clearly impressed with whatever the officer is saying to their sons.

The officer stands and turns around. It's only then that I see his face, and I take a stunned step back.

Chief Wilson?

I recognize his face from Violet's photo. She'd shown it to the group of veterans Troy had taken me to meet over three months ago.

Chief Wilson walks off but doesn't get far before he stops to talk to another family. The brother and sister—both under the age of seven—seem excited to talk to him.

The *clip-clopping* of hooves against the dirt ground tears my attention away from Chief Wilson and any other thoughts I might have about the man.

"Are you okay?" Emily asks me a while later. The horses

whose cart we just loaded with passengers have lumbered off, and we're waiting for the second team to return.

Little kids' laughter comes from somewhere in the line. Two six-year-old girls are playing hopscotch on the uneven ground next to it as they wait for their turn on the wagon ride. They giggle, not caring that there is no actual hopscotch pattern. I smile at how happy they are, and I try to ignore the faint smell of grilling meat and mini donuts from the nearby food vendors. It's making me hungry.

"I'm fine. I just miss Bailey." I pluck an imaginary piece of hay from my tank top so Em doesn't see the partial lie in my eyes.

I do miss Bailey. That much is true. But I can't shake the conversation I had earlier with Violet.

"I bet it's also because you miss a certain someone else." Emily's mouth curves into a know-it-all grin.

I know exactly who she's referring to, and the thought of him makes me go all gooey-warm inside. "Yes, maybe that too. But what Troy and his brothers are doing is important. They're saving lives."

Emily adjusts the rim of her straw hat, her two pigtails brushing her bare shoulders. "The good news is, your boyfriend can't get injured this time."

"As far as we know. Medically cleared or not, I won't put it past him to still participate in the actual rescuing."

"Good point. All the Carson brothers are like that. It's part of their alpha-gene complex. But it's also what causes women to flock to them like horny chickens."

A snorted laugh trips over my lips. "Is that even possible? For chickens to be horny?"

Emily's grin returns, only wider this time. "Maybe that's a question for you to ask at the petting zoo." She raises her hand and waves.

I turn to see who she's waving at. A woman in denim shorts

and a flowery peasant blouse is walking toward us. Her golden hair cascades over her shoulders. There's something oddly familiar about her, but I can't place what it is. It's like I've seen her before but at the same time I haven't.

"Hey, Emily," the woman says.

"Hi, Theresa. This is Jessica"—Em nods at me—"the photographer I wanted to introduce you to."

Theresa smiles, the curve of her lips polite and friendly. "It's nice to meet you, Jessica."

Emily's phone pings in her hand, and she quickly checks the screen. "Theresa is a social worker for the county, but she lives in Eugene."

Social worker. Possibilities churn in my head when I think about her job and Violet. Maybe Theresa could help her. But that would mean betraying Violet's trust, and I can't do that. And who's to say Theresa would even believe me if I told her about Violet's husband, a man who's paid to serve and protect but who is abusing his wife?

A warm breeze picks up, brushing my hair into my face. "Not to worry," I say, tucking it behind my ear. "If you still want to talk, I'm free whenever's convenient for you, other than when I'm doing my actual day job."

"Jess works for Troy Carson," Emily explains. "She's also his girlfriend."

A grin as wide as the Pacific Ocean curves onto Theresa's face. "Ahhh, you're the mysterious girlfriend who has my sister's panties in a tangle."

Something unexpected twists in my stomach. I push it aside and shoot Em a quizzical glance. "Sister?"

"Katelyn Bell," she clarifies.

Sisters. That explains why Theresa looks so familiar.

The *clip-clopping* of horseshoes announces the arrival of the next team of horses with their wagon.

Emily and I say goodbye to Theresa and help load the

group of passengers onto the wagon. They sit on the bales of straw piled in the middle. Once the wagon is loaded, the horses plod off.

A young boy standing at the front of the line shares some fun facts about dragons with me. Most of it I don't catch because the words flow from him faster than water falling off a cliff.

"I know someone who will be happy to see you." Emily's amused voice is loud enough to be heard over the endless stream of the boy's facts.

I look over my shoulder to see who she's talking to. Troy's standing behind me, his gaze lingering on my butt. My heart does a bouncy little two-step, and my body heats a thousand degrees. His eyes flick up to mine, and he smiles.

His brothers are with him, dirt smudged on their faces. Their navy T-shirts, with the Maple Ridge SAR logos on the chests, are also dusty.

"Thank you for educating me about dragons," I tell the little boy and excuse myself.

Then I'm on my feet, walking to Troy. "I take it things went well since you're smiling."

"Yes. Other than the part where I prefer to be searching for the missing individuals and not manning the map." Troy pulls me to him and kisses me. It's family friendly for the benefit of the kids in the line for the hayride, but that doesn't stop my body from reacting as if it were something much steamier. "When are you finished here?"

I check the time on my phone. "In about thirty minutes."

Emily joins Troy's brothers and the couple standing with them. I instantly recognize the husband and wife. I've seen pictures of the beautiful dark-haired woman whose parents immigrated to the U.S. from South Korea. Kim. The photographer whose award-winning photos I idolize every time I go to Zara's apartment.

The tall good-looking man next to her with Zara's copper-brown skin is Jerome. Kim's husband and Zara's other brother. He's holding an adorable six-month-old baby wearing a light-pink hat.

Troy threads his fingers with mine. "There're some people I want to introduce you to." He takes me to where Kim and Jerome are standing and makes the introductions.

Kim's smile is as beautiful as the photos she shoots. "So you're my replacement for Em's business?"

"I'm not sure if replacement is the correct word. I don't think I'll ever be at your level."

"Em, Zara, and Simone think you are, and I'm sure your photos are as incredible as they claim."

Troy gives my hand a light squeeze. "They are. You don't give yourself enough credit, Jess."

"I'm rusty."

"If that's your rusty, I can't wait to see your unrusty pictures." He kisses my temple, and I turn all gooey at the sweetness of the move.

"I would be happy to give you some pointers, if you'd like," Kim offers. "Not that I'm a pro at shooting weddings. I only did a few for Em."

"I've seen some of the wedding photos you took. They're gorgeous. I would love any pointers you can give me." I want to do the best possible job for Theresa's wedding. I don't want to let her and Em down.

I wave at the little girl in Jerome's arms. "Aren't you adorable?"

Her lips curve into a toothless grin.

"I think she's counting down the days until she can crawl and get into all kinds of trouble." Kim smiles at the little cutie, the love for her daughter glowing in her eyes.

Sidney blows a raspberry in agreement.

The sound of approaching hooves has me twisting around.

But it's not the horses and wagon that knocks the air from my lungs. It's Chief Wilson. He's standing next to the white picket fence a few yards from where we're gathered, his eyes locked on me.

The intensity of his gaze causes my stomach to churn, and a shiver gallops up my spine. My muscles solidify, turning me into a statue. I've seen pictures of Medusa's victims, the horror captured on their faces when they're transformed to stone. That expression, I'm positive it's now on my face.

Wilson doesn't move, nor does he break eye contact. His cold gaze stabs me with the force of a pickax. Chips away at the stone. Searches for an unspoken truth.

His eyes flick from me, and it takes a moment to understand why.

Troy advances on him with the speed of someone on a mission, movements pantherlike, dangerous.

And the fangs of dread sink into me.

25

TROY

July, Present Day
Maple Ridge

hief Wilson's standing to the side of the road, his attention locked on Jess—as if he's trying to peel away her layers, to uncover her secrets.

Secrets she doesn't want anyone to know. Would he even believe she was innocent when it came to her husband's death? If he's anything like the guy I once knew in school, the answer is no.

Before I realize what I'm doing, I stalk toward him, half-aware of the noises surrounding us. Laughter and chatter from the little kids waiting for the hayride. The country band playing onstage. Announcements piping through the loudspeakers. None of those things are of interest to me.

Wilson's gaze shifts to me, and he nods. The nod lacks any hint of friendliness. It's barely more than an acknowledgment, even though I've known him most of my life. We've never been friends. Not even close.

I want nothing more than to tell him to stop looking at my woman that way. To stop putting her on edge when she's starting to make real progress with her therapy. But I can't do that without betraying her trust, so I opt for the next best thing.

I glare at him, a raging fire roaring inside me. "Why are you staring at my girlfriend like that?" *Do you know who she really is?*

"I don't keep a running tab of the women you fuck, Troy. Could you be more specific? Which girlfriend?" His icy tone contrasts with the heat in his words.

I step closer to him. A stupid move, but I don't give a damn about that either. "Jessica Smithson." I watch for signs he knows her true identity.

Wilson doesn't put distance between us. If anything, he does the opposite. He doesn't move, but he does seem to make himself look bigger. More intimidating.

Except I have faced worse men than him while in the Marines, so his bullshit strategy fails to work on me.

"Stand down, Carson, or I'll have you arrested." He barks his command like a pissed-off Rottweiler.

"Arrested for what?" My volume matches his beat for beat. A group of six people walking past us stop, their puzzled glances cast our way. Others watch us like we're a spectator sport. The murmur of voices isn't enough to drown out the country music playing in the background.

"I'm sure I can find something." The sound of Wilson's voice drops to a casual level, but the implication behind the words is clear. He nods at something over my shoulder, but his eyes never leave mine. "Trouble does run in the family, after all. I wonder how Lucas and Kellan are doing these days…" He says it in a tone that implies he has anything but their welfare in mind.

The corner of his mouth tilts, not enough for everyone else to see it, but it's enough to get what he wants.

A reaction.

From me.

I shove him in the chest.

The movement might not have been enough for him to land on his ass, but the force causes him to take a step back.

He grabs his handcuffs and yanks my injured arm behind me, not giving me a chance to react. "Troy Carson, you're under arrest for assaulting an officer."

Pain shoots through my shoulder and radiates down my arm. A curse releases from my mouth before I can stop it, giving him exactly what he wants. But I refuse to fight back or tell him he's hurting me. I won't give him that satisfaction.

"You're hurting his injured shoulder." Jess's shrieked words break through the pain-induced fog in my brain.

He ignores her and snaps the metal cuffs on my wrists.

I guess that's what happens when the bully you grew up with becomes a cop.

"You thought *that* was assaulting an officer?" I say through gritted teeth. "You're wimpier than I gave you credit for."

Wilson leans in, his stale breath hot on my ear. "You always were a stupid asshole, Troy." He jerks up on the handcuffs.

The move is enough to cause me more pain, but not enough to be noticed by witnesses.

I don't so much as flinch a muscle, not daring to give away he's hurting me. Not wanting to give him the satisfaction.

26

JESSICA

July, Present Day
Maple Ridge

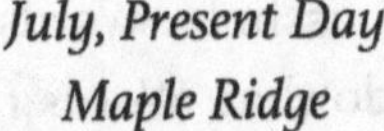

A squad car pulls up, and a handcuffed Troy is escorted to it. The need to help him throbs in my veins, but I don't know what to do. Chief Wilson isn't going to release Troy just because I want him to.

My skin prickles, and I rub at my wrists. My arrest happened over five years ago, but the memory of my wrists being shackled is still fresh. The sun is warm, but it's not warm enough to chase away the chill now plaguing my body.

I take a step toward Troy, but a hand grabs my arm from behind, stopping me. Kellan.

"Leave it, Jess," he says, voice low. "You going over there will only make things worse."

"But Chief Wilson's hurting him. He's going to reinjure the shoulder and—"

"There's nothing you can do."

Kellan's right, but that doesn't give the chief of police the right to hurt Troy. Like being married to Violet doesn't give him the right to abuse her.

Yet he still does and gets away with it.

"Shit, what was he thinking?" Lucas's voice is so low, I can't tell if he's asking his brothers or himself the question. "Wilson's the last person you wanna try to push around. The man is a grade-A asshole."

"You know him?" *Do you know him well enough to give me suggestions on how to get his wife and child away from him?*

Troy slides into the squad car. He doesn't look in our direction.

A murmur of voices grows from the people who witnessed what went down. I catch a few of the words. Words that agree the chief of police is an asshole. Words that wonder what the hell possessed Troy to do that. Words that question the legitimacy of the assaulting-an-officer charge. Troy shouldn't have pushed the man. But assault? Really?

"Yeah. I know him," Lucas says. "We all went to school together. He was in Troy's grade. He was a jerk even back then."

"What's going on?" a familiar male voice asks behind us.

We turn to find Noah and Avery walking toward us, holding hands. Noah's checking over my shoulder, to where the squad car is parked.

We explain as best as we can what happened. None of us actually heard what was said between the two men.

Noah's brow wrinkles into a frown. "Shoving a cop is unacceptable, but arresting Troy seems a little overboard."

"C-can you talk Chief Wilson into dropping the charges?" I ask, vaguely aware I'm rubbing my wrists again. I drop my hands to my sides.

The squad car pulls away.

"I doubt it," Noah says, watching it drive down the street. Wilson isn't in it. He's walking in the opposite direction to us, toward the petting zoo. "I'm still new to the force. I have no say on how things are done."

The small crowd dissipates now that Troy is gone. Lucas taps away on his phone. "I'll call Blake."

"Blake?" I look to Kellan for an answer.

"He's a defense lawyer and a friend of Lucas's. But it's a holiday and the weekend, so Troy won't have bail set until Monday at the earliest. More likely Tuesday since they'll have backlog from being closed Friday."

I deliberate for a second if I should tell Troy's brothers about Violet. But that would mean betraying her trust and possibly make matters worse. Besides, if I did tell anyone, it won't help Troy, and what if no one believes me? We're talking about me accusing the town's chief of police of abusing his wife.

If Violet's too scared to admit it's true, my accusations might make things worse for her, for Sophie, and even possibly for Troy.

Lucas gets off the phone a few minutes later. "Blake's now aware of the situation and is going to do what he can. But there's really nothing he can do until Monday. In the meantime, we might as well make the most of today's celebration."

"Even though Troy's in jail?" I fight back the urge to rub at my wrists again. Rubbing them won't erase the memories of my arrest.

Lucas releases a long, hard breath, his frustration at the situation clear. "Troy messed up, but he'll be pissed at himself if we go home because he got himself arrested. While it might have been a stupid move, he must have thought he had a good reason for shoving Wilson. Otherwise, he wouldn't have done it. So yeah, we'll stay and have a good time. For Troy's sake." The smile that stretches on Lucas's face seems two shades short of genuine.

The second team of horses *clip-clops* toward us, and Emily

and I return to our job of helping people load and unload from the ride. I focus on that and try not to think about what happened between Troy and Chief Wilson. Try not to think about Troy's injured shoulder.

By the time our shift is over, I'm exhausted from trying not to worry about Troy.

Emily is smiling, her gaze directed over my shoulder, but there's something slightly off about the curve of her lips. "Hi, Joanne. Ian."

My stomach drops. *Oh, God.* Troy's parents. They're going to hate me. I don't know what exactly caused Troy to go off the rails and push Wilson, but I have a feeling it had to do with the way the man was glaring at me before Troy stormed over to him. And if that's true, they definitely won't want me dating their son.

They won't want me going anywhere near him.

"Are you two having fun?" Joanne asks us.

"It's been busy, but yes," Emily responds, her voice overly cheerful, even for Em.

I follow her lead and tug my mouth into a near-painful smile. "I'm glad I got to volunteer here." I wave in the direction of the wagon.

"That's wonderful. We're heading out. If you two see my boys, tell them I said hi and we'll see them once Ian and I get back to town."

Emily shares a quick glance with me. "You're going somewhere?"

"We're going to Sacramento for the week. We're visiting some friends down there."

I can almost feel the tension drain from Em on an inaudible sigh at the news. Tension I hadn't realized gripped us both at seeing Troy's parents.

We wish them a great trip, and they walk toward the parking lot of the festival grounds.

"Thank God she didn't ask where the guys are," Emily says. "I'd rather not be the one who tells her what happened to Troy."

That makes two of us. But I'm sure they'll eventually hear what happened—either from their sons or because there were witnesses to his arrest.

"Do you think his parents will be mad?" I ask.

"Probably not. But they will wonder what possessed him to act that way."

And then they'll question their son's choice of girlfriend.

Zara and Simone are finished with their shift at the petting zoo by the time we arrive at the entrance to it. They're talking to two women who could be sisters or cousins, one of whom is holding a child. Both have long blond hair. Both are wearing shorts and T-shirts, but the clothes of the woman not carrying the two-year-old appear to be more big-city chic than small-town casual.

The woman with the toddler takes in our group. Her gaze searches the area. "Where's Troy?"

"Olivia," Simone says to her, "have you met Jessica?"

"No, but Troy has mentioned you." A small smile wobbles on Olivia's face but fails to click into place. "He said you're interested in interviewing me for an article. Because my late husband had PTSD."

Her expression crumples for a second, and my heart breaks for her. Her husband didn't deserve what happened to him. Olivia and her daughter don't deserve what happened to them.

My smile is no stronger than Olivia's, sympathy for everything she's gone through holding the curve of my lips in place. "If you would be willing to. But I know it might be difficult for you. So I understand if you aren't interested."

"Can I think about it? I'm still not sure if I'm ready to talk about it yet."

I nod, a new level of self-consciousness clawing at me.

Olivia is pretty, her face scar free. Troy has known her since they were kids. It's possible he crushed on her when they were younger, before she and Colton hooked up...

"Hi!" The little girl waves at us, interrupting where my thoughts are headed, and she points to Sidney in Jerome's arms. "Baby!" Her mouth stretches into a big grin.

"That's right. That's Sidney," Olivia tells her daughter. "How are you two enjoying parenthood?" She directs the question to Kim and Jerome, which leads to a short discussion between the three of them about the joys of being parents to a baby.

I bite hard on my lower lip, preventing my own comments from spilling, longing for those moments when I held Amelia as a baby in my arms. Her sweet smell. The way she blew raspberries or giggled.

"Hi, I'm Cora," the woman with Olivia says. "Livi's big sister." Her gaze shifts between Avery and me.

Avery and I introduce ourselves, the relative newcomers to the group. It's obvious everyone else already knows Cora.

Olivia switches her daughter to her other hip. "I thought Troy was also coming. And is there a reason you three have dirty faces?" Her question is aimed at Troy's brothers.

Kellan exchanges glances with Garrett and Lucas, the unspoken message between them lost on me. "We were all, including Troy, on a search and rescue. He was going to be here, but he had to leave and won't be back for the rest of the day."

The rest of us keep quiet about where Troy went. He probably wouldn't want her to know about the arrest and worry her. I'm worried enough for the both of us.

"How's California?" Emily asks Cora, swiftly changing the conversation away from Troy.

My body goes rigid and adrenaline pumps through my veins. California. *Fuckers.*

"It's better now that I've left. I just went through a bitter divorce after I discovered the cheating..." She looks down at her niece. "The cheating banana loaf was hooking up with some peanut butter."

Snorted laughs come from the guys.

"So I'm here for the next few months, getting over that, and plotting the next stage in my life. Plus, spending more time with my sis and my adorable niece." She smiles at Nova. Nova grins back.

"Where in California?" I keep my tone as friendly as possible, wrestling with the panic that threatens to betray me. *Please don't be from San Diego.*

"San Francisco."

Relief trickles in, but it's not enough to douse the fear. My hand goes to my hair, and I subconsciously tug on the blond ends. The roots have recently been retouched.

Hopefully between the hair color and scars, it's enough to keep Cora from recognizing me.

I fight the urge to duck my head and prevent her from seeing past my fake identity. Her expression holds no hint of recognition. No sign she has seen me before but can't quite place me.

But even then, it's not enough to untie the tension knotted in my muscles.

That will only happen once Troy is released from jail.

GARRETT DROPS ME OFF AT MY HOUSE A FEW HOURS LATER. Butterscotch trots into the hallway from the living room as I reactivate the alarm, and we go to the laundry room to let Bailey out of her crate.

"You'll be staying with me tonight," I tell Butterscotch. "Your daddy tried to get into a fight with that asshole Chief Wilson, who didn't take too kindly to that. So your father will be spending the next few nights in the slammer."

A chill clambers over my body just thinking about Troy being stuck in there until Tuesday. "You two want to go for a walk?"

I stick close to my house while walking Bailey and Butterscotch, not wanting to go near Violet's house in case her husband's there. Not wanting to give him a reason to investigate me.

We return home, and I reactivate the alarm.

The dogs and I head upstairs and go into the closet in the guest bedroom. I pull open the secret door and crawl inside the hidden space. The dim light from the bedroom doesn't reach this far, but I've been in here so many times, I know where the light cord is, even if I can't see it.

I tug on the cord, and a soft glow spills from the bare bulb. The hiding space makes me think of the cellar in Jacques's barn, where he and Iris hid downed Allied pilots and where Johann hid his Jewish friends.

Was this space added in case Iris ever needed to hide? Maybe lifelong paranoia was a side effect of being an SOE agent. Or was it used for other purposes? Like hiding her journals, the heart pendant, and the medal?

I still don't know where the pendant and medal are from. I've never been one to jump to the end of a book and read it first. That's what searching for the medal online feels like. Skipping to the end of the story, and then reading the book, even though you know how it ends.

The medal I can only guess has something to do with her time in France as an SOE agent. I haven't looked it up online. I'm hoping Iris's journals will reveal how she ended up with it.

Bailey and Butterscotch sniff the floor around the edges of the enclosed space.

"Remember," I tell them, my voice a hushed, playful tone.

"You can't tell anyone about this place. It's special. Maybe not as much as Narnia, but it's still special." I remove my laptop from next to the cardboard box and crawl out of the space. The two dogs follow me.

I close the secret door, ensuring the bookshelf is flush with the wall.

In the kitchen, I place the laptop on the table and turn it on. I go through the photos I took today with my phone, send some of them to the laptop, and make notes of what I could have done better. I also create a list of the photos I want to edit. They're the photojournalistic images I took while no one was paying attention to me. All were taken prior to Troy's arrest.

I skip through a few photos until I land on the ones I took of Emily before we started our volunteer shift. She was laughing like she didn't have a care in the world. The picture is timeless and gorgeous and will look great converted to black and white.

I flick to the next photo. Again, of Em. A few other people are also captured in the image. No one I recognize, other than Chief Wilson.

I hadn't noticed he was watching me at the time. He's at the edge of the frame, which is why I didn't notice him when I took the picture. His expression...shit, his expression. It's like he's trying to peer through my layers, as if that would solve a riddle playing in his head.

He wouldn't have realized at the time that I was taking photos, because I was aiming the camera at Emily and it appeared as if I was just checking something on my phone. It wasn't obvious I was taking photos.

Why the hell was he even looking at me? *Shit. Please tell me he hasn't realized I'm Savannah.*

He could be one of those idiots who believes the conspiracy theories that claim I really did kill my husband, a cop. Is that why he arrested Troy?

No. No. No. That doesn't make sense. You can't arrest

someone because their girlfriend was wrongfully convicted for killing her husband.

Did the cop who saw me talking to Violet this morning have something to do with Chief Wilson watching me this afternoon? Or am I deluding myself, and he's been watching me for a while now? Or was it just a coincidence?

My body trembles with me just thinking about the possible reasons for Chief Wilson's presence in the picture.

I scoot off the chair and sink onto the kitchen floor. I wrap my arms around Bailey, trying to calm the trembling.

Once I've somewhat regained control of myself, I sit back on the chair and swipe through the next few shots on my phone. A few frames later, the chief of police isn't looking at me. He's talking to a white man with light brown hair. I don't recognize him. They could be talking about a million different things, including where's a good place in town to eat.

But something about their expression suggests whatever their conversation is about, it's deadly serious.

You're reading too much into it. A good reporter would never make assumptions based on a photo.

A picture might be worth a thousand words, but that adage only works if I know the meaning behind the picture. Misinterpret it, and I could make things so much harder for myself.

But even knowing this, I can't shake the feeling I haven't misinterpreted anything.

But really—what am I planning to do? Take the photo to the police station—and then do what with it?

The last thing I want is to go there and risk people recognizing my face. The last thing I want is to draw attention to myself from the men and women in blue.

It's not as if my going there will save Violet from her husband.

It's not as if it will make things any easier for Troy.

27

ANGELIQUE

July 1943
France

I awaken the next morning, tangled in the bed covers and Johann's limbs. The heat of his body presses into me, and for a minute, I pretend there is no war going on beyond the blackout curtains. The world is silent other than the chirping of birds and Jacques moving around the kitchen, getting ready for his day.

A day fresh with new possibilities.

A day with the same fears that plagued us last night. As wonderful as it had been, nothing has changed with the state of the world. I might have realised I'm falling in love with Johann, but nothing has changed when it comes to Hitler.

If anything, my feelings for Johann make things more dangerous for us. My allegiances haven't altered. My king and country and sister are still my top priorities.

The sleeping man next to me stirs, and his long dark eyelashes flutter open. "*Bonjour*." He smiles at me, and my heart becomes buoyant.

I return the smile, mine shy and without a hint of remorse for what we did last night. "*Bonjour*."

"I don't suppose we can stay in bed all day and forget our real life?" Amusement lightens his tone, sending relief pulsing through me that he's speaking in French and not English.

Maybe I didn't cry out in my native tongue after all. While I have no doubt he suspects I have connections to the local resistance effort, he hasn't pieced together that I am a spy. I want to keep it that way.

"Unfortunately not." My words float out on a sigh. I close my eyes, attempting to block the memory of my nightmare and the last time I saw Pierre. A tear leaks free and drips onto my pillow at the loss of the man. At the loss of the friendship we'd shared.

Johann tightens his hold on me and kisses my brow. I open my eyes and see the adoration I feel for him mirrored back. A tiny part of me wonders if I'm imagining it, or if he's playing me for a fool and will turn me over to the SS as soon as it benefits Hitler.

With Charles, I experienced moments of doubt late into our relationship about his feelings for me. I ignored my gut when I should have listened to it. This time, my gut is silent. It's the SOE agent, the woman who has been hurt by someone who once claimed he loved her, who is raising the question.

Johann gently presses his lips to mine. "Are you still willing to come to the grand ball with me? It is in two weeks."

Something coils in my belly—either nervousness or excitement. But he is not taking me out on the town and courting me. He's taking me into the pit of vipers where I might learn something valuable for Baker Street's cause...or my identity might be unearthed. "I don't have anything suitable to wear."

A ball for a powerful party leader and his wife requires something fancier than anything I own in France. I have the money to procure such a dress on the black market, but if I buy one, it will only raise questions.

"I can get you a dress."

"Are you sure you want me there?"

"You will be the only pleasant thing about the night." He kisses me once more.

"I'll be there." As much as I would rather not be in the presence of some of the most evil monsters in the Reich, if it benefits the Allies, I will do it.

We reluctantly climb out of the narrow bed. Johann returns to his room, and I hurry to get dressed and go downstairs to make him his breakfast.

Johann enters the kitchen as I put his plate on the table. Food is in short supply for everyone, but the meal on the plate is still more than the average French citizen has available to eat.

He finishes his breakfast and carries his plate to the sink. I take it from him. The sound of crunching gravel draws close to the house. My stomach tightens as it always does at that noise. It means only one thing.

I walk Johann to the front door. He grabs me and pulls me to the wall beside the door. His mouth captures mine, and he kisses me with more passion than the earlier kisses this morning. We are not visible to anyone who might peer through a window. But what we're doing—the kissing—is dangerous. What if we're interrupted, if Jacques opens the door, not knowing we are here, and exposes us?

But even knowing that, I don't push Johann away. I pull him closer to me, allowing him to temporarily distract me.

"How about we watch the sunset tonight?" he murmurs against my lips.

"I would like that."

He leaves, and I wait until I'm positive the military Jeep is gone, then retrieve my bike from the barn.

I pedal into the village to queue for rations. The mood is normally sombre, even more so since the Germans moved here. But with the cloud of Pierre's death hanging over us, the mood is more suffocating than soot.

Condemning stares burrow holes in my back. He was my friend too, yet I seem to be, in everyone's eyes, responsible for what happened.

What did the SS find that gave them cause to interrogate and execute him? He was a member of the parachute reception committee, but he wouldn't have known where the weapons were stashed. Unfortunately, the SS didn't know that when they arrested him, and I don't know if the arrest had anything to do with the weapons or if they found something else with which to incriminate him.

The village is a close-knit community, the villagers slow to accept strangers into their fold. But that doesn't mean for the right price one of them could not easily be tempted into becoming an informant. An informant who might be more than happy to hand me over to the Gestapo or the SS because they know I'm not Jacques's daughter. An informant who would willingly risk Jacques's life for money or status.

If my true loyalties are uncovered, I will face the same risk of execution that ended Pierre's life.

A woman approaches where I am standing in the queue, her toddler daughter balanced on her hip. The woman wears a scowl directed at me. "Why are you in the queue? You don't need to get rations. Not when you're bedding one of them."

Her accusation is a slash across my belly because it is true. I am now bedding Johann, but not for the horrendous reason she assumes. Nor can I defend Johann and tell her he is nothing like the other German soldiers and the Nazis.

I gather all the indignation I can muster. "I'm not bedding one of them. He is billeted in the same house that Monsieur Gauthier and I reside in. And that is only because he hasn't kicked us out as the papers he possesses permit him to do."

An older woman whose loyalties are in question stands farther ahead of us in the queue. Only five other women separate her from the woman who has accused me of sleeping with the enemy. Rumour has it the older woman's son is part of the Milice. She could have been the one who turned on Pierre and handed him over to the SS.

"That's because you're sleeping with 'im," the mother with the toddler bites out.

"You have no proof of that simply because it's not true." I fasten on a mask of incredulity, hiding the fact she is correct, and keep my voice low so not to draw attention of the older woman.

"You're getting special treatment, though, am I right? He supplies you food that is not available to the rest of us."

That part I won't lie about. "It is not as much food as you're thinking. And it's because I cook it for him. I am employed as his housekeeper. But instead of money, he pays me with a roof over Monsieur Gauthier's and my head. Are you saying if he had been assigned to stay at your house, you wouldn't have done the same for the sake of your daughter?"

I subtly nod towards the older woman ahead of us, warning the mother she needs to be more careful with her words.

Her eyes dart to the other woman, and her next words are spoken more softly. "Of course I wouldn't." She might have said that, but her eyes reveal the opposite. She would do anything to protect her child. She's just rightfully angry that I'm the one benefitting and not her.

The young woman in front of me turns, dark shadows smudged under wide eyes. "Has he forced himself on you?" Her voice is not much more than a whisper. Fortunately, she does not require to be reminded of the risk this discussion poses.

"No, I've been lucky. Captain Schmidt has been a gentleman. They aren't all like that." The memory of how Major Müller's gaze leaves me raw and vulnerable tastes sour on my tongue. I cross my arms, the basket in my hand almost knocking the arm of the woman holding the toddler. She moves back a step.

"He's not the only monster who visits the house, is he?" the young woman asks, her eyes wide with horror and sympathy.

"There have been a few occasions when his commanding officer has come over." I quickly scan the village square, ever alert to the arrival of German soldiers who might overhear me or wonder what we're talking about. "I fear what could happen if Captain Schmidt is not at the farmhouse if the Major should show up unannounced."

The young woman sneaks a furtive glance around like I did a moment ago. "I wish there was more I could do about our situation. I feel so helpless. My husband is in prison, and I don't know if I'll ever see him again." Her tone is fired up with a quiet intensity, a fierceness that only the enemy can stir to life.

"We can resist," I tell her. "All over the country people are doing things to make the Germans' lives more difficult. Everyone can do it. The trick is not to get caught. Do whatever we can, no matter how big or small." One of the reasons the SOE was created was to fan the flame of resistance that had started in France at the beginning of the war. They didn't want the fire to burn out before D-Day. Agents were sent to France to keep it going, to add wood to the fire, to help it burn hotter, brighter.

"But how?" the young woman inquires.

"Listen to the BBC French news. Vandalise posters. Slash German tyres."

The young woman nods again, but this time there's a new spark in her eyes.

"I can't," the woman with the toddler says. She looks down at her child.

"Not everyone is able to resist," I gently tell her. "You have to weigh the risks, and you have more at risk than most of us." I stroke her daughter's hair, the light-brown strands soft against my fingers.

"You're resisting them?" A silent awe sits in her tone.

"Yes, I'm doing what I can. But I can't tell you what that is."

"Can you at least tell us if it is what Pierre was doing?"

A pair of Milice officers round the corner. Smiling at the two women, I laugh as though they've just told me something amusing. The woman with the toddler catches sight of them too and does the same. The toddler giggles because her mother is laughing.

"God, what are they doing here?" she asks under her breath. "I liked it better when no one realised our village existed. The SS, the Wehrmacht, the Gestapo—none of them could be bothered with us. Now they're like vermin who have discovered where the cheese is hidden."

"They're afraid," I say. "They know we are all fighting for our country. Not just here, but all over France."

"If they're afraid, they're doing a good job of hiding it." She kisses her daughter's head and walks away, careful not to gain the soldiers' attention.

The young woman shifts to face the front of the queue, our conversation too dangerous to continue.

After I've collected the meagre day's ration, I enter the bookshop and retrieve the message that was left for me in the drop box. I pretend to retie my shoelace and slip the thin strip of paper into the hem of my skirt.

The bell above the shop door tinkles. Monsieur Joubert greets the woman whose son is rumoured to be with the Milice.

I grab a random book from a nearby shelf and go to pay for it. The woman watches me when I approach the counter but doesn't say anything.

This only makes me more nervous.

AT THE FARMHOUSE, I HURRY UPSTAIRS TO MY ROOM. THE SMALL piece of thread I left on the edge of the rug is where I last placed it. No one has disturbed the location and found my hiding spot under the floorboard.

I remove the hidden supplies used to decipher coded messages. I'm the only one here. It takes me a few minutes to figure out what Allaire wrote. The print is tiny, so as to fit in more words on the minuscule scrap of paper, and I have to move it around in the light streaming through the window to read it.

As I decode the message, I listen for any noise that indicates Johann has returned early or the vineyard has an unwanted guest. Once I've finished, I read the deciphered message.

> I have looked into The Wolf's claims about his grandparents being from Switzerland. It is indeed correct. His mother had an aunt who was also deaf and who died ten years ago. She and her family were living in the region of Pays de la Loire, France. There is no indication that The Wolf's mother and sister went there when they allegedly left Austria. London has advised not to involve The Wolf in our activities at present time. Unclear where his loyalties lie.

Frustration prowls through me, and I pace. Frustration at the words. Frustration that I'm not sure what to believe. Did I let myself get duped by Johann's kind words and selflessness, or is Baker Street just being cautious? Can I trust him and my heart—or did I make a mistake letting him in?

28

TROY

July, Present Day
Maple Ridge

After spending the weekend and Monday in the slammer and Tuesday morning in court for my bail hearing, I head to Jess's house and ring the doorbell.

Barking comes from the other side of the door and grows louder as Butterscotch and Bailey run toward it.

The front door flings open. Jess eyes the sling that once again supports my arm, and her shoulders deflate. "He hurt you?" Her tone is less of a question and more like an accusation.

Butterscotch pushes past her leg and barks at me. Bailey nudges her way past Jess's other leg and parks her ass on the ground.

"You don't need to lecture me," I tell my dog. "I know I fucked up." More than they can imagine.

Butterscotch gives me another bark. Jess snort-laughs. "You tell him, Butterscotch."

Then Jess's mouth is on mine. And she's kissing me like she hasn't seen me in ten years and missed me the entire time. The words I've been longing to say, that I love her, push to the surface, but I rein them in and just enjoy the kiss. My good arm holds her close.

She smells delicious. Smells of strawberries and freedom. Three days in the slammer was bad enough. I can't imagine how she survived all those years locked away in a maximum-security prison, especially knowing she was innocent.

I tenderly kiss her forehead, breathing in her scent once more. "Thank you. I needed that."

"Are you okay? Is your arm okay?"

"It wasn't redislocated, but because the joint was already compromised, Samuel wanted to be sure I didn't screw it up again." After I complained at the police station my shoulder was hurting and I mentioned the injury I'd sustained during the search and rescue, Samuel was brought in to make sure I hadn't done further damage.

"You're back in the sling," Jess says. "For how long?"

"A couple of days."

She moves aside to let me in and shuts the door behind me. "Do you want something to eat?"

My gaze takes in the partially renovated house, with the living room that now opens up to the kitchen, the wooden floor, and the first coat of light-beige paint on the walls. *Dammit.* Her renovations were stalled because of our injuries, and now they'll be stalled a little longer because of my shoulder. If I had controlled my temper with Wilson, she wouldn't have to wait so long for her dream house to be completed.

She reactivates the alarm. "Are you going to tell me what possessed you to attack the chief of police?"

A short and derisive laugh escapes me. "I wouldn't call

shoving him an attack. Granted, I shouldn't have done even that. But he pissed me off, and like an idiot, I reacted."

And like the asshole he is, Wilson arrested me.

"The man's dangerous." Jess's tone is heated, but there's also a hollowness to it that I can't figure out.

"He's not dangerous. Not like the men I've dealt with in the past. He just likes to be in a position of power."

"That's the most dangerous kind of man. Promise me, Troy, you won't do that again." Her voice turns rough, poorly masking the frantic tone beneath the surface.

I cup her face, attempting to soothe her fear. "Hey, he's not going to hurt me."

"Right. You just felt like wearing a sling."

I have no idea where Jess's concern is coming from, so I shrug it off. I get that her abusive husband was a cop and Wilson is an asshole, but we're not talking about the same man. Maybe if Wilson had military training, I'd be more concerned.

"Did you sleep?" I ask. The shadows under her eyes say she didn't, but that's nothing new with Jess. Her sessions with Robyn are helping, but it's not enough. Jess might not experience nightmares every night like before, but she still gets them.

"Did *you*?" she asks, avoiding my question.

"Not really. How the hell did you even sleep in prison?"

"Who says I did? I spent most nights struggling with nightmares and fears of being killed in my sleep. I only fell asleep when my body was too exhausted to do anything else."

"*Shit.* I can't believe you spent five years living like that." I can't believe she didn't come out even more broken.

She gives me a tired smile. "At least I don't have to deal with that anymore."

She should never have had to deal with it in the first place. That's what pisses me off the most. All of that she wouldn't have had to deal with if the cops had done their job and arrested the right person, instead of focusing all their energy on her.

"I'm so sorry about Saturday," I tell her, my gut burning from guilt. "I know how much you wanted to see the fireworks."

Garrett told me when he came to get me from the courthouse that Jess had opted out of watching them. She'd been looking forward to seeing the fireworks. I did that. I stole them from her.

"It's okay. I couldn't enjoy them knowing you were in jail." The pain in her voice fists my heart hard.

I brush the side of her face with my thumb. "It wasn't the same as what you had to survive." Not even a fraction of the hell she'd endured. I can't even begin to understand what she went through.

"I know, but that didn't stop me from imagining the worst."

"I'm sorry, Jess." I'm sorry for all the pain I caused because I let Wilson get to me. "How about I take the dogs out to relieve themselves, and after that, you and I can have a nap?"

Then I can hold her the way I've missed doing for the past three days.

A WARM BODY WIGGLES AWAY FROM ME ON THE BED. I SLOWLY open my eyes. Jess's bedroom is still light like it was when we lay down for a nap. "Where do you think you're going?" I say, my voice drowsy.

If my arm wasn't in a sling, I'd pull Jess to me. *Fucking asshole.* Wilson didn't have to be so rough when he handcuffed me. It wasn't as if I'd been resisting arrest, as Blake pointed out at the station. And as a video that surfaced on social media could attest.

"I figured since you were still asleep, I'd make dinner."

"I can help. Assuming you still want me here after what happened Saturday."

She smiles, the movement defying the downward tug on the

corner of her mouth from the scar. "Of course I want you here. For dinner. Plus, there's something I want to show you." She climbs out of bed. "I did have a question about some of the photos I took at the festival on Saturday."

"You're looking for my brilliant expertise?" I know nothing about photography. I'm more of a point-and-shoot kind of guy.

"No, I want to see if you recognize any of the people in the photos."

Several minutes later, we're in the kitchen, peering at her laptop screen.

"Do you know who he is?" She points to a man talking to Wilson. He's white with light-brown hair, maybe in his early forties, in good shape, medium build, slightly taller than Wilson. There's nothing about him that stands out.

"He doesn't look familiar. Maybe he's from one of the neighboring towns."

She brings another photo up. Wilson is looking directly at Jess, and something unsettling stirs in my gut. It's the same feeling I had when I caught him staring at her on Saturday.

"Why's Wilson watching you?" I ask, curious if she has any idea what his problem is.

"I have no idea. I didn't notice he was doing that until Saturday night when I was looking at the photos."

"Maybe he wasn't thrilled you were taking his picture." I keep studying the image as if the answer is there on the screen.

"He had no idea I was doing that. I kept the phone waist height, and it wasn't obvious I was shooting photos. I doubt he knows I captured him staring at me. What if he knows who I am? What if he thinks I really am a cop killer?" Her voice is a strained whisper and her eyes are wide.

"But you aren't a cop killer. You're innocent."

"Not everyone believes I'm innocent. Plenty of people think I'm guilty. Some think I got a lucky break. Others believe I conspired with my lover to kill my husband. I've seen comments where people have threatened my life because they still believe I'm a cop killer."

"I doubt Wilson thinks you're a cop killer," I say, even though I'm not sure what he believes when it comes to Savannah or if he has an opinion on her at all. "I doubt he has any idea who you are, Jess. Only Kellan and I know, and that's because you told us. Your appearance has changed enough since your arrest and initial media coverage that he won't recognize you. You were released because you were innocent of the crime. So there won't be any APBs requesting police departments be on the lookout for you."

"Robyn knows the truth." Jess's quiet voice is free of accusation, but the ever-present fear is still there.

"Robyn is your therapist. She told you she wouldn't tell anyone, and she won't. I know her. She will keep your secret. What I'd like to know is why Wilson was watching you or if it was just a coincidence."

"Maybe it was a coincidence." She closes her laptop. "Or maybe that's why he arrested you. Because he has an issue with me."

"The only reason he arrested me is because he's an asshole."

Jess wraps her arms around herself. "Just promise me you won't antagonize him again. I don't trust him."

"That makes two of us." But even knowing that, I can't find it in me to make the promise.

29

TROY

July, Present Day
Maple Ridge

Thursday evening, I head to Picnic & Treats, where I'm meeting the festival committee involved with equipment rental and setup.

Jess and Kim are at another table when I enter the café. Kim has a camera in her hand, her long black hair in two loose braids.

I walk over to them and give Jess a quick kiss. "Hey, Kim," I say to the wife of one of my oldest friends.

She smiles the same teasing grin I grew up with, the compassion that's all Kim shining in her eyes. "How's your arm?"

"It's better. I can dump the sling tomorrow. You guys comparing photography tips?" I nod at the camera in her hands.

She hands it to my girlfriend. "Jess is borrowing one of my old cameras and some of my gear for the wedding she's shooting since her equipment was lost in a flood two years ago, and she hasn't had a chance to replace it." Kim is looking at me and doesn't see the guilt and sadness flicker in Jess's eyes. I don't need my gut to tell me a flood wasn't what cost Jess her camera. Maybe her dead husband had something to do with what happened to it.

She can afford to buy a new one with the restitution payment, but she hasn't yet.

The sadness in Jess's eyes swiftly shifts to excitement. "Kim's giving me pointers for shooting the wedding."

"Nice camera." Not that I know anything about cameras. But from the way Jess is practically cradling it like a newborn, I'm guessing it is a nice camera.

"Thanks," Kim says.

"Are you still coming over to my place after your meeting?" Jess asks me.

"I'll be there as soon as I'm finished here." I give her another quick kiss and walk over to the corner of the café where members of the equipment and finance committees have claimed a table.

"How much are we looking at for the equipment and setup?" I ask Emily a few minutes later once the six members of the two committees have arrived. All are regulars at the Veterans Center and have volunteered to help out with the festival. Emily is sitting next to me, studying the numbers on her tablet.

She tells us the amount for the equipment we need to rent —the stage, the tables and canopies for the vendors, the sound system—as well as the cost for the rental company to set up the stage. We're looking at mid five figures.

A low whistle comes from Sheldon. "Damn."

I already knew this last week when I spoke with Anthony

Bell about the sponsorship, but hearing the amount doesn't get any easier with time.

"But the good news is, each vendor is paying a fee to have a table," Em points out. "That will help offset some of the costs. And then we've got a number of sponsors. That will pay for the rest of the expenses. It looks like we won't be in the red before we start the event. I just need to confirm that things are a go, put the deposits on the equipment, and we'll be all set for that part of the big day."

I turn to Taylor, the head of our finance committee and our treasurer. She and her girlfriend, Kim's sister, are the owners of Barside Brewery. She's the one who manages their books. "Is that okay on your end of things?" I ask her.

"Yes. You'll need to cosign the checks, and then we can get them to the suppliers."

Thank God most of the other things we need to deal with—other than some paid promotion and the licenses—are free. The entertainers are all volunteering their time. Even the roadies who work with the rock band Pushing Limits are volunteering to help out.

By the time the group has finalized details for the event, Jess and Kim have already left Picnic & Treats. I thank everyone for coming.

As I walk to my truck, my phone rings. I check who's calling. Anthony Bell. The festival's biggest sponsor. If he hadn't agreed to help out, I'd probably still be scrambling for sponsors to make up the amount we need. "Hi, Troy speaking."

"Hi, Troy. This is Anthony Bell." His voice comes through the line grumbly rough.

I don't know why, but something about his voice sends dread wrapping around my gut and squeezing tight. "Hi, Anthony. What can I do for you?"

He makes some sort of noise that is indecipherable on the phone. "I heard you assaulted the chief of police on the weekend. And well, Bell Automotive is a family establishment, and we can't have our good name linked with something like that. I admire what you're doing with the festival, Troy. But I'm afraid I'll have to withdraw my sponsorship for the event."

Fuuuuck.

"I promise you, Anthony, it was just a misunderstanding. And it definitely wasn't assault."

"Right. I get that you didn't lay your fists on Chief Wilson, but I can't take the risk of bad press from this. I'm sorry, Troy. I wish I had better news, but my decision is final. I have to go now. I have an appointment with a client." The line goes dead.

Fuck. Fuck. Fuck.

The dread in my stomach sets off a cascade of explosions through my nerves, tensing my muscles, giving me heartburn. Now what am I supposed to do?

THE MOMENT I WALK THROUGH JESS'S FRONT DOOR AN HOUR later, my mouth is on hers. I push her against the front door and kiss her long and hard, letting myself forget for a second everything outside the walls of her house. "I think we need to change the no-kissing-at-work policy," I say once we stop kissing, my lips already missing hers.

"You do, do you?" She laughs softly and her eyes sparkle with amusement.

My mouth tugs to one side. "Yep. I think that would be better for our mental health."

She laughs again, a little louder this time. "It might be a distraction my boss won't appreciate."

"Oh, your boss is completely fine with a little distraction now and then. It's good for morale."

She kisses me on the cheek. "I'll think about it...but you've given me some strong points to consider."

Jess threads her fingers with mine and takes me into the kitchen. I don't bother mentioning my phone call with Anthony Bell. I need to figure out how to solve the problem of the lost sponsor without dragging her into the mess I created. She's got enough she's dealing with. I haven't told anyone else about what happened. I want to do some damage control first.

Kim's camera is sitting on the kitchen table. Jess picks it up reverently and puts it away in the camera bag.

"The flood you mentioned to Kim," I say. "That's not how you lost your camera, is it?"

She took photojournalism courses in college. She must have had a good camera back then.

Jess looks away, but not before I see the pain in her eyes. "No, it isn't."

"Will you tell me what happened?" The pitch of my voice drops, my tone gentle and coaxing.

"My husband took away a lot of things I loved. That was his way of controlling me. But my camera...my camera was different. That he smashed because he thought I was having an affair. I wasn't, but he refused to listen and destroyed my camera as punishment. The rest of my gear vanished shortly after that."

A string of curses marches through my head. After everything he put her through, I'm surprised she picked up a camera again.

But I guess that's the point. She didn't. Jess has been using her iPhone camera. And that was only because Robyn had been encouraging her to revisit some of her old hobbies.

I stroke my thumb across her cheek. "I'm sorry for everything he put you through."

I swear, I'll never let anyone else hurt you like that.

A voice in the back of my head calls me a liar. I've already hurt her. I hurt her Saturday when I got myself arrested.

I can't do that to her again.

30

JESSICA

July, Present Day
Maple Ridge

Friday after work, I'm sitting in Picnic & Treats with Simone, Zara, Avery, and Em. Troy and his brothers have already left with the Marine vets who are here for their mountain excursion weekend. They're due back Sunday afternoon.

"I've been working through the online course that focuses on wedding photography," I tell the four women. "But it's one thing to watch the videos. It's another to apply them to real life. I need to practice." I smile at them, channeling Bailey's puppy eyes that are hard to resist. "And I need to practice with brides and grooms. You four and your grooms. Well, more like one husband and three men acting like grooms. Garrett, Kellan, and Noah."

Emily heaves a dramatic sigh. "Once a fake bride, always a fake bride."

Zara snorts and grins at me. "We had to do the same for Kim when she agreed to be a wedding photographer. Maybe that should be our next business. We rent ourselves out to photographers wanting to get into the wedding industry."

I laugh a low rumble in my throat. "At least I won't be working with rookie fake brides."

"You'll have to count me out." Avery shrugs, her lower lip caught between her teeth. "Noah and I have only been together for five months. I don't want to freak him out and have him believe I'm already imagining us walking down the aisle."

I make sure there's nothing in my expression that gives away my relief. If I can avoid being near a cop, all the more power to me. Even if it is Noah.

"Are you...thinking of that?" Simone asks, her face glowing.

Avery shrugs again. "Not really. Well, maybe once or twice. But I don't want to jinx what he and I have by even thinking it."

"Alright," I say. "You and Noah are exempt from helping me practice."

Emily's phone buzzes on the table. She checks the screen. "Simone, Letty asked me to thank you for hooking her up with the wig person you recommended." Emily turns the phone around to show Simone whatever is on it.

"That looks great. Tell her she's welcome."

Zara and I exchange curious glances.

Emily shows us the photo of a woman in her early forties. Her thick blond hair brushes against her jawline. "My old colleague from when I was an elementary school teacher was recently diagnosed with cancer," Emily explains. "She wanted to get a wig. And she wanted something that didn't cost a fortune but is still stylish."

"Wow. That's a wig?" I would never have guessed.

Simone nods. "The woman who designs them does a great job. The best ones are made from natural hair, but those are pricy. Her wigs are the next best alternative."

Simone takes a sip of her drink. "So, how are things going, working with Troy?" The question is directed at me.

Everyone peers at me expectantly, her curiosity mirrored on their faces.

"It's going well. But working in an office isn't my dream job. And I'm not thrilled at the idea of working for the man I'm also dating."

It's one more piece of my life that Troy's part of, along with sharing the same friends. That was the problem I had when I was married. The few friends I had were married to my husband's friends or colleagues. I couldn't even call them close friends, which meant I had no one to turn to. The women were loyal to their husbands...who were loyal to mine.

My only friend in Maple Ridge who isn't linked to Troy is the one friend who is married to an abusive man.

"Why not?" Simone asks. "A lot of husbands and wives work successfully together. Although I do get the part about it not being your dream job."

"I don't want to have to rely on a man for my happiness and money," I explain. "A girl I knew in college ended up marrying a man who became abusive. She had no way to support herself, even if she could've escaped him. He made her give up her career. And then he made her give up her friends. He manipulated her every move."

"What happened to her?" Sadness radiates from Simone, and she shares a quick glance with Avery.

"She died." It's not a lie. Savannah Townsend died the day I was released from prison. My husband and prison broke her. The woman she became is the woman trying to rise from the ashes. Building a new life in a town that doesn't know who she is. "My friend lost so much because of a man. I don't want to make the same mistake." *Again.*

Heartbreak flickers on Emily's face. "We've known Troy

since elementary school. You never have to worry about him being abusive."

"I know. But that doesn't change anything. Fortunately, I'm not interested in getting married, so that partially solves that problem." It's the first time I've said it out loud or even thought it. The possibility of marrying a second time hadn't crossed my mind while I was in prison. I hadn't expected to survive my time locked away.

Growing up, I'd dreamed of one day finding Prince Charming. Too bad my Prince Charming turned out to be a psychopath. I would've done better marrying a toad.

"You don't want kids one day?" Em asks.

"You don't need to be married to have kids." My parents were proof of that.

"So you do want kids?"

What I want is my daughter. But that will never happen. Not in the way I wish it could.

I tear off a piece of my muffin, unable to look at the four women. Afraid if I do, they'll see the pain in my eyes, see the truth about Amelia. "I have no intention of having kids without a loving father to be there for them. I know what it's like to grow up without a father." Fortunately, I had a grandfather to fill that role until I was twelve.

My words are just an excuse. If I hadn't been wrongfully imprisoned for my husband's death, I would have raised my daughter without a father figure in her life. But after losing my daughter, I'm not willing to go down that path once more and risk losing another child—one way or another. I can't go through that pain again.

I glance up from my muffin.

All four women stare at me with a compassion that's beginning to not feel so foreign since moving to Maple Ridge. Compassion had been in short supply while I was in prison. Any hope of it had been stomped out, like a daisy underfoot.

Even when Anne had offered me a place to stay while I was healing, I'd been half expecting her to change her mind. To crush my dream of starting over. And yet, these four women, who don't know anything about that part of my life, seem to get me.

Guilt tugs at me, whispers in my ears, reminds me that as much as they've been there for me, have been supportive, I haven't fully let them in. But I'm not ready for that yet. Not ready to tell them the truth about my past. Not all of it anyway.

"I lived with my grandmother when I was a kid," I say. She was the poster woman of compassionate. "My mom didn't want me. I have no idea who my father is." And I don't care who he is either. "Anyway," I say, needing to get this conversation back on track, "are any of you free next Thursday so I can practice taking wedding photos?"

Zara nods, thankfully taking my cue to switch topics. "Garrett and I are free. His book's due on Monday, so he'll be available after that. He usually likes to take the week off after sending a book to his editor."

"Perfect. Do you still have the outfits you used for Kim's photo shoots?"

I PEDAL UP THE DRIVEWAY LEADING TO A SMALL BUNGALOW AND dismount. An assortment of flowers is blooming in the planters by the front door and from the hanging baskets above the porch.

The porch swing reminds me of Granny's old one. I used to love sitting on it as a kid, gently swinging while she read me a story.

I push my bike past Olivia's car and prop the rusty frame against the brick wall of the house. I unzip the trailer's cover and unfasten Bailey, who's wearing her *Service Dog in Training* vest. My fingers sink into her hair, gaining strength for this interview. I don't know Olivia at all, other than when Simone introduced her to me last weekend after Troy was arrested. But I do know she and her daughter are part of the reason Troy is organizing the festival.

The reason Troy wanted to buy Iris's house and flip it.

Bailey and I walk to the front door, and I ring the doorbell. I wasn't expecting Olivia to call me the other day and tell me she'd decided to go through with the interview. Just knowing she's a close friend of Troy's amps up my nervousness, and I shift on my feet.

The door opens. Olivia stands on the other side of it, a grinning older toddler balanced on her hip. The streak of bright-blue paint smeared on her T-shirt matches the one Nova is wearing across her pink top.

"Come on in," Olivia says, a nervous smile ghosting her face. "The place is a bit of a mess. Because, well...you know." Her gaze drops to her daughter.

My own smile is soft, hiding the heartbreak behind it. "Don't worry. I more than understand."

"Doggie!" Nova reaches for Bailey.

Bailey presses her body against my leg, instinctively knowing what I need even without her advanced level of PSD training.

Olivia lets me into the house, and I toe off my shoes. She leads Bailey and me the short distance to the living room. The house is small and messy and perfect. It feels like a home.

Olivia puts Nova on the floor and begins removing toys and blankets from the couch. Nova stares uncertainly at Bailey, her arm hooked around her mommy's leg. The look Bailey returns is pure playful puppy. She's hoping Nova will want to play with her even though Bailey is wearing her vest, which means it isn't playtime.

I sit on the couch and put my hand on Bailey's back,

soaking in her warmth. Bailey stays still, awaiting my next instructions. I tell her to lie down, and I give her a treat for positive reinforcement.

"Nova loves Butterscotch," Olivia tells me. "But other than that, she doesn't have a lot of experience with dogs. And definitely not with service dogs." She takes Nova to the kid-sized armchair, and Nova climbs onto it. "The puppy is working," Olivia explains to her daughter. "Do you want to play your favorite game?"

Nova nods. Olivia passes her the iPad from the coffee table and helps her start the game.

Olivia sits on the other end of the couch. "Troy told me you're dealing with PTSD." Olivia studies my face, and I suddenly feel naked, exposed. He hadn't mentioned that to me.

"I am, but I prefer not to discuss the cause of it." The words are spoken softly, almost as if they're a secret themselves.

Part of me expects Olivia to change her mind about the interview, and I wouldn't blame her if she did. I'm asking her to open up about the worst time of her life, to bleed for the sake of an article that will hopefully help others in her situation. But at the same time, I'm not willing to open a vein and bleed myself.

She gives a small nod, her thoughts seemingly somewhere else. "Colton and I were high school sweethearts. He was Porthos. I was Aramis. And Troy was Athos. The Three Musketeers. It had been that way since we were kids. We did everything together.

"The summer before our junior year of high school, Troy went away with his family for a few weeks. Colton and I were hanging out in his backyard one night, sitting together in front of the firepit." Olivia's gaze turns dreamy, like she's in another time and place, and the curve of her mouth follows suit. "We were just talking, and he was sitting so close to me. And I remember thinking how amazing he smelled. And the next thing we knew, we were kissing, and it was the most incredible thing in the world." A light flush spreads across her cheeks.

"By the time Troy returned home, Colton and I were a couple. Although it did take us another two weeks before we confessed to him we were dating." Olivia laughs softly under her breath.

Her smile bleeds away, leaving behind Colton's widow, who's still picking up her broken pieces.

I can't begin to imagine how she feels. I'm a widow, but all I feel is relief in that. Olivia and Colton didn't just love each other, they'd been best friends.

Olivia tells me about when she realized she was in love with Colton, about their life together before they got married. About learning she was pregnant with Nova and how much Colton loved his daughter. About how everything changed after the tragic bus accident that stole so many young lives. He was one of the first responders to arrive at the scene.

As clichéd as it sounds, Colton really was the center of Olivia's universe. He was the oxygen she breathed. I can't even fathom what that would be like—to love someone that way, that fully.

She smiles at her daughter, her love for Nova shining wet and bright in her eyes. Love for her daughter and for her late husband.

"I miss him so much," she whispers and sniffs.

I cover her hand with mine. I can't take away her pain, but I wish I could. Like I wish I knew how to take away Violet's pain.

"I don't know what I would have done if not for Nova," Olivia says. "She was my reason for getting up each morning. For remembering to breathe. But the truth is, Colton died long before his heart stopped beating. The PTSD had done that to him. Troy and I tried to get him help, but Colt's pride and pain and stubbornness made that impossible. I don't want any wife, girlfriend, child, parent to go through what Nova and I did."

She brushes away her tears, and I do the same with the couple branding a trail down my face.

But my tears aren't only because of what Olivia shared with me. They're because Amelia had been my reason for getting up each morning when my brain just wanted to shut down during my marriage. Shut down and drag me deeper into a world of depression.

Thinking about her while I was incarcerated had been the oxygen I'd needed to keep on breathing. To keep stumbling through each day. Even after I signed away my rights to be her mother, there was still a part of me that clung to the belief I would one day see her again and she would forgive me for not being there for her growing up.

It was only after I was stabbed that I finally surrendered all hope.

I'd given up on life like Colton had.

"I also don't know what I would do without Troy." Olivia's expression warms at his name, and the sorrow I witnessed in her eyes and the curve of her shoulders fades. "He has stepped up in ways I never expected him to. He's become my brick wall. I was lost without Colton, but Troy found me."

Something about the way she says the last part causes my heart to pinch, but I pretend not to notice the reason for that.

The doorbell rings.

"I wasn't expecting anyone." Olivia stands. "I'll be right back. Are you okay if I leave Nova here with you?"

"Sure. We'll be fine." I smile at the little girl who's been entertaining herself with her mommy's iPad for the past ten minutes.

Nova shows me the game she's playing. A kids' game with cute cartoon fishes. It makes me think of Windermere Lake, which reminds me of all the times I've gone canoeing with Troy. Unfortunately, my renovations haven't been the only casualties of our injuries. I haven't been able to go canoeing or practice yoga or hike. And Troy hasn't been able to work in the same capacity as before.

Olivia returns to the living room with Lance. He's wearing jeans and a gray T-shirt that hugs the swell of his lean muscles. His bangs flop in his eyes, and he rakes his hand through his hair, pushing it away from his face. The guy is definitely good-looking.

"Hey, Jess. Didn't expect to find you here." He flashes me the teasing grin he usually gives me whenever he shows up at Troy's office. He's still entertained that I'm dating his boss—our boss.

Nova looks up at Lance and squeals. She clambers to her feet, and he scoops her up in his arms. "Hey, kiddo. I came to see if you and your mommy want to go out for dinner. Do you think you can convince her for me?"

He tickles Nova, and she giggles.

Olivia beams at the pair. "You know you have her wrapped around your finger. You can get her to do anything you want. Do you mind if I finish this interview first?"

Something tells me it's more like Nova has Lance wrapped around her cute little finger.

"Not at all," he replies, his warm smile firmly in place.

"You can stay if you want." She sits back down next to me on the couch and resumes where she left off when the doorbell rang.

Her face brightens as she tells me all the ways Troy has helped her—like he's helped me. The more Olivia talks, the more obvious it is just how much she relies on Troy. How much she cares for him. Cares for him as more than just a friend.

My gaze flicks to Lance as she talks, and I catch the frustration in his eyes. From the way Olivia talks about Troy, it's clear she cares for him as more than just a friend, but it's also clear from how Lance is looking at her that he has strong feelings for

Olivia. Only, Olivia doesn't notice it because she's looking at me.

Just how far do her feelings for Troy go? It's like she's forgotten I'm his girlfriend.

Or maybe that doesn't matter. Eventually Troy will realize he deserves better than my broken pieces.

The broken pieces I'm figuring out how best to slot together. But like a shattered vase, I might never be whole again.

Some of my pieces might be forever lost.

Pieces that Olivia still has of herself.

31

ANGELIQUE

July 1943
France

London *has advised not to involve The Wolf in our activities at present time. Unclear where his loyalties lie.*

The last line of Allaire's message doesn't surprise me. Johann has been doing whatever it takes to protect those he loves: his mother and sister, Oskar, Margrit, and Sonja. If the Allied forces were putting them at risk, he would fight us to save his friends and family. His loyalties lie with those he loves and not with a particular country.

But a Nazi shot Dieter, Johann's best friend. Hitler doesn't see a place for Jews and disabled people in his Aryan society. There is no reason for Johann to support Hitler and those who worship the *füehrer*—and there is every reason for him to help the resistance against the occupiers.

Last night, he said he hadn't killed anyone yet, but he was still afraid for his soul. Would he feel the same way if he were working with a local resistance group? Would he even be interested in helping them?

It's a question I cannot ask him. Not now. Not while his friends are escaping to a country where they'll finally be safe. Not while his sister's and mother's whereabouts are unknown. And not when I've been given direct instructions not to include him.

I light the candle and burn the original message from the drop box and the one I transcribed. Once the ashes have been disposed of, I work at coding a new message for Allaire.

Message received and understood. Will keep you apprised of the situation. If the blue tits land safely in the nest, it will go a long way in securing The Wolf's loyalties to us.

I secure the coded message and my supplies in the hiding place and reposition the wooden floorboards, rug, and white thread. The courier is scheduled to arrive in four days to check the other drop box for messages to Allaire. It will be another day or two after that before he will receive it, assuming everything goes according to schedule.

I return outside to tend to the garden. The hard manual labor is the perfect distraction from my thoughts. I'm beyond exhausted, and a kaleidoscope of emotions consume me, and with each twist of the wrist, a new emotion becomes predominant. Optimism. Grief. Fear. Hope. Worry. Guilt. Love.

Jacques has already eaten the evening meal by the time Johann enters the house. The *thud-thud-thud* of his booted footsteps don't go upstairs or come into the kitchen. They head to the drawing room. This is followed by a murmur of voices. The two men are talking, but I cannot hear what they are saying.

I put the plate I was washing on the sideboard, dry my

hands with the tea towel, and go to see what's going on. Johann is bent over the side table, his back to me, his body blocking whatever he's working on.

He straightens and steps away, revealing a radio. The dark wood is slightly chipped, the edges worn. It once belonged to someone else until the Germans confiscated it. I don't even want to think what might have happened to its previous owners.

"It's illegal for us to be in possession of that," I remind him.

"We will just have to make sure it isn't found," Johann says. "And if it is found, I will take responsibility for it. But I need to know if Oskar and his family make it to their destination, and this is the only way for you to learn they are safe, *non*?"

"That's correct."

He rubs his hand over the smooth wooden surface. "Don't tell me what the coded messages say. Then German intelligence won't be able to learn anything from me if they should find it here."

I nod, thankful I can now listen to the BBC French news more frequently than before. Since Johann has been living here, I've been reduced to listening to it whenever he's away in the evenings. "We will still need to be cautious," I say. "We cannot risk it being found."

"Agreed."

There's a reason the Nazis don't want the French to listen to the broadcasts. The BBC news is the only way to rally support of those wishing to resist the occupation, to let them know Britain hasn't abandoned occupied Europe to the Germans. It provides hope in a time when there is so little of it.

Jacques, Johann, and I sit close to the radio so we can keep the volume low. The timpani beat of *Dot. Dot. Dot. Dash* begins the broadcast. The Morse code for "V." For victory.

"Ici Londres! Les Français parlent aux Français."

The announcement is followed by five minutes of the world

news, something that has been in short supply in France. The Germans make sure we only see their propaganda. A variety of entertainment—poems, comical plays, commentaries on the war, slogans, songs—makes up the meat of the show. It lasts for about thirty minutes.

"Resist the demands of the Vichy government," the announcer says in French. "They are not your friends. They will bring our beautiful country to ruins with their corruption and drive for power. Resist and fight. Everything you do takes us one step closer to winning back our country. If you work in a factory that makes goods that supply German soldiers, do what you can to make the products subpar."

Johann laughs, the sound a soft rumble in his chest. "That would explain why the tyres are constantly needing to be replaced on some of the German military vehicles. The men were complaining the French don't know how to make tyres like the Germans do."

The final five minutes of the broadcast pertains to my role in the SOE.

"The turkey ate the cow," the radio announcer proclaims. "Claude has a rainbow beard. Monkeys sing with bananas."

Some of the silly messages are just noise, as meaningless as they come across. They are created to distract the enemy, leaving the Germans to scramble and figure out what the messages mean. The other silly messages are signals to agents on the ground, to confirm an air drop is happening as scheduled that evening, the RAF plane having just taken off from England.

None of the messages tonight are applicable to the job I was recruited to do.

The broadcast ends, and Johann hides the radio in the barn. I know he hasn't found our other hiding spots because the security measures I employ have yet to be disturbed.

"Looks like it will be a beautiful sunset," Johann tells me. "Should we go to the pond to watch it?"

"I'd like that very much."

He and I walk towards the pond, neither of us talking. The night is quiet other than the drone of insects. It's a welcome reprieve from the explosions, the rhythmic staccato of marching soldiers, the vibration of an engine belonging to the enemy.

Johann and I sit on the grassy bank, and he laces his fingers with mine. We gaze to the horizon, where the sun lies just above scattered clouds.

"Anja used to believe mythological creatures caused the sunsets," he says after a few minutes, a gentle, brotherly smile on his face. "It was their campfires, she claimed, that created the colours. And when the colours went away, it was because the fires had been extinguished, and the creatures would then dance for hours in the moonlight. The brighter the moon, the longer the dancing lasted. They would sleep during the new moon because there was not enough light to dance."

"I guess she never had a chance to dance herself?"

"No, she danced. She danced all the time. She couldn't hear music, but she could feel it. When she was little, she would go out in the garden and twirl and spin. She pretended she could hear the music the mythological creatures created. Special music only the deaf could hear."

I grin at the joy in his voice. "My sister would have loved her, and she would have loved that story." And my real sister will still love the story if I live long enough to tell her it. Or she would if the Official Secrets Act I signed didn't prohibit me from talking about my time here in France.

Talking about Hazel with Johann makes me feel closer to her. Closer than I have felt since discovering the truth about her and Charles. But I can't tell Johann that. I can't tell him about how I turned my back on my sister and never once gave her a chance to explain. My engagement to Charles had been a mistake, but I was too blind to see that. I didn't love him as much as my sister does.

I didn't love him the way I love Johann.

But the reality is, other than these stolen moments, there is no future for us together. Once I return to England, things will end between us. Of that I am certain.

My heart aches thinking about it, so I don't.

"If you could live anywhere in the world," Johann says as the bottom of the sun dips below the horizon, "where would it be?"

"Anywhere?"

"Yes, anywhere, but not France. You already live here. You cannot pick the country you grew up in."

I release a soft laugh because while I might have lived in France and Austria for several years, England is the country where I spent much of my youth. But his comment confirms I didn't speak English last night. I had called out in French. Jacques hadn't been certain about that when I asked him earlier.

"Canada. Perhaps Quebec since they speak French there. What about you?"

"Oregon. That's in America." Johann's thumb caresses the back of my hand, and a tingly warmth spreads through my limbs from his touch.

"Why America?"

"While I was in university, I made friends with an American who was from Oregon. He told me about the mountains that were so close, they were practically on his doorstep. And there was a lake near his home in the small town he lived in. Maple Ridge."

"You've just described Austria." Humor paints my tone in various shades.

He grins at me. "I know. I also said you cannot pick a

country you grew up in. I know most of America does not look like that, but there are some places that are as beautiful as my home country." There's a wistfulness in his voice that often sneaks in when he talks about Austria. I don't blame him. I loved living there too.

"I also believe America would be safe from having a leader like Hitler. My friend said they have checks and balances to keep a president from becoming a dictator. Even back then, my friend warned me Hitler was dangerous. He was quite vocal about it at the university before returning to America."

"What did the other students think about that?"

"We had a number of political student groups. Some went underground when they realised their views were not appreciated by the majority. These were the communist and social democratic groups. They felt the same way as my friend did about Hitler. When Austria became part of Germany, many of their members vanished or were rounded up and sent to prison camps."

"Were any of them friends of yours?"

He shakes his head. "I didn't align with either of those groups. I wasn't all that interested in politics. Not in the way my friend was. I just wanted to build things. I left politics to those who cared about it. I know now that was naïve thinking."

I return my gaze to the sunset. The sun sinks farther on the horizon, the sky so vibrant, so alive. A contrast to the France we are living in. It's as if the war is slowly bleaching the colour from every living thing around us, leaving a faded shadow in its wake.

The sun eventually disappears, the last of its rays staining the sky with a smear of deep red. I shift my head to look at Johann. He's watching me, and even in the dim light I can see the longing in his eyes.

He strokes his thumb along my cheekbone. He doesn't have to say what he is thinking, I can tell from his touch. I lean into him, wishing to be free of the war. Wishing we were just two people who have feelings for each other. Two people unafraid of what tomorrow might bring, of the decisions we'll have to make.

His lips brush mine in a sweet kiss, and our bodies shift towards each other.

I part my lips and let him in. His tongue glides against mine. And like the sun a few minutes ago as it sank below the horizon, our bodies sink onto the grass, our mouths joined.

32

JESSICA

July, Present Day
Maple Ridge

The first wedding-photography practice session is a casual, outdoor event in Simone and Lucas's backyard.

I reach down from the stepladder, and Simone passes me the last jar filled with fairy lights. I hook it onto the string hanging between the trees, biting my lower lip to keep the pain in my ribs from showing on my face.

She gazes at the jars already strung up. "It looks so magical."

It really does.

Zara and Garrett step out of the house, dressed in their wedding gown and suit.

"Wow, this place looks incredible." Zara raises the floor-length hem of her simple satin gown and walks across the grass, the long slit in the side revealing golden flashes of her leg.

Zara's the one who looks incredible.

Her braids are fastened up in an elegant style and her makeup is glamorous, complete with long fake lashes, which she's currently using to give Garrett playful, flirty eyes.

"God, if Garrett can't see how gorgeous she is," Simone whispers, "I might have to hit him on the head with the floral centerpiece."

The corners of my mouth twitch into a smile. "Can I take photos while you're doing that? It might add a nice touch to Em's portfolio."

Simone's abrupt laugh is too soft to be heard by anyone else in the backyard.

Zara glides over to the end of the aisle we'd set up with white chairs on either side of it. Garrett takes his place at the wooden archway, which Emily decorated with a simple floral arrangement of fake flowers.

We spend the next hour shooting various photos. Occasionally, I try for the same shot several times, like a movie director who makes his actors shoot a scene over and over and over until he's happy with the results. And I take tons of notes so I can replicate the best pictures when I shoot a real wedding.

I don't make the pair kiss—much to Simone's disappointment. I catch her pout when I end things before it gets that far, and I can tell what she's thinking.

"The last photos I want to take are of the bride and groom dancing." The sunlight has dimmed and the lights in the jars glow like fireflies. It really is romantic.

Garrett and Zara walk to the center of the lawn. The lights hanging from the trees twinkle softly in the background above their heads. There's no real dance floor, but no one will realize that with the angle I'm shooting the photos from.

Behind me, the back door to the house slides open. Without turning around, I know it's Troy, Kellan, and Lucas. They were at the Wilderness Warriors site, getting ready for the weekend trip with the next group of military vets.

Emily turns on the music and Garrett and Zara dance for a few minutes while I capture those shots. They're a beautiful couple. And so at ease with each other.

Everything about this mock wedding is beautiful. So why don't I feel the same level of excitement I used to feel behind the lens?

Is it because the wedding isn't real?

Or is it because it's never been your dream to be a wedding photographer?

Sure, it wasn't Savannah's dream. But I'm not her. I'm Jessica. Why can't this be *my* dream?

We finish up, and Simone goes over to her husband and kisses him. Zara and Garrett duck into the house to get changed.

"Can you hold the stepladder while I get the jars down?" I ask Em as I step onto the first rung of the short ladder.

An arm scoops around my waist and pulls me to the hard body behind me. My skin instantly tingles at the contact.

"I can get them." Troy's husky voice brushes across my ear and ignites the happy nerves between my legs.

I glance over my shoulder. "Right. If you want to reinjure yourself." My words pour out like hot caramel melted over ice cream, not quite the sound I was going for. "But I'm thinking we might want to avoid that."

Troy lowers his mouth to mine and prevents any further discussion.

The kiss only lasts a few seconds, but it's the best few seconds of my day. I twist around, taking care not to accidentally hurt his arm. "Loved the kiss. But it's not changing anything. You're not climbing the ladder."

"Kellan," Troy calls to his brother, who is walking toward

the table where Emily directed him to go. "Can you help Jess with those lanterns?" He points to them.

And I try to ignore the growing hollowness in my chest that's been there since I gave up everything after marrying the wrong man.

A hollowness that didn't shrink while I was shooting the practice wedding photos.

33

JESSICA

July, Present Day
Maple Ridge

Saturday morning, Bailey and I head to the park to work on her training. The sun is bright, but I'm wearing my yoga pants and long-sleeved T-shirt because we're nowhere near the high for today.

"Hi, Jessica," a woman's voice says as I'm praising Bailey. Bailey's doing a great job heeling and ignoring the other dogs playing catch on the grass.

I glance up and shield my eyes from the sun with my hand. Olivia's sister is standing in front of me with Nova in her arms. "Hi. Cora, right?" Like her clothes the other day, her jeans and floral blouse look more city-chic than small-town casual.

"That's right. My sister mentioned you're training your dog to be a service dog."

I nod. "I've been diagnosed with PTSD. Troy thought I might benefit from having her."

Crinkles form between Cora's eyes. "Wouldn't it be better if you had a dog that was already trained as a service dog? This one's just a puppy." She points to the eleven-month-old puppy in question. "She's too young to start the advanced training for PSD certification."

"You know about service dogs?"

"No, I...I read an article about the topic not that long ago. It was about Prison4Paws. A select group of inmates train the puppies from when they're about only thirteen weeks old. The puppies stay with the inmates until they're about a year or more, and then the dogs leave to go to their next stage of training. From a young age, the puppies are being conditioned as future service dogs."

I would have loved to have done something like that while I was locked away. As far as I know, my prison had nothing like Prison4Paws.

"She was going to be trained by someone else," I explain, "but things changed, and she's mine."

"But she's not a fully-trained service dog."

Cora didn't ask a question, but I answer anyway. "No, but she will be."

"And then you'll give her to someone else who has PTSD?"

"No, she'll still be helping me out. PTSD isn't something you overcome overnight. It can take years, even with therapy."

"And you're getting therapy?"

I kneel next to Bailey and stroke her, easing my fingers between her silky strands. "I am."

"I'm glad to hear that. Livi's husband refused to acknowledge he was struggling. Maybe if he had gotten help..." Her voice fades, regret and unanswered questions left dangling in its wake.

"It's because of Troy that I'm seeing a therapist. I was in denial about the PTSD when I first met him." And for a while after that too.

"Livi mentioned you've only lived here a few months."

I nod, the unease I feel around strangers kicking in. It was different when I was talking to her sister yesterday. I was the one asking questions. But I didn't have to do that too often. Olivia seemed happy to tell me everything without much prompting.

"Were you in the military like Troy?" Cora asks.

"No."

"Paramedic or EMS?"

I push to my feet. "No." The word stretches out on a slow breath.

"How did you get PTSD?" Cora's eyes widen. "Oh, my God. I'm sorry. That's none of my business."

"That's okay." My tone remains polite, friendly, but I really wish she would stop asking me questions. I already told Olivia I didn't want to talk about the cause of my PTSD. I get the feeling Cora's questions have nothing to do with her sister.

Cora looks at me expectantly, waiting for me to divulge my past. I can see it in her eyes, the curiosity.

I have no intention of giving her what she wants.

Cora smiles, her teeth super white against her mauve lipstick. "I think it's great you have a boyfriend like Troy who's able to help you. I bet a lot of men wouldn't do that for a woman he just met."

"You're probably right. But you know Troy. He's that kind of guy." The kind of guy who likes fixing buildings and people. "He's an advocate for those struggling with PTSD. That's why he's organizing the festival, to raise money to help provide services for those with PTSD. And to help their families. Like your sister and niece."

I'm just lucky the state is covering my therapy. If it weren't for that, in the beginning, before I got the restitution payment, I'd still be drowning like Cora's brother-in-law was until his suicide.

"Troy really is a special guy," Cora says, and I can tell she's not only saying that; she believes it.

"He is."

Nova fusses in her aunt's arms. Cora lowers the little girl to the ground. "What made you decide to come to Maple Ridge?"

Nova squats in front of Bailey and giggles.

"It sounded like a great place to live, especially with the mountains nearby."

"Where were you living before Maple Ridge?"

An uneasy feeling pounds inside me like waves churning up debris at the bottom of the ocean. So many questions. But I haven't seen a hint of recollection on her face. No special ability to see past my scars and change in hair color. No special ability to recognize me for the woman I used to be.

"A small town out east," I tell her.

Bailey has been patiently sitting next to me, but when you're an eleven-month-old puppy, your patience only lasts so long. She tugs on the leash, eager to get going again. *Thank God for that!*

"Well, Bailey and I should get back to our training. It was nice talking to you, Cora." I smile down at Nova. "Bye, Nova."

The toddler waves bye-bye to me and does a cute little dance in front of Bailey.

The pair leaves, but as much as I try to focus on my training goals for today, I can't stop wondering if the only reason Troy is interested in me is because I need saving. I'm a novelty to him. A chance for him to play the role of my white knight.

What will happen once I no longer need saving? Will he end things and move on to the next woman who needs his help? For all I know, something had already happened between Olivia and Troy long before I moved to Maple Ridge—or possibly even more recently—and they will end up together.

Bailey and I return home. I go to the fridge to make some lunch and discover a Morse code message stuck to the stain-less-steel door. It takes me only a minute or two to figure out the message.

> *Will be thinking about you tonight while I look*
> *at the stars and the Great Cock Constellation.*

I snort-laugh and place the message on the kitchen table. My phone pings with a text.

Simone: Are we still on for tonight?

I TAKE A SIP OF MY WINE AND PLACE MY FANNED-OUT CARDS ON the coffee table. "Full house."

Avery, Simone, Emily, and Zara groan and drop their cards on the table.

"Are you sure you weren't a card shark in your previous life?" Zara grabs one of the samosas she brought with her and dips it into the yummy chutney she also made.

Chuckling, I grab my own samosa. I could live on these. Along with the other international foods she makes at Picnic & Treats. "Positive. I'm just lucky today."

"Well, either way," Simone says, "I'm glad you could finally join us for Game Night...even if the guys aren't here, and it's actually Saturday and not Friday." She slides me a look that can be interpreted several ways, one being she knows the only reason I'm here is because Noah isn't. *Is it that obvious?*

I lean down to stroke Bailey, who's sitting patiently next to me, even though I know she'd love to go play with Jasper.

A loud squeak comes from the chew toy Jasper's attacking, and he takes it over to where Simone is sitting on the other end of the sectional.

"What's Noah up to tonight?" I ask Avery, my tone casual, something I've been working on when it comes to her boyfriend. At least I can now mention his name without my mouth going dry. I'd call that progress.

"He's gone away for the weekend with some friends. You know, a guys' weekend. No women allowed." She takes a sip of her vodka cooler.

"How did you two meet?" Unlike the other three women at the table, Avery didn't grow up in Maple Ridge. But from what I've figured out, she wasn't in town long before she and Noah began dating. Pretty much like Troy and me.

"He rescued me from a ditch. I grew up in Portland, so I wasn't used to big dumps of snow. Well, Maple Ridge got a big dump back in February, and I lost control of my car and ended up in a ditch. He happened to be driving by and stopped to see if I needed help. I didn't know at the time he was a cop. He was a good-looking guy—"

"Who she thought wanted to get into her panties," Simone says, the equivalent of a snicker in her tone. "And damn, the girl gave the poor man attitude. Instead of leaving her there like some guys might have, he called a tow truck and decided to wait with her until it showed up."

"But she was still giving him attitude." Zara picks up the story next. "And it was very cold. So Noah hoisted her onto his shoulder and walked to his warm truck."

"Naturally, I thought he was a serial killer, and I started to fight him and kicked him in the nuts."

Zara, Simone, and Emily all wince in sympathy for Noah.

Avery grins, but the smile is sheepish at best. "Okay, not my finest moment. Anyway, he goes down, dropping me in the process...and somehow, we roll into that damn ditch. He ends up on top of me. A state trooper picks then to drive past and stops to see if we need assistance. That's when I discovered Noah was a cop. The trooper knew him."

"Oh, but that's not the best part," Emily chimes in, lifting her wineglass as if to toast what comes next.

"I was so embarrassed at how I kicked him in his nuts." Avery's smile widens. "I made him some brownies the next day and went to the police station to drop them off for him. He took a bite of one, declared they were the best brownies he'd ever tasted, and asked me out on a date."

"And you've been together ever since?" I ask.

"Yep. One date became two. And I quickly realized he was a nice guy, despite being a cop." She shrugs. "I've never been a fan of cops. I've had a few bad experiences with them in the past. But Noah is nothing like them, so I gave him a chance."

Maybe she's right. I need to give Noah a chance. He's not my late husband. He's never done anything to make me feel threatened or unsafe. Just the opposite.

I nod at her, my message clear—I'll no longer go out of my way to avoid Noah. But the same can't be said for the rest of the Maple Ridge police force.

They haven't yet earned my trust.

"ARE WE STILL ON FOR TOMORROW?" SIMONE ASKS ME AS I SLIP on my sandals.

"Yes. I'll see you around two thirty?"

"That sounds good."

Zara and I step out of the house into the cooling night air. It's already dark by the time she drops Bailey and me off at my home. Fatigue dulls my thoughts, drains the energy from my body, and a yawn powers through me. But even my exhaustion and the two glasses of wine I've had tonight aren't enough to get me to go to bed yet. I'm in no rush to relive yesterday's nightmares.

I enter the house, reactivate the alarm, and turn on lights as

I walk to the kitchen. The lights chase away the shadows haunting the house at night.

Bailey stops and stares at the door leading to the backyard.

"You wanna to go out to do your business?" I click her leash onto her collar, turn on the patio light, and deactivate the alarm again. I open the back door, and we step outside.

I walk her over to the patch of grass used for her business, ever conscious of my surroundings. I listen for every sound that's out of place, every smell that deviates from normal.

Without warning, Bailey lurches toward the oak tree, but doesn't get far because of her leash. "Bailey. Stay."

The obedient puppy does as she's told.

"Good girl."

She might be staying, but something still holds her attention in the gloom of the shadows. Adrenaline courses through me, hijacking my heart rate. Goose bumps painfully prick my skin.

I reverse a slow step, my gaze locked on the shadows of the tree. The same place Bailey is still watching. *It's probably just a squirrel.*

Something moves in the shadow and it's not a squirrel. It's a person. I gulp in mouthfuls of air and gage the distance to my back door. Bailey whimpers.

My eyes adjust to the shadows. I can make out the person's oversized black hoodie. The hood covers their head, and their shoulders are slouched, as if the person is in pain. They've got a large bundle blanketed in their arms, and a beige bag is slung across their shoulder.

Not just a bag...a diaper bag. A diaper bag I've seen before.

"Violet?" My voice sounds loud to my ears but I'm sure I didn't say her name much above a whisper.

She steps closer and the light from the back door lands on her, revealing her bruised and swollen face.

My stomach lurches, and a horrified gasp erupts from my

lungs, echoing through the cool night. It's too familiar. Painfully familiar.

If Violet's husband's anything like mine was, the fresh bruises on her face aren't the only injuries she's dealing with.

She can't go back to him. I won't let her. I'll do whatever I can to keep her safe. Chief Wilson has hit her for the last time.

I slowly approach her and quickly realize the blanketed bundle is Sophie asleep in Violet's arms.

I gently touch Violet's shoulder, letting her know she's doesn't have to do this alone. "Let's get you inside. You'll be safe in my house."

She doesn't say anything. Her body is trembling, telling me everything I need to know.

"Does he know you came here?"

She shakes her head. "He was called in at work for an emergency, and his replacement hadn't arrived yet at the house." A tremor grips her voice, the sound small and hollow, and it tightens around my heart.

"Replacement? Do you mean the cop who approached us the other day at the park?" Or does her husband have more than one person keeping an eye on her?

She nods, the movement small. "I didn't know where else to go," she says, keeping her voice low.

My gaze darts to the house on the right. The windows overlooking my backyard are dark, and no one seems to be looking out of them. "You did the right thing coming here. Don't worry. You won't have to go back to him. Your days of being his punching bag are over." I'll make sure of that.

"I probably shouldn't stay." Her head jerks, turning to the side as if she heard a sound I missed. "He'll find me. It's not safe for me to be here."

"Did anyone see you?" I ask, the pitch of my voice low.

"It doesn't matter. He'll know. He knows everything."

I don't tell her that I doubt it's true. It always felt like my husband knew where to find me. Knew what I was doing. She has her reasons for feeling that way, just like I did.

"You'll be safe here. I have somewhere you can hide if he comes to my house. He won't know you're here." As long as Sophie doesn't begin crying. I haven't tested to see if Iris made the secret room soundproof.

I put my arm around Violet, sheltering her from the world, and I take her and Sophie into the house.

I activate the alarm. The tension in Violet's body deflates a tiny bit at seeing the security system. *Thank you, thank you, thank you, Troy*, for being so insistent at having it installed. Violet's husband won't be able to enter the house without me knowing.

I close the curtains in the kitchen and living room. "The first thing we're going to do is take photos." I point to Kim's camera on the kitchen table. "Then you'll have proof. Although I'm not sure how permissible they are when it comes to the courts. Maybe a doctor or police officer needs to take them for them to count."

"I can't talk to the cops," Violet whispers as if worried my house is bugged. "They can't be trusted. And if I go to the hospital, they will have to file a report with the police. I can't risk that."

She's right. If she were anyone else, taking her to the hospital would hopefully be enough to get things rolling to keep her safe. But I don't know if it's enough when her husband is the chief of police.

"Alright. I'll do what I can." I take Violet and Sophie upstairs to the spare bedroom but don't turn the light on. The curtains were taken down in anticipation of the renovations that are now stalled.

Violet lays her daughter on the bed. Sophie barely stirs and goes back to sleep.

"Did you know Iris?" I ask, the volume of my voice quiet. "She used to live here."

"No. From what I've occasionally heard about her, she died years before I moved to town."

"Well, she built a special hiding space in the closet. I don't know why she did that, but thankfully, she did. It's the perfect hiding place for you and Sophie. Just in case."

I lead her into the closet, turn on my phone flashlight, and show Violet how to open the secret door. "All you have to do is pull on this handrail, and you can close the door from the inside. No one will know you're in there."

I remove the cardboard box with Angelique's journals, medal, and the heart pendant, and place it by the bedroom door. I also remove the few other things I've been hiding in the space, like my laptop and the wooden box with Amelia's things inside. "Until I can get you to a safe house, we have to make sure no one knows you're here. You won't be able to leave this house. You understand that, right?"

It will be like Oskar and his family and the Allied pilots who hid in Jacques's barn. I silently thank Iris for teaching me what to do through her journals. For giving me the strength to follow in her path, for giving me the inspiration to hide Violet here. For building this space, though I'm sure this isn't what it was originally intended for.

Violet nods. "Thank you for helping me."

"You're welcome. I wish someone had helped me escape my husband." If they had, I wouldn't have lost all those years I can't get back. I would be spending my time with my daughter, instead of trying to prove I'm worthy enough to see her again. "Do you have anywhere you can go? A relative who doesn't live near Maple Ridge and your husband doesn't know about?" Who am I kidding? He can find that information out if she hasn't already told him.

"None I can think of. He knows where my family lives in

Portland. And I don't remember the last time I talked to my cousins, uncles, or aunts. I can't even tell you where they live now."

That doesn't matter. Her husband might have the resources to track her down if she went to her relatives. She wouldn't be safe with them.

"We'll come up with something else. My only concern is Sophie. It's one thing for you to disappear and start a new life where your husband can't find you. But if you disappear with your daughter, you might be charged with kidnapping if you're ever found."

"It's a risk I'm willing to take to protect her. We'll disappear like you did. I'll make sure he never finds Sophie and me." Her whispered words hold an edge of determination, barely recognizable under the tremor that hasn't left her voice.

We go to the bathroom, where I photograph the roadmap of abuse on Violet's body. She winces from the injuries; some I suspect I can't see. But every time I ask her if she's sure she doesn't want to go to the hospital, she nods.

"You might have fractured ribs," I tell her.

"It doesn't matter. No hospitals."

I don't push it because I've been in the same place. Same abuse. Same injuries. Same husband. A husband who was a cop. A husband who believed he was the law and I had no rights.

After we're finished with the photos, I add food, drinks, blankets, pillows to make the hiding place more comfortable in case Violet and Sophie need to hide in there for a length of time. I also give her an old flashlight Iris kept in the kitchen drawer and a bunch of old AA batteries that still have some power left.

We have no idea if any of my neighbors saw her outside, but once Violet and Sophie are reported missing, this could be one of the first places the cops search.

Because I'm Violet's friend.

It doesn't matter, though, if that's the case. One way or another, I'm going to protect Violet and her daughter. I'm going to help them start a new life, a life far from here.

I just need to figure out how I'm going to do that. And I have to make sure no one finds out they're here.

I pick up my phone from the bed and send Simone a text.

Me: Sorry, something came up. I have to cancel tomorrow

34

___

TROY

July, Present Day
Maple Ridge

I mentally curse my dislocated shoulder. And Chief Wilson. I might have enjoyed the Wilderness Warriors trip this weekend a bit more if not for them both.

And while I'm at it, I curse him some more for putting the festival in jeopardy. I still haven't come up with a plan to make up for what the loss of the Bell Automotive sponsorship has cost us. So far, the damage hasn't spread to the other sponsors. Thank Christ for that. But I still need to find a new sponsor.

Maybe I could talk to either Theresa or Katelyn and see if they can help change their old man's mind.

"That was a great trip," August says as my brothers and I load the men into the rental vans. "I'll be here next summer for sure." The twenty-nine-year-old SEAL vet has a below-the-knee amputation, but he didn't let that hold him back from

275

climbing. This was his first time doing it since losing his leg three years ago.

"Glad you enjoyed it." I hoist my daypack into the trunk of the van. It was the only thing I could carry on the trip, and it barely had anything in it. I felt like a goddamn wimp.

All I can think about during the return trip to the cabins with my group of men is how I'll be seeing Jess soon.

How I'll get to kiss her. Get to make her come. Get to bury myself inside her.

My brothers and I unload the vans. The vets will be leaving tomorrow morning. Tonight is our last night together as a group. Suzanne, a retired Air Force lieutenant who had at one point dreamed of opening a restaurant, is already cooking the meal. And she doesn't disappoint. The food is incredible.

I pull out my phone and text Jess.

> Me: I'm at the cabin. Will be finished here
> in about two hours. Will head to your
> place after I pick up Butterscotch from
> Katherine's

Jess doesn't reply, but she's probably busy with Simone. The two women had plans to hang out this weekend.

I put my phone away and join everyone by the campfire, where our visitors, Suzanne, and my brothers regale each other with stories about our time in the military.

It's another hour before a text from Jess finally pings on my phone.

> Jess: Sorry. Rain check? Have a
> headache. Going to bed early

> Me: Are you okay? Maybe I should come
> over to check on you

> Jess: No. I'll be fine. Nothing a little sleep
> won't cure. See you at work tomorrow

> Me: See you tomorrow. Hope you feel
> better soon

I bounce my fingers against my thigh, restlessness growing inside me. It's only been two days since I last saw her, but I miss her.

"Bad news?" Garrett asks me.

"Huh?"

"You're looking like a grumpy bear. I figured you got some bad news."

I smirk and still my fingers. "Grumpy bear?" I put my phone back into my shorts pocket. "No, nothing major." At least I'll see Jess tomorrow. Prior to our accidents four weeks ago, we'd spent the weeknights working on her renovations. That's been temporarily put on hold. But now that I'm officially her boyfriend, I get to spend time with her without using the renovations as an excuse to see her.

I can't take her canoeing or biking like we were doing before the accidents, but we can always watch something on TV together.

Or sit by the firepit, Jess in my arms, and watch the stars and talk. Talk and get to know each other better.

And I can make things up to her after she missed the firework celebration. Because of me.

I ARRIVE AT MY OFFICE EARLY THE NEXT MORNING. JESS ISN'T here yet.

I dive into my awaiting paperwork—the part of my job I'm not a big fan of. It feels even more tedious than normal as I wait for Jess to walk through the door, my ability to concentrate at a new low.

My office door is wide open so I can hear when she arrives.

The main office door clicks open thirty minutes later as I reread a paragraph for the third time. I glance up from my computer.

Bailey and Jess enter the outer office and go to her desk.

I push out of my desk chair and walk through the doorway. "Mornin'. How's the headache?"

A smile flickers on Jess's face like a match flame that hasn't quite caught hold of the kindling. "It's much better, thanks."

"You sure? You seem...off."

"No, it's all good. I'm probably just a little tired. That's all."

I close the distance between us and pull her to me. "I missed you this weekend." Christ, how I've missed her.

The flame catches and her smile brightens. "I missed you too. How was the—"

My mouth is on hers, not giving her a chance to finish the question. Making up for lost time.

If Jess didn't have a strict policy against fucking on my desk or anywhere else in the office, I'd be taking a quick break and making the most of it buried inside her.

But then, kissing her had also been against her company policy, so there's always hope.

My hand goes to the nape of her neck, and I deepen the kiss. My other hand rests on the curve of her spine, and I pull her to me so not a single drop of space exists between us. A soft moan vibrates through her and burrows in me.

"Are you positive you don't want to drop your no-sex-at-work policy?" My lips curve into a lecherous grin.

She laughs, the sweet sound going straight to my cock. "Absolutely positive. I have a strict no-sleeping-with-the-boss policy."

"A policy you have violated more than once in the past few weeks."

"Right, which is why I have to be stricter about the no-sex-at-work policy."

I kiss her exposed neck. "Do we get to ignore the policy tonight? Your place?"

"Actually, that won't work."

"Okay, my place." I'm not sure I can survive another night without her in my arms.

She presses her teeth into her bottom lip and looks toward the window overlooking the mountains. "That won't work either. Rain check?"

Disappointment turns to dry cement in my gut. "You have something planned?" I casually ask, keeping my curiosity from scorching my words. But I can't stop feeling as though this has something to do with her past and her difficulty with trusting people—especially me after I screwed things up by going after Wilson.

"Yes," she says rather quickly.

I wait for her to elaborate but she doesn't. Not that she owes me an explanation. "How about tomorrow?"

"Tomorrow won't work either."

"Wednesday?" She can't practice yoga while her ribs heal.

"I'll have to get back to you on that."

"Alright. Let me know when you can fit me into your busy schedule." The disappointment in my gut grows heavier and heavier.

Her eyes widen, and it takes me a moment to figure out why. *Shit.* I'd meant for that to sound whatever-works-for-you casual, but it came out bitter. Broody.

"I'm sorry, Jess. I didn't mean for it to come out that way. You don't need to justify to me why you're busy. I'm glad you're not hiding at home anymore. You deserve to have a life again. It doesn't always need to include me."

Jess winces, but then smiles. "It's just a really busy week. And then you'll be gone again on the weekend. But hopefully next week won't be as bad."

"I guess that means I need to make the most of our time together while I can."

So I kiss her one more time, our tongues gliding together, but I can't shake the gut reaction that something is going on. She might be returning my kiss, but she's also pulling away from me because of what happened with Wilson.

35

JESSICA

July, Present Day
Maple Ridge

I poke my head into Troy's office. "I'll see you tomorrow." Guilt burns at the back of my throat at how I'm lying to him about not being free tonight. Just like I lied last night when I texted I had a headache.

I can't risk Troy going to my house and discovering Violet and Sophie hiding there. I want to trust him. I really do. But I can't. Not after he got himself arrested because he pissed off the chief of police, Violet's husband.

"I can give you and Bailey a ride home." Troy opens his desk drawer where he keeps his truck keys.

"That's okay. I have to go to the store first. And I'm looking forward to the bike ride home. I'll see you tomorrow." My tone is coated with an extra dose of cheery.

"Okay." He closes the drawer.

I turn to leave, Bailey by my side.

281

"Oh, Jess."

I swivel around, praying he's not planning to join me at the store. "Yes?"

Troy stands from his desk chair and walks over to me. My question is answered with a kiss that leaves my legs feeling like they no longer belong to me—in a good way. Our tongues dance my favorite tango. And for a fraction of a second, I forget why he can't come over to my house. Why I can't spend the night with him.

But then Violet's bruised face and everything she's been through, everything she'll still need to survive against, reminds me why I can't spend the night with him.

Until I figure out how to get her to safety, no one can come over to my place. And I don't feel comfortable leaving Violet and Sophie alone for longer than necessary in case they need me. Violet is hurt and might need my help with Sophie.

And I need to start working on her escape route. I won't have time for that if I stay overnight at Troy's.

Somehow, I find the will to pull away from Troy. "See you tomorrow." I maneuver my mouth into a smile and pray the truth of what I'm up to isn't graffitied on my face.

"See you tomorrow."

The sky is blue when I step outside the building, but storm clouds are gathering on the horizon.

"We need to get some groceries before we go home," I tell Bailey and bike to the store with her in the trailer.

I pick up some extra food for Violet and head for the baby aisle, rewarding Bailey as we move through the store, treating it like a regular training session. Praying that her *Service Dog in Training* vest doesn't draw unwanted attention.

I glance around, searching for anyone who might recognize me. The place is busy, but I don't see anyone I know.

I grab a package of toddler-sized diapers and hurry to the cashier. I pay for everything and head for the exit. But as I walk out, Simone enters the store. *Fuckers.* The package of diapers is too big to hide behind my back.

Her gaze drops to the package in my arms and shoots up to my face, her eyes wide. "Are you...are you pregnant?"

I swear she says it loud enough for everyone in the store to hear, although that's probably my imagination.

I laugh, but to my ears it sounds more desperate and forced than genuine. "I think it's a little early for me to buy diapers if I'm pregnant. Which I'm not. And these are way too big for a baby, especially a newborn. They're for toddlers. It's definitely too early for me to buy those. If I were pregnant." I'm babbling a train wreck of words, but I can't seem to stop.

"So why are you buying diapers?"

"They're for...a neighbor. Sh-she wanted them in case her granddaughter visits this weekend." I inwardly cringe. *Shut your mouth, Jess, before you make things worse.* "I've got to get going. Bye." I rush out of the store, not giving her a chance to ask me any more questions that will cause me to dig a deeper grave for myself, and I assist Bailey into the bike trailer.

I cover the diapers with her blanket and scan the area for signs of Chief Wilson or any other cop. Violet and Sophie have been missing for almost twenty hours.

By now, he will have filed missing persons reports. I don't think he will have filed a kidnapping complaint against Violet yet. That would cause people to wonder why she would kidnap her daughter.

Unless...unless he's been doing what my husband did prior to my attempted escape with Amelia. Planting seeds of doubt. Making his colleagues believe I was depressed. Questioning my sanity.

Those little seeds of doubt knocked me down the one time I did attempt to escape with our daughter.

Social services was brought in. I almost lost her because of that.

And then, I did lose her, even though it wasn't by my husband's design. Lost her as my daughter.

I climb onto my bike and slowly pedal home. My hypervigilance takes over, like an old friend who's always in the corner of the room, ensuring I'm safe. I keep peering over my shoulder, half expecting to find a police car tailing me.

I turn onto my street, only to discover a police cruiser slowly driving toward me. I look down at the road ahead of me, avoiding eye contact. My heart's pounding a chaotic beat, the loud rhythm echoing in my ears.

Just keep pedaling. Don't give the officer a reason to think you've done something wrong. You haven't done anything wrong. You're trying to save a woman's life.

The black and white vehicle stops, and I inadvertently glance up. The driver's window is open and the cop is looking at me. *Nothing to see here. Keep driving.*

A tremor grips my body, and I tighten my hold on the handlebars.

The officer is several years older than me, his dark hair already turning gray. Worry lines crease his brow. "Ma'am, have you seen a woman in her early thirties with a young toddler?"

I pretend to contemplate his question. "Sorry, I haven't. But I was just coming home from work." I don't bother to mention I was at the grocery store. The less he knows about my activities the better.

"If you do see her, please contact nine-one-one."

"Is there any woman in particular you're looking for? Or are you looking for any women in their early thirties with a young toddler?" I have no clue how many women in Maple Ridge fit that description.

"It's Violet Wilson. The chief of police's wife."

I widen my eyes and infuse fear into my tone—which isn't too difficult given I'm already there, but for different reasons than the officer is thinking. "Is she okay? Is she missing?"

"I can't say. Do you know her?"

I'm about to deny I know her but change my mind. It wouldn't take much for the officer to discover the truth. "A little. She was in my yoga class until she quit." More like, until her husband forced her to quit going to yoga.

"And you haven't seen her after that?"

"Other than when I ran into her the other day at the park, no, I haven't seen her since she quit yoga."

"Do you know any place she might go?"

Again, I pretend to think about his question, looking at the sky in case the answer is there. An answer that will satisfy him and cause him to keep driving. At some point—if he hasn't yet —he's going to notice I'm shaking and wonder why. "We...we talked mostly about yoga. So I really have no idea where she might've gone."

He nods. "Okay. Thank you." He drives past me, and it takes all my willpower not to collapse.

I want to stand still and wait for my body to stop trembling and for my heart rate to return to normal before moving on. But that's not normal behavior for someone who just answered a cop's questions and has nothing to hide.

I pedal home and continue up the driveway to the garden gate. I can't tell if my neighbors are in their kitchen and can see me, but there doesn't seem to be signs of life there.

I open the gate, the rusty hinges squeaking louder than normal, and wheel the bike and trailer into my yard. I take them to the door and unzip the trailer cover. Bailey waits for the command that she can get out and jumps over the edge of the opening. She sniffs the ground.

I remove her vest, signaling that her training is over for the day. Then I unlock the door and go inside.

A cavernous silence surrounds me. My breath stalls, and for a heartbeat, I wonder if something happened and Violet and

Sophie are no longer here. But the alarm is still activated, which goes a long way in reassuring me.

I enter the code so the security company doesn't think someone is breaking into my house and go back outside. I remove the groceries and diapers from the trailer, take them into the house, and put them on the kitchen counter. I put the bike in the garage and bring Bailey inside the house.

I walk through the downstairs. It's exactly as I left it. The place isn't toddler friendly, but the tools Troy and I were using for the renovations are in the garage or in his truck, waiting until we can resume the project.

"Bailey, heel." I walk up the stairs, Bailey by my side, and enter the guest bedroom. The naked window faces the street.

Would it look suspicious if I rehung the curtains and closed them? I hadn't shut them at any point before taking them down, but perhaps that doesn't matter. My neighbors might not even notice if I suddenly start closing the curtains in the evening.

Maybe I should rehang them tomorrow. If someone notices the curtains are in the window again, they might just think I changed my mind about getting new ones.

Violet is curled up on the pink bedding with Sophie next to her. Both are asleep.

Sophie stirs, and her eyes sleepily blink open. She rolls onto her side, sits upright, and begins babbling. Her small purple octopus and floppy lamb lie next to her. She grabs the octopus while still babbling to me.

Not wanting her to wake Violet, who looked exhausted when I left for work this morning, I press my finger to my lips and gently scoop Sophie into my arms. She smells like baby shampoo and childhood dreams. She smells like Amelia did at that age.

I close my eyes, pretending for a second that she is Amelia.

"What time is it?" Violet's sleepy voice asks from the bed, and I open my eyes.

"It's after five. Did you get much sleep?"

She pushes herself to sit on the bed and puts her feet on the floor. "A few minutes. I must have dozed off. How was work?"

It's such a simple question that for a heartbeat, it's easy to forget our dangerous situation.

"Ma. Ma," Sophie says and resumes babbling.

I place her next to Violet on the bed, deliberating how much to tell Violet about what happened on my way home.

Sophie uses her mother's arm to pull herself to her feet.

Violet kisses her on the top of her head. "Hey, sweetheart. Did you have a good nap?"

Sophie just grins at her.

"He's looking for you," I say, not wanting to interrupt the peaceful moment, but she needs to know what's going on. "I was biking home and a cop asked me if I had seen a woman in her early thirties with a young toddler."

Violet nods, not at all surprised. How long was her husband searching for her before getting the police involved? How many lies has he told over the past few months or years to get the department on his side should Violet attempt to escape him?

I don't doubt he's as evil and conniving as my husband was.

"Why did someone want to kill your husband?" Violet's tone is soft, and she catches me off guard with the slight change in topic.

"I really don't know." I sit on the bed, Sophie between us.

"Maybe someone suspected he was hurting you and killed him?"

"A vigilante? It's possible, but highly unlikely. I was set up to make it look like a murder-suicide. Except I was the one who unknowingly took the drugs. And after my arrest, the idea I was an abused wife seemed to be a shock to everyone who knew my husband and me. On the outside, we appeared to be the perfect couple. None of his friends and their girlfriends or wives bothered to get to know me enough to see the cracks in the shiny surface."

Or more likely, his friends knew not to get too close to me. His possessive streak scared them away.

"And he chased my friends away during the early part of our marriage," I say, "except I didn't clue in at the time that's what was happening. I just thought we were drifting apart because I was married and they weren't." Perhaps that was true to an extent, but there was also more to it than that.

"He didn't talk much about work." I lift my shoulders in a quick shrug. "He was a cop, so I'm sure there were plenty of people who didn't like him. But he was a regular beat cop. He wasn't investigating a crime ring. He wanted to be a vice cop, but he had been passed over for that promotion more than once."

And I witnessed firsthand how angry he'd been about that.

"So, he didn't have a list of enemies like some cops might?" Violet asks.

"Exactly. And that's also what the prosecution claimed. He was well liked. Why would anyone want him dead?" I shrug. "They clearly didn't know the man the way I did."

"You're lucky. You could start your life over without having to worry that your husband's hunting you down." She shudders at her new reality.

I put my arm around her, telling her it will be okay, even though I can't find it in myself to put words to the lie. I don't know if she'll be okay. I don't know if any of us will be okay. If we're caught, I'll be charged as an accomplice to kidnapping a child.

"That might be true," I tell her, "but I also don't want anyone to know my real name. I don't want the media knowing where to find me. And I..." I swallow the rest of my words, their taste bitter. Because it's ultimately something Violet must be thinking. We don't want anyone wondering why we stayed with our husbands for so long. Wondering why, if they were really abusing us, we didn't just leave.

She nods and covers my hand on my lap with hers.

"I don't want people to see me for my past. To judge me for something I had no control over," I whisper through a dry throat. "I've been careful to cover my tracks. Fake ID. Change of hair color. Moving to a small town. Keeping off social media."

"What about your banking information?" Violet asks, her face beyond pale. It's a good thing she's sitting. Sophie, on the other hand, is growing restless and squirms out of her mom's arms and crawls onto the bed.

"Someone set that up for me, but they had connections." And I'm not sure they would help me when it comes to Violet. Not when there's a child involved like there is in this situation.

Violet deflates at that. "I don't even know how to get a fake ID."

"I know someone who might be able to help." But that means telling Kellan what I'm up to. I trust him. But do I trust he won't tell Troy? "We might need to hold out a few days, though. If we're lucky, your husband will think you've left town. Does anyone know you were coming to see me yesterday?"

"No. The only way anyone would know I'm here is if they saw me. But I was careful to make sure no one did."

"That's good." I glance down at Sophie, who's looking out the window at the bird in the nearby tree. No one on the street or in the houses across from us can see us where we're sitting. "I bought Sophie some diapers and Cheerios. I didn't see anyone in the store who I recognized, so no one can connect me to your disappearance." I'm sure Simone won't say anything. She believed my lie about the diapers. I would order them online, but I don't want to risk the boxes being left on my front porch for everyone to see. "And I'm going to check into women's emergency shelters in the area that might be able to help you. And then we'll figure out how to get you into one." The tricky part will be Sophie. Her husband still has the right to see his daughter. That will need to change. "Did anyone else see your injuries?"

Her eyes fill with the same shame I felt due to my husband's abuse. "No. I was scared what would happen if anyone did. There would be consequences. For me."

So other than the photos I've taken, it will be his word versus Violet's. Unless I can get her help before they heal.

"Do you know any family lawyers you can contact?"

"Lawyers?" The word falls out battered and bruised and defeated.

"You're going to need someone who knows the legal system and who can help you."

"I don't know anyone. I can't even afford a lawyer."

I squeeze her hand. "Give me a day or two, and I'll see what I can figure out."

Sophie loses her grip on Violet's arm and sits down hard on the bed. She cries out, the high-pitched noise either a protest or demand.

The doorbell rings downstairs. Violet's spine straightens and her muscles turn rigid.

"It's probably just Delores," I tell her. "She drops by unannounced all the time." I stand and walk over to the window.

A police cruiser is parked in front of my house, and my body turns cold. Cold enough to refreeze the polar caps. The red and blue lights aren't on. From where I'm standing, it's impossible to see who's at my front door. But I know...know without a sliver of doubt whoever was in the vehicle rang the doorbell.

"It's the cops!" I barely push the warning through my tightening throat.

36

ANGELIQUE

July 1943
France

"Are you ready for this?" Johann asks, and his eyes linger on my hand, almost as if he's caressing it with his gaze. It's much safer than a real touch the driver might witness.

"Yes," I reply, a slight breathlessness to my voice, the same way it's been every time Johann's looked at me since we became lovers two weeks ago. "Just like we practised."

The past fortnight has involved many rehearsals for tonight —many tips on ways to behave, what to expect...and many occasions of indulging in his touch.

My stomach clenches as the black car we're in approaches the Ritz Hotel in Paris. Johann and I arrived in the city yesterday for the ball that takes place this evening, and I have not been able to shake the feeling I'm being watched.

The driver stops the car in front of the main entrance and

291

opens the door for Johann. Johann climbs out in his full-dress uniform that looks wrong on him. It is one he does not belong in, but the people here tonight have to believe he does.

I focus on the man I love and not on what the grey uniform stands for. He assists me from the back seat. The hem of my green silk gown swishes just above the ground. He offers me his arm, and we walk towards the entrance under the watchful eye of several soldiers.

I draw in a slow breath. *You've been trained for this.*

Perhaps not so much the part where I'll be socialising with some of Paris's elite in hopes of learning something that could benefit Baker Street. My SOE training did not prepare me for that, but I will get to draw on my experience of being the daughter of a former diplomat. I had attended a few soirees while my mother was alive.

At the same time, I need to remember in the Germans' eyes I'm a simple French widow who spends her days helping her father in the vineyard.

We enter the ballroom, and Johann leads me to a couple I don't recognise. Like Johann and several other men here, the officer is in full military dress uniform. His medals gleam in the light from the grand chandeliers above our heads.

The woman by his side is tall and slender, her blond hair pulled back in a chignon. She raises a delicate hand to touch the diamond pendant above the neckline of her haute couture dress.

They all salute each other to a round of "Heil Hitler." I repeat the words, and a piece of me dies. But if I refuse to say them, my actions could bring to question Johann's loyalty to the *füehrer* and cause me some undesired attention.

"Helene, this is Captain Schmidt," the man who I believe to be General von der Osten says to the woman in crisp German. "Captain Schmidt, may I introduce you to my wife, Helene von Rundstedt."

Johann gives her a curt nod. "It's a pleasure to meet you, Frau von Rundstedt," he responds in German. "And this is Madame Angelique D'Aboville." My introduction is made in French.

Helene smiles, the subtle curve of her lips polite and seemingly genuine. "*Bonjour*, it is nice to meet you, Angelique." Her heavily German-accented French is practiced if not a little stilted. Her gaze sweeps down my simple gown of green silk and the black gloves that end a few inches below my elbow. "Your dress is lovely, dear."

"Thank you. Yours is too."

"Do you speak German?" she asks.

"I'm afraid not."

Disappointment flickers on her face, and her expression settles once more into a polite smile. "That is too bad. My French is not very good."

"Don't worry yourself with this one," her husband tells her in German. "There are plenty of women here with whom you would do well to get acquainted with."

"You're right," she says on a put-off sigh. "Hopefully Herr Hitler bans French so they're forced to speak German in this country."

I'm certain the majority of France would have something to say about that.

I listen to a rather dull conversation between von der Osten and Johann on the topic of Parisian theatre, while I pretend I have no idea what they're talking about. Helene listens with great interest, interjecting her own opinion now and then. I get the sense she's an intelligent woman and possibly dangerous to both France and England. I suspect she has her husband's ear when it comes to politics.

I smile pleasantly, as though I'm not wishing they would move onto a topic that will be of interest to Baker Street and the resistance networks throughout France.

Several other officers join our group. Johann introduces me to them in French. But even so, they choose to converse in German. A few of them attempt to talk to me in French but quickly grow bored of speaking in a language in which they are not fluent.

Major Müller joins the group. "I have received word the battalion will be transferred to the Eastern Front in a matter of months," he proclaims at one point, chest puffed out like it's an honour to be fighting the Russians. It is not a sentiment I have overheard being shared in the village among other German soldiers. They seemed nervous at the prospect—much like Johann's best friend, Dieter, had been before he attempted to desert the Army.

Johann doesn't seem particularly excited at the news. He doesn't say anything, but his quiet reserve isn't missed by me.

The conversation shifts to the Jews who have been rounded up in Paris and sent to various labor camps in France.

"I can't believe those creatures were allowed to run around the country like rats," Helene says. "Herr Hitler did the right thing getting rid of them."

Johann stiffens next to me. His reaction is not enough to alert the group he does not agree with her anti-Semitic attitude, but it is enough for me to know he's struggling not to say anything to contradict her. The rest of the group agrees with her, the zeal of their voices ranging from a hearty agreement to something more boisterous. That has Helene smiling, clearly satisfied by their responses.

After a few minutes of additional chatter about other groups she feels are beneath her, Helene and von der Osten excuse themselves to talk to another couple.

"Are you enjoying yourself, Madame D'Aboville?" Müller asks the question in French, but the curl of his mouth on his otherwise bland face warns me he plans to play with me like a cat with a canary.

"Very much so. Thank you, Major."

"I don't suppose you would care to dance with me while Captain Schmidt speaks with Captain von Kubizek?" He gives Johann a look that says neither Johann nor I have a choice in the matter.

I take Müller's proffered hand and let him lead me around the dance floor in a waltz. My back is stiff, letting him believe I fear him. I do fear them all, for what they can do to me, for what they have done to the agents who've been captured and disappeared. But this—the fear he wants me to feel—is part of his game.

"This must be quite thrilling for you," he says in a tone sharpened to a fine point. "A huge step up from the quaint country dances you are used to."

"It has been enjoyable." It would be more enjoyable if they would discuss something useful to my role in France.

"You have ambitions, is that not true?"

I smile sweetly at him. "I do not know what you mean. Are you referring to my father's vineyard? That will pass on to my brother."

"And what about your ambitions with Captain Schmidt?"

I fashion my expression into that of surprise. "Captain Schmidt? I have no ambitions when it comes to the man. I am here because he asked me to attend with him." And he did that because one of the other officers during the dinner he hosted at Jacques's farmhouse had been vying to bring me, more out of amusement than for any other reason.

Müller eyes me thoughtfully as we glide along the dance floor. "Captain Schmidt has the ability to rise further in the ranks. Do you see yourself by his side when he does?"

"It's not something I have thought about." I glance to where Johann is talking to several officers of higher rank. More than anything, I want to be by his side, but not for the reasons Müller thinks. I have no ambitions, even within the SOE organisation. I'm just trying to survive the war like everyone else and to bring it to a swift end, with England on the winning side. And to see my sister again.

"You're an intriguing woman, Madame D'Aboville."

"I'll take that as a compliment."

"As you should."

The dance thankfully comes to an end, and I make my way over to Johann. He smiles at me and introduces me to the group. When I am asked if I speak German, I tell them I do not, and they resume their conversation in the language.

And I go back to resembling a bouquet of flowers on the side table—beautiful but barely noticed when one walks past them.

"We need to get more French citizens to turn on these rebels," a tall officer with grey hair says. "Make it clear that if they remain silent about individuals they suspect are members of the group, that is a form of collaboration and will not be tolerated. Anyone suspected of collaborating with the enemy will be sentenced to death. Anyone who turns in a suspected rebel will be rewarded."

"We've been doing that," another officer replies curtly.

"Apparently, you have not been doing it enough. And you need to find ways to infiltrate their networks. Their leaders are arrogant and foolish. Use that to your advantage." The grey-haired man looks around the room, perhaps checking no wait-staff is nearby before he lowers his voice. "I've received word from intelligence that one of the Gestapo agents has convinced a member of the rebels that he's on their side."

"Madam D'Aboville, would you like to join us for a stroll in Le Grand Jardin?" one of the wives asks in French.

I do my best to keep one ear on the other conversation while responding, "Thank you for the offer, but I think I will stay here with Captain Schmidt."

"...don't realise the agent is Gestapo," the grey-haired man continues. "He has convinced Monsieur Baudelaire to deliver to the agent for safe keeping the weapons and explosives that England sent them. But instead of a safe handoff like the rebels will be expecting, the Gestapo will make arrests and confiscate the enemy's stash of weapons."

My pulse thunders. This—this is exactly the sort of tipoff we need. It could save so many lives.

The two wives murmur to their husbands. The men nod, but their attention seems to be less on the women and more on the conversation at hand.

The women walk off towards the French doors, laughing between themselves, while the men ask the grey-haired man questions. And I remain the bouquet on the side table, long forgotten and deemed insignificant by the men, absorbing everything they say.

Johann is quiet through the discussion, almost stiff.

The conversation shifts to something trivial about European architecture. "Would you care to dance, Angelique?" Johann asks me.

"I would like that very much." I flash him a soft smile, relieved to escape these men for a few minutes, and we step onto the dance floor.

Johann takes me into his arms, his hand on my upper back, my hand on his shoulder, and we dance the waltz. For a moment, everything else around us disappears, and it feels as though Johann and I are the only two people on the floor. I have to remind myself not to look like a woman who is in love with her dance partner, especially after my conversation with Müller. But that doesn't stop my body tingling from Johann's touch.

The evening eventually comes to an end, and he and I return to the hotel where we are staying. We don't talk in the vehicle. I just stare out the window at the barren streets.

Everyone else in Paris has to respect curfew, which began several hours ago.

Johann walks me to my room, which is connected to his. "Did you want to...?"

I nod. "I need a few minutes first to freshen up. I'll knock on the adjoining door once I'm ready."

He kisses me softly on the lips and unlocks my room door. I smile at him, the movement as soft as his kiss, and step past him. No sooner has the door clicked shut than I am rushing to the desk. I write a brief coded message for Allaire, taking care to leave no indentation on the surface beneath.

Nazis have infiltrated a resistance circuit. Baudelaire will unknowingly be handing over weapons to Gestapo. Ambush planned.

The cut-out will come to my room tomorrow to pick up the message for Allaire. In the meantime, I hide the small piece of paper in the secret compartment of my purse for safekeeping.

I quickly wash my face so as not to take too long and make Johann suspicious, and I knock on our adjoining door. I'm wearing nothing more than a robe when he enters. He no longer has on his uniform. He has changed into the trousers belonging to Jacques's son. His bare muscular chest and stomach are on display for me to appreciate, and I'm relieved he took the time to remove all reminders of the entrapments that have nothing to do with the man beneath.

He enters my room and pulls me into an embrace. I allow myself to relax into him. But even then, uncertainty still lingers as to whether Allaire will be able to change the course of events the Germans have planned. Will he get the message in time and be able to convince Baudelaire he is in danger? Egos are growing bigger every day, and some men think they have things under control when they do not. They end up believing they know better and ignore orders from their leader within the resistance group. I have heard of that happening more than once since I arrived in France.

"I'm sorry you had a boring time tonight." Johann kisses my temple.

"You didn't know they were only going to speak German. I suppose in time they will expect us all to speak it, and German will become France's official language."

"I hope not, but I suspect you are right."

"Did you have a good time at least? It looked like you were involved with some pretty intense conversations."

Johann releases me. "Most of them were boring and politically based. Everyone wants power, and they don't care how they achieve it."

I cock my head to the side. "Is that why politics doesn't interest you?"

He holds up his hands. "These were made for designing things to make the world a better place. They weren't meant for me to climb the political ladder."

"How is it you're a captain if you aren't interested in climbing the political ladder? I know nothing about the military, but isn't that what it's all about when you're aiming to advance in your rank?"

He leans in so his mouth is against the shell of my ear. "In my case, it was about being good at what I do and about staying alive." His gravelly, low voice sends a shiver of need through me. "And if the Nazis believe I'm on their side, I have a better chance of surviving this war." His mouth coasts along my cheek, his warm breath fanning my skin. "If I hadn't been captain, I would not have been able to stay with you and Monsieur Gauthier. My rank gave me that option. And it was one I chose to exercise, if only to give me a sliver of peace for a few minutes a day from the horrors I've seen and the choices

I've had to make." His voice, although still strong, splinters a tiny bit.

"It will be that way for so many people," I say. "Innocent people who have lost their lives or their families. Boys who have been forced to grow up too quickly and become men. Children who will grow up without a father. Orphans who have lost everything."

My grandfather told me when he was still alive about how men returned from the Great War a shell of the person they had once been. They had gone crazy and had to be locked away in an asylum. And those who hadn't been locked away relied on alcohol and opioids to numb the memories.

No one comes home a winner in war—especially from a war started by a madman.

I embrace Johann in what I can only hope is comfort. Neither of us will come out of this war in one piece. I've witnessed things like he has that I would rather forget. My actions have resulted in the deaths of others, even though it wasn't intentional. And I doubt the nightmares will ever fully go away.

"Can we not talk about this for now?" he asks. "I just want to hold you and make the most of this time we have together before my unit is sent away."

"What do you mean?" An unexpected slither of dread leaves my chest feeling heavy and tight. "Where are they sending you?"

"Nowhere yet. But there is talk we will be sent to the Eastern Front in a few months. Even the engineers." His look confirms he doesn't want to discuss it. So, I let him do the one thing he is happy doing—I let him kiss me.

Our lips move together, and we sink onto the bed.

37

TROY

July, Present Day
Maple Ridge

Monday afternoon, I tie Butterscotch's leash to the bike rack outside of Picnic & Treats. He plunks himself down in the small patch of sun on the sidewalk. "I won't be long," I tell him and scratch him behind his ear. "Promise."

"Hey, Boss."

I stand in time to see Lance leave the café with Ethan, the newest member of the Maple Ridge Search and Rescue team. "How's the job site going?" I ask Lance.

"Good. We're more than ready for you to come and inspect the work so far."

"That was my goal for today, but I was catching up on paperwork. I'll be there tomorrow morning. Bright and early."

Lance chuckles. "That's why I never want your job. I hate

301

paperwork. Have you met Ethan Philips?" He directs a chin nod at the man.

"I have. We've worked together a few times locating lost hikers." I didn't realize Lance knew him. Ethan has only lived in Maple Ridge since the beginning of the year. "Good to see you again."

Ethan gives a single nod. "You too, Troy."

I say goodbye to them and enter Picnic & Treats. Zara isn't working the counter, so I text her. She replies she's in the staff room and for me to come on back.

She's sitting on the couch when I enter, her paperwork spread out on the large coffee table in front of her.

She stretches her arms above her head and tilts to the left, lengthening the other side of her body. "Hey, what's up?"

"I came by to get Jess's favorite dessert to drop off at her house. Thought I'd come to say hi while I was at it."

Zara tilts to the other side. "Wow, you have it pretty bad for her, don't you?"

I drop into one of the armchairs. "Because I'm bringing her dessert?" I'm not about to admit to Zara the dessert is my excuse to see Jess outside of work, even if it's for only a few minutes.

Zara lowers her arms. "What exactly are you hoping to happen between you and Jess?"

The question comes out of nowhere and isn't one I was expecting or prepared for. "We're still getting to know each other. We're taking things slow." Until Jess fully trusts me, that's about all we can do after everything she's been through.

Zara eyes me speculatively. "You know, between you and your brothers, you're the only one I thought would get married."

The corner of my mouth lifts into a smirk. "And because Lucas got married, you think we've met the Carson brother marriage quota?"

"No. But if you're hoping to one day get married and have children, Jess isn't going to be that woman."

"Aren't you jumping things a little? Jess and I are just dating. You can date without the whole marriage thing thrown into the mix."

"True. But it's always helpful if you know early in the relationship the other person's long-term relationship goals. If you want to one day settle down and the woman doesn't, it's better to find this out early before you waste too much time on a relationship that will go nowhere."

"How do you know Jess doesn't want to get married?"

"The topic came up about a week and a half ago when we were talking to Simone, Em, and Avery."

Fair enough. "Okay, so she doesn't want to get married. That doesn't mean I'm going to dump her because our long-term plans don't match. I'm not looking to rush off and get married. And my life won't be over if I don't tie the knot." Jess did mention well before she and I became involved that she wasn't interested in settling down or having a family. I can't say I blame her after what happened with her first marriage. Part of her must be terrified of it happening again.

"And your parents won't be disappointed if they never get to be grandparents?"

"Lucas and Simone might decide to adopt," I point out. "I wouldn't rule them out yet."

"Alright, as long as you know what you're getting into with Jess."

And there's the zinger. The real reason for Zara's questions. I don't know how much she knows about Jess's past, and I'm not about to ask her in case she knows nothing. "I knew what I was getting into when I first witnessed her have a flashback. I knew something bad had happened to her. I didn't want her to go through what Lucas did. And that's why I'm paying for her therapy. So yeah, I know what I'm getting into with Jess."

Zara slants me a look that's more unsettling than an unexploded land mine. "You mean your company insurance is paying for her therapy."

I don't respond. Lying to Zara is never a good idea as eleven-year-old me learned the hard way.

Her eyes widen with an *Oh, shit.* "Does she know you're paying for it?" Zara's cutting tone warns she already knows the answer. "Crap, Troy. I thought you had switched it to your company policy."

"I haven't figured out how to do that without telling her the truth." That I've been paying for her therapy because I hadn't wanted the cost to be a deterrent for Jess to get help. But that was before she got the restitution payment—something Zara doesn't know about.

And after Jess received the payment? I didn't know how to bring up the truth without upsetting her, because then I'd have to admit I hadn't been totally honest with her.

"So you're going to keep lying to her? You lied about Bailey, telling her she was training Bailey for someone else when Bailey was hers from the get-go."

My muscles tighten the way they did when I was a Marine and we were preparing to go into battle. "Your point being?"

"My point being, she wasn't happy when she found out you lied about that. What's gonna happen when she finds out you've been paying for her therapy?"

"She's not going to." The dark look I level at Zara says it all and then some. "Is she?"

"I won't lie to her, Troy."

"I'm not asking you to lie. I'm asking you to keep this to yourself."

Zara grunts and crosses her arms tightly in front of her, her own battle pose. "That's still lying."

"Doesn't matter. I'm doing it for her own good."

Zara mutters something I don't fully catch beyond *Idiot*

alpha men. "You're playing with a grenade, Troy. And I'm sure you know the dangers of that."

"This is different. No one's getting hurt."

She shakes her head, and I know she's back to thinking *Idiot alpha men* again. "God, Troy. I hope you're right. I *really* hope you're right."

38

JESSICA

July, Present Day
Maple Ridge

"It's the cops!" I tell Violet, my voice a hoarse whisper. I can't see from where I'm standing at the bedroom window, but I'm positive that's who rang my doorbell. My voice is low and cracked, my words squeezing past the rapidly beating heart jammed in my throat. "You and Sophie need to stay in the secret room until I tell you the coast is clear. But we should use a special code phrase. How about, 'Monkeys eat peanut butter sandwiches'? Don't open the door unless you hear me say that. Okay?"

Violet nods, blood drained from her face.

Grinning, Sophie pushes away from Violet, her legs wobbly on the mattress. "Key. Key. Key," she says, possibly trying to imitate *monkey*. She loses her balance, lands on her butt, and lets out a disgruntled shriek.

No, no, no, no. I grab her floppy lamb, hoping it will keep her quiet, and hand it to her. That seems to be enough to distract her from screaming. I quickly help them into the hiding space and close the door behind them. I shut the closet door and hurry downstairs as the doorbell chimes again. Bailey comes with me.

I check through the peephole, praying it's Delores and not a cop who's ringing the doorbell. My prayer is not answered. It's a cop, just not the same one I saw while biking home. He's about Troy's age, mid-thirties. The cop and my husband look nothing alike, but that doesn't dampen the rush of fear assaulting me.

"I'm turning off the alarm," I call out, my heartbeat not slowing the slightest, and turn to the code box on the wall. My hands shake as I punch in the numbers on it, and I accidentally hit five instead of six. *Focus.*

I get the code correct on the next attempt. "Sit," I tell Bailey. She does as she's told, and I unlock the door and open it. "S-sorry, I was in the washroom." My hand tightens on the doorknob.

His gaze instantly moves to Bailey, and his eyes narrow marginally. "Get your dog away from the door." The dropped-volume command in his tone sends another wave of fear clawing at my skin.

"Sh-she's training to be my service dog. She needs to stay by my side." I have no idea what the normal protocol is in situations like this, but I don't want to be without her.

"Then she needs to be on a leash."

Well, if you'd given me more notice...

"Okay, give me a second." I close the door and contemplate leaving it shut.

I glance upstairs, silently pleading for Sophie not to shriek or for either her or Violet to make noise. So far, it's quiet.

I click Bailey's leash onto her collar and take a quick moment to hug her. The cop doesn't seem patient enough to wait for me to put Bailey's training vest on her. "It's going to be okay. It's going to be okay." I repeat the words slowly and softly to myself a few more times and straighten to my feet.

I open the door again. Bailey remains sitting by my feet. My hands are no less shaky than before.

"Do you live in this house?" The cop's appearance might be nothing like my husband's, but his voice is the same block of ice.

"Yes. I-is something wrong?" My gaze wants to check over his shoulder to see if my neighbors are watching. But he's big and bulky and I can't see past him.

He studies me for a fraction of a second. It's long enough to send my pulse thundering in my ears and it feels like my heart is attempting to burst out of my chest.

Think about Amelia. I imagine her running through the San Diego waves, giggling. I skip and dance alongside her, laughing and enjoying our temporary freedom. The scent of coconut sunscreen mingles with the salty breeze.

It works. Slightly. My pulse still pounds in my ears, but it's slower and quieter than a moment ago. The trembling remains the same.

"I'm looking for a missing woman and her seventeen-month-old daughter. They were last seen yesterday around noon. Have you seen them?" He shows me a recent photo of Violet and Sophie on his phone. Violet is smiling, but there's an emptiness in her eyes that tells me the smile is fake. For the camera's benefit.

It's a look that screams for help. That begs for someone to release her from her own private hell. It's not the kind of photo you would expect to be shown when looking for a missing person.

Or...her husband is using the photo for his benefit, setting Violet up for the biggest fall of her life. *Clearly, she's not mentally stable, your honor. My wife shouldn't be allowed custody of our daughter.*

I nod, unable to take my eyes off the picture, unwilling to let the officer peer into them. "That's Violet Wilson. She used to be in my yoga class."

He lowers his phone, not giving me a choice but to look up at him. "Have you seen her since then?" he asks.

"This is a small town. I bump into her at the store from time to time."

"Did you see her yesterday?"

"No." *Please tell me no one saw her coming here. Please tell me—*

"Is there any reason you're nervous?"

"N-no." I fight the urge to rub my clammy hands on my thighs.

"Is there a problem, Officer?"

Troy. He's carrying a white box with the Picnic & Treats logo on it.

What's he doing here? I didn't see him walk up the path leading to my front door, but here he is. *Thank God.*

The cop pivots. "Hey, Troy. What are you doing here?" His voice is friendlier than it has been the entire time he's been talking to me.

"Hey, Roy. I came to see my girlfriend." Troy nods at me, his expression somewhat relaxed, but not as relaxed as it normally would be. His gaze remains on the cop.

"Have you seen Violet Wilson and Chief Wilson's daughter, Sophie?"

"Not for a few days. Why?"

"They're missing. They haven't been seen since yesterday." Roy's voice is even, but not even enough to mask his concern at their disappearance.

Troy's brow creases into a slight frown. "Maybe they're visiting relatives."

"They haven't seen her or heard from her in the past few months."

God, her family must be freaking out of their minds right

now. They have no idea where Violet and Sophie are. The less they know about her disappearance, the better. Then they are less likely to accidentally give anything away to the authorities.

"Does Chief Wilson think they've been kidnapped?" Troy asks.

If Wilson suspects that's the case, why hasn't the police department issued an Amber Alert? Even if they have reason to believe his wife has kidnapped his daughter, he should be issuing the alarm.

"That's one scenario we're investigating." The cop's attention shifts back to me. "Now, will you explain why you're so nervous?"

My throat tightens, blocking the words I don't want to say.

"She was raped out east by someone pretending to be a cop." Troy says it so smoothly, I almost believe him myself. He steps past the cop to place his free arm around me, and I sink into his comforting touch. "She has PTSD and can't differentiate between a genuine cop in uniform and someone who is faking being one. To Jessica, you're all the same."

The cop looks at me for confirmation, and I nod, unable to do more than that. His expression softens. "Sorry you went through that."

"Thank you." The words push out in a dry croak.

"If you see Violet Wilson or her daughter, please contact nine-one-one."

Both Troy and I tell him we will. The cop walks down the path to the sidewalk and moves on to the next house. He's gone, but my body won't stop shaking.

Troy rests his hand on the curve of my spine. "Let's get you into the house."

Panic resurges in me. *No. No. No.* The last thing I need is Troy coming inside. "I'll be fine, Troy. I'm tired. I think I'll just go to bed early." I fake-yawn, cementing fiction to fact.

Something flickers on his face, but he smooths out his

expression before I can get a firm grasp on it. "I thought you had plans tonight."

"I do, b-but I'm going to cancel. Thank you for telling him what you did. About the cop." Troy's quick thinking saved me from having to create another lie. And what Troy said wasn't completely off the mark. I was raped by a cop. I was just married to him at the time.

"You're welcome. I brought you this." He hands me the white box. "It's your favorite."

Guilt pummels my insides and my stomach churns at the lies I'm being forced to tell. To my friends. To Troy. To the people who are supposed to keep everyone safe.

"Thank you." Smiling, I reach up and kiss him.

It was supposed to be a brief kiss. An I'll-see-you-later kiss.

Troy has something else in mind. He deepens it, and every part of me tingles with need. I don't want to stop kissing him. I want to crawl inside him. To feel safe. But as much as I want to drag him into the house and spend the evening wrapped in his arms, I can't.

I pull away. "Bye." I step inside the house and shut the door before he can say anything else.

Closing my eyes, I lean back against the wall and wait for my stomach to settle. The past few minutes play out in my mind, and my stomach churns again, only this time with the threat that I'm going to hurl.

I put the box on the hall table, race upstairs, and make it to the bathroom just in time. I heave into the toilet, my body shaking from the crash of adrenaline and all the lies burying me alive. Tears wet my face.

Once the heaving is finished, I stagger to my feet, splash cold water on my face, and brush my teeth. *God, what am I doing?*

I take several long, slow breaths, and once I've collected

myself, I leave the bathroom and walk toward the guest bedroom.

I change my mind at the last second and make a quick detour to my room.

I remove the envelope from the wooden box hidden in my closet and pull out the photos of Amelia. The baby picture. The photo of when she was a toddler. The photo of when she was five years old and drawing a picture with crayons.

I trace her sweet face in each photo. "This is why I'm hiding them," I whisper, the words barely more than the movement of my lips as I stare at the photos. "This is why I'm risking everything to save Violet and Sophie."

Why I'm risking my freedom and the chance to see my daughter again. If Violet and Sophie are found here, I'll be charged with aiding and abetting. Craig and Grace will definitely not let me see Amelia then. And even before that, the cops might scrutinize me since I know Violet, and eventually they'll recognize me as Savannah. My past identity could be leaked to the public. And then how will people see me: as a victim, a survivor, or a dangerous ex-con?

But despite all I'm risking...I can't let her husband win.

39

JESSICA

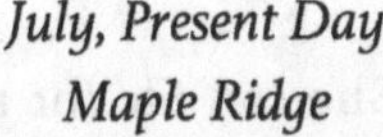

July, Present Day
Maple Ridge

"Hello," I say to the woman on the other end of the phone. Violet is sitting next to me on the bed, playing with Sophie. The early evening sunlight streams through the window, the recently replaced curtains open since no one can see us from the street when we're sitting on the bed.

"I have a friend whose husband physically abuses her, and she and her toddler need a safe place to go to rebuild their lives," I tell the woman.

It's the tenth call I've made in the past four days to a women's emergency shelter.

"Is she still living with him?" The woman's tone is warm and compassionate. Like it has been for those nine other calls I've made to the various shelters.

"No, she's currently staying with me, but it's not safe

313

enough." Patrol cars have been driving down the street several times a day since Violet disappeared with Sophie. Thank God they don't have radio-seeking equipment like the Gestapo used.

I don't think they do. I'm not exactly up-to-date on the latest surveillance equipment.

"Unfortunately, our shelter is full. Have you tried...?" She lists a place I've already called.

And the hope I've been desperately clinging to disintegrates. "They're full too," I say, even though it won't change anything.

"There's not enough funding and too many women who need to be placed. Has she filed a report with the police? She'll need that if she plans to apply for full custody of her child." This isn't the first time I've been told this.

"It's complicated."

"Hun, it always is. She can file for a restraining order. But that doesn't always work. Abusers often ignore the orders. How long has your friend and her daughter been staying with you?"

My body freezes at the question, frigid water pumping through my veins. Does she know it's Violet? Can they trace the call?

Am I putting Violet and Sophie in danger?

Shit. Shit. Shit.

I end the call, the weight on my shoulders growing heavier with each passing day.

"Any luck?" Violet asks, optimism in her tone, though it's clear from the defeated curve of her shoulders she already knows the answer.

"No. Everywhere I've tried is at capacity."

"Even if they have a place for us, I'll still have to file assault charges against my husband, which I can't do." She releases a hard sigh. "This is hopeless. And I'm putting you in danger, Jess. If Alex figures out I'm here, he'll go after you."

"He's not going to figure it out. We just have to get you out of Oregon. And then you'll need to go underground for a while." A long while.

"I don't have enough money for that. I can guarantee my credit card has been canceled."

"I know. That's the first thing he would've done when he realized you got away. But I have money." I can give her some of the restitution money. Plus, there's the money I had put aside for the renovations. They've been put on hold anyway because of Troy's shoulder and my bruised ribs. "It's enough to help you and Sophie get a new start."

"I can't do that. You need the money too."

"You can do that, and you will. There was no one to help me escape my husband. I know how Alex's type of mind works. He'll never stop hunting for you. The harder we make it for him to find you, the better off you'll be."

A text comes through on my phone.

Zara: Are you still on for Game Night?

Now that I'm no longer avoiding Noah and I'm giving him a chance after what Avery told me, I said I would join the group for Game Night. But that was before Violet and Sophie ended up at my back door.

Me: Next week. Something came up

Okay, the shelters are out as a likely option. I'll have to take things into my own hands.

I call Kellan. *Please pick up. Please pick up.*

The phone rings a few times. "S'up?" he asks, answering.

"Are you alone?"

"I'm on my way to Zara's. You need a ride?"

"Is anyone else in the SUV with you?"

"No, it's just me."

"Can...can you swing by my place after Game Night? Alone. And you...you can't tell Troy about this call. You can't tell anyone." I squeeze my eyes shut against the pain of lying to Troy. He deserves better than this. *Lies. Lies. Lies.* My skin itches at all the lies I've been forced to tell—starting when my husband's abuse began.

But these lies will save Violet. Will prevent her from losing her daughter.

And...I could end up in prison again if something goes wrong. I'll be giving up my chance of ever seeing Amelia, of being part of her life.

I watch Violet gazing adoringly at *her* daughter. The love shining back at her polishes my steely resolve.

"I told you, Jess, I won't lie to my brother."

"I know. But this is important." I blow out a breath. "It's a matter of life and death."

THE DOORBELL RINGS, AND I LET KELLAN INTO THE HOUSE. I close the door behind him and reactivate the alarm. "Thanks for coming. There's someone I need you to see. Upstairs. But first, I need you to promise me you won't tell anyone. Like I said on the phone, it's a matter of life and death."

"I promise." Kellan says it so straightforwardly, placing his full trust in me, even though trusting people is a challenge for him. Like it is for me.

God, I hope I'm not about to destroy that faith he has in me. I value Kellan's friendship above a lot of things, but this—what I'm trying to do—is bigger than all of it.

Kellan follows me upstairs to the spare bedroom. Light spills from under the closed door. I draw in a lungful of air, praying I haven't made a big mistake bringing him here, and open the door.

Violet is on the bed with Sophie in her arms. The curtains

are closed. The bruises on her face have faded a little, but they're still hard to miss.

"Jesus Christ," Kellan mutters and looks at me for answers.

"Her husband is abusive. She escaped him but she can't get into a shelter. All the ones in the area and beyond are at maximum capacity or can't take women who aren't in their jurisdiction. She needs to get as far from Chief Wilson as possible so he can't track her down and torture her. Possibly kill her. I was hoping you could help us. She needs fake IDs."

Kellan rakes his fingers through his hair and says something under his breath I don't catch.

"I have no idea who arranged for mine," I explain. "And I have no idea how to contact the individual who helped me get out of San Diego. Can you help us?"

I don't want to involve Craig and Grace—not if I'm hoping to be allowed back in Amelia's life. This, helping Violet, might be too much as far as they're concerned. I can't take that risk.

"You realize this is kidnapping, right?"

Violet and I both nod. Sophie waves her little hand at him.

"I don't have a choice." Violet's voice is small, her tone begging for him to help them, pleading for him to understand. "I can't go back to living with him, and I can't risk him getting partial custody or any sort of visitation rights. Sophie and I need a clean break."

The Chief Wilson I saw at the Fourth of July celebrations was great with kids, but who's to say that same man won't end up hurting Sophie the way he hurts her mother?

"Where will you go?" Kellan asks.

Violet turns her gaze to me.

"I'm still figuring that out," I tell him. "Ideally on the other side of the country. The farther the better."

"Are you planning on telling Troy what you're doing?" Kellan folds his arms across his chest and levels me a look that gives me chills but doesn't dent my resolve to help Violet and Sophie.

"No. It's too risky."

"How so? He spent two tours in Afghanistan. You can't get much riskier than that."

"How about the way he handled things when he shoved Chief Wilson in the chest?" I give Kellan a pointed glance of my own that says I'm not backing down from my decision. "I'm worried he'll do something that will cause more problems for Violet. Or he could get into bigger trouble with the law than he's already in. My husband was like Chief Wilson. He liked to win. Every time. And he didn't like losing his possessions."

"So you're never going to tell him?"

I shake my head.

"He suspects something's up. He was asking everyone tonight if they know what's going on with you because you keep canceling on him." Kellan's gaze goes to Violet, and his eyes soften. "I'm guessing you're the reason for that."

Violet hugs Sophie a little tighter, and I can't shake the fear I'm adding to her feelings of guilt because I'm ignoring my friends so I can help her.

I reach for her hand, squeeze it reassuringly, and turn back to Kellan. "I can't risk anyone coming over and finding Violet and Sophie here. And they're already here alone during the day. I don't want to leave them longer than that. I know what it's like to be scared and isolated."

Kellan is silent for a long moment, his face giving nothing away. The weight of his silence presses down on my chest, makes it difficult to draw in a breath.

"I have some connections who can help with the ID," he finally says after a beat. "Any idea what state they'll end up in?"

"I'm working on that." Once I figure out how exactly I'm going to get them away from here.

"Decide where they're going, and then I'll talk to my connections."

A small amount of the weight releases from my chest. "Thanks, Kellan. I hope this doesn't cause you any problems."

He doesn't say anything, which is answer enough.

40

TROY

July, Present Day
Maple Ridge

Early Sunday evening, I drive to Jess's house after leaving the Wilderness Warriors building. Butterscotch is still with the veterans since I plan to be back in an hour or so. I need to see Jess. I need to check that she's okay. And most of all I need to kiss her. Other than when I've seen her at work, the last time we've really talked to each other was last Monday, when Roy was at her house, asking her questions about Violet Wilson.

I can't explain it, but it feels like Jess and I are back where we started when I first saw her at the lake almost four months ago. She doesn't trust me.

And she's still withholding secrets.

If she can't trust me, what kind of future can we have together?

I ring the doorbell. And wait. And wait. And wait. Bailey's barking comes from inside the house.

I press the doorbell again. This time I don't have to wait long before the door unlocks, and Jess opens it partway. But not enough for me to see past her.

An uncertain smile flickers on her face. "Hi. I didn't realize you were planning to come over."

"I wanted to make sure you're okay." My brothers and I were away last night with a group of retired vets, so I haven't seen her since Friday at work. "Can I come in?"

Her face pales, and she looks over her shoulder. She opens the door wider and steps outside, partially closing the door behind her. "This isn't a good time, Troy. Can it wait until tomorrow at work?"

Her comment takes me by surprise. "Christ, you make it sound like I'm your boss who's asking you to do something work related after hours instead of your boyfriend who wants to see you." The words come out harsher and grumpier than I'd planned, and I instantly regret them.

She winces, and several emotions flicker on her face, none I can get a firm grasp on—other than possibly guilt. "Sorry, I didn't mean it that way. But...but this really isn't a good time."

"Is it something I can help with?" I don't mean to sound like a desperate idiot, but I missed her, even though I was only gone one night.

"No. It's something I need to do on my own." Her voice hardens like she's getting impatient.

A muffled, high-pitched noise comes from inside the house. Jess's eyes widen for a fraction of a second, and she casts another worried glance over her shoulder.

I take a step forward, ready to investigate what caused the sound. "What was that?" My gaze darts up the staircase.

She puts her hand on my chest. "It was nothing. Just Bailey. Upstairs."

Bailey's nose pokes between Jess's leg and the doorjamb. The noise comes again from upstairs.

"That wasn't nothing, Jess." My Marine instincts kick in, and I make a move to push past her to investigate the sound.

She blocks me with her body, her forehead pinched into a scowl. "Troy, this isn't going to work."

I frown. "What isn't going to work?"

"You. Me. I...I don't think I can be your girlfriend anymore." She swallows. "In fact...in fact, I know I can't be your girlfriend."

My chest tightens, squeezing the air from my lungs. "You don't mean that." Shit, she'd better not mean it. She's just...she's just overreacting. About something.

Sadness flashes in her expression, so quick I wonder if I imagined it. "This. Us," she says, her voice cracking. "It's moving too fast for me, Troy. I need a break."

"A break? Already? We haven't been together all that long." *Breathe before you screw this up even more.* "I'm not your fucking late husband. You don't have to push every man away just because you're afraid they'll turn out like him."

"I don't push every man away. I haven't pushed your brothers away."

"You aren't dating my brothers!"

She flinches, and my stomach twists into a painful knot. I think back to Friday night and the past two days in the mountains. *Kellan.*

When we were kids, whenever Kellan did something that would get him in a shitload of trouble, he had a certain tell on his face I recognized. It was the same tell he wore this weekend whenever his gaze landed my way.

But I know my brother would never hook up with a girl I'm dating. So what the hell is going on between them?

"You've been distant this past week," I press on, my voice gruff. "Why?"

"I told you, I've been busy."

"Why do I get the feeling there's another secret? No matter what I do to prove you can trust me, you still keep secrets from me."

"Well, I guess I can't keep secrets from you if we're no longer dating." Anger scolds her words.

"So that's it?" Bitterness snakes its way through me, spreading its poisonous venom. "You're going to put that goddamn wall back up again?"

"I guess so." She winces and releases a hard breath. "I'll keep working for you until you can find my replacement. I...I mean unless you don't want me to come in tomorrow."

A small part of me wants to tell her not to bother to show up. But I can't do that. She needs a job, and I have no intention of being the asshole who leaves her unemployed. No one will want to hire her if they think she's a quitter. She already quit working for Zara because it was too stressful with the PTSD.

"You don't have to quit working for me. I'm not the asshole boss who fires his employee because she won't date him. We can be cordial to each other." Except my tone doesn't suggest I can be cordial, the pain in my heart stealing my ability to keep my tone neutral.

"Thanks, Troy." Her voice is a soft whisper that grips my splintering heart with sharp talons. "I'll see you tomorrow." She opens the door wider and retreats inside.

I stand on the porch for a minute, going through everything that just happened. Then I stalk to my truck, climb inside, and reverse out of the driveway onto the street.

I keep driving until I get to the cabins where Butterscotch is waiting for me. I grab a beer from the icebox by the firepit where everyone is sitting and drop my ass into an empty chair.

"How's the old woman doing?" one of the guys asks with a chuckle. "Must be pretty serious between you two, given how fast you flew out of here when we got back."

"She's fine." I chug down some beer. "It's not serious. I just wanted to check on her."

My gaze flicks to Kellan, who's suddenly fascinated with the label on his beer bottle.

"**What do you mean she quit therapy?**" I ask Robyn on the phone. Disbelief and the residual anger from what happened two nights ago simmer beneath the question. I'm standing in the hallway of the house one of my crews is currently renovating, and I can feel their curiosity burning into my back.

I haven't seen Jess in the past two days, the pain from our breakup too raw. Instead, I've avoided the office when I know she's there. And Kellan has been avoiding me—or he's been too busy to reply to my texts and phone calls.

I open the front door and step outside. The street is empty of cars and pedestrians, but the low hum of a lawn mower comes from the house several doors over. Far enough away the teen pushing it can't hear me.

"She phoned this morning and told me that while she appreciates everything I've done for her, she's ready to end our sessions." Robyn's frustration at the situation sits unguarded in her tone.

"Did she give a reason?"

"You know I can't discuss that with you. I'm only telling you this because you were paying for them."

I let my head fall back against the front door. "Can you at least tell me if it's okay that she quits the sessions?"

"No. I can't."

"Okay. You can't tell me as her therapist. But can you tell me as your friend?"

A long sigh comes through the phone line. "Alright, in my

professional opinion, no, she's not ready yet to quit seeing me. We were making progress, but she still has a ways to go."

Shit. Then why the hell did she quit?

"Did she figure out I was paying for it?"

A crow lands on the grass a few yards from where I'm standing. It caws loud enough to wake the dead in the cemetery on the other side of town.

"No. But if I were you, I'd come clean about that." Robyn's tone is not that of a therapist but as the friend who whipped my ass in soccer in middle school.

"Because she has trust issues?"

"I can't tell you that, Troy."

"How about grunting it? One grunt, she has trust issues. Two grunts, she doesn't."

Robyn groans.

"So, she does have trust issues."

"Hey, I wasn't answering the question. I was just groaning because you haven't changed since we were in school."

She can't see me, but I still grin. I always did know how to push her buttons. "I'll take that as a compliment."

She snorts.

Robyn doesn't need to tell me Jess has trust issues. It's obvious she does. "I know about the abusive husband," I tell her. "And I know she was wrongfully convicted for his murder."

"She mentioned she had told you all of that." Robyn's tone is back to professional therapist.

Great.

I can't even get a firm read on Robyn to determine if there's anything else she knows and I don't. Not on the phone. Maybe if we were meeting in person, I'd have better luck with that.

"Look, as her therapist, I can't tell you anything. But as your friend, I will tell you I'm concerned about her. I can tell she's stressed about something, and I'm worried about her mental state. She's come a long way since we've started the sessions, but she's still...she's still very fragile. I'm worried whatever is going on in her life will be too much, and she'll regress. Regress hard."

"She broke up with me on Sunday." Just saying those words is a land mine to my heart. "Whatever is stressing her caused her to end our relationship. But she won't tell me what it is." She did tell me some bullshit, but I don't buy it. There's something else going on with her. But I'm afraid of pushing the wrong buttons and losing her permanently.

"She never mentioned that to me. I really don't know what to say, Troy. She still has a long recovery ahead of her, and this will only set her back. She needs help, but she also needs to be willing to get it. And right now, it doesn't sound like that's the case."

"Is there anything I can do to help her?"

"Be her friend. If she lets you. That's all you can do for now. I have to go. I have a client. Bye, Troy." She hangs up before I can ask any more questions.

I stare at my phone for several minutes. I can't even ask Jess what the hell she's thinking quitting therapy. To do so means admitting I was the one paying for it.

How the hell am I supposed to help her now? Now that she has practically barred me from her life?

41

ANGELIQUE

July 1943
France

War ruins one's ability to sleep for long periods. Those lazy Sunday mornings, when all I want to do is sleep in, no longer exist. The nightmares, the 2 a.m. parachute drops or acts of sabotage, the bombing, the fear, all contribute to sleepless nights and waking before my body is ready.

I blink my eyes open, desperate to chase away the image in my head of the last time I saw Pierre. My heart is beating too fast. Air refuses to enter my lungs. I can't see the time on the clock on the bedside table, but I know it's early morning. Even the birds aren't up yet.

I sit upright, struggling to draw in a long breath. I rest my brow on my bent knees and hug my legs. The room is dark due to the blackout curtains, which only heightens the panic coursing through my body.

Movement next to me on the bed reminds me I'm not at home in England. I'm in a hotel room in Paris after a night of being invisible while listening to what the Nazis have planned.

I sense Johann sit upright. He gently sets his hand on the curve of my upper back. "Angelique?"

"How is it you never have nightmares?" My cracked voice fights its way through a dry mouth.

He doesn't answer right away, but even in the pain-filled silence, I know what his answer will be. "I do. All the time."

My breathing eventually evens out, and Johann coaxes me to lie down and snuggle against his warm body. He doesn't bother with empty platitudes that everything will be all right. There's no point. We both know nothing is further from the truth. I cannot even guarantee the next time he's on an exercise with his battalion, he won't be killed because of the actions of a resistance group or SOE agents.

Even if he tells me where he'll be and I know he's in danger, I cannot say anything at the risk of the Allies operation. My feelings for him change nothing.

"There's something I need to tell you." His hot breath brushes my ear, his voice a deep murmur.

"What's that?"

"There's an ambush planned against the French rebels. Their leader believes he'll be handing over a supply of weapons to another group of rebels for safeguard. But it's a trap. The man, Monsieur Baudelaire, will be delivering the weapons to a Gestapo agent. The Gestapo is planning mass arrests."

If Johann could see my face, he would see the wide-eyed shock. If his body wasn't pressed to mine, I could allow relief to loosen my muscles. My body tenses instead as I continue with the charade I don't understand German. That I didn't understand what I heard last night at the party. "Why are you telling me this?" I whisper.

Why are you helping the Allies?

"You helped my friends get out of the country. Maybe the person who helped with their escape knows someone who could prevent the ambush."

"I'm not a rebel, if that's what you're thinking." That much is the truth. It's too dark to see his reaction, to know if he believes me. He's taking a great risk revealing what he heard. He always takes risks where I'm concerned.

He doesn't respond, and I let it be. He didn't have to tell me what the officers were talking about last night. My gut tells me I can trust him, but that doesn't mean I can tell him my secrets. It's better for both of us if he's in the dark about them.

His mouth brushes my brow, and we fall into a comfortable silence, wrapped in each other's body, until sleep finally pulls me back under.

WHEN I WAKE AGAIN, LIGHT STREAMS THROUGH THE WINDOWS, the blackout curtains now open. Johann is sitting in the chair next to the window, staring out at Paris, wearing his regular hateful uniform.

At the sound of my movement, he glances at me, solemn creases stretched across his brow. "It doesn't look like a good day for a walk." He returns to gazing out the window.

I frown at his comment. The sky is blue without a single cloud in sight.

He pushes himself out of his chair and walks to the bed. He sits next to me and brushes a strand of hair off my forehead. "There's a Milice officer watching the hotel from across the street. He's been there a while."

The thought of him there, possibly waiting for me, sends my heart thumping heavily in my chest, the vibrations felt in my ribs. The Gestapo is setting up a trap for Baudelaire, and I cannot help the feeling that I, too, am approaching a trap that at any moment will be sprung. The danger has always been there, only now it feels that much more real.

"I wonder who he's looking for." I keep my tone casual, the skill honed from months of living in occupied France. It does nothing to calm my heartbeat. "Have you been up long?"

"Only about half an hour."

"And he's been there the entire time?"

Johann nods, lips rolled into a line. "He was watching the main entrance when I first opened the curtains, and he hasn't moved since."

If he's waiting for someone of interest to the police, then he's not here alone. There will be officers watching the other entrances too.

I make a move to climb out of bed, the sheet wrapped around my chest, wishing Johann and I didn't have to go anywhere. Wishing we could just stay in bed and make love like we did last night until the officer tires and goes away. Until I forget all about the officers and the war and the hate.

Johann pulls me onto his lap and kisses me. I embrace him, holding him close, not wanting to let go. The touch of his lips makes me forget what I'm supposed to do. The sheet puddles around my waist, and I get lost in the kiss.

It doesn't last long enough, but from the way his body reacts pressed against me, if he hadn't pulled away when he did, we would likely be having a very late breakfast.

Smiling shyly, I hurry to my bathroom.

I step out of it several minutes later, dressed. Someone knocks at my room door. Johann walks to the door and opens it.

"I have Madame's coffee, Monsieur," a young female voice says.

"Oh, yes, I did order that," I respond so Johann does not suspect anything is out of sorts.

He opens the door wider, and a maid enters. Her dark hair

is pulled up in a low chignon and the rest of her description matches the one Allaire sent me last week.

Her gaze settles on me. I give her a barely perceptible nod and walk to where I left my purse. I remove from the secret compartment a franc note and the coded message I wrote last night for Allaire.

She places the tray on the side table, and I discreetly hand her the message. "*Merci.*"

"*Merci,* Madame." She gives me a slight curtsy, and her gaze darts to the tray. I return her unspoken message with a tiny nod, and she leaves.

"Would you like some coffee?" I ask Johann.

"I don't suppose it's real coffee, is it?"

The corners of my mouth pull into an amused smile. "It smells like chicory water."

"That's what I thought. I'll pass, *merci beaucoup.*"

I pour myself a cup, even though I'm not all that interested in drinking the water. Without being obvious about it, my fingers nimbly search for the message somewhere on the tray.

They brush across the tiny, folded piece of paper, and I palm it in my fist. I take a sip of my coffee, waiting for the opportune moment when I can read the note.

Johann removes the folded newspaper that was delivered with the beverage. "I'm going to read this in my room. You can join me when you're ready." He carries the newspaper through the open connecting doors.

I go to the bathroom and quickly work on transcribing the message Allaire sent me.

Go for a walk with Captain Schmidt to the pond in the Tuileries Gardens. You are not to meet with anyone, including me. You're out for a pleasant stroll with your officer sweetheart. Will watch if you are followed.

I rip the message into small pieces, put them in the ashtray, and light them with a match. I wait until they're nothing more than powdered ash and flush them down the loo. I join Johann in his room.

"Is there anything interesting in there?" I nod at the open newspaper in his hand.

"Apparently the Germans are winning the war." He raises an eyebrow. "And they're claiming to have won battles the other side also claims to have won, according to Friday's broadcast." He folds the paper and tosses it onto the bed. "It's hard to know what and whom to believe these days." He pulls me onto his lap.

"I think we should go for a walk after breakfast," I tell him. "It's a beautiful day, and I would love to visit Jardin des Tuileries. Perhaps see the pond."

He frowns, and his gaze shifts to the view outside the window. "Are you sure about that?"

"If he's still there when we leave and he follows, then we know he was waiting for one of us. I cannot imagine why he would want to watch us. We haven't done anything wrong. Not unless it is a crime for a French widow to be with a German officer." I lightly press my lips to his. "And what is more romantic than to stroll about the gardens on a beautiful day?"

Johann brushes his lips along mine, a small curve to his mouth. "If that is what you wish, then that is what we shall do."

We go downstairs to the café and eat croissants and berries for breakfast. The windows overlook the corner where the Milice officer is standing. My hands tremble, given he's possibly waiting for me.

No, you cannot think that way. If you look nervous, the officer will believe you have something to hide. And if he wasn't interested in me before, he will be now. I inwardly curse myself for being such a ninny just because of the conversation I overheard last night. My life was at risk the moment I stepped on the Lysander back on British soil. I can do this.

But some fear is beneficial. Fear keeps one from being overly confident. It keeps arrogance that can lead to mistakes at bay.

Johann and I leave the café. I loop my arm with his, and we head towards Jardin des Tuileries. People rush past to get to their destinations. I catch the occasional individual casting me hateful glares, thinly veiled with a mask of indifference. *Collaborator. Traitor. Whore.* Johann might not notice the accusations in their eyes, but I can't miss them.

Aware that anyone could be watching us from either side of the war, I chat with Johann about nothing important. I smile and laugh and do everything I've been taught to do to throw off suspicion.

Johann and I arrive at the gardens and wander around. The midmorning sun beats down on us. Allaire approaches. His eyes give no indication he is paying attention to us. He suddenly stops and crouches to tie his shoelace.

When he straightens, he gives a barely perceptible shake of the head and resumes walking.

No one is following Johann and me. Thank goodness.

So why are the Milice watching the hotel like bloody starving vultures?

Johann and I spend half an hour strolling through the gardens. We walk past other couples. Some of them are young soldiers with smiling girls at their side. It's feasible the girls are also part of a resistance group, interested in any useful gossip the soldiers might share. Or they could be collaborators. Or simply young women who fell in love with a man in a uniform.

Johann and I return to our hotel. The Milice officer is no

longer where we last saw him. "Where did he go?" I ask under my breath. Allaire said the officer wasn't following me or Johann, but I don't like how the man only vanished after we left the hotel.

"He didn't leave," Johann says flatly at the same time as I spot the man standing directly outside the building.

A man in civilian clothing charges from the hotel, almost knocking into a woman on the sidewalk. The officer screams for the man to halt. He doesn't. He darts across the street. A whistle blows, and other officers appear from around the corner of the hotel and pursue him.

Johann laces his hand with mine and tugs me along. The eyes of the man they're chasing momentarily lock with mine. I don't move, my muscles seizing. I've seen him another time, another place—only I don't know when or where or why.

He is no match for the officers. One knocks him to the ground.

A black car pulls up beside the man. And I watch in frozen horror as they beat him with sticks, yank him to his feet, and shove him into the back of the vehicle.

Cold stark fear squeezes the air from me, chills my blood. I could be next. If the Milice catches wind of my true identity, I can expect the same level of cruelty. A cruelty I might never survive.

How do I know him?

42

JESSICA

July, Present Day
Maple Ridge

Thursday midmorning, I fill in measurements on the online order form for the cabinets one of Troy's clients requested. Uncertainty and regret make my skin itch and remind me I was an idiot for quitting therapy two days ago. But I didn't have a choice. It was that, or put Violet and Sophie's lives at risk.

The secrets. The plan—still a work in progress—to get the pair out of town without Violet's husband locating them. What it could cost Violet, Kellan, and me. All of it has made me more anxious. And I was afraid I'd break down during therapy, and all my secrets would spill like oil from a tanker. Destroying the lives of those I care about.

Robyn would be required to inform the police of my actions. I couldn't afford that. Violet and Sophie can't afford that.

I'm just trying to protect them. Violet. Sophie. Kellan. Even Troy.

Especially Troy.

I miss him. God, how I miss him.

I miss how it feels to be in his arms. How it feels when we kiss, when we laugh, when we spend time together. I miss the evenings spent working on the renovations with him. They feel like they were a lifetime ago.

It's been four days since I ended things with Troy. Four days since I last saw him. He hasn't been at the office all week.

Correction. He's been at the office. Before I get here. And after I leave for the day.

The phone rings, and I answer it. "Carson Construction. How may I help you?" I singsong into the phone as if my heart isn't ripping in two from just thinking about Troy.

"Hi, Jessica," a woman says. "Can I speak with Troy please? This is Theresa Bell."

"Oh, hi, Theresa. Sorry. He's not in the office right now. Can I take a message?"

"Yes, please. Tell him I spoke to my father about him canceling the festival sponsorship, but unfortunately, I can't get him to budge on his decision. Can you tell Troy I'm really sorry? I saw the video from the Fourth, and I agree with everyone else. Chief Wilson overreacted to what Troy did."

I'm vaguely aware of telling her I'll give Troy the message, but the majority of my brain is numb as I attempt to piece together everything she's saying. Festival sponsorship. Canceled. When did this happen? And why is this the first I'm hearing about it? Especially when the loss of that money is a huge deal.

They were our biggest sponsor.

And Troy still refuses to accept any more of my restitution money to cover the cost beyond the five grand I donated.

We end the call, and I go back to doing some simple

accounting that's part of the job. There's a reason I went into investigative journalism in college and not math. I love writing. And I love the research involved with producing a good investigative piece. Math and numbers? They bore the hell out of me.

If only this job relied on more of the former than the latter.

I focus on inputting the numbers a supplier just sent me into the spreadsheet, and I try not to dwell on how Violet and Sophie are alone in my house. I'm so focused on making sure I'm typing the numbers correctly, I barely register the click of the door shutting over the keyboard-tapping quiet of the office.

"Jessica Smithson." The dagger-sharp demand in the male voice cuts through the near silence, and I startle.

I look up from the computer screen to the man standing in front of my desk. Chief Wilson.

My body turns into a stone statue. My heart stops for a fraction of a moment, and then resumes beating—faster, and hard enough to chip away at the stone.

He might be darker blond than my husband was, but that's where their dissimilarities end. They're both tall and spend their time honing their bodies in the gym. Turning their muscles lethal to anyone considered beneath them. I recognize those same ice-blue eyes. The ice blue that turned even icier when my husband's anger was directed at me.

Right now, Wilson's eyes are the blue of a calm ocean. I shiver, not so easily fooled.

It's not my husband. It's not my husband. It's not my husband. I keep repeating this as I discreetly massage my thigh under the desk, hoping the trick is enough to prevent me from slipping into a flashback.

Bailey whimpers. I give her a look that warns her to stay lying down on the floor next to me and keep quiet.

"Yes, what can I do for you, Chief Wilson?" The words come out sandpaper-rough, leaving my throat raw, my nerves exposed. I'd reach for the glass of water on my desk, but I'm afraid the tremor in my hand will give away the fact I'm involved in his wife and daughter's disappearance. And I have no delusions about the reason he's here.

He steps closer to my desk. "I understand you're a friend of my wife's."

"We know each other from when she was in yoga," I reply in the way of a nonanswer.

He knocks over the small container on my desk where I keep my pens. The move is deliberate, full of a veiled annoyance. "When was the last time you saw her?"

I knead my thigh harder. "July Fourth."

Bailey whimpers once more.

"And you didn't see her after that? Perhaps at the grocery store?" He places his fists on the desk and leans forward, his breath hot on my face. His broad body fills most of my view of the room and the door to the outside world.

"No, I haven't seen her since." I will myself back into the form of a stone statue. A statue that won't squirm on the chair and give away I'm hiding something. Give away I'm lying.

The corners of his mouth turn up. It's not a friendly smile. It's a shiver-inducing smile. A smile that makes my stomach churn, my heart creep into my throat. "Is that so?"

Fuckers, does he know something?

My eyes widen slightly, and I work to wipe away the surprise on my face.

Chief Wilson leans forward another inch, not easily fooled. I can feel the heat pour off him, the flames flickering from hell. "My daughter is missing." His eyes soften with pain and grief, stunning me.

The shock only lasts a fraction of a second. Then his smile widens, torment and torture glinting in his eyes, replacing the pain. I make the mistake of looking at them too closely. As if they hold the answer for how to take him down. But all I see reflecting from the dark, bottomless pupils is fear. Violet's fear and my own fear of the man.

The office door opens, startling me. I wasn't expecting anyone. Like I hadn't been expecting Chief Wilson to show up.

"What's going on?" Troy asks, his tone one-stop short of snapping at the man.

The chief's smile doesn't fade as he straightens to face his new foe. "I was just inquiring if your assistant has seen my wife and daughter since their disappearance."

I reach down for Bailey and stroke her, my attention still on the two men.

"What? You think she kidnapped them and hid them in her desk drawer?" A wry smile shifts on Troy's face, and his tone adds a silent, *You really are an idiot.*

Chief Wilson's retorting sneer is enough to cause even the most hardened criminal to take a step back. "What about you? When was the last time you saw my wife?"

"That would be the same time I told the last officer who asked me that question. I haven't seen your family for several weeks." Troy's brow creases into a concerned frown. "Your wife has been missing for over a week, and you're telling me you still don't have a clue where she is?"

If the chief had been any other man, one who didn't repeatedly abuse his wife, I'd have expected to see at least a smidgen of worry and pain flicker on his face when Troy mentions Violet. But not even a hint of those emotions crosses Chief Wilson's expression.

His nostrils flare. His face reddens. He's angry. Angry she bested him. Angry he still hasn't figured out where she's hiding. "We're investigating leads, which is why I'd appreciate it if your assistant would cooperate with my questions."

"I have," I tell him. "I've told both you and the officer who came to my house the same thing. I haven't seen her since July Fourth. I was at the park near Troy's house when I saw her. An officer approached her while we were talking, and she left with him. She seemed nervous. Like he had…like he'd been stalking her." Because the chief of police had sent the officer to keep an eye on her. "Maybe you should be questioning him."

"Which officer?" he asks, even though he surely already knows.

"I don't know his name, but if you want, I can go to the station and identify him." *Preferably in front of witnesses.*

"Alright. I'll arrange for you to come in to do that."

How I manage not to roll my eyes at his insincere comment is beyond me.

Troy crosses his arms, his Marine stance adding to his threatening posture. "Do you have any more questions for us? Or is that it?"

My heart *whomp-whomp-whomps* in my chest, preparing for another showdown between the two men. This was the reason I broke up with Troy—so he didn't inadvertently put Violet at a greater risk.

And now that I know the fallout from their last confrontation—the loss of the Bell Automotives sponsorship—I'm scared of what will happen if there's more conflict between them. Especially if news of it goes public. It could put the festival in jeopardy and hurt the individuals it was supposed to help.

"No, that's everything." Chief Wilson glares at Troy, his hand going to his holster, but he doesn't say anything more.

Fortunately, Troy chooses to also remain silent and keeps his hands off the chief this time.

As soon as the door clicks shut behind Chief Wilson, my breathing comes in fast and shallow. *Oh, God.* What if he gets a search warrant for my house? What if Violet and I missed a clue of her whereabouts lying around? Or Sophie might fuss if they're in that space for too long while the police comb through my house?

"Hey, Jess." Troy says something else, but I have a hard time registering what he's saying. My thoughts and body are turning numb, and I feel like I'm being yanked beneath the surface. My lungs are filling with fear and despair, and I can't kick my legs hard enough to break free.

I hear a faint whimper through the numbness, and Bailey jumps her paws onto my lap and licks my hand. It's enough to snap me out of whatever spell I'm under. But it's not enough to stop my rapid breaths.

Troy crouches in front of me. "You're hyperventilating, Jess. Cup your hands against your mouth and breathe into them like you would a paper bag."

This time his words make sense, and I do as he suggests.

It takes several breaths before things begin to level out again. And the trembling of my body isn't as bad as it was when Chief Wilson was here. *I'm safe.*

I'm here.

Troy's here.

"You okay now?" Troy asks, still crouching.

I nod.

He straightens and gets to his feet. "Any idea why Wilson was questioning you?"

I shake my head. "Maybe he was bored." My attention is focused on my hands.

"And *you* think quitting therapy right now is the right thing to do? I mean, look at what happened with Wilson asking you questions." So many emotions grate in his voice. Anger. Frustration. Confusion.

But it's the guilt, which I don't even think he realizes is there, that raises my hackles. "How do you know I quit therapy?"

Troy flinches, and I know right then that I've been played for a fool. "Why would Robyn tell you I quit therapy? Isn't that confidential information?"

He unfolds his arms, and his gaze darts to his office behind me. The man who has fought the enemy in Afghanistan can't even look me in the eye. "That's because the state wasn't paying for your therapy. I was."

I stare at him for several long seconds. *God, please tell me I misunderstood him.* "What do you mean you were paying for it?" The words sound like they're trudging through quicksand.

"I knew you wouldn't get help because you couldn't afford it, so I told Robyn I'd pay for the sessions. I asked her not to tell you."

"Because...?" Steam rises inside me, pressure building to a dangerous level.

"Because I figured once you discovered the truth, you would quit going."

"Even after I got the restitution payment?" The volume of my voice skyrockets. "You could have told me the truth then, but you didn't." He'd just continued with the lie that the state was paying for my therapy.

Troy doesn't reply, possibly because there's no clawing his way out of the deep pit he has created.

I let out a hard breath, but it's not enough to release my annoyance after this new revelation. I know I'm keeping a secret from him, but it doesn't affect him directly. What he did isn't just a secret—it's manipulation. "So instead, you decided to be manipulative like my husband, just so you got your own way. This job, the therapy, Bailey. Everything is about what *you* want. I know I'm broken, Troy, but it's not your place to decide how to fix me."

"I'm not trying to fix you," he says, his voice a low growl.

I push to my feet, my legs as shaky as they were when Chief Wilson interrogated me. "Really? You've done nothing since the beginning but try to prove I'm broken and attempt to fix me. News flash, Troy. I don't need you to prove I'm broken. I already know that. No one survives the ten years of hell I went through and comes out in one piece." Hot tears prick my eyes at the truth behind my words. I've been a crumpled mess most of my life, although I didn't realize the severity of it until my husband showed me.

Troy's expression is that of a man who is lost and knows no matter which direction he steps, the cliff will crumble under his weight. "I didn't want you to end up where my best friend did."

"I know. But I'm not Colton. And saving me won't bring him back. I can't even trust you. This is why you should never have anything that's dependent on a man. Your job. Your friends. Your car. Your house. Because once he decides to take it away, you lose everything."

He holds up his hand as if that will stifle the flow of my words. "You're overreacting, Jess."

I narrow my eyes at him in warning, but he continues to douse gasoline over the fire his words ignited. "What I did for you, I would have done for any of my friends."

"Would you have slept with them too?" For all I know, he has slept with at least one of them. Maple Ridge is a small town. There aren't a lot of options.

"I slept with you because I want you," Troy says. "Plain and simple. I've never been interested in Simone, Zara, or Emily in that way. They've always been like sisters to me. And I've never been interested in Avery either."

"What about other women? You've been helping Olivia—"

"I'm not sleeping with her, and I never have." His tone is stiff, and accusation burns in his eyes.

"Never claimed you had." Although if he asked, I know she would jump at the chance. That much is obvious. "Fix Olivia. Don't try to fix me." From what I've heard, her husband was amazing until he was dragged down by PTSD.

She doesn't have the trust issues I do.

She still has her beautiful daughter.

Troy would be better off with her than he would with me.

I'm messed up. Olivia isn't. I'm pulling my life back together again, piece by piece. She and I are in two different places.

And I'm trying to give Violet and Sophie a new life. As long as I'm doing that, there's no room for Troy in my life—which is why I broke up with him.

I check the time on the computer. It's getting late, and I have to pick up some food and other essential supplies on the way home. "I need to go. And just so we've got it straight, I will be paying you back every cent you paid for my therapy."

"That's not necessary, Jess."

"Yes, it is," I snap.

I turn off the computer, grab my purse, and hook Bailey's leash onto her vest. "Oh, and Theresa Bell called. She couldn't convince her father not to pull out of his sponsorship agreement." I level a glare at Troy, reminding him that he too has been keeping another secret. Reminding him I know the price of his animosity toward Chief Wilson.

A price I have no intention of letting Violet and Sophie pay.

Troy stands there motionless, my last words clearly enough to put out his fire. I walk past him, not giving him a second glance.

And the hot tears from a few moments ago stream down my face as I walk out the door.

I remove my phone from my purse and text Simone, attempting to push everything that just happened with Troy from my mind. Right now, I need to focus on helping Violet and Sophie.

Simone responds as I approach my bike.

Simone: I'm free anytime Saturday.

43

TROY

July, Present Day
Maple Ridge

Garrett and Lucas walk into Barside Brewery thirty minutes after I arrived. I'm still at the bar, talking to Kim's little sister, Evie.

Evie tucks her dark, shoulder-length hair behind her ear, her purple streaks bright in the light shining above the bar. Her smoky makeup emphasizes her bedroom eyes that leave most guys drooling on the bar top. Including the man two chairs down from where I'm sitting.

She leans forward to take his order, flirting with him a little. Taylor, from the far end of the bar, rolls her eyes. She doesn't complain about her girlfriend flirting with the men. It brings in the tips. And all the men in Maple Ridge know Evie is taken. It's the strangers—like this man—who are clueless.

Garrett slaps me on the back. "You want to sit at the bar or play pool? Hey, Evie." He nods at her.

345

She moves away from the man and pours her charm on Garrett and Lucas, the grin less flirty than the one she used on the other man. We're like brothers to her. "You guys want your regulars?"

"Sure."

"Yup."

I chug what's left of my beer and put the glass on the counter. "I'll take another one too. Thanks."

She nods at me with a smile.

"You gonna tell us what has you sitting in here on a Thursday night, drowning your sorrows with beer?" Garrett asks.

"I fucked things up with Jess, she dumped my sorry ass the other day, and we just had a fight."

Both men wince, the expression more of an *ouch, sorry to hear that* than anything else.

"What happened?" Lucas leans back against the bar.

"I'm not exactly sure." Or not sure what to tell them. They don't know about her past, and I'm not about to bring it up. Only Kellan and I know the truth. It's up to Jess to tell my brothers, as well as anyone else. "She has major trust issues. And well, she found out I've been paying for her therapy, and she got mad, claiming I was being manipulative."

Garrett's eyebrows jerk halfway up his forehead. "You were paying for her therapy?"

Evie puts the three filled glasses in front of us. We thank her, and Garrett pays for this round.

Lucas looks past me to the guy sitting not far from us at the bar. "Let's go over there." He tilts his head at an empty table far enough away that we won't have to worry about people over-hearing our conversation.

We grab our beers and take our seats at one of the sturdy round tables near the cornered-off section with the pool tables. The dim lighting where we're sitting matches my mood.

"So, you were paying for Jess's therapy?" Garrett nods for me to explain.

"I knew it was the only way to get her to go in the beginning. I wanted to remove as many obstacles as possible that would prevent her from getting the help she needed."

"Fair enough. But doesn't your company medical plan cover it?"

"She wasn't my employee when she started therapy. Because I didn't want her to know I was paying for it from the very beginning, I couldn't exactly switch her over to my company's plan. I'd initially told her the state was covering the cost."

Both my brothers wince.

"She believed you?" Garrett lifts his glass to his mouth.

I turn my beer on the cardboard coaster, condensation trickling down the side of the glass. "Yup. Every. Single. One of my lies." My frustration and lack of regret at helping her soak through each word.

"How did she figure out you were paying for it?" Lucas asks.

"I found out the other day she'd quit therapy. When I returned to my office this afternoon, Alex Wilson was interrogating her about Violet and Sophie's disappearance. Jess has a bad history with cops, and that's part of the reason she has PTSD."

"What kind of bad history?"

"It's not my place to tell you." I take a long sip of my beer. "But it's enough that Wilson's presence in my office was clearly freaking her out. After he left, I brought up how she'd quit therapy. Except, I shouldn't have known about that."

"So you had to 'fess up to paying for it," Garrett says, filling in the blanks.

"Yup." And true to her word, Jess wired me the money a short time ago. I only accepted it because I knew it was important to her that she pay me back.

Lucas picks up his glass. "So, you and Jess are really over?"

Behind him, an older couple takes a seat at a table for two, but they're still far enough away they can't hear us. The country music playing through the speakers also helps with that.

I return my attention to my brothers. "In her mind we are. I'm not ready to give up on her yet. I understand why she's scared. Her past hasn't given her a good reason to trust men."

"And where does Kellan fit into all of this?" Garrett asks.

"What do you mean?" I keep my voice even, not wanting to give anything away. Especially not the part where it pisses me off Jess trusts him more than she does me. Always has, it would seem. Given how much they have in common when it comes to their families and spending time in prison, it's not hard to see why. But that doesn't mean I have to like she has confided in him instead of with me.

"You think we haven't noticed how close they are?" Lucas replies. "What? You think she's into him instead of you?" The last bit comes out with the equivalent of an eye roll in his tone.

"They have a shared history." Close enough to one. "He understands her in a way I'll never be able to. But both have made it clear to me they don't see each other as anything other than a friend."

"You don't believe them?"

"No, I believe them. But something's going on with her, and I bet Kellan knows what it is."

"So ask him."

I throw Garrett a *Do-you-really-think-that's-gonna-help?* glare.

Garrett isn't fazed by it. "You've got nothing to lose."

"I've got everything to lose. He's made it quite clear he's on Jess's side, no matter what. She doesn't trust me as it is. She's not going to trust me if I push Kellan for answers."

"I hate to say this," Lucas says, "but maybe you and Jess aren't meant to be. I mean, it's obvious you care a lot for her. Possibly even love her. But sometimes that's not enough."

He's right. Sometimes it isn't enough. I'd hoped this wasn't one of those times. But maybe Jess will never be ready for love. I can't blame her for that after what her late husband put her through.

I don't answer Lucas since I'm not in the mood to put words to what I'm thinking. So I just shrug and stand. "I'm up for a game of pool. Who wants to join me?"

Garrett and Lucas grab their beer and join me at the pool tables. Katelyn is there with one of her friends and Olivia's sister, Cora. Cora and Amy are playing pool together. Katelyn is watching them. All three are wearing shorts and tank tops. All three have the attention of several men sitting nearby.

Cora winks at two men, both of whom I recognize. They work for one of the logging companies in the area.

Katelyn grabs two cue sticks from the wall. "How about you and I play, Troy?" Her head tilts to the side, and she peers at me beneath long, thick lashes. She flicks her loose curls over her shoulder and flashes me a smile.

"Sure. Why not?" I take the stick from her and set up the balls.

She goes first. Both of us are decent players. I win the first game. She wins the second one.

I drain my third beer and go to order a fourth one, even though I probably shouldn't drink anymore. I need to be at the job site early tomorrow because I have PT in the afternoon with Lucas.

I return to the pool table with my drink as Katelyn sets up for another game.

"Garrett and I are heading out," Lucas says a short time later. "You want a ride home?"

"I'm going to stick around for one more game." I take a long draw of my beer.

Lucas looks pointedly at the glass in my hand.

Katelyn pauses, setting up her next shot. "I can drop him off on my way home. I've only been drinking water." She sends the green striped ball into the far pocket.

"Okay. We'll see you tomorrow." Lucas smacks me on the back. "Don't worry about Jess. I'm sure you two will figure things out. You're good together."

"Thanks, bro." I give him a one-arm hug. Ditto with Garrett.

They leave, and I turn to Katelyn. She has an expression on her face I don't know how to decipher. So I don't. "Guess it's just you and me."

Amy left about twenty minutes ago, and Cora is sitting at the table with the two loggers. She laughs, the sound breathlessly high, almost a giggle.

I frown. "Is she gonna be okay?"

Katelyn glances over her shoulder to their table. "She should be. She's not drinking alcohol either. Plus, she has a black belt in karate. If anything, they're the ones you might need to worry about."

Cora laughs again at whatever the men are saying. They don't look drunk, and she certainly doesn't.

I return to focusing on my next shot.

The green ball I'm aiming to send into the far pocket seems a little blurry. I squint, align my stick with the blurry white ball, and jab it.

The white ball rolls toward the green ball...but misses it by an inch.

44

TROY

July, Present Day
Maple Ridge

The bright sunlight blasting through my bedroom window is the first thing I notice when I wake up. The jackhammer going off in my head is a close second.

I groan and close my eyes for a moment as I clear the cobwebs from my head. Just how much did I drink last night?

I shift positions, and my knee brushes a warm body under the covers. *Jess.*

Despite the pounding headache, I smile. She must have shown up at the bar and we made up. I dig deep in my foggy memory to remember what happened, but all I pull up is a blank.

It doesn't matter. We're back together. That's what's important.

My cock hardens, not at all deterred by the headache. It's

dealing with a different kind of ache. One that will be relieved once I'm buried inside her.

I slide the sheet down, exposing Jess's shoulder. A butterfly tattoo peers at me, the wings a delicate swirl pattern.

When the hell did she get a tattoo? And...and the hair's all wrong to be hers. Wrong shade of blond.

I jerk away from the sleeping body in front of me...who isn't sleeping anymore. She flips over. And fuck. Katelyn?

My cock goes limp, and it feels like I've been sucker punched in the gut.

The sheet that was around Katelyn's body has slipped and is no longer covering her. I keep my eyes glued on her face, but I can tell that her breasts are exposed. She's naked. I'm naked. *What the hell happened last night?*

I scramble from under the covers, despite my stomach's protest. It lurches, but that has nothing to do with how much I drank.

I grab my clothes off the floor. Katelyn's are also strewn everywhere. The pounding in my head increases. It too has nothing to do with the alcohol in my system and everything to do with why I don't remember anything after Katelyn drove me home.

Smiling, she props herself up on an elbow. "How're you feeling, Troy?" Her voice is soft and low, but my remorse, resentment, resignation echo loudly in my brain. I barely hear her.

"What are you doing in my bed?" The words come out in a quiet, sleep-scratchy rumble.

Her eyes widen and hurt shines back at me. "Don't you remember?"

"No, I don't remember a thing. Other than playing pool at Barside last night." I yank on my jeans, not bothering with my underwear.

"I drove you home, and you insisted I come inside. So I did.

And the next thing I know..." She leaves the end of the sentence hanging, but the implication is clear.

My head hurts too much for me to even utter a single curse. I want to sit on my bed, but that might not be a good idea with Katelyn sitting there naked. I lean against the wall and slide to the floor.

Goddamn hell. I should have gone home with Lucas when he offered me a ride.

I bury my face in my hands and attempt to rub away the memory of finding Katelyn in my bed. Or better yet, erase from history she and I had sex.

"What's wrong, Troy?" Her tone is a sweet lullaby that's supposed to soothe, but it only compounds on my nightmare.

"I have a girlfriend."

"Girlfriend? You told me last night that you and Jessica broke up."

"We did." I bounce my forehead on my fist. Nope, that doesn't do much for my headache. The headache that worsened with Katelyn's revelation. "But as far as I'm concerned, Jess and I aren't over," I tell her.

But we will be now. Jess has been hurt enough by men, especially those who were supposed to love and protect her. She's not going to let me back into her life after she learns about my latest fuckup.

"When you told me last night you would be my date for my sister's wedding, that was a lie?"

Just file it with everything else about last night I don't remember.

"If I told you I would go as your date, then I will." Except...I might not remember much about last night, but there is one thing I do remember. "Isn't Jess your sister's wedding photographer?"

"That's right."

Fuck. No. "I can't go as your date to the wedding my ex-girl-friend is working at."

"Why not? It's not like you guys were in love. You've only been together a month or so. I'm sure she won't care. Because if she cared, she wouldn't have dumped you."

I lean my head against the wall for a beat, inwardly cursing myself for being an idiot. When that doesn't solve my problem, I grunt under my breath and stand. "I guess my truck's still at Barside?" My gaze goes to my bedside tables, but my phone isn't on either one.

"That's right."

I don't give Katelyn a second glance and go downstairs. I find my phone on the floor near the front door and pick it up. Lucas and Garrett both texted to make sure I got home okay.

It's still early, but I know they both should be up by now. Okay, not Lucas. He's probably enjoying a quickie with his wife before he heads to the Veterans Center.

I send Garrett a text.

> Me: Can you take me to Barside so I can
> pick up my truck?

He responds while I'm in the kitchen tossing back a painkiller and water.

> Garrett: Sure thing. I'll be at your place in
> about 20

> Me: Thx

I return to my room. Katelyn is still in my bed, reclined against the pillows and checking her phone.

I grab my clothes for the day. "I'm having a shower now. Then Garrett's picking me up. You can leave whenever you're ready." That's not my favorite plan, but I'm not going to be an ass and kick her out...even if I want to.

She looks up from her phone, her eyes sparkling in the sun shining through the window. I guess I'd been too drunk last night to remember to close my curtains.

"I thought we could get together after you've finished work," she says. "Maybe have dinner."

"We're not dating, Katelyn. We had sex." Very forgettable sex, apparently. "I'm sorry, but I'm not looking for a new girlfriend."

She laughs, but it's not Jess's laugh, and that only puts me more on edge. "I was thinking more like having dinner as friends. Nothing more. That's allowed, right? There's no rule that says you can't go out with female friends after a breakup. Or are you in mourning and can't even hang out with Zara, Emily, and Simone?"

Zara. Emily. Simone. *Oh, crap.* They're Jess's friends too. Her husband isolated Jess from her friends when they were married. It was why she had a difficult time escaping him. What's going to happen now that Jess and I have broken up? Will we remain friends? Or will Zara, Emily, and Simone feel like they're being forced to decide who they can spend time with?

"No, I'm not in a period of mourning," I say, my voice gruff. "But that doesn't mean I'll have dinner with you. And I'm not going to your sister's wedding as your date."

Katelyn shrugs, not seeming at all concerned by my response, her attention back on her phone. "My father told me he pulled the festival sponsorship after what happened between you and Chief Wilson. How about you go as my date to my sister's wedding, and I convince him to reinstate the sponsorship?" Katelyn looks up from her phone, smiling in the way Emily does when someone gives her chocolate—her addiction. "We can discuss things at dinner tonight."

I cross my arms over my chest. "Theresa already tried to get him to change his mind." I bumped into her a few days ago in town and had asked her if she could talk to him, hoping she would have better luck than I'd had.

Katelyn lifts her chin, her expression smug. "She obviously didn't try hard enough. So do we have a deal? Dinner and the wedding, then I'll talk to my father."

"Why can't you talk to him first?"

She rolls her eyes. "Because the wedding is in two days, so his focus is on that and not on anything else. The last thing he wants to talk about is sponsoring your festival. But afterward? Then he'll be more receptive to me talking about it. Your choice, Troy. Dinner and being my date and I'll talk to my father...or turn your back on all three?"

My chest raises and lowers on a long, deep sigh. "Okay, on all three counts." The veterans who are booked for this weekend with Wilderness Warriors live in Maple Ridge, and we aren't leaving on the overnight excursion until late tomorrow morning.

"Perfect." She smiles and scoots out from under the covers.

I don't stick around to see how naked she is. I head to the bathroom. And pray that once I'm finished scrubbing my body in the shower, I'll discover last night never happened.

That this morning was nothing more than a bad dream.

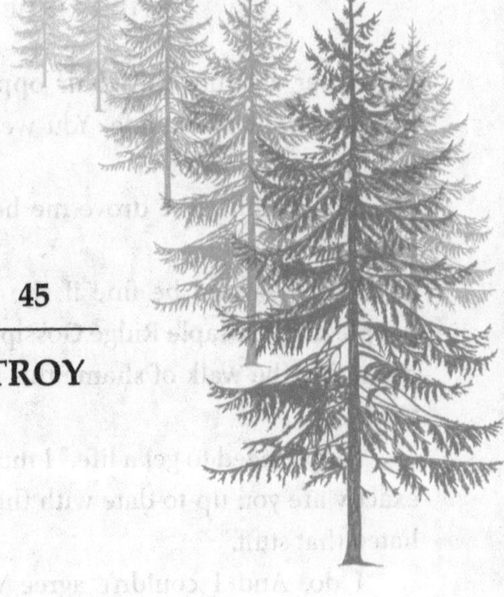

45

TROY

July, Present Day
Maple Ridge

Zara places two plates full of appetizers on her coffee table. She's hosting Game Night this week, which means she's trying out new foods on us that she wants to introduce at Picnic & Treats. We're her guinea pigs.

Except I'm not exactly hungry after eating dinner with Katelyn an hour ago.

"What's this about you now dating Katelyn Bell?" Zara gives me the evil eye she's been perfecting since we were kids.

Everyone else stares at me from the couch and armchairs, their expressions exhibiting a host of emotions. Shock, disbelief, and anger being the most prominent ones. Even Butterscotch seems pissed at the news.

"I'm not dating Katelyn." I reach for my cola on the coffee table.

"That's not the news going around Maple Ridge." Zara

357

drops her ass into the chair opposite mine. "You were with her last night at Barside. You were also spotted leaving with her."

"That's right. She drove me home because I didn't want a DUI."

"Which would be fine if she hadn't spent the night. Five people on the Maple Ridge Gossip Grapevine reported spotting her doing the walk of shame this morning. After you'd left for work."

"People need to get a life," I mutter into my drink. "And why exactly are you up-to-date with the latest gossip? I thought you hated that stuff."

"I do. And I couldn't agree with you more about them needing to get a life. But that doesn't change the fact that you had dinner with her before coming here."

Everyone else continues staring at me. Not one of them tries to put an end to the interrogation.

"As friends," I clarify. "We had dinner only as friends. We needed to discuss something."

"True or false? You're going to her sister's wedding on Sunday as her date."

Christ. How the hell does Zara even know any of this? "I'm going as her friend. Nothing more. We're not dating." I put the glass down without taking a drink and lean back in the armchair.

"Then why were her friends talking about how you two are now dating?" Zara grunts, trying to laser a hole between my eyes. "You and Jess just broke up, and you're already dating other women. And having sex with them. Well, one woman. Katelyn."

"What difference does it make if I'm dating other women?" I demand, my rough tone scraping the air. "Jess. Broke up. With. Me." Just saying the words out loud feels like a chisel is being hammered into my chest.

Kellan glares at me like I've stolen the software he's been working on and sold it to the highest bidder.

"She might have broken up with you, but that doesn't mean she's over you." The fine grit to Simone's words doesn't remove my thick layer of guilt. Guilt because I screwed up and had sex with Katelyn. But not because I had dinner with her before coming here. I'm allowed to have dinner with friends, regardless of whether I'm dating anyone or not.

"Doesn't matter if she's not over me. She doesn't trust me enough to try to make our relationship work. Anyway, like I said, I'm not dating Katelyn. Her father, Anthony Bell, was going to give a large donation for the With Hope festival. But after what happened between Chief Wilson and me during the Fourth of July celebrations, Anthony changed his mind about the money. The festival needs that money. Every dime of it. I didn't have much luck changing his mind. I'm hoping Katelyn does."

"You've lost me," Garrett says, frowning. "What does that have to do with you going to the wedding with her?"

Emily groans. "She told you she would convince her father to change his mind, but you have to be her date first? You could've asked Theresa. She would have done it without any strings attached."

"She tried." The words heave out on my frustrated sigh.

"And you think Katelyn will succeed when her sister didn't?" Lucas shakes his head with the same disbelief that's in his tone.

"Who knows? But it was a chance I was willing to take. For the sake of the festival."

"What happened between you and Jess?" Emily asks after a moment, looking like her heart is the one broken instead of mine. "You guys were perfect together."

I shrug because hell if I know. "Guess we weren't perfect enough."

"Do you love her?"

"Em, leave it alone." Kellan's tone is lethally calm, but there's something under the surface that gives even me the chills. I've never heard him talk that way to her.

Her replying scowl is enough to turn most men to ice. It doesn't faze my brother.

"It doesn't matter if I love her," I respond, not even slightly entertained by their standoff this time.

Emily's expression brightens, and a smile curves her mouth. "Sure, it does. Love always matters."

Despite everything, I chuckle, a rumble deep in my throat. "You always were the romantic."

"Even though it hasn't done me a lot of good." She raises her vodka cooler as if to propose a toast. "But we're not talking about me. We're talking about you. If you love someone, you fight for them. You don't give up. You don't date or have sex with Katelyn."

"I'm. Not. Dating. Katelyn." Dammit. How many times do I have to repeat it before they believe me?

"So you've said. But you haven't actually denied sleeping with her. Does that mean you did sleep with her?"

"Did I wake up with her naked and asleep next to me? Yes. That happened. Do I remember having sex with her? No. Most of last night is a blur."

Kellan still doesn't look particularly thrilled by tonight's revelation. No one does.

Has Jess heard the rumor about me and Katelyn? This is a small town. If she hasn't already heard the speculations, she will have by tomorrow.

An urge ignites inside me to go out on the balcony and scream at the stars. I douse it. I don't need everyone, including Zara's neighbors, to witness my frustration. I feel sick. Sicker than this morning when I woke up with a hangover.

"Can we just start the game?" I ask, wanting to get the night over with.

Zara removes the pack of cards from the box and shuffles them.

An hour later, everyone in the room has whipped my ass in poker. It was a targeted attack. Of that, I'm positive.

Not in the mood to play another round, I call it an early night. I don't even wait to get home before sending Katelyn a text.

Me: Just a reminder. We're not dating

I turn over my engine and head home.

A text comes through while I'm driving. As soon as I park the truck in the garage, I kill the engine and read it.

Katelyn: Is the reminder for me or you?

Me: Your friends. You might want to tell them we're not dating. They seem to think we are.

Katelyn: Okay

Katelyn: Do you want to come over tonight?

Me: I'll see you Sunday for the wedding

Katelyn: Okay. Goodnight, Troy

Maybe I should date Katelyn. If the woman I'm in love with isn't interested in me, why should I stay single? Why shouldn't I have sex?

Maybe next time I fall for a woman, she won't be too afraid to take a risk on love.

Fuuuuuuck.

I slam my hand hard on the steering wheel, giving myself another reason to curse. Out loud this time.

Christ, I don't know what I'll do about Jess...and I don't know what I'll do if Katelyn can't convince her father to change his mind about the sponsorship.

I need to come up with a Plan B when it comes to the money. And I need to come up with it quickly.

As for Jess—I'm not ready to give up on her yet. I'll fight for her once I get back from this weekend's Warriors excursion.

She's the only woman I want.

46

ANGELIQUE

July 1943
France

The night after returning from Paris, Johann, Jacques, and I sit in front of Johann's radio, waiting for the BBC French broadcast to begin. Johann and I are sitting on the faded settee, our bodies not touching.

My muscles are still tense from yesterday when we witnessed the Milice capture the man who had been in the hotel where Johann and I stayed. That was not the first time I'd witnessed the brutality of the Milice or SS or Gestapo. They take great pleasure in ensuring their cruelty is seen. What better way to ensure the French people keep in line?

But why did he look so bloody familiar?

The question has replayed in my head countless times since I saw the man arrested yesterday. Perhaps I've seen him during one of my visits to Paris. But he had to have done something notable for him to stand out in my mind. And why did he

363

appear to know me? In that briefest moment when our eyes locked, I had a feeling he recognised me too.

I think back to my months of SOE training, and that's when it all slips into place. He had just completed his training when I was new to the program, and he'd left for his mission well before I left for mine. I didn't realise he was still in France.

An icy shiver runs through me at what happened to him. Ever since I landed on occupied soil, the enemy has come close to capturing me on so many occasions. Does this mean my turn is imminent? Will my fate mirror his?

A fate that will end with my tortured body dumped somewhere, my remains possibly never identified. Hazel won't even know what happened to me. She won't know I loved her.

If I could, I'd write her a letter to be passed on to her should I die. But that is not feasible. It would be too dangerous for the person with the message, for Hazel should it fall into enemy hands.

I don't regret for a second being in France, doing what I can to end the war. I would do it all again, even if things had gone down differently between Charles and me. I just wouldn't have fallen in love with Johann.

No, that is not true. I would have still fallen in love with him. Nothing would change how Charles and I were wrong for each other.

Neither Johann nor I told Jacques what we witnessed yesterday outside the hotel. Like everyone in France, he knows what the enemy is capable of. He doesn't need the reminder. He's tense enough as it is.

The Morse code *Dot. Dot. Dot. Dash* emits from the radio, signalling the broadcast is beginning.

"Ici Londres! Les Français parlent aux Français."

The broadcast continues with the usual contents: the update on what is happening in the world, the political commentaries, the poetry, a comical play about Hitler being a foolish clown, the calls for France to fight the enemy, to not let the enemy destroy the country like an out-of-control disease.

And then comes the moment we're waiting for.

Cumquats make delicious squirrel pastry.

The elephants are rampant in July.

The monkeys are dancing on rainbows.

My breath whooshes out of me. "They made it," I say in a daze. "They made it. They're safe." I grin at Johann. "Oskar, Margrit, and Sonja all made it to safety. They're alive."

"Thank God!" he says on a hard exhalation, and we jump to our feet, embracing.

Johann squeezes me tighter. "Thank you." He releases me and turns to Jacques. "And thank you for everything you did for them. You could have turned them in, which is what some people would have done. But you didn't. You didn't turn them in, even though they're Jewish, and you didn't turn me in for helping them. Thank you."

"Didn't see any point in doing that," Jacques responds gruffly, but there is no missing the slight quirk of his lips on his weathered face. "The Germans would execute you, and then we would be forced out of this house when another German took your place." He glances around the drawing room, sadness weighing down the corners of his mouth. "And I would lose what's left of my memories of my wife and family."

Jacques unfolds from the wingback chair and leaves the room. His movements are slow, and his footsteps falter as if each step causes him pain. If not for the war, he wouldn't be forced to manage the vineyard on his own. He would have his son here helping him. He would have capable men doing the physical labor. My heart aches for everything he has been forced to endure.

I turn and find myself in Johann's arms once more.

"I only hope my friends and their daughter finally find the

happiness they deserve." His words are murmured at my temple.

I don't dare tell him the anti-Semitic feelings so widespread in Europe are not much better in England. The only difference is the atrocities occurring in the concentration camps don't exist in Britain. That king and country aren't forcing them to wear a star on their arm, shutting down their businesses, or preventing them from studying at university.

England is still the safer alternative to where they were living, but the distrust for Jews due to the lies told to the German people will also haunt them in my homeland. Hitler's poisoned words and politics had been embraced by many in Britain before the war, and the distrust only grew with time.

I don't tell Johann any of this. I just let him enjoy the knowledge his friends are safe. It's all I can give him. He's still in the dark about the fate of his mother and sister. Even I cannot help him there. It's impossible to know where they went and if they are still alive. It's impossible to know if we can save them too.

Just as it's impossible to know if we will be able to save ourselves, if we will survive the war.

September 1943
France

I SIT UP IN BED A LITTLE TOO QUICKLY AND A WAVE OF NAUSEA hits me. It feels like I've been tired for too long, almost since the war began, yet lately, it seems almost more so—as if the hounds of sleep are always nipping at my heels.

Johann is away for the next few days, and it's the new moon.

That means I will hopefully be sabotaging a railroad tunnel tonight. Sleep won't be happening until after the job is finished, which will be sometime after two o'clock in the morning.

I breathe slowly through my mouth, and the nausea gradually subsides. Taking care not to move so fast this time, I stand and get ready for the day. Memories linger in my thoughts of the past two months following the grand ball in Paris. Memories of stolen moments with Johann, the tender words spoken between us, the embraces, the kisses, the quiet lovemaking. The walks to the pond to watch the sunsets. The murmured discussions about a future together—a future based more on dreams than reality.

I greet Jacques and prepare porridge for him from the small quantity of oats we have left. It's runnier than either of us would like, but it's more than most people get these days. It's been nine weeks since Johann learned that Oskar and his family are safe. Nine weeks he's been breathing a little easier. The same cannot be said for the rest of us.

I sneak a little extra helping of my porridge into Jacques's bowl. He has plenty of work to do in the vineyard today, and he needs as much energy as he can get. All I need is more sleep.

"Would you stop giving me all your food?" he grumbles and starts coughing. The cough began a week ago and hasn't relented yet. If anything, it's getting worse.

"I'm not giving it all to you." I show him the contents of my chipped bowl. "See?"

He gives me the gruff look I'm familiar with when it comes to his expressions, and I cannot help but smile. Nothing gets past this man.

"You need it more than I do," I amend. "I'm going to drop by Dr. Deschamps's office tomorrow and tell him your cough isn't getting better."

"It will be fine. I don't need to see no doctor." He glares at me, making his opinion on the topic clear. I shake my head. As long as I'm living under his roof, it's my job to keep him alive until his son is freed from the German POW camp.

"You should eat more," Jacques says. "You've got lots of bicycling to do today."

Tonight's sabotage requires I cycle a fair distance. The satellite network in the area where it will take place recently lost one of their members. I am her replacement for the mission.

I allow Jacques to spoon the extra porridge I gave him back into my bowl. He's stubborn, and this is one battle not worth fighting. Fortunately, porridge is one food that doesn't make my nausea worse.

Nausea. Exhaustion. I've been blaming them on my late nights, the nightmares, and the lack of food, but what if...I count to when I roughly remember my last menses. With everything going on, I'd lost track of it.

I'm late, but that is understandable with the stress of my job and the diminished food supply. Even the food Johann provides isn't much. It's not designed to feed all three of us. It's only meant to benefit him.

The fatigue and nausea are easy to blame on the consequences of war, but those two symptoms combined with tender breasts can mean only one thing. *Bloody hell.* I'm pregnant. About eleven or twelve weeks if my maths is correct.

I draw in another slow breath. It's all I can do not to weep and curse out loud. I had hoped to one day be a mother, but not now. Not in the middle of the war. Not when the world is filled with ignorance and hate. Not when I have a job to do to help stop the Nazis.

But since there is nothing I can do about the dilemma for now—I have a mission to get to—I eat a spoonful of porridge and push all thoughts of the pregnancy aside. "I won't be back until tomorrow," I tell Jacques. I don't tell him where I'm going. He doesn't need to know.

"Be careful." He doesn't look at me when he says it. He focuses on eating his food. We both do.

We finish our meal, and I quickly clean the dishes. Jacques heads to the vineyard. By the time I leave the house, my stomach is a bit more settled. Settled enough that I'm able to pedal the seventy-five miles to the safe house where I am staying the night.

Which means I have plenty of time on the journey to dwell on my situation. So many questions buzz around in my thoughts. I'm going to be a mother. But what does that mean for my work with the local resistance circuit and the SOE? Of course, I will need to inform Allaire that I am pregnant. It is better he hears it from me than from someone else.

My duties will need to be reassigned so I can continue my work with the resistance circuit. My ability to perform my physical duties as an agent will be greatly compromised once I become heavily pregnant. It won't be possible to squeeze down narrow shafts then.

And where will I live? For now, I am staying with Jacques and Johann. But according to Major Müller on the night of the dance in Paris, Johann's battalion is supposed to be moving to the Eastern Front soon. Johann hasn't received the direct orders yet, but he knows it is coming shortly.

Once Johann is gone, what will happen to me?

Some of the villagers already believe I'm a collaborator because I live in the same house as a German officer. A baby in my belly will only be seen as evidence to support the notion.

Others might believe the baby is the product of rape by a German soldier. Plenty of French babies coming into the world now are due to that very reason.

And...will my being pregnant change things between Johann and me? How will he feel about being a father?

All these unanswered questions tie me up with ribbons of uncertainty and concern and regret.

I park my bicycle at the side of the small building, out of view from the street. One of the windows near the front door is cracked, as is the beige stucco wall. The building three doors down wasn't so lucky. The casualty of a recent air raid.

I knock on the door. It opens a minute later, and I find myself looking at a woman about my age, holding a young baby to her breast. "*Bonjour*, I'm Carmen. My uncle Bernard has begun violin lessons."

"Nice to meet you," she replies without a hint of a smile. "I'm Bridgette. My husband is in the kitchen, cooking dumpling stew."

She opens the door, lets me in, and nods in the direction I need to go. I walk along the short hallway. She follows me.

Male voices spill from an open door, and I enter into what was once a child's bedroom. Or maybe it still is between local resistance group meetings.

The blackout curtain is pulled shut, hiding from the outside world the group of men and the map on the table in the centre of the room. Hiding all hints they're plotting to blow up a train tunnel.

The four men gathered around the map look up and peer at me with a mix of open distrust and relief.

"This is Carmen," Bridgette tells them. It's not her real name. None of us are using our real names. She leaves the room.

"Jean Paul said you are skilled at setting off explosives in tunnels," one of the men says.

"That's correct." I don't elaborate further. They don't need to know all the details.

They introduce themselves.

"Is it true you gained information about plans for an ambush during a weapons exchange?" Philip, a man of about twenty-four years old, inquires. "And because of that, the maquis ambushed the Gestapo instead of the other way around?"

I nod. "That is true."

"From what I've heard, you saved a lot of lives."

Allaire took the necessary steps to ensure those members of the resistance got to live another day. I sent him a subsequent message explaining that while I was the one who overheard the German conversation not meant for my ears, Johann also told me about it the next morning, following the party.

The reply echoed the first one he sent me about Johann.

London still advises that we don't involve The Wolf in our work at present time since it is unclear where his loyalties lie.

Bridgette enters the room, carrying a glass of water. The baby is no longer feeding. She's asleep in her mother's arms. Bridgette hands me the glass.

"Thank you," I say, grateful for something to quench my thirst after the long bike ride.

The baby stirs, and the man who introduced himself as Laurent glances at the child, his expression full of adoration. And for a second I let the sweet image slip into my thoughts, but instead of Laurent, it is Johann gazing adoringly at *our* child. In my mind, I kiss him on the cheek and tell father and daughter how much I love them. Johann smiles at me, his love for us burning bright in his eyes.

Someone coughs, and I'm brought back to the here and now. I slowly sip the lukewarm water, my stomach settled for now. The nausea has resurfaced several times during the day over the past few weeks, and I don't want to risk it striking tonight.

"What's the security like for the tunnel?" I ask. "Can we expect trouble from the local authorities?"

"With the increase in attacks lately on the factories, bridges, and train tracks," Laurent explains, "the local authorities aren't taking any chances. They've increased the reward money for anyone who reports suspicious activity, and they have brought in more soldiers to guard anything perceived as a potential target."

"That is how we lost Giselle," Philip says. "The woman living near her turned her in. Giselle had done nothing suspicious that would bring attention to her, but the collaborator would sell her children to the devil himself if it meant she could make some money." His tone is heated, as if someone had thrown petrol onto a fire. But there is also another emotion in his voice. White-hot grief.

Not grief because they lost a good agent. The pain in his voice and on his face suggests Giselle meant more to him than just an asset to the resistance circuit.

"I'm sorry for your loss," I tell him. This is why falling in love during a time of war is not a good idea. But with love comes hope. And hope is what gives us the strength to keep fighting, to make it through each day. "How will you be protecting me while I place the explosives in the tunnel?" I ask the four men.

"Patrols are lighter at night." Laurent points to a piece of train track on the map about five miles from here. "Especially here. If we travel along this path, it's likely they won't see us. And if they do, we can easily take them down before they sound the alarm."

"We've been watching their routines for the past two weeks," Philip adds, "and they never deviate from them. We will have a twenty-minute window when no one is watching the tunnel up close."

"Up close? Are you saying even during that time, there will

be at least one guard watching the ventilation shaft from afar?" I take a sip of water.

Laurent nods. "But he won't be able to see you. Not from where he'll be standing."

"Can you not just eliminate him?"

"Too risky."

Philip and Laurent go over the plan with me. It seems sound enough. I ask a lot of questions to make sure we have everything straight.

"We should rest up for now," Laurent tells the group.

Bridgette takes me to an empty guest room. I lie down and close my eyes, praying the war will be over before the baby is born. Wondering what life will be like for me as a pregnant woman in occupied France.

I'm dreaming about Johann and our baby and England when someone shakes me awake. The room is dark, other than the faint glow from the candle in Bridgette's hand.

"It's time to get ready," she tells me.

It's well past curfew when the four men and I set out along the road, keeping to the trees and undergrowth. Had it been daytime, dozens of German soldiers would be traipsing through the wooded areas, watching for people planning to do exactly what we're doing or attempting to flee the country.

Unlike during parachute reception parties when the full moon brightens the way, the new moon casts the world in deep shadows. Shadows that hide us and our knapsacks filled with explosives and the detonator.

We cautiously head towards our target: a tunnel for a railway that connects Germany with the Atlantic Ocean.

A tunnel that once destroyed will greatly inconvenience the Nazis.

47

JESSICA

August, Present Day
Maple Ridge

I press Simone's doorbell. It's late Saturday morning, and Lucas is away for the overnighter with the Wilderness Warriors.

I need Simone's help with Violet and Sophie, and I'd rather Lucas didn't know about it—or anyone else. It's enough that Kellan is involved, but now I also need Simone's assistance.

The front door opens. Simone's wearing a floral sundress, her long reddish-brown hair pulled up in a ponytail. I biked over and look far from glamorous in a pastel-blue T-shirt, and shorts that cover the round scars on my upper thighs. They do nothing to hide the red scar there from the accident six weeks ago.

Jasper's standing next to her, happy as always to see Bailey. Bailey sits patiently beside my leg, wearing her *Service Dog in*

Training vest, waiting for my command to enter the house. I can tell her puppy patience won't last much longer. She's itching to play with her friend.

Simone smiles. "C'mon in."

Bailey and I follow her into the dining area of the open-concept house. Sunlight shines through the living room window, creating a spotlight on a vase of pink lilies in the center of the table.

But it's not the flowers that leave me inwardly groaning. Zara and Avery are sitting at the dining table, with an assortment of food, including samosas from Picnic & Treats, in front of them.

Emily isn't here, but that's probably because she's busy setting up Theresa's decorations. The wedding is tomorrow.

Simone grabs the pitcher from the table. "Strawberry lemonade, Jess?"

"Yes, please." I take the empty seat, my insides twisting. With Avery here, I won't be able to talk to Simone about the wig I need for Violet.

Simone passes me the glass of lemonade. "You mentioned you have something important you want to talk to me about?"

"It...it doesn't matter anymore. I was..." My gaze flicks to Avery and my palms itch. I rub them against my shorts, and my gaze drops to my plate.

"Jess," Avery says, her voice soft. "I promise whatever you want to tell us, I won't tell Noah or anyone else."

My heart hits a speed bump, and my head jerks up. "I don't know what you're talking about." I reach for one of the samosas, hoping it will be enough to change the topic.

"What's going on, Jess? Is it Troy?" Simone's tone is as gentle as Avery's. She takes a samosa from the serving plate, her eyes tenderly probing mine.

I shift my attention to the lilies on the table, afraid of her seeing the truth in my eyes. The flowers are beautiful. Only five months ago, I couldn't have fathomed the thought of ever seeing something so beautiful again. "No. It's. Uh." I lick my suddenly dry lips and look up at Simone. "I need to contact the person you mentioned the other day where Emily's friend got her wig."

A relieved smile curves Simone's mouth. "Sure. But you don't have to be nervous about needing a wig." Her eyes widen and her mouth drops slightly open. "Do you...do you have cancer?"

"No, it's nothing like that. It's...I...someone I know needs it to help them disappear."

"But not you, right?"

I choke out a sad laugh. I can't help it given the irony of the question.

"Can you tell us what's going on?" Zara sits up taller. "Maybe we can help you."

Avery covers my hand with hers. My hand is shaky. Hers is warm and soft, the gesture somewhat calming. "I realize you haven't known us for long, Jess, but you can trust us to keep your secret."

In the few months I've known them, they've done nothing to betray my trust. I swallow past the lump that's hardening in my throat. "It's vital you don't tell anyone what I'm going to tell you. And that includes Lucas, Garrett, and Emily."

"You want me to lie to my husband?" Simone's tone isn't harsh or disbelieving. It holds the equivalent of a cringe—as if she had already suspected I was going to ask that of her.

My muscles tighten and my stomach hurts. "Yes. Kellan knows everything I'm about to tell you. Troy knows some of it, but there's something bigger he doesn't know. And I need it to stay that way." Then I utter the seven words that swayed Kellan to my side. "It's a matter of life and death."

"I won't tell anyone unless you're okay with it," Simone says. Zara and Avery concur.

I take a deep breath and let it out slowly in a soft *whoosh*. I wish none of this was happening. I wish Violet's marriage was happy. Wish I wasn't hiding secrets that could land me back in prison. Wish I wasn't putting these three women at risk, asking them to lie for me.

And I wish I didn't have to worry about trusting them and having them betray me.

I roll my lower lip between my teeth, still uncertain how to start this. I tossed and turned for a better part of the night, figuring out how to broach this conversation with Simone. I hadn't planned to tell anyone else about my past or about Violet and Sophie.

As if Bailey senses I need her, she comes over to me, and I sink my fingers into her silky hair. I take a deep breath, but it's not enough to chase away my fear that I'm making a mistake trusting these three women. Especially Avery, whose boyfriend is a cop.

Angelique had to trust members of the local resistance group and the *Cashmere* network. She had to trust the escape line would be able to get Oskar and his family out of France. Had to trust the guides weren't going to hand the family over to the Gestapo. I draw strength from all of that.

"I know where Violet and Sophie are." My voice cracks, the words getting stuck in my dry throat. I would drink some lemonade, but my hands are too shaky to pick up the glass without sloshing the liquid everywhere.

I clear my throat. "Before I tell you where they are, I need to tell you something only Troy and Kellan know. But please understand I'd rather no one knows the truth...because I'm not that woman anymore." I give a self-deprecating laugh because I still don't know who I am. Not after everything I've been through. "Do you know the name Savannah Townsend?"

Zara shrugs. "It sounds familiar. But that's all I've got."

Simone shakes her head. "Same. The name is familiar. Is she a relative of yours?"

Avery's astute gaze studies my face, and it's as if the name slots all the puzzle pieces together for her. "Her husband was an abusive asshole. And a cop. Someone killed him, and his wife was framed for his murder. She spent five years in prison for a murder she didn't commit." Avery's eyes go glossy.

"She had a toddler daughter," I tell Avery, the heaviness in my heart giving weight to my words. "But she gave her up for adoption to the girl's uncle and aunt because she never expected new evidence to surface, proving she was innocent like she'd been telling anyone who bothered to listen. She lost the one thing that was most precious to her. The one thing she loved more than her own life and freedom."

I rub my hands against my shorts as if that's all it will take to make this situation go away. For the nightmare to end. "I know where Violet and Sophie are, but I need a disguise for them to help them escape Maple Ridge and Violet's abusive husband. That's where the wig comes in."

Shock widens Simone's and Zara's eyes, rendering the two women apparently speechless.

"You do realize her husband and the Maple Ridge Police Department are looking for them?" Avery's voice cracks in a whisper.

"And Noah too. But I can't let them find her. Violet's life depends on it. Hers and Sophie's lives depend on it." My tone pleads for them to keep my secret.

"So those diapers I saw you with two weeks ago...?" Simone's eyes widen, and she relaxes back on the dining room chair as if the answer is suddenly clear to her.

"I was buying them for Sophie. And I've had to buy her more since then. I'd get them online, but my neighbors might get suspicious if the delivery person leaves the boxes on my stoop and it's obvious what's in them. I've been lucky so far when I've bought them in the store—other than when you saw me that day."

"I'm sure we can figure something out to help with the diaper situation," Simone says.

"Thank you. That would really help." Her words knock off a small amount of the heavy load on my shoulders. It won't be fully gone until I get Violet and Sophie far from Oregon.

"So what does Savannah Townsend have to do with Violet's and Sophie's disappearance?" Zara's brow furrows. "I mean, other than the obvious—Violet's and Savannah's husbands are cops. Well, was in Savannah's case."

I locate on my phone the photo of Amelia that was taken when she was twenty months old. I caress her sweet face and hand the phone to Zara. "I'm Savannah Townsend." The name tastes foreign on my tongue. I haven't felt like Savannah in a long time.

I don't think I've seen Zara more surprised than in this moment. Her mouth is a perfect O of pinkish-brown lipstick. The expression is mirrored on Simone's face. Avery just seems...sad.

I point at the photo in Zara's hand. "Her name is Amelia." I choke on the ache in my heart from saying her name out loud. "She's my daughter. Or she was until I gave away my rights to her and let my brother-in-law and his wife adopt her. I'd been sentenced to twenty-five years in prison and had given up hope of anyone realizing I was innocent. I didn't want her to grow up thinking her mother was nothing more than a murderer. I didn't want her to grow up ashamed of me or scared I would try to see her once I was finally released." Except the latter is exactly what I'm hoping to do if Grace and Craig let me.

The pain on Simone's face causes me to hiccup back a building sob. "She doesn't know you're her mother, does she?"

I shake my head, the never-ending grief crushing me. "Her

adoptive parents felt it would be better if she didn't know about me, and I agreed with them. When I was still married to my husband, she was the only thing that kept me going. The only thing that kept me from giving up on life. I was attacked while in prison and nearly died because the one thing worth living for was no longer mine. I'd given up on life."

Tears break through the dam at the memory of that day. Of watching the blood—my blood—spill across the gray concrete, of welcoming my death. I hadn't realized at the time I would soon be a free woman.

"But I guess God had other plans for me," I tell them. I don't believe in God, but that was the one time I let myself believe that something bigger than all of us does exist.

I wipe my slick cheeks with the back of my hand. For all the good that does.

"I had a daughter once." Simone's voice is so low at first I'm not sure I heard her correctly. She clears her throat, her attention on her plate. "I was twenty-two and pregnant with Lucas's baby. But he didn't know it at the time. When I was five months pregnant, I was involved in a multi-car pileup because of a drunk driver. I lost my baby, and I lost my uterus due to an emergency hysterectomy to save my life."

Her pained eyes meet mine. They hold so much grief and understanding, my tears start up again.

"Her name was Lily." Simone's gaze flicks briefly to the vase of lilies on the table. "I know what it's like to lose a child and feel like you've lost everything. I'm sorry you had to give up your daughter because of the actions of someone else. That's why you're so determined to save Violet and Sophie, isn't it? You don't want Violet to lose her daughter too?"

I nod. "Maybe she'd have a better chance of keeping Sophie if her husband wasn't the chief of police. But he knows how to play the system to his advantage. Like my husband did. That makes it even harder to escape."

"Does Troy know about your daughter?" Simone picks up her samosa but doesn't seem to be any more interested in eating it than I am in eating mine.

I swirl mine in the chutney but don't make a move to put it in my mouth. It's to give my hands something to do. "No. And Kellan doesn't either. Only Violet knows." And Robyn. "I failed Amelia in so many ways. But at least because she's a minor, the media has left her alone." Thank God there are no threats online targeting her—that I'm aware of. "I'm trying to get to see her again...even if it's just as a friend of the family. But so far, her adoptive parents have been against the idea because... because I spent five years in a maximum-security prison. It changed me.

"That's why I don't want anyone else to know that I'm...was Savannah Townsend." I abandon my samosa on my plate. "If anyone finds out...finds out I didn't leave my husband...that I failed my daughter..." Shame flares and consumes me like it does on a daily basis. "If anyone finds out I spent five years in maximum security, in a system that changes you...and not necessarily for the better." The shakiness in my hand worsens, knowing everyone could so easily turn their back on me.

"You have nothing to be ashamed of, Jess," Simone says. "And you didn't fail your daughter. Just the opposite. What you did took tremendous courage. What you're doing for Violet and Sophie takes tremendous courage."

I draw in a long breath, filling my lungs with what can only be hope. "Thank you. The prison didn't release to the media or anyone else news that I was attacked while I was there. The media didn't have a recent photo of me after my release, and they didn't know I'd dyed my hair or about the scars on my face. Between those things and keeping a low profile, I've kept people from recognizing me."

"Troy knows all of this?" Zara asks, her shock at my news no less than it was at the beginning of the conversation. Other emotions also color her tone. Sorrow? Regret? Grief? Anger on my behalf? The one emotion void in her tone is pity. And for that, I'm grateful.

"He knows most of it...other than the part about my daughter and that I'm hiding Violet and Sophie." I explain to them my reasons for keeping him in the dark. "He might know about Amelia, but if he does, he hasn't mentioned it. He told me he wouldn't google my name. He knew I wanted to keep all of that in the past. The media hasn't mentioned my daughter since shortly after my husband's murder."

Zara's gaze flicks to Simone for a brief moment and back to me. "Are you sure you don't want to tell Troy what's going on?"

"Positive. It's better that way for all concerned."

"Other than the wig, what else can we do to help?" Simone picks up her glass.

"I could use some help in figuring out how to get Violet and Sophie out of Oregon," I tell them. "The women's emergency shelters in the area are all full. Violet needs a safe place where she and Sophie can go and her husband can't find her." I look at each woman in turn, hoping one of them has a suggestion. "Her family lives in Portland, so she can't go there. It will be too easy for Chief Wilson to locate her if she does."

Jasper wanders over to Avery. She pets him behind the ear. "They won't be able to travel out of Maple Ridge via public transportation. Someone is bound to recognize them and report them to the police."

"We need something like what they did during the Second World War," I say, "when downed Allied pilots tried to return to England. Escape lines through France led to the Pyrénées Mountains in Southern France, and the pilots hiked into Northern Spain and made their way to Portugal. The escaping pilots were passed from one helper to the next along the escape line until they got to the mountain range."

"So the same idea as the Freedom Railway and the conductors who helped escaped slaves get to the north and Canada," Zara adds. "That's not a bad idea. But let's hope this is easier to pull off than it was during the time of slavery and the Second World War."

I'm not sure if it will be any easier or less dangerous than it was back then. There are more challenges now when it comes to disappearing and starting over.

"I can talk to some people I know about arranging potential safe houses," Avery says.

Zara sweeps a cluster of thin braids behind her shoulder. "Same here. I have some connections in New Orleans who might be able to help us. Can't get much farther away from Maple Ridge than that."

I sag in partial relief, praying this will work and no one is caught in Chief Wilson's web of terror. He won't torture them like the Gestapo did when they captured and interrogated anyone they suspected working with the Allies, but he could easily destroy someone's life if he really wanted to. "Thank you. You can't begin to understand how grateful I am. How grateful Violet will be. Because of her husband, she'll lose everything. I just want to make sure Sophie isn't added to the list."

Avery picks up a mini quiche from a plate in the center of the table. "Your husband. He's the reason you're so nervous around Noah, isn't he?" She takes a bite.

I shift on the chair at the reminder of who her boyfriend is. "I know Noah isn't my husband and I know he wasn't responsible for me spending five years in prison, but I can't help it. I'm working on it, but it's not easy because I know he's a cop...even when he isn't in uniform. I just...cops make me extremely nervous."

A small smile curves on Avery's mouth, the sadness in her eyes giving away she's not a stranger to some of what I've gone through. "I get it. My father was an alcoholic and focused most of his abuse on my mother. She was finally able to get away from him and took my sister and me with her. But it took her five attempts because every time we left him, she'd second-guess herself and return to him. I think she was as scared to be without him as she was with him."

Avery puts the half-eaten mini quiche on her plate. "It's never easy to escape an abuser...even when you have escaped them. But just so you know, Noah will never judge you because of your past. None of us will. But if you ever need someone to talk to, I'm here for you."

Her words take some more of the weight I've been experiencing for too long from my shoulders. "Thank you. I'm taking my recovery one day at a time and figuring out who I am."

Avery's mouth melts into a wide smile. "It will come. I remember my mother went through the same thing. And eventually, each day was brighter than the last. She became the woman she'd always wanted to be. She went back to college and got her degree in social work and took art classes. Tons of art classes." Avery makes a sound bordering on a giggle. "And now her house and studio are filled with paintings of nude men and women. It's quite startling, actually. I'm looking forward to Noah's face when he finally sees the place." She laughs once more, and her laughter is contagious as we imagine his expression.

I brush away the tears that are the result of laughing so hard and opening up to the three women. And with each tear shed, the tension drains from my muscles, giving me a moment's reprieve.

For the first time in I don't know how long, I don't feel so alone in my pain. Troy has been incredibly sweet and supportive. But this—what these women are doing, risking—is different. It's heartwarming. Inspiring. I feel like I have sisters again.

Sisters my parents never gave me. Sisters that I had in my best friend when I was younger—before that was taken away.

"Alright," Zara says after we've recovered from laughing so hard. "Let's get to work on getting Violet away from her husband."

And we instantly sober at what we're about to face.

48

JESSICA

August, Present Day
Maple Ridge

I enter the living room belonging to the parents of the bride and swallow back a yawn. A side effect of last night's bad dream.

I survey the natural lighting. With the picturesque windows spanning the length of the wall, it's perfect for the style of photos I'm aiming for. Light and airy. Magical.

The four bridesmaids, dressed in rose-colored gowns, are talking excitedly among themselves. Theresa's father is sitting on the couch, sneaking in some Sunday afternoon football on TV. Katelyn isn't in the room. She's upstairs with Theresa.

Doing my best to be invisible, I shoot several candid photos of the bridesmaids laughing and smiling. And I sneak in a photo of the priceless expression on Anthony's face as he watches his team score a touchdown. He's wearing a tux, the bow untied, which only adds to the charm of the photo. It's my favorite one I've shot so far today.

I open my mouth to plead for Anthony to change his mind about the festival sponsorship. But what am I going to say? Tell him he's making a big mistake—that Chief Wilson is an abusive husband? It's Theresa's wedding day. He's not going to want to discuss the sponsorship on his daughter's big day.

I shut my mouth and go upstairs to Theresa's old bedroom. Katelyn is there with her mom, fussing over the bride. She glances at me long enough to smile and returns her attention to Theresa's veil. Em is also in the room, going over last-minute details with the trio.

"The dress is gorgeous," I tell Theresa. The full-length gown is off-white with several dozen buttons running down the back.

While Theresa continues to get ready, I take more photos—the precious moments of the mother-of-the-bride with her two daughters.

Eventually, Emily and I head out in her car for the next part of my wedding-photography plans.

"You and Troy...you really are over?" Em asks, driving along the neighborhood street. The words are spoken like they're rare and delicate flowers she's trying not to trample. And she appears truly heartbroken, which would also explain why she kept looking at me like she expected me to dissolve into tears while we were at Theresa's parents' house.

She's not too far off. It's taking everything I have not to do exactly that. "Yes. Things were getting...um, intense." I had only planned for it to be a break, but then things fell apart between us when we had the argument. The ache in my heart worsens at just thinking about how things went so wrong.

Emily rolls her lips together and keeps her gaze on the road. "I love your dress. It's pretty."

A short chuckle tumbles from me. It's not like she's never seen the dress before. "Thank you. Anne Carstairs gave it to me as a gift after I bought her great-aunt's house. It's my favorite dress. If I was five years old, I'd feel like a princess in it." That's the best way to describe how the dress makes me feel.

Emily laughs and turns down the street where the wedding ceremony and reception are taking place.

She parks the car on the driveway in front of the house and helps me with my gear.

Once inside, I shoot numerous photos of the groom, his groomsmen, and his family as they prepare for his part of the day. They're having so much fun, it's hard not to get pulled into their joy and laughter. This is what weddings should be about.

"Okay, everyone," Em announces a short time later. "The bride and her family are on their way. It's time for you to head to the garden."

I follow the group outside to where the guests are gathering. I photographed the stunning details this morning, so I don't have to worry about that now, other than a few shots with the change of lighting.

My gaze lands on Troy, and a rush of jumbled emotions congeals inside me. Relief, regret, happiness, sorrow. I haven't seen him since Thursday at work. I want to run over to him and kiss him, but my resolve locks me into place.

I'm doing the right thing by pushing Troy away. What I'm doing for Violet and Sophie is bigger than my own happiness.

I stretch my lips into a facsimile of a smile. Unless you look too closely and catch the cracks in the shiny veneer, it's passable for the real thing.

He smiles back, but it's missing the brilliant luster I'm used to.

Katelyn steps up to him and embraces him. I don't have time to dwell on that. Her presence means the bride and the bridesmaids are almost here. I rush around to the front of the house to prepare for their arrival.

The next three hours are a blur. I'm constantly on the go,

unable to slow down and think. Think beyond what shots I want to take, the aperture and speed settings I'm using, the best lighting, the best angle for each shot.

I don't want to miss those magical moments every bride wants to see long after her wedding day is over. I'm flitting this way and that way, capturing as many of them as I can in the photojournalistic style I love. Each photo tells a beautiful story.

"Why's Troy here with Katelyn?" I ask Emily when I finally have a second to breathe. She's been clinging to him like a barnacle at the bottom of a boat.

Emily busies herself with a flower arrangement that already looked good.

"Em?" Her name is drawn out in a warning. A warning I don't want to be lied to. Which is rich given all the lies I'm currently keeping track of.

God, when did I become such a big liar? My gut tightens in reply.

Sometimes lying isn't a bad thing. Not when it can save a life.

"They're...they're dating," Emily says. "Or at least that's the rumor. Troy denied it when Zara brought it up Friday night."

The tightening in my gut grows and spreads to my chest. "Katelyn doesn't seem to think it's a rumor."

Emily watches them for a second, creases wrinkling her brow. "No. She doesn't."

"How long has the rumor being going on for?" My gaze shifts to Troy and Katelyn, who are now talking to her parents.

"Since Friday."

Friday? That would explain the odd glances Simone and Zara kept slipping each other yesterday when I went over to Simone's house. They were trying to decide if they should tell me.

"What else does the rumor say?" I turn to Emily in time to catch the pain on her face before she smooths it away. The world swirls around me, and I close my eyes. "They've slept together, haven't they? Recently, I mean."

An oxygen-robbing silence is my reply. I open my eyes to see the truth written all over Em's face.

"He claims he doesn't remember having sex with her, but he did wake up naked in bed with her."

"He doesn't remember having sex? Wow, just how bad was it?" I mumble the last part under my breath, but she must have heard. She cackles, and I can't help the smile that flickers on my face.

But once I remember who we're talking about, the smile vanishes.

A week. He could have at least waited a week after I ended our relationship before he jumped into bed with another woman.

A ballad starts to play through the speakers, and the bride and groom begin their first dance together. I shoot more photos. I'll have so many photos to edit after tonight, I might never have to leave my house again.

Which means I'll never have to see Troy and Katelyn together as a couple after tonight. I guess if there's a bright side to the work I have ahead of me, that would be it.

I yawn, the lack of sleep and the stress from the last few days quickly catching up to me. *Just a couple more hours to go...*

The sound of glass shattering on something hard intrudes on my weary thoughts, and past blurs with present.

My husband is standing in front of me, still in his uniform, his face mottled with rage, the end of his Glock directed at me.

And my body turns ice-sculpture cold.

49

TROY

August, Present Day
Maple Ridge

Katelyn drags me onto the dance floor, but my heart isn't into it. I keep stealing glances at Jess. She's visibly exhausted, as if she hasn't slept for several days.

I want to ask her what's going on, but she made it clear that her life is none of my business.

The sound of a glass breaking has my head jerking in the direction the noise came from. Two waiters bend down to pick up the fragments.

Jess is standing a few feet from them, eyes wide and staring unseeingly at something in front of her. People are looking at her like she's a curiosity. A statue.

Anthony moves forward, hand raised as if to touch her. It's only then I realize I'm rushing toward Jess.

"Troy?" Katelyn calls out from behind me.

"Don't touch her!" I say to Anthony as I put my arm between them. "She's having a flashback, and you touching her might make things worse." I turn to face the woman I love. She's trembling and doesn't seem to be aware of her surroundings. "Jess, it's Troy. You're safe." My voice is level and calm, the opposite to how I feel getting to stand so close to her.

"What's wrong with her?" Katelyn says quietly next to me.

"Jess, it's Troy. You're safe. Whatever you think you're seeing, it isn't real." Not anymore.

Jess slowly blinks, and I can see on her face the moment she remembers where she is. She closes her eyes and mutters to herself.

"Are you all right?" I ask her.

Her eyes fly open and dart from me to Katelyn. "I-I need to get back to work."

I put my hand on her arm. "You need a break." The feel of her soft skin against my fingertips is an electric shock to my heart. It jump-starts the organ, which hasn't been beating properly since Jess ended things between us.

"I'm fine, Troy." The words sound strained, forced, like they're being pressed through clenched teeth.

Jess pulls away and brushes past me without giving me a second glance. She heads for the tent opening.

I take a step toward her, but Em catches my eye. She shakes her head and goes after Jess.

Katelyn places her hand on my arm. "Maybe I should go talk to her." She hurries after Jess and Em before I can tell her that's not a good idea.

I turn to explain to Anthony that Jess has PTSD and to apologize for my reaction when it looked like he was going to touch her, but he's no longer there. I scan the tent, unable to locate him.

I shrug off my need to explain things to him. I have no

intention of using what just happened with Jess to convince him to reinstate his sponsorship.

Theresa breaks away from her husband and turns to watch her sister disappear out of the tent. She walks over to me and flashes a tight smile that says so many things, none of which I can unscramble. "What's going on between you and my sister?" She asks it so casually, her words throw me off at first.

"Nothing. We're just friends." *And she promised if I came to your wedding as her date, she would convince your father to change his mind about the festival sponsorship.*

"Since when were you two friends?" Her tone isn't harsh or demanding or sarcastic. It's soft and worried.

I frown, confused by her comment. "I've known her a long time, and I volunteer at the Veterans Center where she works. I'd say based on that alone, we're friends."

"That's funny because I don't ever remember her wanting to be your friend, Troy. Boyfriend, yes. But never something as simple as being your friend."

The frown pinches tighter between my eyes, and I have a feeling I'm about to be hit with a shit-eating headache. "What are you saying?"

"I'm saying that things aren't always what they seem with my sister. Is it true you slept with her?" There's no judgment in Theresa's eyes, just an unexplainable apology.

"When did that become public knowledge?" My tone is harsher than expected, but it's not directed at Theresa. *Goddamn small towns.*

Theresa winces. "So it's true?"

"Apparently," I mutter.

"What do you mean?"

"I mean exactly that." I don't feel like explaining to Theresa how I don't remember having sex with her sister. At. All.

Theresa looks toward the tent opening for a second, then turns back to me. "Just be careful. My sister likes you a lot. And while I love my sister, I don't always agree with her methods. I saw how you were with Jess. I'd hate to see that get messed up because of Katelyn."

I almost bark out a humorless laugh at how she's a little too late with the advice. Things are already messed up, and it has nothing to do with Katelyn.

I was the one who screwed up everything after things fell apart between Jess and me.

One of Theresa's bridesmaids comes over to get her, and I head to the tent's exit.

Several people have also escaped the tent and are enjoying the mountain scenery. I scan the area. The sun has started setting, but it's still light enough for me to spot Jess, Emily, and Katelyn sitting on a bench by the pond.

From where I'm standing, it looks like they're having a friendly discussion. But as I draw closer, I notice Jess's pained expression.

I stop, unsure if I should check on her or leave them alone to talk.

Emily's head turns my way. Relief appears on her face— only for her expression to darken. She wants to knee me in the nuts.

I ignore her reaction. "Hey, ladies."

Jess unfolds from the bench. "I should get back inside. Theresa is tossing the bouquet soon, and then I'll probably head out."

She walks past me. But since I have no intention of letting her get away without me fighting for her, I gently grab her arm.

She sucks in a soft breath, the longing in her expression mirroring everything I'm feeling. I'm not the only one experiencing the buzz beneath the surface from the skin-on-skin contact.

I let myself get lost in Jess's eyes for a heartbeat, but now isn't the time for me to show her what she means to me. She won't listen to me here, in front of everyone. And I have to think things through first. Plan what I'm going to say to her the same way I plan out my renovations.

I let go of Jess's arm, even though my body and heart are begging me not to. I don't stop her when she slips away. I level my gaze at Katelyn.

I'm vaguely aware of Emily saying something, but I'm too focused to hear what she says. She hurries after Jess, leaving me alone with Katelyn.

"I didn't have sex with you, did I?" My voice is dark and dangerous, masking the fear simmering inside me. Fear I'll never be able to repair what Katelyn helped me destroy.

"Sure, you did." She smiles at me, but the curve of her mouth lacks sincerity. The corners flicker like they're battling to stay in position, but the weight of her regret is pulling them down. The same regret and uncertainty wars in her eyes.

"If that's true, then why don't I remember having sex with you? Unless I somehow banged my head, giving myself amnesia, there's no way I would forget something like that."

The regret and uncertainty vanish from her eyes, replaced with a steely resolve. "You were drunk, I guess."

"I was drunk," I echo, the words sounding empty. "If a man has sex with a woman who's too inebriated to remember it the next day, it means she was too drunk to consent. And that makes it rape."

Katelyn's eyes widen. "Are you saying I raped you?"

"No, I'm saying it never happened. If I was too drunk to remember having sex, it means I was too drunk to get it up. Which means nothing happened. I don't know why you were naked in my bed. Or even why I was naked. But I do know we never had sex." I fold my arms across my chest.

Mascara-darkened lashes lower over narrowed eyes and her body goes rigid-straight. "Are you calling me a liar now?"

"Which is it, Katelyn? Did you take advantage of me while I

was drunk? Or are you lying to everyone about what really happened Thursday night?"

She huffs, her body remaining stiff.

"Look, I don't care what your reasons are for lying. I just care that you're hurting someone who means a lot to me. I agreed to be your date because you said you would convince your father to change his mind about the festival sponsorship." Which I'm beginning to believe was a lie. She wasn't going to do that. And even if she did try, she won't be able to convince him. "I've made it clear nothing is going to happen between you and me." I take a step back. "Keep away from Jess. And you're going to tell everyone the truth. You and I. Never. Had. Sex."

"Hey, it's not my fault people assumed we did." She lifts her shoulders in a weak shrug. "I didn't actually start the rumor."

"But you also didn't stop it. You were the one who started the rumor we're dating, weren't you?"

Another shrug, but she has the decency to look somewhat contrite.

Shit. I don't have time for this. I've got a relationship I need to figure out how to fix.

I turn on my heel and stalk toward the tent.

50

ANGELIQUE

September 1943
France

A stifling silence surrounds us as the four men and I creep towards our target: a tunnel, through which a railway track connecting Germany with the Atlantic Ocean passes through. Explosives weigh down the knapsacks on our backs.

Two of the men split off from the group. Their job is to dispose of the guards should the Germans return to the area sooner than scheduled. Or if it takes me longer than planned to execute my task.

Laurent, Philip, and I arrive at the grassy slope that hides the tunnel from above, and we listen for signs of danger. The next train isn't due to arrive for several more hours, but that's not what has me the most concerned.

I glance to where the German soldier, with his eyes on the ventilation shaft, should be standing. Standing as if nothing has

397

changed since Laurent and his sabotage team came up with the plan for attacking the tunnel.

The German is stationed twenty yards away, barely visible in the dark. I hope Laurent and Philip are right about the German's inability to see what we're up to once I am swinging from the parachute harness—a deadly spider dangling from her web. I doubt I'll survive the fall if the ropes are cut.

I remove my knapsack and put it on the ground by my feet. Then I step into the harness, fasten the straps, and check the secureness of the rope. I'd rather not plummet to my death if I can avoid it.

Once Laurent and Philip have everything ready, they help me climb into the brick structure, hoisting me up as if I weigh nothing. My fingertips scrape along the rough surface as I grope around in the dark.

Palms clammy, I swing my legs over the side. The German soldier doesn't fire or shout out an alarm, and I release a slow, even breath.

I can do this.

I signal with hand gestures for Laurent and Philip to lower me. The shaft is narrow, and I'm the only member of the team who can fit inside it. If there is ever an advantage to the starvation diet the Germans have reduced us to, this would be it. But how much longer will I be able to do this before my pregnancy prevents me from fitting in tunnel shafts?

I ignore the question for now and make my way down the tight brick enclosure, forcing myself to breathe slow and easy. I'm not usually claustrophobic, but I seem to be making an exception this one time.

The knowledge that my life is in the hands of Laurent and Philip isn't helping. I trust them as much as I can in the short time I have known them. It's the Germans I do not trust. All it takes is for one of them to discover Laurent or Philip at the entrance to the shaft, and my life is as good as forfeit.

I wiggle my way out of the bottom of the shaft until I'm dangling in the middle of the tunnel. I swing to and fro, a circus act minus the audience. No one is in here. Thank God for that. The guards are stationed outside at either end. They weren't expecting anyone to climb down the shaft to blow up the railway tunnel.

I examine the scene in front of me, doing the reconnaissance work I was trained to do. I shine my torch up the shaft and turn it off and on two times, signaling for Laurent to pull me up. The two men haul me up as I wiggle my way through the shaft to the top.

At the opening, I draw in a deep lungful of cool night air and crawl out. I drop nimbly to the grass, my feet landing with a soft thud on the ground, the sound too quiet to be heard by the German soldier watching the area.

We lower the explosives into the tunnel, aware that we're running out of time—both when it comes to the soldiers checking the area and the countdown until the explosives detonate.

As soon as the explosives and detonator are in position, the three of us run. Stealth is slightly less important at this point compared to speed. None of us want to be here when the show begins.

The damp grass muffles our footfalls. We're nothing more than three dark shadows running in the night. As long as nothing goes wrong with the explosives, our mission has been a blooming success. The meeting spot is four hundred yards away, and we can watch the show from there.

"Halt!" The thunderous command shatters the quiet.

We don't stop or slow down.

We sprint.

The loud bang of a gunshot punctures the air. The exhaustion that has been plaguing me for the last few weeks is shoved aside as a newfound energy fuels me onward.

Another bang. Only this time the noise is accompanied by a burning pain in my calf.

I push past the intense discomfort and limp-run through the forest, not daring to slow my pace. My injured calf will be the least of my concerns if I'm captured.

The crashing of undergrowth, the yelled commands, and the thud of boots against the hard dirt ground warn us of the Germans' rapid approach. If we're lucky, none of them have figured out why we are up here. They'll focus their search on the hill and not on the contents of the tunnel.

We hurl ourselves down the steep incline, rolling and skidding under the cover of night. Small rocks and twigs scratch and dig into me, but they are better than the alternative.

We land at the bottom of the incline in dazed piles, alive for now. Above us, shouts of confusion make their way to us. We scramble to our feet and keep running. The danger is less real than it was a moment ago, but that doesn't mean we can stay here, standing around waiting to get shot from above.

Once we're far enough away to slow to a walk, my hand goes to my stomach and the baby growing within. The move is protective, comforting, as if to tell the baby that if they survive this, they will survive anything life throws at them.

I half expect to experience a sharp pain in my belly, warning me I'm about to lose the baby, but nothing comes. I don't have time to dwell on that or how I feel about it. Laurent, Philip, and I pick ourselves up and stumble towards the meeting point a safe distance away.

We barely make it to the spot before a spark of light flashes from inside the depths of the tunnel. The light then blossoms into a beautiful dance of destructive flames and the billow of black smoke. Metal and brick buckle and burn, and the shock-wave from the explosion collapses the tunnel in a mess of rubble.

The place is a chaos of colours and sounds, all of them

breathtaking because it means one thing: we have just severed one of the railway arteries to the battle in the Atlantic Ocean.

"Show me your leg," Philip says to me, volume low, tone tight.

"I'm fine. The bullet only nicked me."

"I'll let you know if you're fine. I'm not going to have you pass out on me due to loss of blood. Plus, the Germans' dogs will lead them to us if they catch scent of it." His command-rough tone has me thinking twice about ignoring him.

I lean my hand on the thick trunk of a tree and let Philip examine the wound.

He rips my trouser leg, curses, and removes a canteen of water from his knapsack. He pours the cool contents over the wound, washing away the dirt that clung to it when I rolled down the hill.

He removes a strip of clean fabric from his knapsack. "It's not sterilised, but it will have to do. It's better than you bleeding out." He wraps the fabric around my leg and fastens it with a knot. I barely feel anything, the rush of exhilaration from the successful operation numbing the pain.

"A bullet hit her," is the first thing Laurent tells his wife after Philip and I enter the safe house. His voice is quiet so as not to alert the neighbours to our late-night activities nor awaken his sleeping daughter.

He nods at me and continues into the house without another word. The other two men have already gone their separate ways.

Philip helps me to the room where I briefly slept earlier. The rush of exhilaration from a short time ago has faded to nothing, leaving in its wake the burning pain I experienced when the bullet grazed my leg. My limp is no less pronounced, the impact of a dozen or so bruises scattered over my body.

"Let me tend to your wound first, and then you can sleep," Bridgette says softly to me. She turns to Philip. "Off with you."

Philip leaves the room, shutting the door behind him.

I nod to Bridgette and undo my trousers. I carefully peel them off, cautious not to dislodge the makeshift bandage, and turn so Bridgette can inspect it.

"Lie on your stomach."

I do as I am told. She unwraps the cloth and lifts the lantern above my calf. The murmur of Philip's and Laurent's voices come from outside the bedroom, but I can't hear what they are saying.

"It's not too bad," Bridgette informs me. "I'll clean it and wrap it, but you will need to stay here for a few days so your leg is healed enough for you to cycle home. That is assuming the wound doesn't become infected."

Bridgette doesn't know where I live—none of the men do. They only know I reside in a village far enough away, and it took me several hours to pedal here.

Bloody hell and damn. I need to get home before Johann finishes his current operation. I don't want him to worry, which I know he will do if I am not there when he returns. And what if Müller drops by unannounced and inquires as to my where-abouts? He will grow suspicious if Jacques cannot tell him where I went or when I am due to return.

Bridgette returns a few minutes later with the first-aid supplies. We don't talk much beyond a few whispered words. Usually after an operation like this, I experience a second wind that lasts for hours. This time, I can barely keep my eyes open.

I want to ask her questions about being pregnant, but I'm not ready yet to tell anyone the news. I still need to digest it myself and decide what to do about the baby. Decide what to do about my role in ending the war. About what to tell Baker Street. About whether I should tell Johann.

Bridgette gently cleans the wound, dabbing at it with a wet cloth. At the stinging pain, I squeeze my eyes shut and grip the sheet tightly in my fists. It's not the first time I've been hurt since arriving in France, but it is the first time I've been shot.

"The wound is relatively shallow," she tells me, "but the path is jagged and cannot be stitched cleanly. The bleeding has stopped. It won't stay that way if you don't give it a chance to heal." She finishes cleaning it and wraps it up with a new cloth. "I'm going to fetch some more blankets so you can sleep."

Part of me—a large part of me—wants to ignore Bridgette's advice and leave, but that would be foolish given the distance I need to cover. What would it hurt to wait a day or two? A few months ago, I wouldn't have thought twice about pedalling the long distance with a gunshot wound, but that was before I was with child.

Her arms are full when she returns. She covers me and leaves again. It only takes a few minutes for exhaustion to overtake me, and the memory of the exploding tunnel lulls me to sleep.

MY LOWER LEG IS ACHING WHEN I WAKE SEVERAL HOURS LATER, the pain only just bearable. The house is quiet, other than a female voice softly singing a lullaby in the room next to mine.

I sit up, and a wave of nausea hits me. I sink back onto the bed. Being shot clearly hasn't done anything to ease the morning sickness.

The bedroom door opens, and Bridgette enters, her baby in her arms. "You're awake!"

I ease myself upright again. My body is tired, but not as drained as I was earlier. "What time is it?"

"Ten o'clock in the morning. You've been asleep for over twenty-eight hours."

Shock widens my eyes, and my gaze flies to the curtain-covered window. "I have?"

She nods. "I was worried your wound was infected, but you didn't spike a fever. Can I check the wound?"

"Yes."

She lays a blanket from the bed on the floor and lowers her daughter onto it. The baby's little face peers up at the ceiling. Bridgette then has me roll onto my side so she can inspect my leg. The baby doesn't fuss about not being in her mother's arms. She just coos and gurgles.

"How old is she?" I ask, smiling at the little one.

Bridgette unwraps the bandage. "Five months."

"She's beautiful." I have a sudden desire to brush my finger along the baby's soft cheek. The light fluff on her head is blond and her eyes are blue.

"She's the only good thing that has come from this war." Bridgette inspects my wound while I watch her daughter. "It's looking better, but you still need another two or three days of rest before you are able to pedal home."

"My papa will be worried." The words feel so natural coming from my lips. Jacques really has become like a second father to me.

"We can get word to him."

I consider her offer for a moment. Jacques won't be the only person worried about my unexpected disappearance. But he has always known a day would come when I would either have to leave France or move to a different part of the country.

Johann will also wonder what happened to me. But it would be foolish and possibly dangerous for someone to get word to Jacques. If Johann and some of his comrades—or Müller—happen to be at the farmhouse, it could be deadly for the courier and Jacques if someone other than Jacques or Johann should read the message.

I shake my head. "It's probably better if you don't."

"Are you sure?"

"I am."

The baby kicks her legs in the air. Will Johann's and my baby look like that sweet little angel?

Baby. I can't imagine what Johann's reaction will be if I tell him I'm pregnant with his child. It's not as if either of us came to France expecting to become a parent. Not when we're surrounded by nothing but oppression and death.

The baby rolls onto her stomach and puts her hand in her mouth.

"I'll get you some soup," Bridgette says, "and then you should get some more rest." She scoops her daughter off the blanket and leaves me to sit with my thoughts.

For the first time since acknowledging I'm pregnant, I let myself consider what my baby's and my future will be. Assuming we both survive this. I haven't even told Johann I love him. How can I? We're supposed to be enemies, not lovers.

I hate everything the Germans are doing and their disregard for life. But none of those things are Johann. He has proved that to me over and over and over again.

He's fighting for Germany because he doesn't believe he has a choice.

He's fighting for Germany on the slim chance it will save his mother and sister.

He's risking everything for them because he loves his family.

The baby...the baby is part of his family. Will his love for his family apply to his child?

Or perhaps it would be better I don't tell him since it was never the SOE's intent for me to stay with Jacques for the duration of the war. When I finally leave, what would that do to Johann? How would he cope, knowing I've taken his child away from him—and possibly into danger?

Perhaps...perhaps it would be better if Johann doesn't know the truth.

For all of our sakes.

51

JESSICA

August, Present Day
Maple Ridge

"Are you okay if I leave after the bouquet toss?" I ask Theresa as soon as I return to the tent. I'm tired and I just want to go home and check on Violet and Sophie.

And if I have a chance, I plan to read more of Iris's journals. I want to escape reality for a while and find out how Angelique survived the war. Perhaps there will be something helpful in the entries when it comes to getting Violet and Sophie out of Oregon.

What I'm not planning to do is anything that involves thinking about what Katelyn told me a few minutes ago. About her. And Troy.

"That's definitely okay," Theresa says. "We're ready to do the bouquet toss now." She signals to the DJ.

"Okay, all you lucky ladies," the woman announces into the

406

microphone. "It's time for the bouquet toss. Everyone on the dance floor if you're hoping to be the next bride."

A dozen or so women of all ages crowd behind Theresa. I position myself for the best shots and take a series of photos as the bouquet is snatched out of the air by a long-limbed woman.

"Yes!" she shrieks, resulting in chuckles among a group of men on the sidelines and one very audible groan.

I scan the disappointed faces only to realize Katelyn isn't here. Neither is Troy. They must have stayed outside. They're probably making out in some dark corner of the backyard.

Aaaand that's my sign to bail.

I say a quick goodbye to Theresa's family, thanking them for the opportunity to photograph the wedding, and I leave with Emily. She's also finished for the evening.

"You did an incredible job with the wedding," I tell her as she reverses out of the driveway. "Everything ran so smoothly."

"Thanks. Does that mean you're open to shooting more weddings?"

Am I?

I enjoyed shooting this one. But I don't see this becoming my career, even part time. The thrill I thought I would experience, the thrill I had during my journalism degree, just wasn't there. Not in the way I'd hoped it would be.

"Sure. As long as the bride and groom are only interested in the photojournalistic style like today. I'm not looking to be a full-time wedding photographer."

"Fair enough."

That still leaves me with the question of what I want to do for the rest of my life. It isn't working for Troy. That's for sure. Even if I hadn't ended things with Troy, being his full-time assistant isn't my dream career.

Emily drops me off at my house, and I walk across the street to collect Bailey. That's another reason I'm not sure if being a wedding photographer is for me. I can't have her with me on the job, which makes training her more difficult. And if she had been with me tonight, she might have prevented the flashback...or pulled me out of it sooner.

I shudder—not because I remember what happened. I don't. But because they're still coming, and now that I've quit therapy, they'll keep ruling my life. There's nothing I can do about that, though. I can't risk going to therapy and saying something that will get Violet or me in trouble.

I ring Delores's doorbell. A moment later, Bailey's bark comes from the other side of the door. Delores opens it and smiles her grandmotherly grin. "Hello, Jess. How was the wedding?"

Bailey doesn't wait for the command to go outside. She rushes toward me, and I mentally sigh. Guess we have to work on that skill some more.

I hug her, relieved to have her by my side again.

"It was good. Emily did a great job with it, and the bride and groom looked so happy."

I know not all marriages end up like mine and Violet's or end in divorce. I hope Theresa's marriage will be the happily-ever-after sort.

I stroke Bailey, sinking my fingers into her fur. "Thank you for looking after Bailey."

"My pleasure. She's such a sweet thing." Delores hands me Bailey's leash.

While I click it on Bailey's harness, Delores retrieves the few supplies and toys I left with her for while I was at the wedding. I thank Delores once more, then Bailey and I cross the street to my house.

The house is dark except for the living-room light sneaking past the thin gap in the closed curtains. The light that's on a timer.

I unlock the front door and reactivate the alarm. I unhook Bailey's leash. She stays by my side as I walk to the kitchen like she's been trained to do. She's my shadow. A shadow I'm happy to have.

The kitchen light is on, but Violet isn't in the room. I head upstairs. There's no sound coming from the room she and Sophie share. No light bleeding under the door.

I quietly open it to find Violet asleep on the bed. Sophie is sleeping in the play pen that we use as a crib.

I carefully shut the door, not wanting to wake them, and grab my laptop from my bedroom. I need to download the photos from Kim's camera before I go through them.

The doorbell rings while I'm in the kitchen, setting up the laptop. I wince, praying the noise didn't wake Violet and Sophie.

And then I frown. I'm not expecting anyone.

The frown smooths out. It's probably Delores returning one of Bailey's toys that was forgotten at her house.

I go to the front door, flip on the porch light, and peer through the peephole. Chief Wilson is standing on the front stoop, wearing jeans and a navy T-shirt. He just looks like a regular man and not the chief of police, but that doesn't stop my heart rate from going into overdrive, pounding loud enough for everyone in the house to hear. *Oh, God. Oh, God. Oh, God.* What does he want?

I can't even pretend I'm not home. He knows I am because I just turned on the light above his head. *Fuckers.* What the hell was I thinking? Angelique would never have made such a stupid mistake.

I deactivate the alarm, unlock the door, and open it only a couple of inches. "Hi? Can I help you?" The question comes out as a choked squeak, the guilt and fear in the words ringing endlessly in my ears.

"Where is she?" The thunder-loud demand in his voice startles me and shakes the house to its foundation. Or maybe it's me who's shaking.

"Where is who?"

"My daughter, dammit. And my wife. You know where they are." His expression is weary. His disheveled dark-blond hair looks as if he has repeatedly shoved his fingers through it.

"Wh-why would you think I know where they are?" I ask, my pulse stammering in my ears.

"Because I have good friends who work at the grocery store. What does a single woman need toddler diapers for?"

Shit. "They were for a friend."

"I saw the empty box in your recycle bin." His quiet voice simmers with danger and is more terrifying than his previous tone.

Fuckers. I hadn't expected him to snoop through my trash.

"Now don't make me repeat myself, Savannah. Where is my daughter and my wife?" One moment he's standing on my stoop, glaring at me. The next he's pushed his way into my house, his gun leveled at my chest.

I stand frozen, afraid to move even a fraction of an inch—because of the gun and because he knows. He knows who I am.

How? How? How? I've been so careful. I've done everything I can not to draw any unwanted attention or to give away my true identity.

Bailey barks.

"Lock the dog away or else I'll shoot it." The sharp-staccato of his words sends adrenaline surging through me. But it's not enough to set off my fight instinct. Even my flight instinct appears to be broken. I stand completely paralyzed, unable to will my body to move.

What do I do? What do I do? What do I do?

Chief Wilson lowers his gun to point at Bailey, and I have no doubt he'll kill my dog if I give him a reason to.

"Bailey, laundry room." My legs shaking something fierce, I stumble-walk her to the laundry room where her crate is.

"Put her in the crate." Chief Wilson's tone hasn't softened. If anything, it's sharper, louder, and I startle at the force of it.

I open the crate door, praying to everything holy Violet heard her husband, and she and Sophie are now hiding in the secret room. "Crate, Bailey."

Bailey gives me a pitiful look that says she'd rather stay by my side. Realizing that's not going to happen, she gives an unhappy whimper and enters the crate.

Chief Wilson slams the door shut with his foot. "Lock it!"

Bailey releases another whimper, which reaches in and squeezes my heart. I fumble with the lock and snap it shut.

Chief Wilson walks over to the washing machine, bends, and snatches from the floor a small stuffed purple octopus I hadn't noticed had been forgotten there. Sophie's octopus. *Oh, shit.*

"Where's my daughter and Violet?" His tone is tightly coiled and lethal, and I swallow. Hard.

"I-I don't know."

He holsters the gun and grabs my arm, his fingers digging painfully into my flesh. He shakes me. My head whacks the drywall, and for a second, I see spinning stars.

"Where is she?" This time he's louder and spittle hits my cheek, but I don't so much as flinch. And now...and now it's not Chief Wilson who's in front of me. It's my husband. Big and brooding and brutish.

He grabs my hair and drags me into the hallway. "Where is she, fucking bitch?"

He shoves me to the ground and kicks me in the stomach. But I anticipate the move, having been a victim of it too many times, and roll out of the way. His boot glances off my stomach. The contact is enough to bruise, but not enough to do internal damage.

I'm not so lucky with the next strike. He aims for my thigh.

It doesn't break. *Thank God.* But I will be left limping for a few days.

If I survive.

Please wake up, Violet. Please hide before he searches the house.

The next blow is with his fist. He hits my cheek. I feel the skin split. Just one more scar to add to the others that mark my years of abuse. I can't even bring myself to care about it anymore.

I attempt to fight off his next blow, kicking and flailing and squirming. It's not because I believe I'm going to win. I'm not. I can see it in his eyes. He's not going to let me escape. There's only one thing he wants.

And I'm standing in the way of him getting it.

Good. No one was there to protect me from my asshole husband. I lost everything because of him.

That thought is enough to build the fire in my own furnace, and the surge of adrenaline finds a new purpose.

I fight. Fight as though it's my husband I'm trying to defeat. My husband who was the monster who cost me everything.

Needing to grab something to use as a weapon, I roll to my side and attempt to push to my feet.

Another kick—this one lands just below my ribs, preventing me from standing. I collapse and gasp for air, trying to draw it into my lungs. Trying to summon my battle-weary inner strength to help me.

"You fucking bitch. I'm going to lock you away for aiding and abetting a kidnapper. I'm. Her. Fucking. Husband. She belongs to me." He grabs my hair and pulls his other fist back, ready to land another punch.

"No. She. Doesn't." I sob out the shaky words. Tears sting the cut on my cheek. "She deserves to be free." Free with her daughter.

"Stop!" Violet's scream rips through the air, and for a heartbeat, it feels like the molecules of time are suspended.

Nothing and no one is capable of moving. The shock of Violet's voice, the realization she's not hiding—it's too real. "Leave her alone. I'll go with you, Alex. But don't hurt her anymore." Her voice is small and broken and stripped of all hope.

He releases his grip on my hair and straightens. "Where's Sophie?" The name comes out icy and gruff.

I scoot across the floor away from him, heaving lungfuls of air into my aching chest. My ribs hurt, my face hurts, my body hurts, but not enough for me to have suffered serious internal damage. I know...I know from experience I'll live.

The adrenaline fueling my drive to fight peters out, and I'm left shaking and pulling myself into a corner, my butt still on the floor. Blood trickles down my face. I swipe at it with the back of my hand.

"Please, Alex." Violet's voice is a faint whisper, barely heard over the pulse rushing in my ears. "I'll go with you, and I promise I'll never leave you again. Sophie and I will stay with you forever." Her voice cracks, and I close my eyes, unable to look at the pain and defeat on her face.

I've failed. I didn't do enough. I should have moved them sooner. Should have...should have done a better job hiding the evidence they were staying with me.

I reach for Bailey, only to remember she's locked in her crate. I've never felt more alone than I do now.

"Please, Alex." The words are a feather on the breeze. So light and airy, I wonder if I imagined them.

Booted footsteps approach me. My body stiffens, reminding me how bruised I'm going to be tomorrow. I mentally flinch at the pain but keep it off my face. Or I think I do.

"If you tell anyone what happened, and that includes your boyfriend," Chief Wilson says, his voice a quiet warning. "I *will* deny it, and I'll deal with Violet and make you look responsible for her death." The words are spoken with such malice, I don't doubt a single one. "And I know people within the system who will make sure your stay in prison is brief."

The implication behind his words isn't missed, and a wave of dizziness assaults me.

I've been given a life sentence. He's going to stalk me the way he stalks his wife. The way my husband stalked me. They are one and the same. The same monster who needs to be in control of everything.

"Do you understand?" His voice is low, the threat felt deep in my bones.

I nod and pry my eyes open, but I keep my gaze locked on the hardwood floor.

"Look at me!" Chief Wilson kicks my calf, but not as hard as he kicked my thigh.

I do as I'm told. At the fiery pits of hell burning in his eyes, I shrink in on myself.

"I won't reveal you're Savannah Townsend, but come near Violet or my daughter again, and everyone in Maple Ridge will learn the truth about who you are."

I nod, keeping my eyes on him, not daring to let them go to Violet. If I give him any reason to out me, it might result in the media tracking me down. And that—the chaos it could cause— might be all it takes for Craig and Grace to close the door on the possibility of my being in Amelia's life again.

"I'm going to call in for a squad car," he says. "Then I'm going to tell them someone broke into your home, searching for something, and roughed you up. The cop will take your statement. And so there's no confusion, he's a buddy of mine and will have no qualms about arresting you for attempted kidnapping. You and anyone else who was helping."

His eyes give nothing away. I nod my understanding.

"Of course, nothing will come of the investigation." He turns to Violet. "You're to tell everyone you were visiting your family in Portland. Our wires got mixed, and I never got the message you left for me. You had no idea I thought you were kidnapped."

She nods like a puppet whose strings are being yanked.

I don't point out the holes in his story. Holes I'm sure he'll skillfully deal with before he goes public with his lies.

He calls into the station about the break and enter and tells the dispatcher he will stay on the scene until Officer Dunbar arrives.

Bailey whimpers from her crate in the laundry room. I look up at Chief Wilson, silently pleading for him to let me get my dog.

"The dog stays where it is." His tone is a stark wasteland that sends a chill through me.

It doesn't take long for the other officer to show up. He doesn't question anything his boss says. But why would he? It's the same cop who approached Violet on the Fourth of July when I saw her in the park and she told me I was right about her husband.

He's the one who has been stalking her when her husband can't.

Instead of taking my statement, the chief of police tells the other officer and me how things went down. He'd been driving past with his wife and daughter, and I flagged him over. The tale he weaves sounds convincing enough to anyone who doesn't know better.

Violet sits on a chair, trying to soothe her agitated daughter, who woke after Officer Dunbar arrived. Sophie's holding the purple octopus with one hand. The other arm is clutching her stuffed lamb to her body.

I remain in the armchair, feet pulled onto the seat, arms hugging my bent knees, doing my best to keep my trembling under control.

I try slipping away to my happy place to escape this nightmare. But the doors to it have been bolted shut, forcing me to stay in the here and now.

After they've finished concocting the story and reminding me what's at stake, they leave, taking Violet and Sophie with them. I try to catch Violet's eye, but she's staring at Sophie in her father's arms, tears streaming down her cheeks. Sophie's also crying, her little sobs breaking my heart.

Fragments of memories rise and haunt me. Of waking up on the floor. Of Amelia crying in her room. Of finding a gun and picking it up, scared Amelia would come out of her room and accidentally hurt herself with it.

Of being in a daze, unsure what was going on.

None of my memories tell me who killed my husband. None of them will help me save Violet and Sophie.

A new sob wracks my body.

Violet and Sophie. Their names repeat in my head like the rings on the water after a stone sinks beneath the surface. I've failed them. Failed them like I failed myself all those years ago. Like I failed Amelia.

Once again, the abuser has won.

52

TROY

August, Present Day
Maple Ridge

I enter the tent where the wedding reception is being held and scan the area. There's no sign of Jess.

"Have you seen Jess?" I ask Theresa as she and her husband step off the dance floor.

"She and Emily left a few minutes ago."

An elderly man, who I recognize as one of Theresa's grandfathers, comes over to join her and her new husband. I make my excuses and head out to where my truck is parked on the street.

I should probably go to Jess's house to talk to her about Katelyn, but I need time to figure out the best way to fight for her.

Tomorrow.

I'll go over there tomorrow and show her how much I love

her. I'll make sure she knows I'll be there for her once she's ready to let me in again.

My last ex-girlfriend and I broke up because we realized our relationship had run its course. We spent less and less time together, and that hadn't bothered either of us. In retrospect, the only thing that had kept us together for as long as it did was the sex.

And in time, that became more of a booty call.

I never loved my ex-girlfriend. But I am in love with Jess.

Once I arrive home, I take Butterscotch into the backyard to do his business. Then grab a beer from the fridge, drop my ass onto my couch, and surf through the channels.

I have no idea what I'm in the mood for—other than hockey. But it's not even preseason yet, so that's not going to help much.

I land on a World War II documentary about the Enigma code breaker and decide to watch the show. I have no idea why, other than it makes me think about Jess and her unexpected interest in the Second World War.

I've been watching the show for about fifteen minutes when the doorbell rings. Hoping it's Jess, I go to answer the door. But instead of her, I find Kellan standing on my porch. He glares at me like my presence is somehow pissing him off.

"Any reason in particular you're scowling at me?" I don't bother to wait for a reply. I leave the door open and return to the living room and the documentary.

As expected, Kellan follows me. I drop onto the couch. He doesn't bother to sit down. "What the hell are you watching?"

I grab my beer bottle from the coffee table. "A documentary about code breaking during the Second World War. It's really interesting." My tone sounds far from convincing, my frustration surrounding the situation with Jess tarnishing it.

Kellan still doesn't sit. He parks his body between me and the TV. *Asshole.*

I lean to the side to peer past him. Kellan blocks my move as if we're on the ice and he's preventing me from scoring.

"What the hell?" I grumble. "I'm watching that."

"Not anymore, you're not." He grabs the remote from the coffee table and clicks off the TV.

I point the mouth of the beer bottle at him. "When did you turn into such a pain in the ass?"

"I've always been one. You were just too blind to see it. You're an idiot, by the way."

"Why do I have a feeling my being an idiot has nothing to do with you being a pain in the ass?"

"No one can accuse you of being a dumb idiot. Just an idiot."

"Thanks." I think. I take a gulp of my beer and put the half-empty bottle on the table.

Kellan still doesn't move. I force out a heavy breath and stare him down, hinting it's time he gets to the point of this visit.

"What the hell are you doing with Katelyn?"

I groan and drop my head on the back of the couch. "Christ. Not you too. There's nothing going on between us. And all the rumors you've heard to that effect are wrong."

"You didn't have sex with her Thursday night?"

"I've never had sex with her, period."

"But Jess thinks you did have sex with her?" Kellan folds his arms and adopts a legs-apart stance, his expression reminding me of my CO during my last tour of duty in Afghanistan.

"Are you planning to stand there and interrogate me all night?"

Narrowed blue eyes bore into mine. "Yes."

"Is there anything specific you want to say or ask me?"

"Fuck," Kellan mutters under his breath. He has that look I recognize. He's debating his options. I wish he would deliberate faster.

"My sentiments exactly." I grab my beer again. I have a feeling I'm going to need it for this discussion if Kellan ever starts it. Or continues it. Or whatever it is we've been doing so far. "Look, it doesn't matter if Jess thinks I'm having sex with Katelyn. Jess dumped me. She doesn't have a say in who I screw or if I'm allowed to fuck or not." Of course, this isn't how I'm going to lead things when I talk to her tomorrow.

I was an idiot when I accused her of not trusting me enough to let me in—even if I was right.

I'm just not sure what it will take to get her to trust me the way I need her to.

Kellan curses some more under his breath. "The reason she dumped you is because she thought she had to."

What the hell? "Not exactly following you here, Kel."

He grunts and pinches the bridge of his nose like this conversation is giving him a headache. I know the feeling. "Jess is hiding Violet and Sophie in her house. Violet's prick of a husband has been abusing her. And given Jess's own past with an abusive husband, she's helping Violet and Sophie escape."

I stare at him for a fraction of a second, then lunge to my feet. *Of all the fucking stupid...*

I grab the front of Kellan's T-shirt in my fist, but of course he doesn't budge. We're both evenly matched in height, weight, and strength.

Or we would be if I wasn't recovering from a dislocated shoulder.

"Do you realize that asshole's been sniffing around her house? If he even suspects..." I can't finish the thought. I have faced the enemy countless times while in the Marines, but never has fear coursed through me the way it does now.

Kellan's hand knocks my arm away like he's swatting at an annoying gnat. I don't put much effort into stopping him. He's not the one I need to worry about. He's only the messenger.

"This is why she didn't want you to know. She was afraid you would overreact and put Violet in danger."

"Violet?" I snap, the thread of restraint about to unravel. "What the hell about Jess? We've got to get Violet and Sophie out of there before her husband figures out where they're staying."

"Agreed. Jess asked me to get Violet some fake IDs. But I can't do that until Jess knows where Violet and Sophie will end up. Avery, Simone, and Zara are trying to locate safe houses as far away from here as possible."

"Zara, Avery, and Simone even know about this?" Dammit. I was her boyfriend and I'd been kept in the dark all that time. I could have done something to help. But instead, Jess pushed me away. Refused to let me in. Buried herself under more secrets. Shit. When will they ever stop?

"They were hoping to set up an underground railroad to get Violet and Sophie to safety."

The World War II books. That must be where Jess got the idea.

"How close are they to doing that?" I ask over my shoulder as I head to the garage. "I'm going over to Jess's. You can stay here or come with me."

Kellan grunts, clearly not onboard with my plan, but he still follows me. "They're working on it. Simone, Zara, and Avery only found out yesterday about what's going on."

I head to Jess's house in my truck. Kellan follows in his SUV. I'd be lying if I said Jess's inability to trust me doesn't hurt. I've done everything I can to help her, to make her life better when I'd had no idea what had happened in her past. But even then, it wasn't enough for her to open up to me. About anything. About what she's doing for Violet and Sophie.

As we drive down Jess's street, a police cruiser pulls away from her house. My hands tighten on the steering wheel. *Shit. Shit. Shit. Please let her be okay.* I stop my truck a few houses from hers. Kellan parks right behind me. The cruiser goes around the corner.

I couldn't tell who was driving the police cruiser, but Jess wasn't in the back seat as far as I could tell. Which means the cops still don't know she's hiding Violet and Sophie.

I park my truck on the driveway. Kellan parks behind me. I've barely turned off the engine before I'm sprinting to the front door.

I ring the doorbell and wait for a count of three. When no one answers, I turn the doorknob. It's unlocked and opens.

Screw waiting for her to come to the door, I fling it open and rush inside. Kellan is right behind me.

"Jess?" I call out as I check the alarm. It's still disengaged. I frown. It's not like Jess to not turn it on after she closes the door. "Jess!"

Bailey barks from the direction of the laundry room. I start to head that way. Maybe Jess is in there, doing laundry, and the cop hadn't been here after all.

"Jess?" Kellan says softly.

I glance over my shoulder to see what's up. He's walking to the living room. Jess is sitting in an armchair with her arms wrapped around her legs, head on her knees, as if trying to keep herself together.

Oh, shit.

I race to her and kneel beside the chair. "Hey, what happened?" I gently stroke her hair, unable to prevent myself from touching her. It's too damn hard not to.

She looks up, revealing her bruised, tear-soaked face. White gauze is taped to her temple, a small amount of blood seeping through. The cut on her cheek isn't bleeding, but it was at one point. Someone has cleaned it up.

Jess doesn't turn to either of us. Her unfocused gaze is directed toward the kitchen.

And she's shaking.

Shit, how she's shaking.

"She's in shock," I tell Kellan. "Pass me a throw."

He grabs one hanging from the back of the couch and hands it to me. I wrap it around Jess's shoulders.

"What happened?" My voice is gentle, nothing like the one screaming in my head. I caress her unbruised cheek with my thumb, drying away some of the tears.

"Someone broke in and beat me up." Her tone is flat and robotic, like she's reading from a script she hasn't yet memorized.

Kellan crouches on the other side of her. "Where are Violet and Sophie?"

"She decided to return to her husband." Jess continues to stare ahead, barely blinking. Her tone remains robotic. I've never heard her sound like this. "I made a mistake. Violet and Sophie were fine."

Kellan and I exchange confused glances. Why would Violet be hiding in Jess's house all this time if everything was fine?

"It's all my fault," Jess whispers, more to herself than to us. I'm not even sure she's fully aware we're here. "It's all my fault. It's all my fault. It's all my fault." Her eyes are red and she's heartbroken. So goddamn heartbroken.

I stroke her face. It feels like a miracle to be touching her again. "It's not your fault. Nothing is your fault."

I look at my brother. His tight expression confirms we're thinking the same thing. Wilson's the one who hit my girl and told her to lie about what's really gone down with Violet.

White-hot heat flares in me, and my hands itch to murder the asshole. I shove the urge away. That lack of control is why Jess broke up with me instead of asking for my help. I place my hand on her waist.

She flinches and pain registers briefly on her face.

"Can I take a look?" I caress the spot with my thumb so she knows what I'm talking about.

She nods, the movement robotic like her voice.

I inch up the hem of her T-shirt and the throw, exposing more than I was expecting. This is the first time I've seen her back, even though I've had sex with her on more than one occasion. There's a scar, ugly and red, near her kidney. It looks only a few months old. Fresh bruises darken the skin on her side, like she's been kicked or hit with something.

I close my eyes for a beat, trying to find the strength to ask my next question. "Did he...did he touch you or hurt you in any other way?"

Jess's eyes widen and she rapidly shakes her head, seeming to understand what I'm asking. "No, nothing like that."

Relief eases a tiny amount of my fear and anger.

"But he knows who I am. He knows I'm Savannah Townsend. He said he won't let out who I am unless I give him a reason to out me."

A string of curses parade through my head. I know how important it is for her to keep her past identity a secret. "I'm sorry, Jess. We'll have to do what we can to prevent that from happening. For now, you're coming to my place. I'll sleep on the couch."

"No, I don't want to be alone," she says, her tone bordering on frantic. "I want to stay with you. And...and you can't say anything to anyone about what I told you. He'll kill Violet if I so much as mention it to anyone, including the cops. Including you." Her trembling intensifies, the pretense of her original story now dropped. "He plans to frame me for her death."

I've known Jess since she first moved to Maple Ridge. The woman in the chair isn't the same one I met at the lake. That woman was terrified. This Jessica has a resilience about her that didn't exist then. She's scared, no doubt about that after everything she's gone through. But there's still a strength to her words, even with her body trembling. Strength and a hint of trust that wasn't there before.

Another bark comes from the laundry room. Shit, I'd forgotten all about Bailey. I catch Kellan's eye and nod for him to get her.

He pushes himself to his feet and heads for the laundry room.

"Just so you know," I say, lightly stroking Jess's bruised face. "Katelyn lied about everything. I never had sex with her. I was only at the wedding as her date because she promised to talk to her father about the festival sponsorship if I went with her. We were never actually dating."

Bailey comes bounding into the living room and jumps her paws onto Jess's lap. Jess throws her arms around Bailey, and I can't deny the flash of jealousy that Bailey's the one she hugged first and not me.

I stomp down the emotion. I should be happy she even wants me to stay with her tonight after everything she's been through. But it won't only be tonight that she'll be staying with me. Wilson is a threat. A threat that won't go away until he's locked behind bars.

"I still need to help Violet and Sophie." Jess looks between Kellan and me, determination stamped on her face, the bruises unable to hide it. "As long as they're with him, they're not safe. I can't let Violet lose her daughter like I lost mine. There's got to be something I can do to help her. To help them both without her husband revealing my real identity." A small sob escapes her.

Most of what she said is lost on me. Only one word repeats in my head like a never ending echo. "Daughter?"

Pain and heartbreak fill Jess's eyes, and she nods. "I have a daughter. Or I did. Those photos...those photos you found in my nightstand...I told you she was my niece. She isn't. Not biologically. She's my daughter. But she's not mine anymore." The last part comes out as a strained whisper.

The sound of her voice, of how much she's hurting, guts me. I wish I knew how to erase her pain.

"What do you mean she's not yours anymore?" I ask. Kellan's confused expression tells me this is also news to him. He sits on the couch opposite her. I take the chair next to hers.

"Legally, she belongs to one of my husband's brothers and his wife. Craig was estranged from my husband. He believed me when I first told the cops that my husband had been abusing me." Jess explains how her husband had used their daughter to keep Jess from leaving him, how he planted safeguards to paint her in a bad light, to make it look like she had postpartum depression and was a risk to her daughter's safety. She explains how her brother-in-law had arranged for her to come to Maple Ridge, how Craig and his wife had been her daughter's guardians and Jess had given away her rights to Amelia. The intense pain and devastation on Jess's face rips at my heart.

Tears stream down her face again, and she tries to wipe them away. "I'm hoping that eventually I'll be able to turn my life around, and Craig and Grace will let me be part of my daughter's life. Even if it's just as a family friend. That's why I was so excited to decorate the second bedroom upstairs. Why I want to build the window seat. It's for her. For Amelia."

"Does anyone else know she's your daughter?"

"I told Avery, Simone, and Zara. Beyond that..." Jess shrugs, the lift of her shoulders weighted and slow. "The media knew I had a daughter, but she's a minor so they can't talk about her. It's why I didn't want you to google my name. I wasn't ready to tell you about her."

Christ, Jess sacrificed her happiness and freedom so she could protect her daughter and not lose her. But that's exactly what happened in the end. No wonder she's so determined to save Violet and Sophie.

I move off the chair and sink to my knees in front of her. I take her hand, needing to fix, rebuild, and fortify the trust between us. Jess had her reasons for keeping me in the dark, reasons I hadn't given her much choice in. If I hadn't overreacted and shoved Wilson, she might not have felt like she had to keep the truth about Violet and Sophie from me.

"Whatever you want to do when it comes to Violet and Sophie," I tell her, "I'll help you. I don't know yet how we're going to do that, but we will get her out of her situation. I promise."

53

TROY

August, Present Day
Maple Ridge

I help Jess pack her belongings to bring to my house, along with Bailey's supplies. Wilson gave me the perfect excuse to keep Jess at my place with his fake story about someone breaking into her home.

He might have warned her not to tell me what happened, but he can't complain that her boyfriend wants to protect her after someone destroyed her sense of security.

In her bedroom, I shut the flap on the cardboard box. Kellan left ten minutes ago. "Just so we have this clear, I still want to be your boyfriend." *I still love you.* "That never changed." I step closer to her but don't touch her. I want to, but now's not the time for that. "And I'm sorry you felt like I was being manipulative just to get what I wanted. I hadn't meant for you to feel that way. I should have been honest about who was paying for your therapy and about Bailey from the start. I just wanted to help you, but it was wrong of me to not be straight with you."

I'm not thrilled she broke up with me and put her life in danger, but I do get why she ended things between us. I was the one who screwed up, shoving Wilson the way I did. I didn't leave her much choice if she wanted to help her friend.

"The fact that you're here—with me—and not rushing off to push Chief Wilson around...that's big," Jess says and then narrows her eyes. "You're not going to retaliate, are you?"

I inwardly flinch at how much of her trust I need to regain. "No. As angry as I am at what he did to you, going after him won't solve anything."

She nods. "Good. As for the manipulation part, promise me you won't do that again. I need to make my own decisions and not have them made for me. Despite what my late husband thought, I am a capable adult."

"I know you are. And I promise."

"Thank you." A flutter of a smile touches her lips. "Are you sure you want to be my boyfriend? Now that you know the truth about my daughter?" A palpable pain scratches her voice at the last part.

I carefully pull her into a hug, like she's a delicate blossom. "Of course I do. I want every part of you. Including your daughter. Does that mean you're my girlfriend?"

She nods. "It does."

I brush my mouth over hers, grateful to be able to kiss her. "I'll help you turn the guest room into the dream room you've been planning. And I'm sure when the time is right, when her adoptive parents let you into her life again, Amelia will love it."

My gaze skims over the darkening bruises on her face. "We really should get your injuries checked out at the hospital. And have them documented in case we can eventually use them against Wilson." I trace my fingers over her ribs and the bruises along her side. "And I want to make sure he didn't damage your healing ribs." Or inflict other damage we can't see with the naked eye.

"That's probably not a good idea." Her voice is soft, fragile.

"Why not? I just want to make sure you're okay."

She looks toward the window, the curtains closed to the world. "It's late."

"The funny thing about hospitals is they're open twenty-four seven. It's never too late." I coerce a half smile to curve onto my face.

"What about Chief—"

I seal away the rest of that sentence with my finger on her lips. "There's nothing he can do. How will it look if the chief of police discourages victims from receiving medical attention? Especially victims of violent attacks. We just can't tell them the full truth about what happened. For now, you can't name Wilson as the assailant."

I press a kiss on her lips, tender and persuasive. "I can check if Samuel's working tonight and make sure he's the one who sees you. Okay?"

Jess gives a slow, tentative nod, not fully convinced going to the hospital is the right thing to do. But I meant it when I said Wilson can't prevent her from seeking medical attention. And as her concerned boyfriend, who's not supposed to know what actually happened, I'll have something to say about it if Wilson causes more trouble.

No one would expect anything less.

"Good." I send Samuel a text. He responds a short time later. "He agrees you should be checked out. He'll see us at the hospital."

BAILEY AND BUTTERSCOTCH ARE WAITING FOR US WHEN WE arrive at my house after the trip to the ER. Wilson didn't seriously injure Jess, but he came close. He could have caused serious kidney damage. Samuel ordered tests in case there is more damage than realized, but it'll be several days before she gets the results.

Jess yawns, exhaustion from her ordeal creating half-moons under her eyes. I want to cradle her in my arms and protect her from the world. Protect her from all her past demons.

"I'm ready for a hot shower and then bed," she says, turning to the stairs.

"I'll take the dogs outside to do their business. I'll be quick." I don't want to leave Jess alone longer than necessary. She nods, the movement slow and barely perceptible. I watch her tread upstairs.

Once the dogs are finished, I head to the bathroom. The shower is running in the master bathroom, water raining against the tiles. That's not the only sound coming from there. The gut-wrenching sobs are barely heard over the water, but they're still hard to miss.

I push open the bathroom door and step into the steamy room. Jess's clothes lie in a pile on the floor, her sobs coming from the other side of the fogged-up glass door.

I swiftly strip and pull open the door. Jess is standing under the spray, water sluicing over her hair and down her body, her face tucked in her hands. The water is obviously hot, but she's still shaking.

I step inside the shower and close the glass door behind me. Careful not to scare her, I put my hand on her shoulder. She doesn't startle but turns and steps into my embrace.

Her forehead rests on my shoulder and she keeps sobbing. I kiss the top of her head, sharing my love with her. One hand slides to the curve of her spine. The other arm holds her close.

I don't feed her fake platitudes. I don't know if everything will be all right. And Jess knows better than to accept false hope. So, I just hold her.

She eventually turns her face up to mine. Christ, even with all the bruises that motherfucker left on her face, she's still so beautiful. My lips briefly meet hers again—and I fall in love with her even deeper than before.

"I love you." The words slip from my mouth, unexpected, confident, faithful. Jess's eyes widen, so many conflicting emotions swimming in them. But I don't want to pull the words back, yank the wisps of them from the air, hide them until she's ready to hear them. Besides, it's too late for that. I can't turn back time. Nor do I want to. I want her to know I'm here for her.

Always will be.

"Don't worry if you don't feel the same way," I say, knowing I can't ask that of her. Not after what she's suffered at the hands of her husband. "I just needed to tell you I love you, no matter what." No matter how many other secrets she's still keeping from me.

She nods but doesn't say anything. My chest tightens, but I breathe through it, careful to keep the emotion from my face.

I grab the bottle of body wash from the ledge, pour the spring-scented liquid into my palm, and rub it into a lather. Then I take my time gently washing her body.

"I can't believe you lost a festival sponsor," Jess says out of nowhere, her voice a dry whisper. "All because you shoved a man who's been abusing his wife for years. Where's the fairness in that?"

I don't reply because I don't have an answer. To any of it. But she's right. The festival lost a sponsor because Bell Automotives respects family values, and Chief Wilson is the Antichrist of them. But there's nothing I can do about that.

Not without putting Violet and Sophie in greater danger than they're already in.

Jess pours the soap into her hands and follows my lead,

slowly washing my body the way I'm washing hers. Our touches are intimate, intimate but not sexual.

They're about removing all the unpleasant memories from the past few days.

About rebuilding what we have between us.

About sharing my soul with her.

54

JESSICA

August, Present Day
Maple Ridge

I open Troy's oven and check on the lasagna I made while he was at PT with Lucas, working on his shoulder.

"That smells incredible." He slips his arms around my waist from behind.

I shut the oven door and swivel in his embrace. The bruising from yesterday's beating is sore but not unbearable. I kiss him. Long and hard, to the point where I'm dizzy.

But it's worth it.

And the love...the love Troy feels for me, the words he told me last night, is poured into the kiss. His love wraps me in a soft blanket, soothes my battered and bruised self-esteem. The self-esteem that's only beginning to heal after all these years.

I couldn't say the words back to him last night. And I'm still not ready to say them. The last time I said the words to another man, I ended up regretting it. I know...I know it won't be the same with Troy, but the thought of saying the words makes my stomach hurt.

So I don't. I just let myself get lost in the soul-quenching kiss.

"I definitely approve of the kiss." A content smile curves on Troy's lips, but it only lasts for a moment. "Can we talk now about you returning to therapy?"

"I can't go back." The words rush from me, defiance and panic branding each one.

Small divots form between his eyebrows, not deep enough to count as a full frown. "Yes, you can. You need to. I was at Theresa's wedding, Jess. Remember?"

How can I forget? "It's not that simple. I quit because I was scared I would accidentally tell Robyn about Violet and Sophie. I was afraid if I did that, it would screw things up for them and I would end up in prison. Again. It was a risk I couldn't afford to take."

"You can't keep living like this, Jess. You deserve better."

"I know. But Violet and Sophie deserve better too. And as long as Chief Wilson is pulling the strings, I can't risk it. I can't risk mentioning anything to Robyn that could cost Violet and Sophie their lives." But not saying anything might also cost them their lives.

I can't live with that either. I'm damned if I say anything and damned if I don't.

"Once we've got Violet and Sophie out of their situation, will you restart therapy?" His tone isn't asking a question. It's a demand. Not in the way my late husband demanded I obeyed him. But it does warn me that Troy plans to get his way when it comes to therapy.

All because he doesn't want me to end up like his best friend, Colton.

The doorbell rings, saving me from having to respond. Even

if we get Violet and Sophie out of Oregon, I can't risk talking to Robyn again.

Troy goes to answer the door.

Zara, Avery, Simone, and Emily step into the kitchen soon after. One glance at me and their eyes widen in surprise and horror. Only Kellan knew I was here. Troy and I haven't told anyone else what happened last night. Nor have we mentioned we're back together. We were waiting until everyone arrived. Troy texted them this morning, inviting them for dinner.

"Oh, God. What happened?" Zara can barely choke out the words. She looks at Troy as if he has all the answers, but there's another emotion in her eyes. The same emotion Avery and Simone share.

They know.

Or they suspect they know who was responsible for my bruises. Only Em is in the dark about them.

"We'll tell you as soon as Troy's brothers get here," I share with the four women.

Male voices come from the foyer. The four men enter the kitchen a moment later where the rest of us are hanging out. Garrett and Lucas stop talking as soon as they see me.

"What the hell happened?" Lucas asks, not mincing words. His gaze darts to Troy.

He's not the only one. Garrett's also staring down his brother, silently demanding an explanation.

I look over to the living room window, which faces the street. It's too early to shut the curtains without raising suspicion. "How do we know Chief Wilson or his goon isn't out there watching the house?" My voice is a rough whisper, the memory of his threat last night distorting it.

God...if he even suspects we're talking about him and what really happened instead of the twisted version he concocted, he'll kill his wife and daughter. I don't doubt that.

My heart pounds. And it feels like someone is holding a pillow over my mouth. I can't get air into my lungs.

A hand rests on the curve of my spine. "Breathe, Jess. Look at me." Troy catches my chin with a crooked finger and turns my face to his. "They aren't parked on the street doing surveillance. Kellan and I have already checked. Wilson will hopefully believe you took his warning seriously. We're having dinner with our friends. Nothing suspicious about that."

"And what if he doesn't believe it?" I wrap my arms around myself, suddenly cold.

"Then nothing you do will change that. He was always going to carry out his threat, no matter what you did."

"Is someone going to explain what's going on?" Garrett looks like he's on the verge of pacing. He's as wound up as I am, and he doesn't even know what Troy's talking about.

Troy slips his fingers between mine and leads me to the couch. We sit and everyone else takes a seat. Our fingers remain intertwined.

But even then, my heart rate refuses to slow to a normal pace. "There's something I need to tell you. Something you can't tell anyone. And I mean *anyone*."

I spend the next several minutes getting Emily, Garrett, and Lucas up to speed on the past ten years of my life. My marriage and my daughter. The abuse, the murder conviction, the prison hell.

And I tell them about Violet and Sophie, about our plans to get them away from Maple Ridge and Oregon, and about what happened last night. About the threat Chief Wilson gave me should I attempt to help Violet again.

"Shit." Lucas shoots Simone a look that says he can't believe she didn't tell him.

Garrett forces out a hard breath and shoots Zara an unreadable glare. Probably for the same reason.

"Violet and Sophie need to escape their situation," I tell

them. "But because her husband's the chief of police, he knows how to work the system to his advantage."

"How can we convince her to leave him again after what happened yesterday?" Emily asks. "She's gotta be even more scared of him after she witnessed what he'll do to make sure she doesn't escape."

"And even if we can get them away from here," Troy says, sounding rather doubtful about that, "Violet will be wanted by the police, and possibly the FBI, for kidnapping a child. She'll aways be looking over her shoulder."

He lightly squeezes my hand, reminding me the constant looking over my shoulder hasn't changed even now, and likely never will. I'll always be wondering if one day someone will recognize me as the woman on the news.

I'll always be wondering if they'll see me as a cop killer, even though I'm innocent.

See me as someone who's dangerous because I spent five years in maximum security.

See me as someone who they don't want in their community.

"I can't leave her in that house," I tell them. "Do you know how many women die each year because of domestic violence? And what if he turns his rage on his daughter when she gets older? Even if he doesn't, the impact of seeing him beat her mother will hurt Sophie in the long run. Twenty-five percent of children of abusers go on to follow in their mother's footsteps. She could one day end up in an abusive relationship if the cycle doesn't end. I can't let that happen."

I pray every day Amelia doesn't fall into that statistic. She was so young when her father died. I can only hope she doesn't remember the physical and verbal abuse, and how I was always scared, afraid of doing or saying the wrong thing.

"You should talk to Blake," Lucas says. "If anyone can help us with Violet and Sophie, it'll be him. He might know some legal loopholes we can exploit. Or he'll knows someone who can help us."

Troy nods, his expression thoughtful. "It wouldn't hurt to ask him. If we're talking in hypotheticals, he won't need to report us."

"Blake won't report us for trying to save a woman from her abusive husband," Lucas points out. "And that has nothing to do with him being my friend."

"Why wouldn't he? Doesn't he try to prevent wife beaters from going to jail?" My experience with defense lawyers hasn't been bright and sunny. Mine was unable to help me as much as he tried.

"Not Blake. There're certain types of cases he avoids. Anything that deals with domestic abuse and crimes against kids falls under that category."

"What about kidnapping?" Because that would definitely fall under the latter category.

"In this case," Lucas replies, "he would agree the motive justifies the means."

"Alright. You talk to Blake." Kellan nods at Lucas. "And we'll keep an eye on Violet. If things turn dangerous for her again, we'll get her and Sophie out, chief of police be fucked."

AFTER OUR FRIENDS LEAVE FOLLOWING DINNER, TROY TAKES Bailey and Butterscotch out to do their business.

And I make a decision.

Two weeks. Two weeks of hiding Violet. Two weeks of coming up with excuse after excuse of why I couldn't be with Troy. Two weeks of my body yearning for his touch.

Troy opens the back door and lets the dogs into the house.

"You know that Jacuzzi in your bathroom?" I say nonchalantly. He nods, hope flickering devilishly in his eyes. "I was thinking of soaking in it." I take a step closer to him and run my fingers down his chest. "And I wouldn't mind company. If that's okay with you." Plus, the heat will feel amazing on my sore muscles.

"Hell yes," he mutters and pulls me in for a slow, hungry kiss. And I return each stroke of his tongue with a plead for so much more.

He pulls away as my legs begin to disintegrate from the heat of the kiss. "Are you sure about this? You were pretty beat up last night."

"I'm positive this is what I want." *You're what I want.* "But if this isn't something you—"

He slams his mouth against mine. And the kiss...the kiss leaves my body vibrating with need. The need to have him. To be with him. To touch him.

He threads his fingers with mine, tells the dogs to stay downstairs, and leads me upstairs to his bathroom. He turns the water on in the Jacuzzi and walks over to give me another powerful kiss. His fingers slip under the hem of my T-shirt, and he gently traces up my sides, taking care to not irritate the bruises there.

The skin under his T-shirt is deliciously hot to my touch, his hard ab muscles belying the strength and power that's all Troy. Power filled with kindness and heart. God, how I want him.

He removes his T-shirt and tosses it to the floor. I do the same with my T-shirt, and Troy's eyes heat.

I cup my hand on his hard length, which strains beneath the fabric of his jeans. Troy groans. I grin.

He reaches around and unhooks the back of my bra. I unzip his jeans and slip my hand into the opening.

"Jesus, Jess." The words slide out on an erotic hiss. "You're going to kill me before we even make it to the Jacuzzi."

"Not exactly my plan. But I've missed you." With him so

close, my hands on his skin and his on mine, I'm unraveling one thread at a time. I moan.

Troy turns off the water, and we strip out of the rest of our clothing. His heated gaze pours over my body like hot syrup, coating every part of me—the unblemished skin and the scars.

"Christ, you're beautiful, Jess." He strokes his thumb over my peaked nipple, and a needy whimper falls from my parted lips.

He steps into the tub of bubbling water and holds out his hand to me. I climb in, and we sink into the heat, with Troy behind me. I lean back between his legs, his hard length pressed between the curve of my butt cheeks.

The water bubbles and caresses my bruised body, kissing it better. I groan, feeling more human for the first time in the past twenty-four hours.

"You all right?" Troy's rough voice fans hot against the shell of my ear.

I smile. "Definitely."

We sit for a few minutes, letting the water work its magic. One of Troy's arms is wrapped around my waist, keeping me in place. His other hand strokes the bare skin of my arm, and he lightly kisses my ears, my neck, my shoulders.

"I love you." He whispers the words on my skin with each kiss, branding me with them.

I glance over my shoulder, a silent apology in my eyes at how I'm not ready to say the words.

Understanding burns in his. "I know. I'm a patient man. I can wait." He seals his promise with the press of his lips on mine.

His hand moves from my arm to caress my breasts. The nipples pucker at his touch. He pinches one, and need shoots straight to my core.

I drop my head back on his shoulder, arching my spine. My

nipples poke out of the water, the cooler air causing them to pucker even more.

Troy kisses my temple, but it's not enough. I shift around, straddling him, and kiss him. My lips move with his, my hunger for him urging me on.

His hand skims down my body, and he gives my ass a light pinch.

I grin against his lips. My hand folds along Troy's length, and I stroke him.

"Jesus!" The word flows from him, heat filling each syllable.

His hand moves between my legs, and he caresses my clit, teasing me until I'm squirming on his hand, searching for sweet relief.

His finger slips inside me, and I almost rocket out of the tub. Another finger joins the first, and he thrusts them in and out of me, pressing into my soft heat.

Mother of all things holy. Two weeks. How did I last that long without Troy? Without this?

I run my thumb across his swollen tip, thriving on the velvety softness. He groans.

I open my mouth to say I want him inside me, but it's too late. I'm too...I'm too close to the edge. I...I can't...last. Any. Longer.

And with one more thrust of his fingers, his thumb pressing my clit, I cry out and tumble happily into the star-filled abyss.

My pleasure echoes off the bathroom walls as the aftershocks roll through me in crescendoing waves, one after the other after the other.

Troy removes his hand, giving me a moment to recover.

"I need you inside me," I whisper on his lips.

"We should probably get out of the Jacuzzi for that. The condoms are in my bedroom." He helps me out of the tub. I started using the pill a few weeks ago, but it's too early to rely on it yet.

The air is cooler than the water, and I shiver. Troy grabs a towel and wraps it around my shoulders.

We go into his bedroom, anticipation humming through my veins. I pile Troy's pillows against the headboard, and he climbs onto the bed. He removes a couple of square foil packages from the bedside drawer, places them on the comforter, and I straddle him.

Our fingers and mouths resume their teasing and caressing, and it doesn't take long for Troy to be hard once more and for me to be writhing at his touch. He rolls the condom on, and I position myself, his tip at my entrance.

I sink onto his length, gradually taking him in, my moans the accompanying symphony.

Two. Weeks.

That's how long it's been since I last had sex with Troy.

I'll never make that mistake again.

55

ANGELIQUE

October 1943
France

S unday morning, Bridgette walks into the bedroom and opens the blackout curtains. It's been four days since the bullet grazed my calf, leaving a two-inch path in my flesh.

Yesterday, when she examined my leg, she told me to give it another day. The wind and rain hammering the window also conspired against me returning to the farmhouse.

But today, the sky is cloud free and I cannot stay any longer. Even the morning sickness is giving me a reprieve so I can bike to Jacques's vineyard.

Bridgette unwraps the bandage from my calf. The pain has improved considerably during the past three days, transforming to a stinging ache that is more bearable. If the bullet had been a fraction of an inch closer to the bone, I would not have been so lucky.

She inspects the healing wound. "I think you should stay for another day or two."

I twist around to look at it. It's not even close to healed, but as far as I'm concerned, it's good enough for me to get home. "I can't. I have to get back. But I promise I'll pedal slowly."

Shaking her head, she heaves out a short breath, consternation lining her face. "You won't stay no matter what I say, will you?"

I grin because she sounds like Hazel did whenever I got sick and grew tired of her mothering me. They both share the same exasperated huffed tone. "Probably not."

She fists her hands on her hips, and a small grunt escapes her. "God, the lot of you are impossible."

An abrupt laugh comes from the doorway. Laurent enters the room, their baby in his arms. He kisses the crown of his wife's head. "She thinks we're a stubborn bunch of imbeciles. She might be right about that."

She glares at him, but that only succeeds at making him laugh harder, something he probably doesn't do enough of.

"Well, you do take a lot of risks." The sadness in her tone weighs down the room, defusing the lightness Laurent was clearly aiming for.

"I know," he says softly. "I wish it wasn't like this. But I don't just want this war over. I want our daughter to know what it is like to be French and free. I want her to grow up not wondering where her next meal will come from, or be forced to pledge her allegiance to a dictator."

Bridgette cannot argue against that. None of us can.

"I'm grateful for what you have done for me, Bridgette," I say. "I really am. But I need to get back to the house I'm staying at. I need to return to my job of ridding us of the vermin."

"Alright, then. I'll rewrap your leg so the bandage stays put while you cycle home. But I cannot promise you that you won't cause more damage to the wound. I am a nurse. I am not a doctor. I can only do so much."

"I know. It's a risk I must take. But I will take it easy, and I'll push the bike up the hills if they prove to be too difficult."

The sun isn't high in the sky yet by the time I climb on my bicycle, my dress barely hiding the bandage on my lower leg.

"Come on, *ma petite*," I whisper to my baby. "Let's get home before Johann and Jacques become overly fretful."

THE JOURNEY TO THE FARMHOUSE IS SLOW AS I TAKE CARE NOT TO overly tax myself. I arrive more than eight hours later. My calf aches. My body aches. And I'm so very tired.

I lean the bike against the barn and turn to the house. All I'm interested in doing for now is napping before I make the evening meal.

Johann steps out of the farmhouse, spots me, and stares at me for a heartbeat as though I'm one of the mythological creatures his sister loved so much. Then he is sprinting to where I am standing.

Without a word, he gathers me in his arms and kisses me, seemingly not to care that we're in the open.

The kisses aren't sweet or hungry. They're powered by a core-deep desperation. I loop my arms around his neck and return his kisses with the same fervour. I had needed so badly to be in his arms again.

"I thought you were dead," he says, and guilt lurches inside me. "Jacques said you were due back three days ago. When you didn't return..." Johann resumes kissing me, and I eagerly return each one. "I really thought you were..." A long kiss. "I love you, Angelique. I thought you were dead. I thought I'd lost someone else I love."

He continues kissing me, not giving me a chance to squeeze

in a word. His words buoy me, carry me to the heavens. But at the same time, they fill me with dread. Love alone might not be enough when it comes to the war. Not enough to help us survive, to end the death and destruction.

Not enough to ensure we both come through on the other side in one piece.

Johann eventually stops kissing me and rests his brow on mine.

"I love you too," I whisper.

His arms tighten their hold on me, and his words switch to an onslaught of murmured German.

"What are you saying?" I ask, even though I don't need him to translate.

"Sorry, I was just telling you how much I love you. Where have you been? Jacques and I have been frantic with worry. We didn't know where you were. No one visited Jacques to let him know what happened to you." He cups the back of my head, his tender touch causing me to forget everything else.

"I was injured. I needed to recover for a few days before I could pedal home. Did any of your men or Major Müller notice my absence?"

His brow creases, and he pulls away. "Injured? Where?" His gaze searches my body, his hands on my arms.

"Johann, it's important, did anyone else notice my absence?"

"Not that I know of. Müller hasn't been here. Where are you hurt?"

"My calf." I lift the hem of my dress, revealing my bandaged leg. Blood has seeped through the once-white cloth.

The amount of blood isn't enough to cause concern, yet the frown deepens on Johann's brow. "How did you get injured?"

"It doesn't matter." I hardly want to admit someone from his side of the war shot me—no more than I want to explain what I was doing shortly prior to being hit. "And the wound isn't all that bad."

"I'll be the judge of that." He sweeps me up in his arms, not giving me a chance to respond, and carries me into the house.

"This isn't necessary," I protest weakly, lacking the energy to struggle out of his arms. It's a wonder I don't fall asleep in them. I've had plenty of rest over the past four days, but it just doesn't seem to be enough now that I'm pregnant.

He lowers me onto my bed and carefully unwraps the bandage. He curses in German once it's removed, and I pretend not to understand him.

"You see. It's not all that bad." I twist to inspect it. The wound is still raw, and a small amount of blood is leaking from the scab.

"What happened?"

I shake my head. "I cannot tell you. Please accept that."

"I have some first-aid supplies in my room. I'll clean the wound and replace the bandage. Then you need to promise me you will rest for a few days so it can heal."

My lips curl playfully to one side. "Is that your engineering expertise speaking? Or the medical background I don't know about?"

"And if it doesn't get better," he says, ignoring my comment, "I'll fetch the village doctor."

He leaves and returns with the first-aid supplies and a small bowl of water. He's no longer wearing his uniform. He has changed into Yvon's clothes. I appreciate the thoughtfulness of the gesture.

"I should wash up first." I could use a long soak in the bathtub, with a luxurious bar of soap, after the long bicycle ride home. But this is wartime, and that means the only luxury I get to enjoy is a scrub at the sink with plain water.

"I'll help you once I tend to your wound."

"How is Jacques's cough?" I ask.

"About the same."

At least it didn't get worse while I was away. But I was hoping it had improved during that time, even if only slightly.

After Johann cleans the wound, he fetches another bowl of water and a cloth.

He helps me out of my clothes and tenderly washes my skin. My pale flesh is a patchwork of bruises and scratches. He doesn't ask me again what happened, but the fire in his eyes tells me he wants to know. He already suspects the worst.

He kisses me. In contrast to the earlier kisses, this kiss is gentle, full of love and contentment.

"I'm pregnant," I whisper, the words slipping out so easily but surprising me all the same. "I'm pregnant with your baby."

His eyes widen. There is no disgust or anger in them. Only surprise and wonder, joy and fear. The same emotions that battle inside me.

He moves down my body and plants a tender kiss on my stomach. "*Bonjour*, little one. I'm your papa, and I'm looking forward to meeting you." He speaks in French, the warm melodic rhythm of his words wrapping me in love.

And for a several minutes, I ignore everything outside the windows and pretend our life is simple. Pretend we can be a family—husband and wife and child. Pretend we don't fight on separate sides of the same war. Pretend. Pretend. Pretend.

Pretend everything is all right. And I love him. That's all I want to do for the next few minutes.

Johann kisses my stomach once more, then removes his clothes and lies beside me. His arms embrace me, holding me to him. He kisses me, and his hand caresses the spot where our baby sleeps.

My hands trace the beautiful hard lines of his body. The hard lines that have helped Jacques around the vineyard whenever Johann has had a few moments of precious free time. "I want to make love to you," I murmur against his lips.

"Your leg—"

"My leg will be fine. But I need this. I need you."

He nods, a sweet, playful smile on his face. "Whatever the woman wants, she shall have."

Our hands explore and memorise each other's bodies as our tongues worship and dance. We take our time, desperate to prolong the moment between us.

JOHANN GATHERS ME IN HIS ARMS, AND HIS CALLOUSED THUMB draws small circles low on my belly. "You are really going to have my baby?" The wonder and joy in his whispered words have faded, replaced with a knot of other emotions beyond the initial happiness, as if the seriousness of the situation has finally sunk in.

"It's true." I release a long breath, my thoughts and questions and worries over the past few days colliding. I'll only be able to hide my situation for so long, and then my baby will be viewed as the bastard child of a Nazi. I'll be marked a collaborator—which might make my role with the local resistance circuit difficult. I will have lost their hard-earned trust, and if that is the case, I am cross with myself at what that could cost me and my work in the region.

"How do you feel about it?" The roughness of his voice wraps his vowels in worry and hope. A crossroad between what we want and reality. Between dreams of the future and the darkness of our here and now.

"How do I feel about having a piece of the man I love growing inside me? Or how do I feel about it happening when the world is at war, and I don't know what tomorrow will bring?" I am not the first French woman to become pregnant by a German soldier—either because she was raped or because she willingly bedded a German for love or for some other reason. Although in my case, I am not French. Only my forged *carte d'identité* claims I am.

"Yes, the latter part does complicate things," Johann says, his words ending on a sigh.

"I already love him or her very much. What about you? You haven't had as long as I have to get used to the news. I've had a few days to think about it."

Johann's thumb strokes my cheek, and the knot of my emotions loosens slightly. "I'm happy. Worried. The same as any good father would feel upon learning the news from his wife. I want to marry you, Angelique, but our countries won't let us. Not now. Not while the war is on. I know of another officer who has fallen in love with a French woman. He was told marriage is not possible."

Even if Germany did permit him to marry a French woman, our marriage would not be legal. I am not Angelique D'Aboville. I cannot tell him that, though. And if London recalls me, there will be nothing I can do unless I choose to ignore their command. At some point, I will be leaving France. I will be returning to England and repairing my relationship with my sister. Could Johann ever come with me? Or has this war with Germany ended all hope of that?

"We'll figure things out." First, I need to ensure this world is a better place for our child.

Johann kisses my temple. "No matter what happens, I won't lose you. My unit will be reassigned to another region soon, but I will find you and our baby once this war is over."

I smile at him softly, keeping the fear from my face at what the rest of the war will bring. "I know."

"How far along are you?" He rests his hand protectively on my belly.

"About three months. He or she is due late March or early April."

"I should talk to your father. He has warmed to me a little, but I am not sure he will be too thrilled with this turn of events."

I bite my lip, keeping the guilt off my face that Jacques isn't my real father. I know my own father, if he were still alive, would be disappointed with me.

He wouldn't be the only one. Most people who matter won't be delighted at the news. What will Hazel think? When we were teenagers, we dreamt our future children would grow up together. But it's possible she won't want anything to do with me after I return to England—pregnant or not—because I haven't spoken to her in over a year.

"You might want to hold off on that a little longer," I tell Johann. "Give him some time to get used to us together first." I need to inform Allaire of the situation before anyone else learns about it.

I'll do that tomorrow.

Dread snakes its way through me at having to tell Allaire how badly I messed up.

I nudge the emotion aside and for now remain blissfully in the bubble. The bubble I would be in if circumstances were different. If the father of my baby weren't a Wehrmacht officer and our countries weren't at war.

56

TROY

August, Present Day
Maple Ridge

The next morning, Jess and I drive to Eugene to meet with Lucas's college friend, Blake. Lucas called him last night and told him Jess and I need to talk to him about something important. Because Blake's schedule is filled for the day, we had to leave before sunrise to meet him first thing.

"Early mornings should be against the law," Jess grumbles. "Especially after you've had multiple orgasms the night before."

I chuckle, guilty of waking her at 3 a.m., but not regretting it for a second. "We'll grab some coffee first. Lucas figured that will go a long way with his caffeine-addicted friend."

We pick up drinks for the three of us from Blake's favorite coffee house and enter the law firm where he works. A woman with a puff of short white hair is sitting behind a computer. She looks up at us and smiles. "Good mornin'. Who do you have an

453

appointment with?" Her words are infused with a slight Northern Irish brogue.

"Blake Wright. We're Troy and Jessica."

Her smile widens, wrinkles crinkling around her eyes. "I would ask if you'd like some coffee, but I see you've already visited the coffee gods and bought Blake a small sacrifice." She buzzes him to let him know we're here.

He steps out of his office a minute later. He and I man-hug.

"This is Jessica." I avoid giving him her last name for now. I don't know his receptionist enough to trust her.

He takes us into his office and shuts the door. "Have a seat and tell me what I can do for you two." He sits in the chair behind the desk and takes a sip of the coffee we brought him.

"Just to be sure, nothing we tell you will be shared with anyone else?" I ask. Lucas hasn't told him much about the situation. I thought it would be better for Blake to hear it from us.

Blake puts his coffee down and leans forward, folded arms on his desk. "Normally, that only applies to lawyer-client confidentiality. But I'm going to treat our discussion as though you're my clients."

We spend the next ten minutes filling him in on everything. Not a single detail is skipped. Jess does most of the talking. Blake asks the occasional question and jots notes on a legal pad.

"Your friend's situation is tricky," he says once we're finished. "But I agree, she needs to get out of her current circumstances. She and her daughter need to get to a safe location. And the hospital or police would need to take photos of your injuries, Jessica, as well as your friend's. To document them so they can be used at trial."

"A friend of mine, who's a doctor at Maple Ridge Hospital, took photos of Jess's injuries when I took her there Sunday night." Samuel only knew that she might eventually need the photos. He also knew we couldn't tell him everything at that point.

"Do you think your friend will corroborate what happened Sunday night when her husband entered your house?" he asks Jess.

"I don't know. She's scared. She tried to escape him, but he found her. He won't give up so easily. Men like him don't want to lose their possessions. He would rather kill her than lose her."

"That's what I'm worried about. I can talk to the DA and see what she says."

Jess's face pales and her fingers clench and unclench against her skirt. "And what happens if it gets back to my friend's husband? He'll kill her. Or he'll do a great job of making it look like she's a danger to her child."

She doesn't say it, but we know from Wilson's threat Sunday night he will frame Jess for Violet's murder. She could end up in prison, once again, for a crime she didn't commit.

"I'm guessing the odds aren't great the cop who showed up at Jess's house and allegedly filled in a false report will admit to it," I say.

Blake leans back in his chair. "It depends on what grounds he filed the false report. If he was coerced into filing it, he might come clean. It's impossible to say."

"My friend told me the other cop has been stalking her when her husband is busy," Jess explains. "He approached her at the park a few weeks ago when she was talking to me. She was scared of him."

A slight frown pulls onto Blake's face. "Unless there's proof her husband has physically abused her, the husband can always claim the other cop was the one terrorizing your friend. Then it becomes a case of he said, she said. Her husband isn't stupid. He probably has something that will pin this all on the other cop. Something the other cop may or may not know about."

Blake steeples his fingers in front of his chest. "My biggest concern right now is what will happen to your friend. I wouldn't defend a client like her husband, but there are plenty of defense lawyers who will. Those are the individuals I'm most concerned about. They will do anything in their power to make the victim miserable," he says, lowering his hands to his desk. "Unless there's evidence her husband is a rotten cop, his police record could save him and do nothing to protect your friend."

Jessica's expression says none of this is news to her. It was how her husband got away with his abuse.

"I really thought I could help her escape him so she could start her life over." Jess doesn't look at Blake or me. She's staring at her lap. "I knew it would be difficult, but I really believed I could help her. Like the resistance networks during the Second World War were able to get Jews out of the country to safety."

Her gaze flicks up to Blake and then me. "I thought I could make a difference. I thought...I thought if it was possible during the war, I should be able to do the same for my friend and get her away from her husband."

I bite my tongue so I don't point out so many Jews were killed when they were caught hiding or fleeing from occupied countries. And the same for anyone who was caught helping them.

That's one thing Hitler, Jess's late husband, and Chief Wilson have in common. They were bullies. Psychopaths. They didn't care who they hurt. They wanted control and they wanted to be the ones in power. And still do in Chief Wilson's case.

Now, I have to make sure Jess doesn't become his next target.

The woman he decides to get rid of.

The woman who might be his downfall.

"I can recommend a family lawyer," Blake tells us. "She has worked a number of domestic abuse cases similar to your friend's, but unfortunately, as good as Cassandra is, that doesn't guarantee your friend will win custody of her daughter."

And this leaves us right where we started.

Jess and I thank Blake for his help and return to my truck.

"Now what?" she asks. "I can't just sit at home and do nothing to help Violet and Sophie."

"You won't have to. We'll go back to the original plan of arranging for a series of safe houses. They won't be able to stay in Maple Ridge once we get them away from Wilson. We'll need to immediately get them out of Oregon."

This time, we'll need to be more prepared than Jess was the first time Violet and Sophie got away from Wilson.

This time, we won't wait until they escape him before we do something to ensure they're safe.

I STEER MY TRUCK ONTO THE LOT FOR THE LARGE SINGLE-STORY, brick-and-glass building. Green fields stretch on either side of it, reaching as far as the horizon. The sky is deep blue with the midmorning sun.

"Bell Automotives?" Jess stares through the windshield at the building in front of us.

"Theresa didn't have any luck convincing her father to change his mind about sponsoring the festival. If anyone could've done it, it would have been her. When that failed, I was desperate enough to believe Katelyn might be more successful, which is why I agreed to go to the wedding as her date."

"Did she convince her father to sponsor the festival?" Jess asks, sounding pretty hopeful.

"I don't know. I haven't heard from either of them since the wedding. But I'm not sure she was ever planning to talk to him about it."

Jess flashes me a sad smile. "Even though you went as her date to Theresa's wedding?"

"Yes, even then. I'm not ready to write him off just yet. And since we're in the neighborhood"—after driving back from seeing Blake in Eugene—"I thought I'd try once more to talk to him."

"And if talking to him again doesn't work?"

"Then it looks like I'll have to go with Rose and Delores's suggestion. The auction to win dates with hot single men," I deadpan.

Jess laughs, the sweet, rich melody wrapping around me. "I'm sure those two and Samantha won't complain."

"I'm sure they won't." I chuckle.

"Any idea how you're going to convince Anthony to change his mind?"

"Not a single one." I reverse the truck into an empty stall.

We climb out of the front seats, and I take Jess's hand. Now that we're back together and I know all her truths, I have no intention of letting go of her again. Next time she gets nervous and tries to pause our relationship, I'll get her to talk things through first.

We enter the building and head to Anthony's office.

At the display of classic cars, Jess pauses in front of the light-blue Chevrolet from the 1960s. Two of the other cars date back to the 1930s. Their polished exteriors shine under the bright showroom lights. "Wow, those are incredible. I can't believe that Anthony restored them himself."

"That's what he's best known for. His passion for old cars as a kid became his career and that passion shows. It's why he's so successful. Each car isn't just a car to him. It's a piece of history. It's a piece of himself by the time he's finished restoring it. You can see the love he poured into each one." My fingers itch to trace across the glossy surface of the maroon 1934 Ford DeLuxe Roadster, a testament of Anthony's love for what he does.

Jess gives my hand a light squeeze. "It's like what you do, Troy. I've seen the passion on your face when you renovate old houses. And especially when you're finding a way to make a home more accessible for someone with mobility challenges. And then there's organizing the festival when you're already busy with everything else." She smiles at me with an adoration that steals my breath away. "I've never known anyone as passionate about helping people as you are. I mean, look at Wilderness Warriors."

"And it's not only that," she continues, the uncertain woman who barely spoke when I first met her four months ago no longer holding her back. "You're helping families who might feel like they no longer have a voice. You're doing so much for the community." An emotion clouds her eyes, its presence so brief, I don't have a chance to fully grasp what it is. Worry?

Her smile returns, her eyes glittering.

I kiss her forehead. "Thank you," I murmur against her skin. I'm not sure she understands how much her words mean to me. They're the life raft in the choppy festival waters I still have to navigate through.

We turn to head for Anthony Bell's office, but he's standing right behind us, his mouth slack, eyes round. Like he can't believe what he's looking at.

Shit.

The last time he saw me was at Theresa's wedding and I was Katelyn's date. From his wide-eyed expression, it's fair to say Katelyn hasn't told him *why* I was at the wedding with her. Or maybe it has something to do with the bruises on Jess's face.

"Hi," I say, unsure where to start. "Do you have a moment to talk?"

He slowly nods. "Sure, I have a few minutes. Let's go to my

office. Are you okay?" The question is directed at Jess. "What happened?"

She shrugs it off as if it's no big deal—like she has reacted that way plenty of times in the past. "A break and enter. But I promise you I'm fine." She flashes him a smile that looks to be genuine.

He returns the smile, his even brighter than hers—maybe to make the moment less awkward. "It's a pleasure to see you again so soon, Jessica. Thank you for being Theresa's photographer for the wedding. She was so excited when you agreed to shoot it."

A flush spreads up Jess's cheeks. "You're welcome. I enjoyed it. You all made it so much fun."

We follow him to his office, and he waves at the chairs in front of the desk, indicating for us to have a seat.

"I must admit I'm surprised to see you two together," he says once we're all seated. "Troy, weren't you just dating my daughter, Katelyn, this weekend?"

Jess and I are no longer holding hands, but I guess I'm not too shocked he's starting there first.

"Katelyn and I were never actually dating. She asked me to go with her to Theresa's wedding as her plus one. She told me if I did that, she would talk to you about the festival sponsorship."

Anthony's bushy white eyebrows jump up his forehead. "Is that so?"

I nod. "Jess and I have been dating for the past month, but for a reason we can't discuss, she had to temporarily put our relationship on hold. That's the only reason I agreed to go with Katelyn to the wedding. As a friend." Of course, if I had known at the time the real reason Jess had put a pause to our relationship, I would never have gone to the wedding with Katelyn—no matter what Katelyn had promised.

Now I'm just praying Anthony hasn't heard the rumors about Katelyn staying overnight at my house. I don't want to go into what really happened, but I will if I have to defend myself. Otherwise, he doesn't need to know what else his daughter did to manipulate me into giving her what she wanted.

Anthony appears thoughtful for a moment. "Jessica was correct when she said you're passionate about making a difference."

My eyes widen a tiny amount, and he chuckles. "Yes, Troy, I did overhear the conversation between you two in the showroom." He rubs his jaw. "There's still the issue of you shoving Chief Wilson. And you did that in front of kids. It doesn't send a positive message to the youth about respecting the police."

His words feel like a vise tightening around my stomach when I know how disrespectful Wilson is toward his wife. And how he has threatened to expose Jess's past life if she so much as hints at how he's hurting Violet.

But I can't say anything about any of that without putting Violet's and Jess's lives in danger. "I understand that, sir. Would it help if I made a public apology and make it clear to kids that what I did was unacceptable?"

"It would. You mentioned the money raised through the festival would help members of the military and first responders in the area who struggle with PTSD."

"That's right."

"And that includes members of the police department?"

"That's right."

Anthony releases a long, slow breath, his chest raising and falling. "Alright. I'll agree to reinstate the sponsorship, but you have to promise me not to hit, shove, or harass Chief Wilson again or any other members of the police department."

"I can do that." I'll just have to figure out another way to help Violet and Sophie that won't involve me violating those requirements and which would put Jess, Violet, and Sophie in harm's way.

Anthony smiles, easing away the stress lines on his face.

"Good. In that case, we're back in business with the sponsorship. I hope it helps you with what you're hoping to achieve, Troy."

I grin, the weight of the last few days lightening from my shoulders for a moment. "Thank you. It will."

I catch the I-knew-you-could-do-it pride beaming in Jess's expression, and the love I feel for her pounds in my chest, even though she's not ready to go there yet.

57

TROY

August, Present Day
Maple Ridge

After dinner, Jess and I settle in to do research on domestic abuse cases where the abusers have been convicted. My phone pings with a group text from Kellan, who's on surveillance duty at Wilson's house. I've already filled my brothers in on the conversation Jess and I had with Blake this morning.

> Kellan: Quiet here. Too quiet. Don't like it

> Me: Is Violet there?

> Kellan: She hasn't left during my shift.
> But Dunbar is here

> Kellan: You should all get down here. I
> think something's going on

Lucas, Garrett, and I respond that we're on our way.

463

I scoot away from Jess on the couch, not really wanting to leave her. But I don't have a choice. Not if I'm hoping to help Violet. Not if I'm hoping to give Jess some peace of mind about her friend. "I have to go. Kellan's watching Wilson's house, and he doesn't like something that's going on."

Jess pushes herself to stand. "I'm coming with you."

"No, you're staying here where I know you'll be safe."

She fists her hands on her hips and scowls at me. "Don't go all alpha male on me, Troy Carson. We both thought I was safe at my house and look how well that turned out." She points to the bruises on her face.

I don't bother reminding her if she hadn't been hiding Violet and Sophie at her house, Wilson wouldn't have turned asshole on her. She did what she had to so she could protect Violet and Sophie.

And that makes me admire her that much more.

"Okay." I want to argue against her coming with me, except there's not enough time for that. "But you have to do exactly what my brothers and I tell you. We're trained. You're not."

She's walking to the garage door before I finish my sentence. "Fine."

Sighing, I walk after her, my long legs quickly catching up to her.

Butterscotch and Bailey follow after us.

I turn to them. "Sorry, you two. You have to stay here." Jess needs Bailey, but Bailey isn't trained enough to come with us. She's still a puppy. A puppy who might give away that my brothers and I are watching Wilson's house.

Jess is in my truck, seat belt in place, by the time I enter the garage. It only takes a few minutes to drive to where Kellan is stationed. He's sitting in his parked SUV several houses away from the target's home. There's nowhere else to position ourselves where we don't look conspicuous. No neighbor's home where we can watch Wilson's house.

Garrett is already here, his car parked farther down the street. He's walking along the sidewalk as if he belongs in the neighborhood. He pauses to check out the front of the house with a For Sale sign on the lawn.

Lucas pulls up behind Jess and me.

Kellan climbs out of his SUV and walks toward Garrett. Lucas and I get out of our vehicles and join them. Jess stays in my truck. The house for sale is the perfect cover. I can pretend we're discussing possible renovation ideas, as if one of us is thinking of buying the house.

"Is Officer Dunbar still in there?" I casually glance at Wilson's home.

"Unless he left out the back, yes." Kellan points at the house we're pretending to check out. "He's not in uniform. It could be a social visit. But given everything that's been going on, it might not be."

The front door of the Wilson's house opens, and Chief Wilson steps out in uniform. He climbs into his car on the driveway and drives away. Dunbar doesn't leave the house.

"I don't suppose he's just running to the store to grab beer," Garrett says dryly.

"Not in uniform," I respond. "He could have been called into the station. Kellan, Garrett—you and I will follow him and see where he's going. Lucas. You go 'round back and keep an eye on the house from there. Jess will stay in your SUV and can let us know if Dunbar leaves." My command comes out fast, the words fired like a round of bullets.

Kellan, Garrett, and I run to our vehicles, and I quickly explain the plan to Jess. She gets out of my truck and jogs over to Lucas on the sidewalk.

My brothers and I follow Wilson, keeping a safe distance from him. We've done this maneuver before and know to split up so it doesn't look like we're tailing him. The perk of Maple

Ridge being a small town is that it's easier to follow him like this without losing him.

He doesn't seem to suspect we're following him. He's not employing any evasion tactics.

It also doesn't appear as though Wilson's going to the station. But just in case, I call to see if they're expecting him.

"He's not on duty tonight," a female on the other end of the line explains after I ask for him.

I thank her. If this trip has nothing to do with work, why the uniform?

I call my brothers on the conference line and tell them what she told me.

"Maybe it's something she doesn't know about," Lucas points out.

"True," I reply. "But I still don't like it."

My brothers agree.

We drive out of town, which makes following Wilson more challenging without looking suspicious. I stop at one point to let him get ahead of me, so it doesn't appear as if I'm trailing him.

"There's a warehouse not far from here," Garrett says through my truck speaker. "He might be going there. Otherwise, he's driving to Spring Falls or one of the ranch houses between here and there."

"Shit, that's a lot of territory to search through if he's not at the warehouse."

"The question is, why is he driving so far out of Maple Ridge in his uniform while Dunbar is at his house with Violet and Sophie?"

At least we know their bodies aren't in his trunk. Kellan would have seen if Wilson or Dunbar had placed anything suspicious in Wilson's car.

Or I hope that's the case. It's possible he killed them before my brothers and I decided last night to do surveillance on his house. I don't voice that thought to my brothers, but I imagine they're thinking the same.

I silently pray that's not the case. Silently pray Violet and Sophie are safe at home.

I know the warehouse Garrett was referring to and head toward it. The three of us arrive ten minutes later and park our vehicles where they can't easily be spotted behind a dense copse of trees. We harness on our years of Marine training and soundlessly approach the metal fence that circles the compound. Our presence is kept well hidden.

Wilson is standing a few feet from his car on the other side of the metal fence. A man dressed in black and with a rifle strapped to his back walks up to him. They exchange a few words, then shake hands.

I gesture for my brothers to split up so we can survey the perimeter. Unlike the dozen men milling around the compound, eyeing Wilson like he's someone they don't fully trust, neither Garrett, Kellan, nor I have guns.

Wilson and the man in black walk to the trunk of Wilson's car. Wilson opens the trunk and pulls out what could be an AK-47. Several of the other men aim their guns at him, waiting to see what he's going to do next.

What the fuck?

The man in black checks it over and nods. He waves at two men several feet from them to come forward. One I recognize. He was in the photos that Jess took during the Fourth of July celebrations. He and Wilson were talking in them.

The man is carrying a dark-green backpack. He opens the bag for Wilson to inspect. Wilson pulls out what appears to be a thick wad of cash and flips through it, checking the bills.

He says something to the man I can't hear, but from the looks of things, he asked him to dump the bag's contents into his trunk. He takes a minute to inspect what I'm guessing to be more money and nods.

Wilson steps to the side, and the men retrieve more assault rifles from his trunk. They also remove a green plastic container that's large enough to hold four oversized bags of flour. Whatever's in the container must be heavy. It takes two bulked-up men to carry it to the warehouse.

I survey the faces of the men in the compound, doing my best to make out their features. A man resembling Ethan Philips from where I'm crouching is with them.

Christ, please tell me I'm wrong. Of all the people who could have been mixed up with these men, it had to be a man I'd come to respect from working with him during our past several SAR missions.

It's possible Wilson is part of an undercover sting, but it's more likely he's been on the other side of the law if his recent behavior is any indication.

I pull out my phone to take photos, but they won't prove anything. Not from this far away.

I need a camera with a telephoto lens. Or I need to get closer to the action.

A twig snaps behind me.

And a surge of adrenaline fires up my synapses, puts my body on high alert.

I'm flat on my stomach, forest debris digging into my skin. There's a chance I haven't been discovered. That my military survival skills have done what I'd hoped—made me invisible.

"Get up and turn around," a male voice barks, louder and sharper than my CO when he was beyond pissed.

Shit. So much for being invisible.

58

JESSICA

August, Present Day
Maple Ridge

I watch Violet's house from the safety of Lucas's SUV, my fingers itching to sink into Bailey's hair and calm the panic pulsing through me. We couldn't risk bringing her with us, and now I'm regretting that decision.

Lucas is still watching the back of the house. I haven't heard from Troy or Kellan or Garrett since they drove away. I'm not sure what to make of that. So I try to avoid thinking about it.

Looking at the exterior of Violet's house, a passerby would never guess the danger Violet faces every day behind the facade. Her house resembles every other home on the street. White picket fences. Cheerful blossoms coloring the gardens and porches. Blossoms that have been tenderly cared for.

A restrained quiet reigns over the house. A nothing-to-see-here quiet. A light is on in the room at the front, but the curtains are drawn, so I can't check if Violet is all right. Or if she's even in the room.

Helplessness wraps around me like an oversized python, squeezing me tighter and tighter to the point I can't breathe. I can't sit here doing nothing. The least I can do is give Violet hope and let her know she hasn't been abandoned. She's not alone.

I search through Lucas's glove compartment and locate scrap paper and two pens. I click on the end of one pen and try writing on the paper. Nothing, other than a slight indentation where I wrote. *Dammit.*

I try the other pen. The ink flows this time, but it's intermittent at best. I write the short message and fold the paper into a tiny square.

I climb out of the SUV and walk down the sidewalk to Violet's front door. I lift my hand to ring the doorbell, but a crash from inside the house causes me to go still.

Then there's a scream.

The woman's scream isn't loud enough to be heard by the neighbors, and no one is on the street to notice it. Lucas might have overheard it from his position on the other side of the house, but I can't be sure.

The sound comes again and galvanizes me into action, without giving a second thought to the risk I'm taking. Violet. Sophie. I need to make sure they're okay.

Praying the door is unlocked, I grab the doorknob and turn it. I take a deep breath that does nothing to calm me, and I brace myself for all possible scenarios I could be stepping into. Many I don't even want to consider.

The doorknob easily twists, and I release the air from my lungs, relief not bothering to wash over me. I cautiously push the door open, doing my best to not make a sound that will alert anyone in the house of my presence.

I enter. Without Bailey by my side, I feel exposed. Vulnerable.

This is the first time I've been in Violet's home. The inside reminds me of the house I lived in with my husband.

The place isn't just tidy.

It's OCD tidy.

I bet if I go into the kitchen, I'll find the towels perfectly aligned and the cans perfectly stacked. Everything has a proper place, and nothing deviates from it.

The moment it does, even by a fraction of a fraction of an inch, there will be hell to pay.

A near-quiet sobbing comes from the room near the front of the house. I don't shut the front door all the way so I don't have to waste time opening it if I have to quickly escape, but the gap isn't large enough to let in sounds from outside that will alert Dunbar someone else is in the house.

I send Lucas a text.

> Me: Violet is in trouble. I'm in the house

I don't bother to wait for his reply. I creep toward the entrance of the room where the sobbing is coming from and scan the hallway for anything that could be used as a weapon. At least when Angelique was sent to occupied France, she'd been taught self-defense before leaving England. She knew how to turn just about anything into a weapon.

A click comes from behind me. I don't have to turn around to know Dunbar is standing there, a gun pointed at the back of my head.

Fuckers.

59

TROY

August, Present Day
Maple Ridge

I glance over my shoulder, and any thought of escaping from my current situation collapses to the ground. The man's pistol is aimed at my head. And there's a reason I never heard him approach. Everything about the man screams former special forces, including his dark-green camo.

My gut tells me he's a hired hand. The type of soldier who'll work for whoever pays him the most, no matter which side of the law that might fall.

The type of man not to be trusted.

Hands raised, I slowly push to my feet. If I'm lucky, Garrett and Kellan did a better job at remaining hidden.

If not, we're all screwed.

"Walk!"

I do what I'm told. The evasive moves ingrained in my

472

motor memory won't do much good here. He'll kill me before I could make the first move.

He doesn't come off as the sort who's interested in chatting or answering questions. So I don't say anything. I focus on how I'm going to get my ass out of here. Alive and not in a body bag.

I enter the clearing, my hands still raised, and stop since I have no idea where I'm supposed to go. The unspoken question is answered by way of a jab between my shoulder blades with the pistol.

We continue through the open metal gate leading to the warehouse compound and approach Wilson and the man he's talking to.

"Sir!" The word fires from the special forces soldier with military precision. "I found someone snooping in the trees beyond the perimeter fencing. Sir!"

Wilson and the other man turn to us. Both scowl. I know the feeling. I'm as unimpressed with the circumstances as they are. The odds that I won't see tomorrow are exponentially high. My brothers can hardly storm the castle armed with nothing but branches. We'll all get shot if they try.

Fuck. Goddamn. Fuck.

"What the hell are you doing here?" Wilson says by way of a greeting. His face is close-to-stroking-out red.

I could turn the table on him and ask him what the fuck he's doing here, but I don't expect that question will go down well, especially if he is part of a sting.

"You and that fucking bitch have been nothing but trouble." Pure naked hostility sharpens his vowels, threatens to butcher me.

The soldier shoves me toward the warehouse. "Move!"

I'm escorted into the building. The musty, metal tang of abandonment lingers in the air. The large, cavernous space is empty, no nearby hiding places should I be foolish enough to make a break for it. The soldier walks a few paces behind me, his pistol aimed at my back.

I've been in some damn serious situations while deployed. Have nearly died a time or two. But I've never been held captive. Never felt so defenseless.

My only hope is my brothers have realized I'm in a shitload of trouble and have called in for reinforcements. Reinforcements that don't answer to Chief Wilson.

"What are you going to do with him?" Wilson asks, sounding surprisingly unnerved at the situation. At least he doesn't have a gun at his back. He'll get to walk away. Walk away and abuse his wife again.

My gaze catches on a doorway that could lead to the warehouse offices. But it's ten or more yards away. These men won't let me get that far before gunning me down.

"On your knees!" The shrapnel-sharp voice behind me is that of the special forces soldier. The air in my lungs rushes out in a hard breath.

Shit. Fuck. Shit. Fuck.

"Don't be ridiculous." Wilson's tone is a mix of commanding and scared shitless. I don't move, waiting to see how this plays out. "You can't just execute him. You do that, and we'll have all sorts of law enforcement converging on Maple Ridge because of an execution-style hit on one of its citizens. You need to make it look like an accident. Something that doesn't result in too many questions."

"You're the chief of police," the man in black says, voice ice smooth. "I'm sure you can cover the trail. That's why I brought you in. You fucked up. You deal with the problem. This is Troy Carson, right?"

I stiffen at my name. I have no idea who in hell the man is, yet he knows me. What else does he know about me?

"That's right."

"His body will be found in the mountains. He slipped off a hiking trail. End of problem."

"With assault rifle bullets inside him?" Wilson's shit-you're-a-moron tone won't win him any fans with this group. "At least make it look like a hunting accident by a poacher."

"I'll be long gone by the time his body's found, so you deal with it in whatever way you see fit." The man in black's attention swivels to me. "Now on your knees, Carson, or else your pretty girlfriend will be the next to disappear. Savannah Townsend, isn't it?"

I arrange my forehead into a confused frown, not wanting to confirm he's correct, even though Wilson already knows the truth. "No idea what you're talking about." How does this man know who she is? And so much about me?

He makes a small, amused sound but doesn't elaborate on what he knows about Savannah and Jess. I wouldn't be surprised if one of his men has killed a cop at some point just to keep their organization out of trouble, so I doubt he would care if she were a cop killer.

"On your knees!" the former special forces soldier barks, and I have no doubt his bite is every bit as bad as his bark.

I start to lower to my knees.

"FBI! Put your weapons down. You're under arrest."

Shock widens my eyes. It's a voice I recognize. Ethan Philips.

I glance over my shoulder. Everyone has momentarily forgotten me, stunned at the turn of events. In that brief nanosecond, their guard is knocked off-kilter.

I take that tiny window where the soldier's attention is pulled away from me, his pistol turning toward Ethan. I lunge at him. He's large, but he's not expecting my attack. And that gives me an advantage.

A very slight advantage. He has protective gear on and has backup from his men.

Ethan and I have nothing—other than my unarmed brothers. Who might not even realize I'm in trouble. At least Ethan has a gun, which is more than I have.

I curse under my breath that my brothers and I weren't better prepared for this mission. But the original mission had been to protect Violet and to get her and Sophie out of the house if we suspected she was in grave danger. We hadn't planned for any of this.

The former special forces soldier points his pistol at me. I slap his hand to the side, grappling for control. I can't even worry about the five other men surrounding us. I just hope I'm moving enough to keep from being an easy target.

I hurl my body weight at him, attempt to kick his foot out from under him. We both go down as a loud bang splinters the air. I don't feel the sting of death, and my target is no more dead or injured than I am. I have no idea who fired the gun.

He and I roll on the floor, fighting to gain control of his pistol.

I'm vaguely aware of the commotion around us, but I'm too focused on not losing my battle and I don't fully register what else is going on in the warehouse.

A tearing pain rips through the previously injured shoulder. A torn muscle? Ligament? Tendon? I grunt-groan and roll once more. Pin the soldier under my weight. My heart is racing. I'm fighting to catch my breath.

"FBI! Drop your weapons!" a female voice demands. "On your stomach. On the ground."

I catch sight of the toes of her shoes in my periphery and take a chance the soldier won't shoot me before she shoots him. I roll off him onto my stomach.

My gaze finds Ethan. He's talking to one of the FBI agents and is the only agent not wearing a vest identifying him as such. The other agents are cuffing Wilson and the men who work for the man in black.

Ethan walks over to the female agent staring down at me. "He's an innocent." He points at me. "The other one is involved in the operation."

Ethan squats beside me. "You okay, Troy?"

I roll onto my back, struggling to find my breath, my shoulder throbbing. Lucas is definitely going to kill me after this. Him and Samuel.

I nod, although based on Ethan's expression, he's not buying it.

He helps me to my feet as I cradle my arm against my body. "Do me a favor?"

"Sure, what?"

"Can you please stick to just rescuing lost hikers next time?" he grumbles with a hint of amusement.

"Are you telling me this entire time you were FBI?" Damn, I hadn't seen that coming.

"Yup. We suspected Chief Wilson was involved in weapons trafficking. What I'd like to know is what the hell you're doing here?"

"Wilson is an abusive asshole," I say as if that explains everything, and my gaze briefly flicks to an FBI agent handcuffing one of the men in black. "He's been abusing his wife for years."

"Shit. Is she okay?"

I grit my teeth at the throbbing pain in my shoulder. "My girlfriend was helping Violet and her daughter escape, but he found them hiding at Jess's house. He beat Jess up as a warning and reported it as a break and enter."

Ethan huffs a noise of disbelief or disgust or both. "That explains why he didn't request the Bureau's help when they went missing. The last thing he wanted was our involvement when he was abusing his wife and involved in criminal activities. Where are Violet and her daughter now?"

"Home. But Wilson has another cop watching her. Sounds

like he's been stalking her when Wilson couldn't. My brothers and I had a feeling Wilson was up to something, and we followed him here."

"Well, that explains what you're doing here." Ethan shakes his head like he can't believe my role in what just went down. "Which officer is with Violet and her daughter?"

"Clive Dunbar."

"Shit," Ethan mutters under his breath as Kellan and Garrett approach with two agents by their sides.

"We've got a problem," Kellan tells me. "Lucas just saw Jess —and she's inside the house with Violet and Dunbar."

My heart stops beating, an ice bullet ripping through the muscle.

60

ANGELIQUE

October 1943
France

I wake the next morning to Johann stirring next to me in the bed we shared last night.

A coughing fit from downstairs sees me fully awake. I promised Johann I would rest today, but I need to cycle into the village and talk to Dr. Deschamps about Jacques's cough. I also need to leave the message in the drop box for Allaire, informing him of my impending motherhood.

God, what will his reaction be to the untimely news? I wince just thinking about it.

Johann climbs out of bed, and my body instantly misses his heat. He removes his uniform from the wardrobe, and I glare at it, silently cursing what the uniform stands for.

He lays it at the end of the bed, and I'm tempted to kick the bloody awful uniform onto the floor.

Johann leans over me, caging me with his hands on either side of my head, and he kisses me long and hard.

The heat of the kisses cools, and they become sweet and tender.

"I love you," he murmurs against my lips. He shifts down my body and kisses my stomach. "I love you too."

An image of this being a different time and place slips into my thoughts. Of me kissing my husband goodbye before he leaves for his job to make the world a better place.

It's a beautiful picture. One I wish were true.

He pulls on his detested khaki trousers, and I climb out of bed. The chilly October-morning air strokes my bare flesh, turning my skin prickly with goosebumps. I wrap the blanket around my shoulders, limp to my room, and quickly change into a different dress than the one I was wearing for the past few days.

I make my way downstairs and enter the kitchen.

"Please tell me you're not going anywhere today," Jacques says, looking out of the kitchen window, his shoulders curved in on themselves as if to protect his heart from more pain. He learned last night about my injury, but he doesn't know it was the result of a German bullet.

"I have some things I need to do in the village, and then I'll be back to help you here."

"You need to rest that leg of yours."

The stairs creak with Johann's descent.

"I'll rest it tonight, Papa. I promise." I start preparing breakfast for the two men.

Johann enters the kitchen. He spots me at the sink and sadness flickers on his face. A sadness that could mean anything and everything. He could be thinking about his mother and sister. About where they are. About what they would think of his news that he's going to be a father—assuming they're still alive.

Or he could be thinking about how his regiment will be going to the Eastern Front soon.

The sadness on his face quickly fades, replaced by a smile that seems uncertain. The tilt of his lips is barely there, the sparkle in his eyes dimmer than usual.

He sits at the table, and I hand him the plate with his breakfast on it.

Johann is finishing his food when the recognizable sound of tyres on gravel approaches the house. My body tenses as it always does at that sound. Jacques wears his usual disquieted expression at the noise. We know it's Johann's driver. It's not the Gestapo or SS. But even after all these months, our reactions haven't changed.

I walk him to the door. Johann pulls me out of view of the kitchen and presses me against the door. My arms wind around his neck; his go around my waist. And his mouth finds mine in a knee-quivering kiss.

Our lips part after several rapid heartbeats, my breath ragged. We don't immediately release each other. We just stare into the other one's eyes for a moment. The words we can't say out loud with Jacques in the kitchen are clear in our gazes.

Johann's arms drop away from my waist. Without a word, he opens the door and walks out of the house. And already I miss him.

The front door shuts behind me as I return to the kitchen. I pick up his empty plate.

I look up and my eyes catch on the disapproving glare of the man who is like a father to me.

"Do you really believe it's wise for this thing between you two to continue?" Jacques asks. The rough purr of the military engine recedes into the distance.

I walk to the sink and place the plate next to it. Outside the kitchen window, the autumn colours glow softly in the light of the rising sun. Their vibrant colours are a contrast to the mood that has settled over France.

"No. It's not wise." I let my head slump forwards and gulp down the lies and the truth. Keeping them from my expression, I turn to Jacques. "It's far from wise. It's dangerous. But the work I do has benefitted from it."

"I'm sure whoever you work for would agree you have to stop this madness. You're in love with the man. And he's in love with you. Nothing good can come from it. For either of you."

His words surprise me. I didn't think it was obvious how Johann and I felt deeply for each other. I can only hope no one in the village has noticed. Because Jacques is partly right. Nothing good can come from it. Nothing good can come from people knowing about it either.

"My work knows about him," I inform Jacques.

"Do they know you're in love with him?" His expression says he knows the answer.

"I'm loyal to London and the resistance effort. Nothing will change that. No matter what I feel for him, England is my home. England and France are where my loyalties lie."

"My daughter fell in love with the wrong man, and it almost broke her." Jacques's tone slices to the bone, and he slams his palm on the table. I startle at the anger and raw pain in his words. "I don't want the same to happen to you."

"What are you talking about?"

Jacques hasn't spoken much about his daughter. I only know she died during childbirth, as did his grandson.

He opens his mouth to say something but is hit with another round of coughing.

"I'm going to speak with Dr. Deschamps this morning about your cough," I tell him once the coughing fit subsides.

"I don't like doctors."

"That doesn't matter."

I busy myself around the farmhouse for the next hour and

then cycle into the village. I park my bike and go into the book-shop first.

"*Bonjour*," I say to Monsieur Joubert, who is stepping out of his office at the sound of the bell above the door. I close the door behind me.

"*Bonjour*, Angelique." He gives me a small nod, the movement a mix of weary and wary and relieved. His eyes do not hold any warning of a threat waiting inside the shop.

I meander to the drop box in the bookshelf and place the coded message for Allaire inside it. I slip the book back on the shelf, walk to another aisle, and remove a random book from a shelf. I pay for it and head to Dr. Deschamps's home.

His wife opens the door and lets me inside. The waiting area only has a few people sitting on the wooden chairs.

"My papa has a cough that hasn't been getting better," I tell Roselina.

"And you can't convince him to come to my husband's office?" She offers a kind smile, knowing Jacques's stubbornness regarding doctors. "I'll see what he can do after he is finished for the day."

I return her smile. "Thank you. That's all I can ask."

I'M IN THE FARMHOUSE KITCHEN, CLEANING THE STOVE, WHEN THE sound of approaching engines cuts off my conversation with Jacques. He's seated at the table, taking a short break from his chores.

Two shiny black cars with swastika flags flapping in the wind stop in front of the farmhouse. Neither car is the same vehicle that was here earlier to collect Johann.

My heartbeat accelerates. My brain screams *run*.

The engines cut off, and the driver climbs out of the first vehicle. But he's not Wehrmacht or SS.

Several other men in grey uniforms join him—and my heart screeches to a halt.

"Gestapo." The hushed word, thick with fear, comes from Jacques. "You need to get out of here."

But the warning's too late. One man walks to the front door. The others move towards the sides of the farmhouse. One agent will continue to the back. If I so much as attempt to escape out of a window, I'm dead.

You're dead either way.

Loud knocking disrupts my thoughts of what to do.

"We know you are in there, Angelique D'Aboville! Or should I call you Carmen?" The agent's words through the closed farmhouse door aren't in French. They're in English.

Oh, God.

They know.

61

JESSICA

August, Present Day
Maple Ridge

I stand perfectly still in Violet's hallway, like a wild rabbit that's hoping the wolf doesn't notice it if it doesn't move.

The front door clicks shut—followed by the louder click of a deadbolt.

"Go into the living room." Dunbar's sharp tone hooks on to my heart and yanks it into my throat.

I swallow, trying to push down the fear of what will happen if I ignore him. He pokes the back of my head with the barrel of the gun, nudging me forward. I enter the room.

Violet is sitting on the couch, mascara streaking her face. There's no sign of Sophie. It's late. Hopefully, she's fast asleep in bed. Hopefully, she's safe.

Fear I'm too late slices my insides with dread and regret. Fear that maybe I didn't act soon enough to save Violet's daughter.

485

Violet's eyes widen...and then squeeze shut for a beat. "Wh-what are you doing here?"

"I heard a scream," I reply. "And came to check on you. The door was open."

"We've got a problem," Dunbar says.

I look over my shoulder to see who he's talking to. He's on his phone, explaining what exactly the problem is. *Me.*

"Let me know what you want me to do with her." He ends the call without acknowledging what the other person said. I can only hope he was forced to leave a voice message, buying me time.

He points with the gun to the couch. "Sit!"

I do as I'm told. I have a feeling things won't be ending well for me, so I don't want to push my luck. Every moment I can stall the inevitable, the greater the chance Troy will return before it's too late.

Dunbar stands in front of us, his face impassive. He doesn't say anything, and I have no clue what to say to defuse the situation. I learned with my husband I was better off not saying anything than I was trying to negotiate with him.

I'm too nervous to even say anything to Violet. The note I wrote for her in Lucas's SUV remains in my hand, the page still folded into a tiny square. There's no way I can give it to her without drawing Dunbar's attention.

Not that it matters anymore. I don't know if help is on the way—or if it's going to arrive too late.

Urgent pounding from the front door causes my body to jolt. Violet starts to get up to answer it.

"Sit!" The cop shoves her back onto the couch.

The pounding comes again. "FBI! Open the door!"

Violet's shock-rounded eyes match my own. FBI?

Chief Wilson. He called the FBI and told them Violet kidnapped their daughter. If my husband could have gotten away with it, he would've done the same. It's the final bent nail in the coffin. The reminder Chief Wilson holds all the power.

Blood rushes to my ears, blocking the sound of the FBI agents on the other side of the front door.

The same thought must have occurred to Violet. She's trembling. I'm trembling.

Dunbar grabs my arm and roughly drags me to my feet. I stumble at the sudden movement but manage to right myself.

The loud bang of the front door slamming into the wall in the foyer startles me.

Before I can react, a thick arm folds around my neck in a solid vise. Cold metal presses to my temple. *Fuckers.* I clutch at the arm, desperate to pull it away.

I squeeze my eyes shut against the memory of the last time the barrel of a gun was held to my head. I mentally shake away the nightmare of that night, not letting my late husband win. I open my eyes.

Three agents—two Black men and a white woman—wearing black FBI vests enter the living room, guns drawn. They stop.

I claw at the cop's arm, desperate for air, but his long sleeves prevent me from doing much harm. The fear I felt a moment ago toward the FBI when they entered the house flickers out like a fire doused with water. The fear and panic due to the gun at my head burns brighter.

"Don't come any closer or I'll kill her." The cop grinds the barrel of the gun into my temple. I wince and stop fighting him, my strength rapidly dwindling.

A sob comes from the couch. From Violet.

The arm at my neck tightens its grip. A white burst of light flashes in front of me. I clutch at his arm again, attempting to pry it off. I. Can't. Breathe.

I feel my life slipping away. Everything turns blurry. I close my eyes and play in my head the last time I was with Amelia at the beach. Of her dancing on the sand and the waves kissing her feet.

Of us giggling like we didn't have a care in the world.

A loud noise jerks me to the present and my body jolts.

The arm slackens from my neck, and I thirstily gulp in air through my raw throat.

My legs give out from under me and my body sags, my reaction time too drunk from what just happened to save me.

One of the male agents lunges toward me. His arm catches around my waist, keeping me from falling to the ground. My gaze shifts to Violet. She's standing in front of me, looking like she's going to faint or vomit or both.

The other agents' mouths are moving, but no words come from them. Just ringing. Endless ringing.

The male agent guides me away from the couch. His mouth moves, so I assume he's asking me questions. I feel like I'm in a giant bubble, and everything outside it is moving in slow motion.

One of the men goes to Violet. The other crouches where I stood a moment ago. My gaze drops to the floor. To where the cop lies, his blood soaking into the carpet.

Her husband isn't going to be happy about that. The words spin in my head, harder, faster, making me dizzy and nauseous. The heavy coppery odor choking the air isn't helping either.

Voices begin to break through the ringing in my ears. Something about Violet's husband being arrested for weapons trafficking. The evidence being flawless. He won't be granted bail. Shock registers on Violet's face. A new kind of shock compared to a minute ago.

She doesn't have to try to escape anymore. She doesn't have to pretend to be someone she isn't.

She's free.

And I won't have to worry about him revealing my true identity. He's got bigger problems to deal with than my past.

I pull away from the female FBI agent and hug Violet. "You're free. He'll never be able to touch you again." The words rasp over my lips, scraping past my sore throat.

A tremble takes over her body and she's shaking more than she was before the agents showed up. But it's a different kind of shaking.

She's crying.

I'm crying.

And we're hugging and laughing and sobbing. It's over. Violet and Sophie are finally safe. They're free to begin their lives over again. Together.

Jealousy crawls its way in, spinning fine threads, creating a web of frustration and sorrow and pain. I sweep the cobwebs aside, taking comfort that a mother won't be losing her child. They'll be able to have tea parties and school concerts and talks about first crushes. They'll get to have a beautiful life together.

Sophie's wails from upstairs burst through my joy. The female agent goes up with Violet to make sure Sophie is okay. And maybe to search the house for more evidence to use against Violet's husband.

"Can I go upstairs to help Violet?" I ask no one in particular, my voice still scratchy and rough.

"You need to go to the hospital to get checked out," the taller of the two agents tells me. The other one is busy searching through the living room. "I've already called in for an ambulance."

"I'll be fine."

His eyebrow lifts in an I'm-not-buying-that way.

I counter it with a that-doesn't-matter shrug. "Can I at least help her till it gets here?"

"You should rest your voice until you get the okay from a physician."

"You're bossy," I whisper, the equivalent of a frustrated pout in my tone.

The other agent releases a loud snort-laugh. "See, I'm not the only one who thinks you're bossy."

That gets a small smile out of me and a glower from his partner. I'd laugh if I knew it wasn't going to hurt.

Sirens wail from down the street, louder than Sophie's protests a moment ago.

"I need to make sure my friend is okay." I load the words with an extra helping of *please*.

"Don't worry, we'll take care of her," the taller agent tries to reassure me. "You were choked. You need to make sure there isn't any serious damage. C'mon. I'll take you outside."

I glance upstairs to where Violet and Sophie are.

"I'll tell her where you've gone."

I nod, the movement robotic, and I let him lead me outside to where the paramedics are rushing up the path.

He explains to them what happened, and the female paramedic has me sit on the stretcher so she can check me out. I protest when she tries to put the neck brace on me, and I attempt to push it away.

"Sorry, but you have to wear it until the ER physician has cleared you," she says, undeterred by my weak attempts to fight her off. I don't want anything around my neck after having a thick arm there. "They have to make sure nothing was broken or fractured when you were choked."

I don't have it in me to argue, so I quit resisting and reach for a dog who isn't beside me. I just want Bailey and Troy and to go home.

"Jess?"

My gaze shifts in the direction of Troy's voice. His clothes are dirt-smudged and he's wearing a sling. Again.

Garrett, his clothes still clean, is with Troy.

"Christ, you're covered in blood." Troy's concerned eyes search my body for the gaping wound that doesn't exist.

I can't even look down to see what he's talking about. I lift my arms. The fabric on my sleeve is soaked with blood and my back feels sticky. I can't believe I'm only noticing that now. I want to scream and rip off my top. To be free of the remnants of the nightmare.

But more than anything, I just want to look at Troy. I'm alive and he's alive and that's all that matters.

I point to his sling with a questioning raise of my eyebrow.

Troy ignores me. "What happened? Is she going to be okay?" His rapid-fire questions are directed at the paramedic.

She glances at me for permission. I give a tiny nod of my chin to let her know it's okay to tell him. She explains what happened based on what the FBI agent told her.

Anger darkens Troy's face, but he quickly replaces it with relief and gratitude and love. All directed at me. He touches my hand. My heart stutters a beat.

He leans in as if he wants to embrace me, but he can't while the paramedic is checking me over.

"Samuel won't know what to do with you two." Garrett slides a glance between Troy and me. "You're both magnets for getting hurt. But I'm glad to see you're okay, Jess." He nods at me.

"What happened?" I rasp and point once more to Troy's sling.

"He can explain on the bus," the paramedic says calmly. "You're going to the hospital." That's mostly directed at me. She gets me to lie down on the stretcher.

I don't argue but reach out for Troy's hand. He squeezes my hand and climbs into the ambulance with me.

FORTY MINUTES LATER, I'M SITTING ON THE CHAIR NEXT TO Troy's bed in the ER, wearing a pair of scrubs and waiting to hear the verdict about his shoulder. I've already been cleared, the neck brace removed, and have been given strict orders to let my still-sore throat heal over the next few days. I'm allowed to talk, but not excessively.

Troy's been doing most of the talking, telling me what happened after he and his brothers followed Violet's soon-to-be ex-husband.

I'm still processing it all.

I drop my gaze to my lap. When I look up after a beat, it's to find Troy's eyes fixated on the bruises around my neck.

I know what he's thinking. It's there on his face. "It wasn't your fault." My voice is hoarse, but it's an improvement over what it was an hour ago.

I stand and brush my lips over Troy's, telling him without words how grateful I am he's alive. If the FBI hadn't shown up at the warehouse when they did, we wouldn't be having this conversation. I'd be mourning the loss of the man I care deeply for, instead of waiting with him to find out news about his shoulder.

The possibility of surgery has been mentioned.

Samuel has also threatened to put Troy in a body cast so the shoulder can heal. I think he might've been joking, but that might not be a bad idea based on Troy's current track record.

The room door opens. But it's not Samuel who enters or one of the nurses. It's Zara and Garrett.

"The nurse said we could come back here." Zara's carrying a bag in one hand, which I hope contains my clean clothes. In her other hand is what looks like a folded section of a newspaper. Her gaze drops to the bruises on my neck, and for a fraction of a second, horror snags her expression before she alters it to something more neutral. "How are you two doing?"

"Good." I cringe at my hoarse whisper that sounds anything but good. But I'm still alive, so I'm holding on tight to that. At least I can breathe—both literally and figuratively—now that

Violet's husband is going to be locked away for hopefully a long time.

I can return to focusing on building my new life.

Garrett, Zara, and Troy talk for a few minutes. I let my throat rest while I listen and watch them.

And that's why I notice something is off about Zara. Her eyes keep darting my way, and I get the feeling there's something she wants to tell me but doesn't know how to broach the topic.

"What's wrong?" I ask when her gaze settles briefly on me again.

Garrett gives her a resigned nod, looking no happier than she does about what they have to tell us.

"Someone left this in Treats." She holds up the front section of the national newspaper.

"And it's against the rules to leave newspapers there?" I venture because I have no idea why a newspaper would stress Zara out.

"It's not the newspaper that's the problem. It's what's in this particular issue..." She unfolds it, hands the paper to me, and points at a picture.

My stomach plummets at the sight of it. How the hell...? How the hell did the newspaper get a picture of me? It's not one of my old photos from when I had brown hair and no scars. When I looked pretty and wore more makeup than I do now.

This one was taken in Maple Ridge. And not only that, it won't take much investigative work to figure out which town I now call home.

Troy rips the paper out of my hand. "Where the hell did they get this picture?"

My eyes go to the title of the article, and then drop to the byline. Cora Harding.

No no no no no. She's a reporter? This entire time...all the questions. Olivia's sister was asking me questions for an article. In a national newspaper.

Letting the world know where to find me.

Letting everyone in Maple Ridge know about my dark past and my shame.

**DON'T MISS THE EXCITING
CONTINUATION OF THE HIDDEN
SECRETS TRILOGY. ONE MORE
TRUTH IS COMING IN MAY 2024.**

For more information about domestic violence and how you can help someone who you suspect is in an abusive relationship, check out websites such as https://fearisnotlove.ca/.

YOUR BOOK CLUB READING GUIDE

BOOK CLUB QUESTIONS

DISCUSSION QUESTIONS

Please note discussion questions contain some spoilers. I recommend not reading ahead if you want to be surprised.

1. Why did Jessica give up her daughter for adoption to her brother-in-law and his wife? How do you feel about Craig's and Grace's request for Jessica to give them time to make a decision about her being in Amelia's life?

2. How do you feel about Jessica wanting to be a part of Amelia's life again?

3. Jessica has faced several losses over the years. How do you feel that has shaped the person she is at the end of the book? How does that compare to who she was at the beginning?

4. Did you agree with how Jessica planned to help Violet and Sophie? Do you have any suggestions of what she could have done instead or what she could have done differently?

5. Did you agree with Jessica's decision not to tell Troy about her plans to help Violet and Sophie? How would you have done things differently or the same?

6. What resources are available where you live that help women who are in an abusive relationship? Do you have any suggestions as to how you can share the information with a woman who you believe might be in an abusive relationship, but in a way that will not risk additional harm to her?

7. In what ways can you help women who are in an abusive relationship? (e.g. donate or volunteer at a local shelter, learn how to listen to someone who you suspect is in an abusive relationship, etc.)

8. There are different beliefs when it comes to domestic abuse. Do you know anyone who you suspect is in an abusive relationship or has been in one? What are some of the signs that gave you pause about that relationship?

9. What emotions did you feel when Johann and Angelique slept together for the first time? What emotions did you feel when they declared their love for each other?

10. Has your opinion of Johann, a German officer, changed from the time he moved into the farmhouse in *One More Secret* to the end of *One More Betrayal*? How and why has it changed (or not changed)?

11. *One More Betrayal* is at the forefront a romance, but it is also historical fiction, women's fiction, and a story of empowerment. What parallels are there so far between the modern-day story and the World War II story?

12. The novel deals with Jessica's goal to start her life over again and how she hopes her daughter will eventually be part of it. Discuss how motherhood and her past have shaped Jessica's decisions and choices in *One More Betrayal*.

13. Successful romantic relationships require trust. In what ways was trust explored in the story? In what ways was the trust between Angelique and Johann reflected between Jessica and Troy?

ACKNOWLEDGMENTS

First of all, I would like to thank you, the reader, for giving The Hidden Secrets Trilogy a chance. The story has been a passion project of mine for the past few years. One that required a lot of research for the two timeline stories, and one that required I plot the equivalent of four books (even though Hidden Secrets is a trilogy). I have loved every moment of it. But a passion project is even more meaningful when an author's words touch a reader's heart, and when readers fall in love with the characters as much as the author fell in love with them.

As always, I want to thank my wonderful editor, Lauren Clarke, for her insight, wisdom, and sheer brilliance when it came to *One More Betrayal*. Her suggestions for the first two books in the trilogy helped me make the story even better than I had first imagined it. I couldn't imagine working on the series without her.

My daughter's therapist taught her the 5-4-3-2-1 relaxation exercise that Jess mentioned in the book. My daughter's therapist also shared with me some insights into domestic abuse that fueled additional research on the topic, so I could make the story as authentic as possible. One of my goals for the trilogy is to help bring additional awareness to the long-term ramifications of domestic violence. The story was better in part because of what my daughter's therapist told me.

I would also like to thank my agent, Dani Sanchez, for helping to bring my dream to life for the trilogy to be available on audiobook. I can't wait to listen to it once it's available.

And lastly, I would like to thank my husband and kids for their support and understanding of why I love disappearing into my story worlds. I especially would like to thank my daughter, Anja, whose name I borrowed for Johann's sister. She has been my biggest supporter from the very beginning.

ABOUT THE AUTHOR

Born in Brighton England, Stina Lindenblatt has lived in a number of countries, including England, the U.S, Finland, and Canada. This would explain her mixed up accent. She has a kinesiology degree and a MSc in sports biological sciences.

In addition to writing fiction, she loves photography, and currently lives in Calgary, Canada, with her husband and three kids.

For news about her books and to sign up for her newsletter, check out her website at stinalindenblattauthor.com.